H

SHADOWS IN THE SUN

Back in 1918 arms dealer James Martingell received a knighthood for supplying the British Army during the war. With the coming of peace, they want to close him down. Not welcoming the prospect of poverty, Martingell resumes negotiations with his old friend, Sheikh Azam ud-Ranatullah, thereby branding himself a traitor to his country. Ignoring all obstacles, Martingell doggedly pursues the one last coup that will make him rich beyond measure. Trekking across Asia through civil war, betrayal, murder and death, he becomes a figure of grim legend.

SHADOWS IN THE SUN

by
Christopher Nicole

Magna Large Print Books
Long Preston, North Yorkshire,
England.

British Library Cataloguing in Publication Data.

Nicole, Christopher
  Shadows in the sun.

  A catalogue record for this book is
  available from the British Library

  ISBN 0-7505-1425-6

First published in Great Britain by Severn House Publishers
Ltd., 1998

Magna Large Print is an imprint of
Library Magna Books Ltd.
Printed and bound in Great Britain by
T.J. International Ltd., Cornwall, PL28 8RW.

CONTENTS

'The bloody book of law
You shall yourself read in the bitter letter
After your own sense.'

William Shakespeare

Prologue

With a rattle of drums and tambourines, the screams of both bugles and men, the beaters moved through the thick scrub. Kabul was many miles behind them now, and this was the real Afghanistan, high, windswept, arid.

'There, your highness! Over there!' shouted Azam ud-Ranatullah.

'Where? Where?' Habibullah Khan, Amir of Afghanistan, twisted his head and indeed his body to and fro, threatening to tumble right out of his howdah at his elephant's feet.

In his middle forties, the amir was a handsome man, just beginning to run to fat. No one had ever doubted his intelligence, or his ambitions for his country. He had proved himself the most civilised and forward-thinking of men. He had introduced railways and electricity, books and Western dress, to his mountain-girt and backward Asian kingdom—yet the blood of his forefathers still flowed in his veins, and nothing could excite him more than the hunt. It was his misfortune that not all of his people wished to be Westernised, certainly when it meant such a heavy dependency on the arms and money of British India, lying like an immense cloudbank to the south. But those who would oppose his reforms could be dismissed as reactionaries.

'There, cousin,' said Amaruddin Khan, seated, like Azam ud-Ranatullah, in the amir's howdah. Amaruddin, a big, heavy-set, hook-nosed man, was a bastard member of Habibullah's family, but he had made himself a close friend of the amir's.

Now the tiger could clearly be seen, breaking cover to bound across the open spaces beyond. 'I have him!' Habibullah shouted, and levelled his rifle. A moment later he fired, but the tiger raced for safety—while Habibullah Khan slumped forward, his head a bloody mess, into the bottom of the howdah.

'Your highness!' Azam dropped to his knees beside the dead man.

'Cousin!' Amaruddin knelt beside Azam, while from around them there came an explosion of noise from the other members of the hunting party. But the amir was definitely dead, half his brain shot away. The two men kneeling beside him looked at each other, then both turned their heads to gaze at the clump of trees from which the fatal shot had been fired, with unerring

8

timing and accuracy to coincide with the amir's own shot at the tiger. 'Where did you find such a man?' the prince asked.

'Zahir has been in my employ for several years,' Azam said.

'And now?'

'He will continue to serve me faithfully, your highness. As I will continue to serve you.'

People were swarming about the elephant; the mahout had brought the huge beast to its knees, to allow the men to clamber up. 'What a tragedy,' said Amanullah Khan, Habibullah's eldest son, who had been riding on the elephant behind. 'Oh, our poor father. What will our mother say?'

'She will seek vengeance,' Amaruddin said. 'And we shall provide it. The assassin must be caught, and made to confess who employed him. I will see to it. Sheikh Azam, you will accompany me.' They left the son kneeling beside his father, surrounded by weeping courtiers and grooms. The two men mounted their horses, and, accompanied by several of Azam's retinue, cantered towards the trees.

Joining the stricken Afghans as the amir's body was reverently lifted out of the howdah and laid on the ground were two young men, who from their pale skins as much as their clothes were definitely not

9

even Westernised Afghans; one, of medium height, thick-set, with red hair, had strong features to go with his powerful body. He wore a green uniform with a green peaked cap. 'A conspiracy,' he whispered.

The other wore conventional civilian dress for an Englishman in India, from white duck suit to white topi, with a Guards tie. He was taller than his companion, but not as heavily built, although his body was muscular enough. His features were neat rather than handsome, his blue eyes vivacious. But they were sombre as he looked over the clustered heads in front of him at the dead ruler. 'Undoubtedly,' he agreed.

'What will you do?' asked the Russian.

'Inform my people in Delhi, just as rapidly as possible.' The Englishman grinned. 'As you will no doubt be reporting to Moscow, Sandor.'

'We must cooperate in this, Richard,' Sandor said.

Richard Elligan appeared to consider. He was only in his middle twenties, and he was very aware that he was on probation here, standing in for the regular attaché, who was on sick leave. He also knew that his superiors in Delhi would not approve of his friendship with the Russian, the representative of all the chaotic, murderous forces that were

10

seeking to control and perhaps rule that vast menacing country. But what the hell, he liked the fellow, and held the opinion that Alexander Galitsin was by no means a dyed-in-the-wool Communist, merely a man determined to survive.

Which did not mean that he was not a potential enemy, especially when a state like Afghanistan, one of the buffers between British India and Communist Russia, might be about to become up for grabs. 'I'm sure we shall, old man,' he said.

'Will he have escaped by now?' Amaruddin asked in a low voice, as he and Azam gained the trees.

'I would imagine so,' Azam said, 'or he has merged into the crowd.'

For here too there were masses of people, milling about, shouting and screaming. Many carried rifles, which they were firing into the air. It would be impossible to determine who had actually fired the fatal shot. 'Then it is good,' Amaruddin said. 'Now ...'

'Now we need to worry about the British, your highness,' Azam said. Amaruddin had drawn rein. He turned his head, sharply. 'The amir has been assassinated, your highness,' Azam pointed out. 'He was in Britain's pay. Is that not why this tragedy has happened? The British will wish to learn the truth of it, and they will wish to continue their domination of our country.'

'Nasrullah will not oppose them,' Amaruddin muttered.

'Then your uncle must be deposed, and Prince Amanullah must reign in his place.'

'That boy?'

'Boys can more easily be controlled than men, your highness.'

'The British will send an army.'

'I do not think so. The war in Europe has not yet been over a year. They are exhausted. Their people are weary of killing and being killed. They have no money. As I have said before, your highness, with the British ailing, and with the Russians in a state of civil war, now is the best time for us to regain our independence, once and for all.'

Amaruddin chewed his lip. 'We need men, and guns.'

'We have the men, your highness.'

'But not the guns.'

Azam grinned. 'I will get the guns. I have contacts in the West.'

'The man Martingell? Did he not refuse to supply us the last time you made contact with him?'

'That is because he was needed by the

British Government to manufacture arms for themselves, to fight the Germans. That war is now over.'

'You have described this man to me as an unmitigated scoundrel, Sheikh Azam.'

'Oh, he is that, your highness. But he is also bold and fearless, ambitious and pragmatic. He seeks wealth and the power that it conveys. As he is an arms trader, that wealth, and that power, can only be obtained by trading arms.'

'And he will sell us guns for use against the British?'

Azam's grin widened. 'As you have just reminded me, your highness, Martingell is an unmitigated scoundrel.'

Part One

Family Matters

'And after all, what is a lie?
'Tis but The truth in masquerade.'

Lord Byron

Chapter 1

Secrets

'Over here, Sir James,' called the photographer.

James Martingell turned towards the cloaked camera. 'A family shot,' he suggested.

'One of you first, sir, if you will,' the photographer requested. James Martingell smiled at his wife and children, and stepped away from them, faced the camera and the resulting small explosion.

He still could not believe this was happening. James Martingell was fifty-eight years old in this spring of 1919, and although his life had followed a relatively even tenor since he had agreed to work for the British Government just before the outbreak of the Great War, he could still vividly recall the adventures of his youth, when he had accompanied Charles Rudd's expedition into Matabeleland, now known as Rhodesia, when he had been imprisoned by the Boers for his complicity in the Jameson Raid, when he had explored Central Africa and sold guns to the great

Tippu Tib in what was now known as the Congo, and above all when he had also sold guns to Muhammad ibn abd Allah, the Mad Mullah, and what had happened afterwards.

All of those early actions had been undertaken in defiance of the British Government; he had been universally regarded as a renegade, the son of a bankrupt, a man who would sell his own mother for a profit. Now all was forgiven. With the certainty of war with Germany looming in the near future, the British Government of the day had sought all the arms it could find, and the Martingell Arms Company was one of the best in the business. They had buried the past to employ him, and so successfully had he filled and refilled the terms of his various contracts that here he was, on the forecourt of Buckingham Palace, a Knight Commander of the Bath. How he wished poor old William, his brother, cut down by Boer fire as he climbed the heights of Spion Kop in 1900, could have been here to see this day. And perhaps even share in it.

'Now the family, Sir James,' called the photographer.

Anne and the children came to stand beside him. Anne was in her forties, her hair, pinned up beneath her broad-brimmed hat, was still pure gold, her

18

features as handsomely composed as always. In all the world, only James Martingell had seen those features dissolve in the heat of passion, or outrage—he had watched her kill more than one man, amongst them her own first husband. Or despair, as when their son—the only child they had mutually conceived—had died when still a babe. He doubted she had ever got over that. But not even he could estimate the depths of her emotions. She was a woman with vast secrets, which all belonged to him, as she was his utterly faithful support in all things. Especially as regards the other children. Because here their mutual secrets were too immense ever to see the light of day.

Winston Pennyfeather—he retained his dead father's name—was now twenty-two years old. He still wore the khaki uniform of a Guards officer, was considering remaining in the army as a career, so he said. He was a tall, somewhat slender young man, his shoulders slightly hunched, his eyes, as blue as his mother's, only from time to time wearing that watchful, withdrawn look common to so many men who had spent time in the trenches of the Western Front. He worshipped his mother, respected his stepfather, and, like the whole world, accepted that his real father had died a hero's death, battling Socotran pirates off

19

the coast of East Africa. He could never know otherwise.

He was also protective towards his sister, even though she was a year the older. Any casual observer would have supposed they were flesh and blood, for Lanne Martingell was both tall and blonde, if slightly more solidly built than her stepbrother. But she also had secrets, which could not be mentioned. Her mother had been a half-caste part-Boer, part-Scottish prostitute. James Martingell knew that Lanne could just remember Martha Alexander. He did not know, and had never dared ask, what else she remembered, and with what emotions. He had rescued her from the misery of life in Dar es Salaam, simply because he was her father. But Anne had willingly accepted the child as her own, seen that she had the best education possible, turned her into a lady; their friendship, and indeed love, had been moulded when they had both been prisoners of the Mullah, with death a daily possibility.

His family! He was proud of them, as he was pleased with himself. And there remained Mbote. The camera having exploded yet again, he summoned the big African to join them for a third photograph. Mbote, as tall and powerfully built as his erstwhile master who was his

20

best friend, was grizzled now, but he wore his morning dress and silk hat as if born to it, as if he had never fired a gun or taken a knife to an enemy. We have become civilised, James thought.

'Sir James! By God, but that must sound good.'

'It does, to be sure, Hazlitt,' James agreed. But his eyes remained cold as he surveyed the man who had joined them, and from whom the family immediately drifted away; they knew when there was business to be discussed.

'Just reward,' Hazlitt said. 'Just reward.' He was a slight man who sported a fair moustache, and looked far more at home in his morning dress than James did in his. 'Now we must turn our back on the past, eh?'

'It would be nice to be able to do so,' James said.

'Certain aspects of it, eh? My people tell me that our last order was never delivered.'

'On orders from the War Office, Hazlitt. I was informed it was not needed.'

'Oh, absolutely. Our business now is to get as many men out of uniform as quickly as possible. And get rid of their weapons.'

'Britain will still need an army, surely,' James suggested.

'Oh, quite. But we have enough to go on with. And arms and ammunition. Surplus material should be dumped, to stop it falling into the wrong hands, eh?'

'It's a point of view,' James said.

'It's a directive, Martingell,' Hazlitt said. 'We know what you have in your warehouses; we paid for them. Enough rifles, ammunition, machine-guns, grenades, and even a cannon or two, to start another war.'

'It would be an awful waste never to use any of those things. Especially as I have *not* been paid for them.'

Hazlitt snorted. 'My man Howorth will be down to see you. There is a designated dumping area off the Channel Islands. The Hurd Deep. He will bring the necessary forms, and see that it is done. How much notice will you need?'

'Why, Hazlitt,' James said. 'You have just given me all the notice I require.'

James turned to follow his family towards the waiting taxis, and was again accosted. 'Sir James Martingell!'

He checked, frowning at the somewhat dapper man, who wore a waxed moustache and an air of importance even greater than his morning dress.

'Claus von Beinhardt, at your service.'

James swallowed, and looked past him at the woman, taller than the man, plump and pink-cheeked—but then, Clementine von Beinhardt had always been a large girl, who was now an even larger woman.

'You do not remember me,' she said roguishly.

'How could I ever forget, Clementine,' James said. 'But I am afraid I do not understand.'

His brain was doing handsprings. This woman had very nearly been his sister-in-law, in the days when he had worked for the House of Beinhardt and been betrothed to the elder daughter, Cecile. But that had all turned sour, as Cecile had died of malaria in East Africa, and he had made off with a hundred thousand pounds, paid by the Mullah for a shipment of guns. Presumably that had been an act of robbery, but he had suspected, correctly as it turned out, that the Beinhardts would have no use for him once their daughter was dead—as far as they were concerned, he had been responsible for that—and that his employment and equally his future would be abruptly terminated. That money had launched his career—and made him a bitter enemy of the Beinhardt family. To have them here, in London, with the War not yet ended a year ...

'I am Clementine's husband,' Claus von Beinhardt said, importantly.

'My congratulations. But your name ...'

'I changed my name to Beinhardt, when we were married. I am now chairman of the board.' He stroked his moustache. 'Or I was.'

James raised his eyebrows, and looked at Clementine, who continued to smile, and perspire beneath her huge hat and through her organdy gown. It was a warm spring day, but he suspected she might be suffering more from apprehension.

Now she gestured the third member of their party forward. 'My daughter, Sophie. This is Herr Martingell, Sophie. I know you have heard us speak of him.'

James gazed at the girl in a mixture of admiration and alarm. He might have been looking at Cecile, save that this girl ...

'Sophie is seventeen years old, James,' Clementine was saying.

The girl wore a white dress, white stockings, and white shoes, and a white hat from which the auburn splendour of her straight hair escaped like a shawl. She had the slender height of her aunt, and the same handsome, strong features. Now she gave a brief curtsey. 'It is my pleasure, Herr Martingell.'

Her English was as perfect as her mother's.

'The pleasure is mine, Fräulein.' Even at fifty-eight, James could appreciate a pretty girl. And when she bore so close a resemblance to the woman he had nearly married ...

'I wonder if we could have a talk?' Claus von Beinhardt asked, somewhat impatiently.

'What about? Not the past, I hope.'

Claus von Beinhardt gave an altogether false smile. 'The past is the past, is it not, Sir James? One should concentrate on the future. But one can learn from the past. There was a time when you worked for the House.'

'A long time ago. I work for myself now.'

'Of course. And so successfully. Whereas we ... there is no future for an arms firm in Germany at this moment. But we have arms to sell ...' He paused, hopefully.

'I am sorry, Count—I assume you have also taken the title of count? There does not seem to be a future for an arms firm in England, either.' He raised his hat. 'Clementine, Fräulein Sophie, I have enjoyed our talk. Have a good visit.'

'Who on earth was that?' Anne asked.

They lunched at the Café Royal, where they were joined by their partner, Philippe Desmorins. When Philippe had operated in Somalia he had a harem of twelve wives. They were history. Now he made do with just one, a diminutive French girl named

Michelle, less than half the age of her husband, who giggled constantly and gazed at the famous, and fearsome, Martingells with huge, frightened eyes. But she was a plump little thing, which was how Philippe liked his women to be.

'You won't believe this,' James said, 'but that was the Beinhardt clan.'

'Good God!'

'Oh, they've given up attempting to get their money back. Or so they say. They want to do business, again. Seems they have fallen on hard times. They even brought along their rather beautiful daughter to help persuade me, I suspect.'

'And did she?'

James blew her a kiss. 'I'm not sure I could cope with a seventeen-year-old, in or out of bed.'

'You saw the Boche off,' Philippe said. He was a small man, with sharp features. James had not taken to him when first they had met, but over the years he had come to value him as a loyal, if often pessimistic, friend and ally. 'But what do *we* do now?'

'I'm afraid it is going to be a little hard for us as well, for a while at any rate,' James said. 'My contracts have all been terminated. I have been informed by His Majesty's Government that the goods I have warehoused for them must be dumped as rapidly as possible.'

'It will surely be possible to, how shall I say, siphon a few off?' Philippe suggested. He had spent the war in France, fighting in the trenches. Unlike James. Now he was looking his age. But maybe that was the effect of having a young wife.

'Supposing I can find a market for them,' James said. 'And there it is, by God!' He stood up, as the other heads at the table turned. 'Sheikh Azam!' James stepped out from the table to be embraced by the Afghan. The two men were much of a height. 'You remember my wife, Lady Martingell?' How good that sounded. 'And M. Desmorins.'

'Of course. You grow more beautiful by the day, sweet lady.' Azam kissed Anne's hand. 'As you grow more prosperous, my old friend,' he told Philippe. 'And can this be the child I rescued from the Mullah?' He bent before Lanne's hand in turn.

'I remember you,' Lanne said. 'Charging into the Mullah's camp at the head of your men. With Papa.'

'A glorious occasion,' Azam smiled. He looked at Winston.

'My son,' Anne explained. Azam shook hands.

'And this is Mme Desmorins.' He kissed Michelle's knuckles, at the same time glancing sympathetically at Philippe; he

27

knew how the Frenchman's previous wives had been slaughtered by the Italians.

'A happy gathering,' he remarked. 'To celebrate your elevation to the aristocracy, James.'

'I'm afraid a knighthood doesn't actually mean that,' James said. 'But it is good to see you. I still feel I owe you an apology for when last we met.'

Azam took the chair hastily brought forward by one of the waiters, and waved his hand, dismissively. 'You had greater things afoot than to supply arms to an Afghan rebel, eh?'

'But I assume this is not a social call. How did you know where to find me?'

'You are a famous man, James. It has not been difficult.'

'Well, you must come home with us. And talk,' James said.

'You have read the news from Afghanistan?' Anne asked, as they prepared for bed in their London hotel.

James nodded, hanging up his morning coat. It had been a long and somewhat alcoholic day. 'I'm for a bath.'

'I'll join you. James, the amir was murdered.'

'Apparently.' James switched on the water. 'The general idea is that the man behind the crime is his brother,

28

and incidentally successor, Nasrullah.'

She stood beside him. 'And when you were supplying Azam with arms, before the War, he was in rebellion against Habibullah. Was that really in aid of Nasrullah?' The Martingell Arms Company had grown out of the Pennyfeather Small Arms Factory, and Anne, as the widow of the first owner and the wife of the second, was a working partner in the business.

'I am pretty certain not. Azam and Nasrullah loathe each other. And Azam and the amir were reconciled,' James pointed out. 'Azam, as I understand it, was actually sitting beside the amir when he was killed.' James sank into the warm water with a sigh of contentment, watched his wife finish undressing with equal pleasure.

'You do not think he was involved?'

'Perhaps he was. I doubt we will ever know the truth of it.'

Anne got into the bath at the other end, sat down, stretched out her legs to caress his thighs with her toes. 'But you will do business with him.'

He shrugged. 'We need to do business with someone, my dearest girl. And Azam is an old and valued friend. Without his assistance I could never have got you out of the Mullah's clutches.'

'I understand that. We owe him a great

debt. But ... I still do not altogether trust him.'

'Leave the trusting to me,' James suggested.

'And what *about* this Beinhardt business?'

'There is no Beinhardt business, and there will not be. They're in trouble, and they're looking for a partner to get them out of trouble. We are not interested. Are we?'

'I should hope not.'

'That's settled, then. Now tell me, what does it feel like to be Lady Martingell?'

'About the same as being Lady Penny-feather,' she retorted; her first husband had been a knight.

James could not blame her for being miffed, or for not trusting Azam. She longed for the quiet, respectable life, such as, remarkably, she had achieved while the entire world had been convulsed in war. But after so many years, her husband had at last become legitimate, and thus respectable. And thus a knight. Political rewards always had a touch of the sordid about them. But they went into the books. She dreaded a return to the old days. James did not suppose it was physical fear, at least for herself. She had survived too much for that. Rather it was a fear that taking the wraps off of what she, and he, really were, two adventurers who had risked their all time and again, and won, time and again, might now be too much for them, and that Winston might learn the truth about his father.

James had often considered that to tell the boy the truth might be the answer to her problem, however traumatic it might be at the moment of telling. As in a surgical operation, one had to look hopefully for a successful result. But of course, even in surgical operations, things can go wrong. This was what Anne had always feared. How did one tell a boy who utterly respected the memory of his father that the man had been a cold-blooded thief and murderer, that far from facing Socotran pirates he had attempted to kill the man who was now his stepfather, leaving his mother with the starkest choice; she had saved her lover at the expense of her husband's death? How would he react? How could he possibly react? Certainly now. Thus the memory, and the subterfuge, continued. Shared with both the captain of the yacht *Europa* and the two crewmen who had been with them when the tragedy had happened. But one of those had died in the War, and James did not doubt the allegiance of the others as long as he continued to employ them and look after their families; they were accomplices in what had happened. But it always grieved him to see his wife, who had so much to live for, haunted by that memory from the past.

On the other hand, now that the war contracts were finished and done with, and the British Government had given him their ultimate reward and politely intimated that they did not wish to deal with him again, the Martingell Arms Company had to do business with someone. He had been an arms dealer all his life. He knew no other trade. And he had a huge factory standing idle. He must either lay off almost the entire workforce, to join the already huge and always swelling mass of men made redundant by the coming of peace, or he must find work for them to do. Manufacturing the rifles, and other weapons of war, that had made the House of Martingell famous. But first, he had under lock and key enough weaponry, as Hazlitt had put it, to start another war. All of which must now be dumped in the sea? He'd be damned first.

'Have you never heard from the Mullah since our set-to?' Azam asked, as he sipped coffee in the book-lined study of James' Worcestershire home. The two men were alone. Philippe and his wife had returned to France, and Anne and the children were out riding.

'He's still around, from all reports. The British and the Italians have been slightly too busy to deal with him the last four years. But they will.'

'He has made no further effort to avenge himself on you?'

James grinned. 'I think he got too bloody a nose the last time. So tell me about your troubles.'

Azam took a turn around the room, footfalls lost in the soft carpet. 'Do you know what I find amazing?' he remarked. 'That at the end of the greatest war in history, England is still a place of utter peace. Oh, I know you have a long list of dead and maimed, and I know you had a few Zeppelins over on the east coast, but yet that countryside we passed through in the train yesterday is absolutely untouched. No enemy has ever burned your crops, since ... when?'

'I imagine you would have to go back to at least Cromwell and the Great Rebellion, and I'm not sure it wouldn't be a lot further than that,' James acknowledged.

'While in Asia, when it does *not* happen every few years it is the unusual event.' Azam sat down.

'Possibly that is because your people regard death, whether by assassination or by battle, as a way of life,' James suggested.

'Possibly,' Azam conceded. 'Yet it is the

realities of life, and death, with which we must deal.'

'I entirely agree. So tell me this, old friend: had you anything to do with your king's assassination?'

'James, that bullet missed me by inches.'

He was lying, as James recognised. Perhaps the bullet *had* missed him by inches, but it was a risk he had taken to clear himself of involvement. 'Then you condemn the assassin?'

'Ah,' Azam said. 'Now that is a difficult question to answer. As you have just conceded, in my country we do not regard assassination in the same light as do you. Where there is an absolute monarchy, differences in political thought cannot be solved by means of the ballot box.'

'The opinion in England is that the late amir was a sensible, progressive man.'

'That is because here in the West you consider progress as the be-all and end-all of all things. In Asia, there are many people who would not agree with you. A majority, I would suppose.'

'And you are one of that majority.'

'I think I am. Why should men change, simply because change is available? Supposing you and I set out to visit Worcester, you by car and me by horse. Oh, you would undoubtedly get there before me, with a hissing and a banging and a consumption of oil and an emission of exhaust fumes. But I would get there in the end. And if we had business to attend to, together, would you not have to wait for my arrival?'

'You'll forgive me for suggesting that is just a little simplistic, Azam. In any event, once progress has begun, it is useless to try to stop it. It will happen.'

'That is why it is often better not to let it begin,' Azam said.

'You were opposed to the amir.'

'I was opposed to many of the things he wished to do, yes.'

'But you served him.'

'He employed me. I am a loyal Afghan.'

'Then I do not see why you have come to me. Will not Amir Nasrullah faithfully implement his brother's programme?'

Azam's eyes were hooded. 'Amir Nasrullah will not, I think, long remain amir.'

'You can sit there and tell me he will be assassinated too?'

'I do not think he will be assassinated, unless he is very foolish. He will be deposed.'

'And what will happen then?'

'Our new amir will be Amanullah Khan, Habibullah's son.'

'Who no doubt is a friend of yours, and is also opposed to Westernisation of his country.'

'I think I can say yes to both of those.'

'And who wishes for guns.'

'Well, any government needs to arm its soldiers, James.'

'Afghanistan obtains all of its weaponry, quite legitimately, from British India,' James pointed out.

'That is so long as my country is prepared to remain, shall we say, an outlying province of British India. This too is not popular with the majority of my people. Indeed, I would say that relationship, established by Habibullah Khan, was the main reason for his assassination.'

'So your new amir would break with Britain. I have an idea that could mean a lot of trouble.'

Azam grinned. 'Did we not have a similar discussion ten years ago, James, when you first agreed to supply me with arms? Then you feared a British invasion. It did not happen, at a time when Britain was mistress of the world. Now she is wounded. Still a lion, perhaps. Still capable of great things, perhaps. But more concerned with defending what she has than with taking on new, and risky adventures. She is nervous. Her people are nervous. Thus Dyer. You know of this?'

James nodded, thoughtfully. 'It came through a few days ago. General Dyer opened fire upon an unarmed mob in Amritsar. Quite a few were killed.'

'And your press and public opinion are calling for Dyer's head. I do not believe that suggests a government, either here or in India, that will dispatch an expeditionary force through the Khyber Pass.'

'But you still need a supply of modern weapons.'

'Of course. There is always Russia.'

'Russia is in a state of collapse.'

'Perhaps. That is not to say she will not rise again. Or at least, some warlord rise to power in the south, and consider us easy pickings. Will you help me? As I once helped you.'

'Believe me, old friend, I want to. But ... I will never get a licence to ship arms to Kabul.'

Azam grinned. 'Did you have a licence the last time?'

'The last time, had the British Government not needed me and my arms company, I could have gone to gaol.'

'That was only because of the Mullah business that they found out at all. I would say you have a warehouse bulging with unwanted rifles and ammunition. You still have your ship?'

'I still have my ship,' James said thoughtfully.

'Well, then ... ten thousand Martingell rifles, one thousand rounds per gun. Two hundred Martingell machine-guns, fifty thousand rounds each. Sixty thousand Martingell hand grenades. I do not suppose you can supply us with cannon?'

'The Martingell mountain gun is well thought of,' James said absently.

'But that is splendid,' Azam cried.

'Five hundred thousand pounds,' James said, quietly.

Azam stared at him for a moment. 'You were always a hard man, James. Are we not talking about surplus stock?'

'Which still has to be paid for,' James pointed out.

'Half a million,' Azam mused.

'For, as I understand it, a kingdom.'

'By Allah, but you are right. The same terms as before?'

'Exactly. A quarter down, a quarter upon shipment of goods to your satisfaction, a quarter upon arrival in ... Chah Bahar again?'

Azam nodded. 'We can do a deal with the Persians. They are not too happy about British influence in the Gulf.'

'And the final quarter upon delivery to the Afghan border.'

'Very good. I will attend to it. When?'

'We will ship within the week, providing the initial payments are made.'

'So soon?'

James smiled. 'As you say, Azam, the goods are all in stock.'

'Half a million?' Anne asked in wonderment. 'James ...'

'I never said the business was less than risky. But that money will pay for getting us out. One last throw, and half a million.'

She shivered. 'I am terrified.'

'Just don't tell anybody. The word is that, in accordance with recommended government procedure, I am taking all of those surplus arms to sea for dumping. That I choose to take an ocean voyage afterwards is my business.'

'They'll find out. They always do.'

'Eventually. Proving it will be their problem.'

'But this time I am coming with you. The children are quite old enough to look after themselves.'

'I assume you mean Lanne. Winston will be rejoining his regiment.'

'He'll still be able to keep an eye on her.'

The two horses walked slowly through the wooded country behind the house; neither rider was in any hurry. 'We never seem to have any time together,' Winston said. 'I shall be rejoining my regiment next week.' Like his stepsister, he wore civilian riding clothes, flat cap and a sports jacket over his jodhpurs, while Lanne wore a blue hunting jacket and a silk hat. She was quite the most beautiful woman he had ever seen, which wasn't saying all that much about a man who had spent the last five years in the army with little time to look at any woman for longer than a few minutes' paid entertainment.

He had actually never given a lot of thought to his stepsister. She had always been there, since he could remember; they had both been small children when his mother and her father had got together. Then he had been away at school so much of the time, and at that time Lanne had been a curiously withdrawn girl, only at ease in the company of that German nanny of hers. Then had come the strange business of their kidnapping by the Somali warlord known as the Mad Mullah, an enemy of Stepfather's. Winston had been at school when the house had been raided by the Mullah's thugs, and he had never really understood what had happened. Even as he had grown into his teens. No explanation had ever been offered, and the questions that sprang to mind were not to be asked by a gentleman of his mother, or his stepsister. They had been prisoners of the Somalis for several weeks. In that time, he knew, Lisette Uhlmann had been taken into the Mullah's harem, and had never been heard of again. Mother and Lanne had been inviolate, as hostages. But had they been *that* inviolate?

Certain it was that when Stepfather had brought them back in triumph, they had been as close as if Mother had been Lanne's natural mother. He had felt rather put out by that, excluded from the intimacy he had previously enjoyed. But would that not have happened anyway, as he had grown up? Then had come the War. As he had volunteered on the very day the Germans had marched into Belgium, and to Mother's horror been accepted—he had lied about his age, as he had then been only seventeen—they had drifted even further apart. Certainly he and Lanne had done so, as she had joined the Land Army and seldom been home on furlough at the same time as himself. Thus when they had met again, only a few weeks ago—he had been given special leave to be at his stepfather's investiture—they had been virtually strangers. And she had changed. She had always been a pretty little girl. Now she was a quite beautiful young woman. To whom, he could not stop himself remembering, he was not in any way actually related. 'But you're not going to stay here,' he ventured.

'Should I not? It's my home.'

'I meant, you'll be getting married.'

'Perhaps,' she said, enigmatically. Their horses stopped of their own accord, on the banks of a rushing stream. 'I love this place,' she said. 'I don't want ever to leave it.'

'So do I. Will you write to me?' She turned her head, sharply. 'I mean, I don't know where the regiment will be posted. And I would so like to be kept in touch with what's happening here. And you, of course.' His face was crimson.

'Why, it's very kind of you to say so,' she said. 'Of course I shall write to you.'

He slipped from the saddle, and stood on the bank to look at the tumbling water, waiting. But she did not dismount as well, as he had hoped. Instead she turned her horse. 'I think we should be getting home.'

'Why? Mother and Father have gone for the day, haven't they? To look at the yacht?'

'I think so.' But she was already walking her horse back through the trees.

Hastily he remounted and caught her up. 'Is Father really going to do business with that dark-skinned chap?'

'I imagine so.' She glanced at him. 'You don't approve.'

'I don't know. It's just that ... well, I might wind up fighting against Father's guns.'

'In Afghanistan? That's five thousand miles away.'

'Do you approve of what Father does?'

'It's what he's always done. And it's paid for all this.' They walked their horses into the paddock, where a groom was waiting to take their bridles. 'I'll see you at lunch,' Lanne said, and crossed the drive towards the house, pausing to frown at the motor car that waited at the foot of the steps; it was not a vehicle she had ever seen before.

She went up the steps to where Mbote was waiting. 'We have a visitor.'

'For Daddy?'

'I reckon so. Arrived only half an hour ago. Said he'd wait.'

'That's ridiculous. They won't be back till this evening.' She took off her hat and strode into the drawing room, stopped in surprise. The young man standing before the fireplace was better looking and better dressed than she had expected; Father's acquaintances were too often seedy and shabby-looking men. Equally, his tie ... she frowned at the familiarity.

'Good morning,' he said. 'Your man said I could wait in here.'

'You have a long wait,' Lanne pointed

43

out. 'And he is not my man. He is not anybody's man. He is a member of my father's household.'

'Then I apologise, Miss ... Martingell?'

'My name is Lanne Martingell, sir.'

'I am Captain Richard Elligan, Second Irish Guards.'

'I recognised your tie,' she said. 'Have you come to see my father?'

'Yes, I have. Do forgive me, but Lanne ... that is rather an unusual name, is it not?'

'I was christened Anne, Captain Elligan. By my father, before he married my mother, whose name also happens to be Anne. So it was decided that I should be called Little Anne, or Lanne for short.'

'Intriguing.' He looked past her at Winston, just entering the room. 'Good Lord!'

'Yes,' Lanne agreed. 'This is my brother Winston. He is a lieutenant in your regiment.'

Winston had already come to attention, with a faint frown. 'I do not believe we have met, sir.'

'No we haven't. I have been serving in India, and then Afghanistan, as an attaché.

'Well ... welcome.'

'Oh, please sit down,' Lanne said.

'Wilton, we'll have champagne. And Captain, if you do intend to wait for my father, I assume you are staying for lunch?'

'She'll take a week or two to work up, Sir James,' Captain Petersen said. 'But she's in good nick. I've seen to that.'

James stood on the bridge of the two-hundred-foot-long yacht he had virtually inherited after Sir Winston Pennyfeather's death, and was pleased. She was a superb old tub, as Petersen was a superb old salt. Both had spent the war in this secluded Welsh bay, riding to their moorings. 'I never doubted she would be,' James said. 'But she must be ready tomorrow.'

'Tomorrow, sir?' Petersen was taken aback.

'Ready, Captain. I don't know when I'll be sailing, but it will be very soon. How about the crew?'

'Well, most of them volunteered for service, of course. But I told them their jobs were all waiting for them when the War was over, and they've nearly all come back. So we should have a full complement.'

'When you say "nearly all",' James said, 'who has dropped out?'

'Well, sir, Jimmy McAvoy and Sam Pope were killed when their ships went

45

down, as you know. Dave Avery, Willie Jones and Emmott Gladwin were all badly hurt, and aren't up to sailing again. I have replacements in hand. Trustworthy fellows, sir. The only chap I've lost track of is Harry Allardyce.'

James frowned. 'How did you do that?' Harry Allardyce had been the coxswain of the yacht's launch when Winston Pennyfeather senior had been killed. With Jimmy McAvoy dead, he was the only remaining member of the crew who knew what had actually happened; Petersen and all the rest had accepted what James had told them. Allardyce had been bought off with a large payment, a guarantee of future employment for as long as he wanted it, and a suggestion of implication which might land him behind bars if he ever decided to make capital out of his secret. He had seemed happy enough, and when his wife had died James and Anne had taken his daughter Jane into their household as a maid. But it was disconcerting not to have him in sight, as it were.

'Well, sir, he was taking to the bottle,' Petersen explained. 'He was a good man, mind.'

'I know that, Captain,' James said.

'That's why I had him stay with me and a couple of the other lads, as skeleton crew, during the war. But like I said, he started hitting it a bit hard. I had a little chat with him, and he quietened down, but then came the night, only a couple of months ago, when the lads were in the local celebrating like. He must've had a jugful, because the first I'd heard of it was there'd been a fight—I wasn't there myself, you understand, Sir James—and Whitey Clark had been duffed up real bad. There was some talk he might not live. The finger was pointed at Allardyce, and he must've known he'd be for it, because he never came back to the yacht. I haven't heard of him since.'

'I wish you'd informed me at the time. Were the police involved?'

'Oh, yes, sir. They're still looking for him, but no one has seen hide nor hair of him since.'

'Damn,' James said. 'Did he have any family? Apart from the girl, I mean.'

'I don't believe he did, sir.' Petersen observed James' concern. 'I know he was a good man, Sir James. But I can't help feeling, well ... maybe it's good riddance. He was always going to go back to the bottle.'

'Yes,' James said absently.

'The police will catch up with him eventually. They always do.'

'Yes,' James said.

'Well anyway, like I was saying, sir, the yacht will be ready for sea tomorrow. It'll mean working all night, mind. But we'll do it. Will it be a long voyage?'

'It will be a long voyage, Captain,' James said. 'But mum's the word, eh?'

'Oh, aye, Sir James. Mum's the word, all right.'

James slid down the ladder, to find Anne, who had been prowling around the cabins and the galleys. 'How're things?'

'Nothing a good airing won't cure. And you?'

'Everything is just about ready to go.'

'I can hardly wait to be at sea again.'

'Yes,' he said. 'We need to have a chat.'

She raised her eyebrows, but allowed him to escort her to the quarterdeck, where, once they were seated and had been served coffee by the steward, they were out of earshot of any member of the crew. Then he told her about Allardyce. 'You think he may cause trouble?' she asked. 'It's strange ...'

'That he's made no attempt to contact Jane? Maybe he has. We shall have to find out about that. In any event, I think we need to find him, and fast.' They gazed at each other, and Anne found that she was breathing very deeply. They had now been lovers for very nearly twenty years, and had been married for fifteen, yet she was never sure how well she knew this man. She knew that he had a violent past history, that he had killed. Well, if he had not been that kind of man they would never have got together, and she would never have been rescued from the Mullah. And equally, he knew that *she* had killed, at his side. But those days were behind them, surely.

'Once we get him on board the yacht, and put to sea ...' she ventured.

'We always have to come back again.'

'We could knock some sense into him.'

'And make him more resentful than ever? It's not just Young Winston, you know. Allardyce knows all about how we ship the guns. Now, our illegal dealings before the war were accepted and written off by the Government, providing we worked for it. But this deal we're about to pull off will again be illegal. And Allardyce will know that.' Anne shivered. 'I think we'd better be getting home,' James said.

'But you mean to kill Allardyce.'

James' face was solemn. 'I mean to take whatever action may be necessary to protect my family and my business.' Then he grinned. 'But first we have to find him.'

Chapter 2

Truths

Winston Pennyfeather supposed that one of the most difficult positions one could be in was having to stand back and watch a beautiful girl who one has just realised is there for the taking being swanned under one's very eyes by a rival who was not only older, more worldly, better looking ... but a superior officer. Richard Elligan was all of those things, and there could be no doubt that he was seriously taken with Lanne. His conversation flowed throughout the meal, as he spoke of his wartime adventures. Richard was twenty-seven years old, and had been one of the first in France, serving with the first battalion of the regiment. He had spent two years in the trenches, before being wounded and invalided out at the beginning of the Battle of the Somme in 1916. During that time Winston had been training with the second battalion. He had got to France just after the Battle of the Somme.

'That must have been some show,' he ventured.

'It was bloody murder, if you'll pardon the expression,' Richard said, smiling at Lanne.

'I agree with you,' Lanne said. 'But at least they didn't send you back.'

'Well, that was the rule, certainly if you were sufficiently badly wounded. I was in hospital damn near a year. Then they found me a job on the staff, and then they sent me out to India, again on the staff.'

'India!' Lanne exclaimed. 'How exciting. I wish I could go to India.'

'Why, I'm sure you shall,' Richard said. 'Didn't you find staff work boring?' Winston ventured.

'There is staff work and staff work,' Richard said, condescendingly. 'Mine has been pretty interesting.'

'And now you've come to see Daddy,' Lanne said thoughtfully. 'But he has nothing to do with India.'

'Well ...' For the first time Richard looked disconcerted. But he recovered quickly enough. 'You managed without a wound, did you, Winston?'

'A scratch here and there,' Winston said, attempting to be condescending on his own. 'Not enough to keep me out of the front line.'

'Bully for you,' Richard said. 'That was a simply splendid meal, Lanne. I don't know how to thank you.'

'I think you should thank Cook. Now, what would you like to do with your afternoon?'

'You don't expect your parents back for some time?'

'I'm afraid it's not very likely.'

'Ah, then, do you mind if I have a look at this splendid estate?'

'I'll show it to you. Just give me a moment to get changed.' Winston's mouth sagged open, and he had to snap it shut. She had claimed to be too tired to go on riding.

'You're sure I'm not putting you out?'

'Of course not. It'll be a pleasure. Won't be long.'

'You have no gear,' Winston said. 'And I'm afraid mine would be too small for you.'

'I think I can manage as I am,' Richard said.

'Oh. Right. Would you excuse me a moment?' He ran up the stairs behind Lanne, hurried along the gallery, knocked on her door. 'It's me. Winston.'

'Well, you can't come in right now. Wait a tick.' He moved restlessly to and fro on the gallery until her door opened. She was still tucking her shirt into her jodhpurs. 'What on earth is the matter?'

He pushed her inside, closed the door

on them. 'You can't go riding with that fellow.'

'Why ever not? And should you refer to a senior officer as that fellow?'

'He is not a senior officer.'

'He is to you.' She sat before her dressing mirror, began tucking her hair into her snood. 'I can tell you don't like him.'

'I don't feel anything about him, one way or the other,' Winston lied. 'But don't you see, he's from India. It has to be to do with this deal Father is bringing off.'

'Oh, rubbish,' Lanne said, completing her coiffure and standing up. 'No one outside the family knows about that deal.'

'Do you really believe that? I bet he's here to find out what Father intends to do.'

Lanne gave him a sweet smile. 'Then I'll find out just what he is here for. I'll be doing everyone a good turn.' She put on her jacket, picked up her hat and crop, and went to the door. Winston caught her arm. 'Whatever are you doing?' she asked.

'You're being very sprightly for someone who only a couple of hours ago was exhausted.'

'I was not exhausted,' Lanne said. 'I was merely tired of riding ... with you. There. You made me say it. You're being quite absurd. Anyone would think you were jealous of me, or something.' They stared at each other, faces only inches apart. He had the wildest desire to kiss her, and then ... but that would be to start something irrevocable, and he had no idea how it might turn out. Certainly it was not practical with Elligan in the house. Waiting. 'Would you mind letting go of me?' Lanne asked, her voice low, but filled with anger. Winston released her, and she stepped past him on to the gallery. 'Please close my door when you leave,' she said over her shoulder, and skipped down the stairs.

Winston closed the door, and stood at the banister to listen to her bright conversation with Richard as they left the house. Never had he been so angry. His sudden desire for her had taken him by surprise. If he had not truly expected her to fall into his arms at the first invitation, he also had never doubted that she *would* fall into his arms if he was persistent enough. He had certainly not expected her to brush him off so completely and brutally. She had been tired of riding with *him*. But not of riding with Elligan.

He stamped down the stairs, found himself looking at one of the maids, her arms full of clean laundry. He could not remember her name, but she was a pretty little thing, with lank black hair and a thin but curiously mobile body. And he had to have her. Someone. Anyone. But she was the one present. 'Come up to my room,' he said.

'Sir?' She was utterly taken aback.

'You're an upstairs maid, aren't you?'

'Yes, sir. But Mrs Beacham ...'

'Mrs Beacham doesn't employ you, girl. My mother does. Now do as I say.'

The girl looked left and right, as if seeking succour. But there was none. After lunch the servants were inclined to retire to the kitchen for a rest from their duties. Slowly, biting her lip, she climbed the stairs to stand beside him. He nodded at his bedroom door, and she went inside. She laid the folded sheets on a chair, and straightened. 'Please don't hurt me, sir.'

'Now why should I want to hurt you?' he asked, standing against her and running his hand round her chin and down her neck. 'You're not going to pretend you're a virgin?'

She flushed, and bit her lip again. 'Only twice, sir. I swear.'

'Then I shan't even hurt you there, right? Undress.' He closed and locked the door, watched her slowly take off her pinafore. 'By the way,' he said. 'What's your name?'

'Jane, sir.'

'Your last name, goose.'

'Allardyce, sir.'

'Now, James,' Anne said, as the Rolls pulled into the forecourt of the house, just on dusk, 'you mustn't hurt that girl.'

'Of course I'm not going to hurt her. If she knows where her father is, then I'm sure she'll understand that he needs help, and will tell us where to find him.'

Wilton the butler was waiting on the front steps. 'Miss Lanne and the young gentleman are in the drawing room, Sir James, milady.'

'Young gentleman?'

'He's been here all day, Sir James. An army officer. Same regiment as Mr Winston.'

'You mean he is a friend of Winston's?' Anne enquired.

'I do not think so, milady. He has come to see Sir James. Urgent, he said it was.'

Anne and James looked at each other. 'Well,' she said. 'We had better find out what he wants. Bollinger, Wilton.'

'They are already drinking champagne, milady. I'll just open another bottle.' He opened the drawing room door for them, waited for them to enter, closed it again, gently.

'Mother! Daddy!' Lanne was on her feet and hurrying forward to greet them. She had changed from her riding gear into a soft blue chiffon evening gown, as Richard had also changed into his shell-jacket. 'This is Captain Richard Elligan, from Winston's regiment, would you believe it?'

Richard shook hands. 'I hope you'll forgive me, sir, for appearing uninvited. But I needed to see you, and I had no idea you wouldn't be here. So I've rather taken up your daughter's day.'

'She seems to have thrived on it,' James observed.

'You will be staying the night?' Anne asked.

'If you would be so gracious to invite me, your ladyship.'

'Of course he is staying the night,' Lanne said. 'He is so interesting. Why, he has spent the last three years in India and Afghanistan. After having been wounded on the Somme.'

'Is that so,' James said. 'I'm sure we shall look forward to hearing your experiences.'

'At dinner.' Anne took a glass of champagne from Wilton's tray, went to the door. 'I am going to change.'

'Perhaps you'd accompany your mother, Lanne,' James asked.

Lanne bit her lip. But she knew better than to argue with her father. 'And where is Winston?' Anne asked, as the two ladies left the room.

'I have no idea,' Lanne said, sulkily. 'He

has been behaving most oddly all day.'

'Tell me about it,' Anne suggested, as they climbed the stairs.

James gestured Richard to a chair, and drank some champagne. 'I always like to get business out of the way before dinner,' he said.

'Oh, absolutely. It is rather a delicate matter.'

'Tell me.'

'Well ...' Richard sipped his drink. 'Does the name Azam ud-Ranatullah mean anything to you?'

'Come now, Captain Elligan,' James said. 'I'm sure we are both above playing games with each other. Before the war I had business dealings with Sheikh Azam. I sold him guns. They were exported illegally, I'm afraid. But you will find, if you do not already know, that the British Government exonerated me of all blame in the matter.'

'I do know that, sir, and I am very pleased that there need be no subterfuge between us. You know, of course, that the Amir Habibullah of Afghanistan has been assassinated.'

'Of course. I have read the reports. Was not Sheikh Azam one of the people in the amir's howdah when the fatal shot was fired?'

'That is correct, sir. As I was seated on

58

a neighbouring elephant.'

'Were you, by Jove. Must have been exciting. Were you a guest?'

'Only in a manner of speaking, sir. I was military attaché from His Majesty's Government of India with the Afghan government.'

'I see. And this in some way relates to me?'

'I have to tell you, sir, in the strictest confidence, that it is the opinion of the Government of India that Sheikh Azam was involved in the assassination.'

'This opinion was put forward by you.' Richard flushed. 'Well, sir ...'

'Forgive me. But you were the man on the spot, were you not?'

'Yes, sir, I was.'

'And you have reasons for making this accusation?'

'Simply that there can be no doubt that Azam ud-Ranatullah is a friend of Prince Amaruddin, who was also in the amir's howdah when the fatal shot was fired. As perhaps you know, Prince Amaruddin has long been a stormy petrel in Afghan affairs. We have had our eyes on both those gentlemen for some time, and I can tell you that they are extremely shady characters. Or perhaps you already know that?'

'I know nothing of Prince Amaruddin

59

or of Sheikh Azam's political dealings within Afghanistan, Captain. I do know that, when we were in business together, he proved reliable, financially, and a very good friend to me and my family.'

'Of course. He assisted you in regaining your wife and daughter from the clutches of the Mad Mullah.'

'He did, indeed.'

'Therefore, may I be permitted to suggest that he may suppose he has a claim on your gratitude?'

'He does have a claim on my gratitude, Captain. However, I repeat, I have no knowledge of or involvement in Afghan politics. Nor do I intend to have any. But tell me this: are you suggesting that Prince Amaruddin, forgive the Americanism— bumped off his cousin?'

'We have no proof of that, sir. But he is the person most likely to benefit from the murder. And his friends, of course. They would hope to manipulate the late amir's successor, whether it be Nasrullah Khan or Amanullah Khan.'

'Your opinion again. Is this opinion endorsed by the Government of India?'

'Yes, it is.'

'I see. But I still don't understand why you have come to see me on this matter.'

'It is simply that we, the Government

of India, feel that an approach may be made to you by Prince Amaruddin, or by Sheikh Azam, for the supply of guns and ammunition to the regime they intend to set up. Has there been any such approach? We know that Sheikh Azam is in England.'

'Is that a fact. Tell me your objections to such an approach.'

'Well, Sir James, the Government of India has an arrangement with the Government of Afghanistan.'

'You mean it had an arrangement with the late Habibullah Khan.'

Again Richard flushed. 'Habibullah Khan *was* the government of Afghanistan.'

'But, sadly, perhaps, is no longer. This is presumably because not all of his people approved of his Government. Especially its relationship with the Government of India.'

Now Richard's flush was sparked by anger as well as embarrassment. 'That may well be, Sir James. The important thing to remember is that any weapons in Afghan hands, or which may be placed in their hands, could be used against British troops.'

'I see. You are saying that if Nasrullah Khan, once he becomes amir, does not toe the line dictated by the Government of India, it is your intention to invade his country and force him to toe that line. I

61

was under the impression that we had just fought the war to end all wars.'

'Do you not suppose these crazy mountain men may invade India?'

'I consider that extremely unlikely. What could they possibly hope to gain? In any event, I would estimate that the Afghans, who believe the British, even in India, to be honourable men who will deal honourably with them, that is by negotiation and mutual agreement, are far more worried about conditions in Russia, which might at any moment throw up a warlord just as intent upon conquering them as the Government of India.'

'Sir, I find your levity on this important matter most unbecoming.'

'Simmer down, Captain. You're not going to tell me that you weren't briefed on who I was and what I believe in before you came here.'

'I was told that you were a renegade gun-runner who had at last become a patriot.'

'At the time, it was both necessary and rewarding. Now it is no longer necessary, and I have recently been informed that it will mostly certainly no longer be rewarding.'

'You have been given a knighthood for your services to the country.'

'A most grateful country,' James agreed.

'I have not been given anything else. Like so many ex-servicemen, I have been turned onto the street to starve. It is not in my nature to do that, Captain.'

'So you will sell guns to these Afghan rebels?'

'Were they to ask me, I would most certainly go into the matter and discover if it was feasible,' James said, carefully.

Richard stood up. 'Then, sir, I shall bid you good day.'

'It is good evening, Captain,' James said. 'And you have just been invited to dinner and to spend the night. It would be both rude and pointless for you to go rushing off into the night. Now, if you'll excuse me, I must change for dinner. I'll send Lanne to entertain you.'

Richard stared at the door as it closed behind his host. Of all the effrontery, he thought. But what had he expected? He had been warned that James Martingell was a renegade at heart, who had cheated and lied and fought, and where necessary killed his way to the top. That he had always proved himself a bold and determined scoundrel did not alter the fact that he was a scoundrel. Well, then, he would have to be brought down. He ...

'I hope your business with Daddy was satisfactory?' Lanne asked.

He turned, and inhaled her perfume. She was quite the loveliest woman he had ever been close to. The daughter of a renegade gun-runner. Sir James was going to wind up in gaol, he was determined. Then what of the daughter? Was she to be protected? Or taken for what she was, a criminal's daughter? In his present mood, it was the latter. Lanne was ringing the bell. 'I think we need another bottle, Wilton,' she told the butler. Then she came closer. 'You look bothered. Don't tell me things *didn't* go well with Daddy?'

'I'm afraid your father makes up his own rules for life, to the disregard of everything else. It may get him into a great deal of trouble, one of these days.'

'Oh, it often has.' She took a glass of champagne from Wilton's tray, and gestured to Richard to do the same. 'But he always seems to get out of it. Say you'll be friends.'

'I think that may be difficult.'

'Of course it will not be difficult. So you differ on business matters. That does not mean you cannot be friends away from business?'

He gazed into those huge blue eyes. 'Is it important to you that we be friends?'

'I would like that,' she said.

'Mrs Beacham would like a word, milady.'

Claudette, Anne's maid, hovered in the doorway.

'Of course.' Anne gave a little twirl in front of the mirror, and was satisfied. She wore her favourite green, with a low décolletage but shoulders. Her hair was upswept. She had not had to indulge in the bobbing made necessary for so many women by factory working during the war, and she had no intention of cutting her hair now. Nor had she permitted Lanne to do so. Lanne's hair, and her eyes, were the clearest possible refutation of any busybody who might raise the facts of her birth. Of course, it meant that when the girl came to marry, which might be quite soon, a gigantic subterfuge would have to be launched, but as only she, James and Mbote knew the secret, she did not suppose there was a great deal of risk involved.

'I'm sorry to bother you, milady.' Mrs Beacham was a short, stout woman, who looked so serene it was difficult to see her taking the initiative in any direction—but she was actually a severe housekeeper who kept her girls under the strictest control.

'I'm sure it is important, Mrs Beacham,' Anne said. 'I hope nothing is wrong with dinner?'

'Oh, no, milady.' Mrs Beacham's tone indicated that the problem was not *that*

65

important. 'It's the girl Allardyce.'

'What?' Anne's head came up, sharply. 'What about the girl Allardyce?'

'She's gone, milady.'

Anne sat down, and Claudette hurried forward solicitously. 'Gone? I do not understand you.'

'She's left, milady.'

'You mean she's handed in her notice?'

'No, milady. She's just gone.'

'You mean she left the house without permission. I'll speak with her when she returns.'

'I don't think she means to return, milady. She's packed up her things, and taken them with her. I don't think she's coming back.'

'But ... there must have been a reason?'

'Well milady ...' Mrs Beacham flushed scarlet.

'You ticked her off, I suppose. For what?'

'Oh, no, milady. I never said a word.'

'But there is a reason?'

'Well, milady, I don't know for certain. But one of the other girls said they saw Jane leaving Mr Winston's room this afternoon.'

'You mean she shouldn't have been there? She's an upstairs maid.'

Mrs Beacham licked her lips. 'Well, milady, Mr Winston was there too. If you

66

follow me.' Anne stared at her for several seconds. Claudette hastily suppressed a giggle. Mrs Beacham gave her a dirty look. She did not approve of the French, anyway. 'Well, milady,' the housekeeper said. 'Young gentlemen will be young gentlemen, I suppose. But he must have upset her something terrible.'

'Yes,' Anne said grimly. 'Where is Mr Winston, anyway?'

'I think he is dressing for dinner, milady.'

'Thank you, Mrs Beacham. Oh ...' Mrs Beacham, already turning for the door, was checked. 'Have you any idea where Allardyce might have gone?'

'No, I don't, milady. I mean, she's been here six years. I don't think she has another home.'

'Yes. We shall have to find her, and make it up to her. Thank you, Mrs Beacham.'

Anne went first of all to James' room, to find Mbote there. Although the two men's relationship was that of friends rather than master and servant, Mbote had always insisted on acting as James' valet. She told them what had happened. 'You want me to go find her?' Mbote asked.

'She needs to be found. But I think we want to handle this very carefully,' James said, 'in view of what we learned today.' He had told Mbote what Petersen had said. 'I mean, if she was raped by Winston ...'

'Please,' Anne protested.

'You may call it assaulted, if you like that word better. The point is that she was fully entitled to leave. She is fully entitled to bring charges. It wouldn't look very good for us to bring her back here by force.'

'There is also the possibility that she didn't leave because of what Winston did, but because her dad has been in touch,' Mbote said.

'Quite a mess,' James agreed. 'I think we should leave things as they are for tonight, certainly until young Elligan departs in the morning, and then we can begin making discreet enquiries in the villages.'

'Just what did Elligan want, anyway,' Anne asked.

James grinned. 'He came to warn us off dealing with Azam.'

'You mean he knows about the shipment?'

James shook his head. 'All he knows is that Azam is in England, and that we dealt with him before the war. Ergo, he assumes that we may well deal with him again. And he, or his superiors, don't like the idea.'

'His superiors being?'

'In the first instance, the Government of

India. But I would imagine Whitehall is in the background somewhere.'

'And you intend to ignore the warning.'

'I have never taken kindly to warnings. There is really nothing to worry about. Just go downstairs and be charming to the lad. He's clearly very smitten with Lanne. There would be a shock to the British social register. But ... it has to happen some time.'

'I hope you are not saying what I think you are saying, James Martingell,' Anne said. 'Now I need to have a word with Winston.'

'In case it has escaped your notice,' Anne told her son, 'this is 1919. Not 1909. Things have changed. The upstairs maids are no longer fair game. You are very liable to wind up being charged with rape.'

'Oh, come now, Mother,' Winston protested. 'She didn't object. All that bothered her was Mrs Beacham finding out.'

'Presumably you can prove that assertion?'

'Well ... you won't find any bruises on her.'

'I don't know how well that would stand up in a court of law,' Anne said. 'Now, come down to dinner and attempt to behave yourself.' She went to the door, checked. 'What on earth made you do it?'

'I ...' Winston flushed. 'I was upset.'

'What about?' Anne returned to stand beside him, her brain tumbling. 'Was it something that girl said?'

'That girl? Oh, you mean Jane? She didn't say anything, Just oohed and aahed and oh Mr Winston.'

Anne gave a brief sigh of relief. 'Then which girl are we talking about?'

It was Winston's turn to sigh. 'Lanne.'

'Lanne upset you? How?'

Winston raised his head. 'Mother, Lanne and I aren't in any way related, are we?'

'Well, of course not. She was born long before James and I got together.'

'I meant legally.'

Anne sat beside him. 'Lanne is your stepsister. You're not going to tell me ...'

Winston seized her hands. 'I adore her, Mother. I hadn't realised—well, being away for so long, I only ever thought of her as a young girl. Since coming home, and seeing her again, seeing how beautiful she is ... Mother, do you think there is any possibility ...'

Anne's brain was now tumbling so fast she couldn't keep pace with it. She had never been quite certain of James' feelings towards his daughter, whose birth had been an entire accident. That he had rescued her from living her life as the daughter of a prostitute, with the certainty that she would follow her mother into degradation and disease, had been because James was that kind of man, a mixture of utter gallantry and utter ruthlessness. But had he ever had any truly parental love for the girl? That he had charged into the Mullah's camp at the head of his Afghan warriors, Azam ud-Ranatullah and Mbote at his side, had been, she had always felt and hoped, to rescue her more than the child, as Lanne had then been. Now ... would he really encourage a liaison, perhaps even a marriage, between Lanne and this Guards officer, simply to protect his own interests?

Over the years, Anne had become as fond of the girl as if she had been her own daughter. She could not contemplate her being sacrificed, with the certainty of utter misery should Elligan continue to oppose James' plans, and therefore being told the truth about his bride—who might by then even be a mother herself. Whereas, if Lanne were to marry Winston ... that would hardly be less of a sacrifice, she knew. She was under no illusions about her son. His father had been a cruel, deceitful, treacherous man. They had married because Sir Winston Pennyfeather had been broke and had assumed that the daughter of a

South African magnate was the answer to his problems, especially where the daughter was young and beautiful, while she had been young enough and foolish enough to have been dazzled by the thought of becoming a Lady. When, after the marriage, Winston had discovered that her father was actually as broke as himself, he had treated her like dirt in every possible way. When she had squeezed the trigger that had sent him to perdition, while she told herself, and James believed, that she had been saving the life of her lover, she also knew that she had been avenging herself for a dozen years of the most utter mistreatment.

Which had produced a child. She could hope that the half of his character he had inherited from her had made Young Winston a more attractive personality. But she could not pretend that from time to time there was not ample evidence that he had also inherited a great deal from his father. She would not willingly ask any girl to be his wife. But there was the attractive thought that if he married Lanne all their secrets would be kept under this one roof, and she would also be able to protect the girl from the worst of his excesses. 'It would have to be handled very carefully,' she said. 'Has she ...?'

'No,' Winston said. 'That is the trouble.

She treats me like a brother.'

'Well, as I say, it will have to be handled very carefully. Starting now, you must be the soul of courtesy and affection to her. Now finish dressing and come down to dinner.'

'About Allardyce ...'

'Leave Allardyce with me. I shall see that no word of it gets to Lanne. But, Winston ... there must be no others, understood?'

'It's one hell of a tangled world, Mbote,' James said, adjusting his tie.

'Yes,' Mbote agreed. 'You wouldn't seriously sacrifice that little girl for the sake of an arms shipment?' Mbote was the only member of James' entourage who could actually remember Lanne's mother.

'She has to marry some time,' James pointed out. 'And whoever she marries will have to be told the truth, some time. It is a matter of whether he is told the truth before or after the marriage.'

'You don't think Lanne should be told the truth, some time?'

'As I said, it's a tangled old world,' James said. 'Shall we go down?'

Lanne had never been wooed before: having spent most of her adult life either in the Land Army or on this somewhat remote Worcestershire estate, the opportunities had been few. She had, in fact, seldom considered men either as sexual objects or as prospective husbands. She put this down to that terrible episode in her childhood, when she and Stepmother and several others of the household had been kidnapped by the Somalis and held for ransom. As she and Stepmother had been the principal captives, they had not been ill treated in any way, save by the sheer fact of being prisoners in a strange and barbaric environment.

But the threat had been there. The Mullah had said that if Father did not appear with the ransom by a stated date, he would give them to his men. She had asked Anne what that meant; Anne had said, 'It's a game.' Even then she had known it was not a game. Since then, as she had learned what would have been involved, she still shuddered at the thought. That had been her first truly remembered contact with the real world. Before then, her childhood had been a sequence of nightmares, out of which it had emerged that Mother—her real mother—had been a *bad* woman. Because of men! Lanne had never been certain why that had been so—it had certainly not encouraged her to look kindly upon the male sex. Would she again shudder the first time a man's hand was laid on her body, even lovingly?

But that she was now being wooed, and by two men at once, was unarguable. She was taken entirely by surprise. Richard Elligan was a handsome, well-born, articulate man. He was also in opposition to Father, but his manners at dinner were impeccable, and his attention to her the ultimate in admiration. Far more surprising was the behaviour of Winston, who had actually tried to manhandle her that afternoon, but who was now all polite and loving attention. She presumed Mother had had a hand in that, as Anne smiled benignly at her son throughout the meal. While Father, surprisingly, smiled benignly at Richard. There was a good deal going on she did not understand.

'It is a simply glorious night,' Richard said. 'Would you care to take a walk in the garden, Lanne?'

'Why ...' She glanced at James, who had signalled Wilton to replace the port with the brandy decanter.

'Why not?' James asked.

'Great idea,' Winston said. 'I'll fetch your wrap.'

'I suspect Richard would prefer to be *à deux*,' James said, still smiling.

'Why, sir ...' Richard gave one of his flushes. 'If you have no objection, Sir James? Lady Martingell?'

Anne knew she had to continue to proceed very warily. 'Of course we do not object, Captain,' she said. 'Besides, Winston and his father need to have a little chat.'

'Indeed we do,' James said. 'Sit down, Winston.' He waited for Richard and Lanne to depart through the French windows. 'Tell me about this business with Jane Allardyce.'

'For God's sake,' Winston said. 'I told Mother. We had a little fun, there was no question of the girl being forced. What's so important about an upstairs maid? She wasn't a virgin, if that's what's bothering you.'

'I'm sure that was a relief to you. What did you talk about, while having this bit of fun?'

Winston gave his mother an impatient look. 'I told you, Mother. She didn't say anything, of the least importance.'

'And afterwards. While presumably you were enjoying a cigarette?'

'She just left. She put on her clothes and left. How was I to know she was going to run off?'

'Oh, quite. Well, you and Mbote will have to find her tomorrow, and persuade her to come back. You'll offer her money.'

'What's so important about an upstairs maid?' Winston asked again.

'We have a position in the county,' James said. 'Which your mother and I intend to maintain.'

They gazed at the moon, and then at each other, and then sat on one of the wooden benches at the far end of the croquet lawn. There was no wind, and the garden was filled with scent as well as shadow. 'I had forgotten how lovely England can be,' Richard said.

'Isn't India lovely? I have always read that it is.'

'Some things in India are quite beautiful. More beautiful than anything in England. But then some things are quite ghastly. And there is a difference between beauty and loveliness.'

'Tell me.'

'Well, in my opinion, at the least, beauty is hard, cold, perhaps unchanging. Loveliness is soft, changing ... it makes one wish to protect it. You are lovely.'

'Why, Captain Elligan. Do you realise we only met this morning?'

'That seems a hundred years ago. I know. I am being quite impossibly forward. But I feel that our time is very short.'

'Because of Daddy? Are you going to try to stop him?'

'Try to stop him doing what? He has broken no laws as yet, to my knowledge.'

'But you are afraid he is going to.'

'If he attempts to ship arms to Afghanistan without a licence he will find himself in serious trouble.' He held her hand. 'Will you help me?'

'To stop Daddy? I don't think I could do that.'

'Even to save him from prison? Lanne, we know he shipped arms to Afghanistan before the war. How did he do that?'

There was only the briefest hesitation. 'I have no idea,' she said. 'I was just a child then.'

But he knew she had lied. Richard sighed. 'I'm sorry. I had hoped that perhaps you and I, working together, could save your family a great deal of trouble.'

'Is that why you asked me to walk with you?'

'Well ...' His flush was hidden in the darkness. 'Of course not. I think ... In normal circumstances, I would like to see more of you.'

She giggled. 'There's a double entendre. And cannot circumstances be normal between us?'

'I shall be returning to London tomorrow. Unfortunately, I shall be there for only a few days. If you were to come up to town during that time, I should very much like to take you out to dinner.'

'I think I should enjoy that. Supposing I did come, where would I find you?'

'Where will you be staying?'

'We always stay at the Savoy.'

'Ah! Right. Then I will find you. When would you be able to come?'

'I shall come tomorrow afternoon. If I give you time to leave, and then catch the noon train, I shall be in the hotel by five o'clock.' He raised her hand to his lips and kissed it.

Richard Elligan left after breakfast the next morning.

'Impudent oaf,' Winston growled, standing on the porch to wave his superior out of sight. He and Mbote were dressed for their quest.

'You got any special orders, James?' Mbote asked, in the privacy of the study.

James indicated the wad of neatly folded five-pound notes. 'Use those, for a start. Promise her nothing like this will ever happen again.'

'And the other matter?'

'If she has made contact with her father, find out where he is. If she is with her father, persuade him to come here and have a chat with me.'

'Persuade, James?'

'Do what you can. No violence. And do not in any way arouse any suspicions that

79

we may be afraid of him or anything he can do. That we know where he is will be a start.'

Mbote pinched his lip. 'There is only one way to deal with a blackmailer. Even a potential blackmailer.'

'I know that, Mbote. But we will pick our time and place. Above all, nothing is to be said or done in front of Winston.'

'And you?'

James grinned. 'I am going to the warehouse to get things moving. I told Azam we'd ship immediately. Since my chat with Elligan, I reckon the more immediately it is the better.'

'Why are Winston and Mbote going off after that girl Allardyce?' Lanne asked. She and her stepmother were seated on the back terrace enjoying a mid-morning cup of coffee. James had already left for the warehouse.

'How did you know that is what they are doing?' Anne asked.

'One of the other girls told me.'

'But she didn't know why. I am glad of that. We wish to keep it as private as possible. The fact is that Jane Allardyce stole some silver, and went off with it.'

'Allardyce? That's incredible.'

'Why is it incredible?'

'Well ... she's been here for years, hasn't

she? She's virtually a member of the family. And isn't her father a crewman on the yacht?'

'Ah ... he was, certainly. But he's quit.'

'Why?'

'Oh, he took to the bottle and fell out with Captain Petersen. We think that may be why his daughter is behaving as she is.' Anne realised she was getting herself into a tangled mess of lies. 'Don't worry about it. Mbote will sort it out, hopefully without a scandal.'

'If she's stolen something she should go to prison,' Lanne said, definitely.

'Yes. Well, we want to avoid that if we can.'

'May I go up to town this afternoon?' The question took Anne by surprise. 'Why, of course you may. Shopping, is it?'

'Ah ... yes. I need some new gloves.'

Anne put down her coffee cup and regarded her stepdaughter with some severity. 'You're going to meet that ghastly captain.'

'Mother! Richard is not in the least ghastly. But ... yes, he has invited me out to dinner.'

'You have arranged a meeting?'

'No, he will call me at the Savoy, tonight.'

'And I absolutely forbid it.'

Lanne stared at her with her mouth open.

'I'm sorry,' Anne said. 'But I would have thought you'd have realised that he is trying to interfere with your father's business.'

'He was given a job to do,' Lanne said. 'And he is doing it. Outside of his job, there is surely no reason why we should not be friends.'

'Lanne,' Anne said, also speaking with great definiteness, 'I do not wish you to see that man.'

Lanne stood up, cheeks flaming. 'You can't stop me. I'm twenty-two years old.'

Anne also stood up. 'I will speak with your father.'

'He can't stop me either,' Lanne snapped, and stamped into the house.

Anne sat down again, slowly refilled her coffee cup. There were times, no doubt reflecting the violent events of her younger days, when she was tempted to take a hairbrush to both of her children. But as Lanne had pointed out, they were adults. More importantly, she knew, and Lanne did not, that speaking to James would be a complete waste of time. The temptation to let the girl get on with it and ruin her life was even greater than using the brush. But the resulting scandal might ruin the entire family.

As for Winston's aspirations, which made far more sense ... She mused as she drank. How much did James love her? She had given him everything, even control of the Pennyfeather Small Arms Company, now renamed the Martingell Arms Company. He knew he owed her his life, and down to a few years ago he had always been a passionate lover. He had risked his own life to save her from an unthinkable fate in Somaliland. But their actual relationship had never been put to the test, mainly she supposed because they both knew too much about the other. Besides, although James, because of his good looks and forceful personality, had attracted a lot of women in his youth, he had been less exposed in recent years—he had never shown the least tendency to stray. Neither had she, since they had come together. But he knew of her own dissolute past, when marriage to Winston Pennyfeather had been an ongoing purgatory, and she had sought some relief in other men's arms. That was history, forgotten and forgiven. Would he forgive her a late flurry, as it were?

Yet it had to be done. Whatever she did would be for the good of the firm and the family, and he would understand that. Surely. Besides, the idea was enormously exciting and attractive; recently James had not been entirely fulfilling. Would she ever eradicate that streak of wild, sensual *desire* which had dictated her entire life—and from which James had most certainly benefited?

She was never a woman who lingered over her decisions. She finished her coffee and went upstairs. Claudette was in her bedroom, laying out clothes. Claudette loved playing with her mistress's expensive wardrobe, and she certainly kept the clothes in immaculate order. 'Claudette,' Anne said. 'Do you know where Miss Lanne is?'

'Oh, madame, I think she is in her room. She came upstairs with a great banging of the door.'

'Very good. Prepare me a bath and a change of clothing. Town clothes, and an evening gown. I will select the jewellery.'

'We are going to town, madame?'

'I am going to town.'

'But, madame, you cannot travel without me.'

'In this instance I am going to. You will have duties to occupy you here. I will tell you what I wish you to do.' She regarded the young woman. 'I have always been a good mistress to you, I hope?'

'Oh, yes, madame.'

'You will not find a better position in England. Or in France, I should think.'

'Oh, no, madame.'

'Then I trust you will remember that. And whatever you have to do will be rewarded, I do promise you.'

'Oh, yes, madame. I will do anything you require.'

'Well, sir, yes,' said the constable in the village. 'The Allardyce girl was here, yesterday afternoon.' His eyes rolled, as did most people's, when confronted with Mbote, even wearing the tweeds of an English country gentleman.

'You spoke with her?'

'Yes, sir, I did. Asked how things were at the manor, like.'

'And what did she say?' Mbote glanced at Winston, who was shifting from foot to foot somewhat anxiously.

'Just that she'd been given time off, and was going home.'

'Where might that have been, exactly?' Mbote asked.

'Well, sir, she didn't say that. But she took the bus for Tattenham.'

'Thank you, constable.' Mbote got into the car, and Winston cranked the engine then sat behind the wheel. 'So far we're ahead.'

'Tattenham,' Winston muttered as they

85

drove off. 'What's she doing there?'

'Probably changing buses.'

Winston drove in silence for some minutes. 'I don't know why we don't call this chase off,' he said at last. 'If she was going to complain to the police about what happened, wouldn't she have done it to Constable Barkin?'

'Probably not. Constable Barkin is in awe of your stepfather, as are most people around here. She'll have wanted to go further afield.' Winston relapsed into an uncertain silence, and a few minutes later they arrived at Tattenham. This was an altogether larger village, and in addition to a bus station even had a ticketing office. 'We are looking for a young lady, Jane Allardyce, who may have come in on the bus yesterday afternoon,' Mbote explained.

'Oh, aye, squire,' said the ticket agent. 'She did that.'

'You remember her?'

'Oh, surely, squire. She comes here regular, like.'

'Why?'

'Why, it's since her dad came here to live.'

'Ah,' Mbote said. 'Could you direct us to his house?'

'House, is it? He has a room at the Widow Bould. It's round the corner and the third on the left.'

'Thank you,' Mbote said.

'You want to watch it,' the agent called after them as they returned to the car. 'He drinks and has a temper.'

'Thank you,' Mbote said again. 'I think, in all the circumstances, that you should remain with the car,' he suggested to Winston. 'Let me go and visit them, and see what I can sort out.'

'I'm not asking you to do my dirty work, Mbote,' Winston declared.

'And if she's accused you of rape?'

'As I said, she'd have done that to Constable Barkin. Anyway, I'm not afraid of Harry Allardyce.'

Mbote considered. James had told him so many things that needed to be avoided. Antagonising Winston was one of them. And Jane Allardyce, whatever her relationship with a father she could hardly know, was more likely to return in the company of a white man, with whom she had already rolled in the sack, than with a large black man—Mbote knew that most of the servants were afraid of him. 'All right,' he agreed. 'But let me do the talking, right?'

'You're the boss,' Winston said, willingly.

'Anyway, we'll leave the car,' Mbote said. 'We don't want to alarm them by turning up in a Rolls.' They followed the instructions and walked round the corner, found the lodging house without difficulty. It looked neat and clean, as fitted the appearance of the middle-aged woman who answered the door. 'I believe you have a Mr Allardyce lodging here,' Mbote said.

Mrs Bould's face, already cold at the sight of a black man on her doorstep, now turned to ice. 'What's that to you?' she asked.

'I'd like a word with him. Or at least, with his daughter.'

'Oh, yes? What's it all about, then? What are you, police? We don't have no black policemen around here.'

'Were you expecting the police?'

'That I was not. What Mr Allardyce does isn't my business. He doesn't do it here.'

Mbote wondered what 'it' was. 'I am personal secretary to Sir James Martingell,' he explained, pleasantly. 'And this is Sir James' son, Mr Winston Martingell.'

'Oh, eh?' She peered at Winston. 'Is that the truth?'

'Of course it is, my good woman,' Winston said. 'We would be very obliged if you'd let us have a word with Miss Allardyce. You may not know it, but she is a servant at my father's house.'

'Oh, eh,' Mrs Bould remarked again. 'I'll call her.'

'We'd prefer to go up,' Mbote said.

She considered. He realised that she would never have admitted a black man into her house before. But she was clearly reflecting that it could do no harm to assist agents of Sir James Martingell. 'Oh, eh,' she decided at last. 'It's the door on the landing.' She frowned at them. 'I'll have no trouble, mind. Or it'll be calling the police.'

'Why should there be trouble?' Mbote asked, and went up the stairs, Winston behind him.

He knocked. 'Who's there?' demanded a man's voice, remembered well enough.

'Mbote.'

'Mbote?' There was a brief hesitation, and even a whispered conversation from beyond the door, then it swung in. 'Mbote?' Harry Allardyce was a big man, but not so big as Mbote.

'Hello, Allardyce,' Mbote said. 'May we come in?'

'We?' Allardyce blinked past him, as if expecting to see a policeman at his shoulder. Winston was half invisible in the gloom of the corridor.

'Who're you expecting?' Mbote asked. 'You there, Jane?'

'Now you look here, Mbote,' Allardyce

said. 'If you've come to make trouble ...'

'No trouble,' Mbote assured him. 'I'm looking for Jane.' Gently he moved Allardyce out of the doorway and stepped inside, motioning Winston to stay where he was for the moment.

'I had to leave, Mr Mbote,' Jane said, from the far side of the room.

'All you had to do was complain to Lady Martingell,' Mbote said. 'She'd have done the right thing. She wants to do the right thing now. I'm to offer you a rise in pay if you'll come back.'

'Hey, hey,' Allardyce said. 'A rise in pay?'

'We really would like you to come back, Jane,' Winston said, following Mbote into the room. 'We—I'll make it up to you, I promise.'

'Rise in pay, make it up then, what's all this, then?' Allardyce enquired. 'You told me you'd been fired, you little runt. Who the hell are you, anyway?' he demanded of Winston.

'Winston Pennyfeather,' Winston said, 'I'm Lady Martingell's son.'

'Winston Pennyfeather, by God,' Allardyce said. Mbote uttered a curse under his breath. 'I saw your dad die,' Allardyce declared. 'I saw your mummy shoot him down like a dog.'

90

Chapter 3

Criminal Matters

Winston stared at the seaman, while Mbote tried desperately to think. 'My father was killed by Socotran pirates, wretched man,' Winston said.

'Socotran pirates,' Allardyce sneered. 'That's the story put about. Paid us well, they did, your mummy and that Martingell. But she shot him. To save Martingell. Ask the black. He was there. Shot him down like a pig, she did.'

'Liar!' Winston screamed, and hurled himself at the sailor. They fell over a chair together while Jane Allardyce also screamed.

'Do something,' she begged Mbote. Mbote grasped Winston's shoulder as the young man pummelled blows into Allardyce's body. Now he threw an arm backwards, catching Mbote across the face. Mbote staggered and himself fell down. Jane jumped over him and ran to the door. 'Help!' she shrieked. 'Mrs Bould! Call the police! They're killing each other! Help!'

Mbote sat up, wiping blood from his cut lip, watched Winston worrying Allardyce as a dog might have done. Allardyce was fighting back the best he could, but Winston was a highly trained army officer, relatively fresh from two years in the trenches, and as fit as a horse. Allardyce's blows were already growing more feeble as Winston's powerful hands closed on his throat. 'Hey!' Mbote scrambled to his feet, again grasped Winston's shoulder, this time ready for a riposte. But Winston ignored him, while still squeezing away. And Allardyce's face had turned white, as he was no longer making any sound.

Exerting all his strength, Mbote jerked Winston to his feet. Allardyce came with them; Winston's hands remained locked on his throat. Mbote released the young man to hit him twice across the face, and Winston at last released Allardyce and fell against the wall. Having called for help, Jane Allardyce had remained standing in the doorway. Now she dropped to her knees beside her father's body as he struck the floor. 'Daddy!' she screamed. 'Oh, Daddy!'

Mbote knelt beside her, but he could tell at a glance that Allardyce was dead. He glanced at Winston, who had slumped to a sitting position against the wall, wiping blood from his face where Mbote had hit him. 'Christ, but you are in trouble, boy,' Mbote said.

'He was lying,' Winston muttered. 'Tell me he was lying.'

Time for a quick decision. 'Yeah, he was lying,' Mbote said. 'Just trying to cause trouble.'

There were feet on the stairs; Mrs Bould, already uneasy, had not had far to go to fetch a policeman. 'Now then,' said that worthy. 'What's all this 'ere?'

'He killed my dad,' Jane shouted. 'That Winston ... he killed my dad.'

The policeman peered at Winston, and then at Allardyce. 'Holy Mary Mother of God,' he muttered, and dropped to one knee. 'Is he dead?' He asked the question at large.

'Yes,' Winston said. 'I killed the bastard.'

'Murderer!' screamed Jane.

'Oh, my Lord,' remarked Mrs Bould. 'I keep a respectable house, Mr Lewin.'

Constable Lewin removed his helmet to scratch his head; he had never had to deal with a murder before. 'I'll 'ave to place you under arrest,' he told Winston. 'You've confessed to it, see?' He looked around. 'You 'eard him confess.'

'Doesn't mean a thing,' Mbote pointed out. 'You never cautioned him.'

'And 'o may you be, if I may ask?' Lewin enquired.

'He is my father's man,' Winston said, deciding, mistakenly, to take charge of the proceedings. 'My father is Sir James Martingell, of Martingell House in the next parish.'

'Is that a fact.' Once again Lewin looked around, for confirmation.

'A right lot of bastards,' Jane suggested. 'He raped me, he did. And then murdered me dad.'

Lewin was clearly inclined to agree with her, not being a supporter of the aristocracy, or even the landed gentry. 'I'm arresting you both,' he decided, 'on a charge of murder.' He raked his memory. 'You don't 'ave to say nothing, but if you do say something, I'll use it in evidence against you. Right?'

'Near enough,' Mbote agreed.

'And none of your lip, black feller.'

'Am I allowed to make a request?'

'Such as what?'

'That Sir James be informed of what has happened.'

'Soon enough,' Lewin said. 'Soon enough. First things first, eh? Now you come down to the station. And no trouble,' he added, suddenly realising that either of the men he was arresting, much less both, could probably break him in two without too much effort.

'Here, what about the stiff?' demanded

94

Mrs Bould, dropping her affected accent in her agitation. 'You can't leave him there.'

'No one's touching 'im until my inspector has seen 'im,' Lewin said. 'You'll lock this door, Mrs Bould, and give me the key.'

It was Jane's turn to protest. 'What about my things, then?'

'They'll 'ave to stay there for the time being, miss.'

'Shit!' Jane commented, also reverting to type. 'See what a fucking awful mess you've caused?' she shouted at Winston. She seemed far more concerned at having to abandon her belongings than at the death of her father.

'Now, then, miss,' Lewin said. 'No trouble. Come along, you fellows.'

James parked the car outside the house and went up the front steps. Wilton waited for him with a glass of sherry. 'Her ladyship out the back?' James asked.

He felt pleased with himself. A visit to the warehouse had established that he could deliver all of the weapons needed by Azam from surplus—the arms he was supposed to be dumping. 'You'll load up immediately, Mr Grayson,' he told the factory manager. 'We need to move this stuff as quickly as possible.'

95

Grayson remained a cautious man. 'It's all above board, Sir James?' he had asked anxiously. 'I was told all this merchandise was to be dumped.'

'So it is.'

'There'll be a licence, then?'

'It'll be here next week,' James said. He had his own printing press and was adept at forging the necessary documents. 'But we load immediately.' Anne, James thought happily, would be pleased.

But Wilton was looking agitated. 'Her ladyship is not here, sir. She has gone up to town. She said to tell you she will be back tomorrow.'

'When did she leave?'

'About eleven, sir. I believe she intended to catch the twelve-fifteen to Paddington.'

James looked at his gold hunter; that train would be leaving now, and it was an express, He drank some sherry. Off to London, without mentioning a word of her intentions to him? That was certainly not like Anne. Whatever could have happened? But no doubt she would explain everything tomorrow when she returned. 'Very well, Wilton, thank you.' He strode into the house. 'Mr Mbote and Winston back yet?'

'No, sir.'

'Hm. They may well be lunching out. Very good. Ask Miss Lanne to join me on the terrace.'

'Ah ...' Now Wilton was looking positively terrified. 'Miss Lanne is in her room, sir.'

'All right. Ask her to come down, will you.'

'She has locked herself in, sir, and is refusing admittance to anyone. She will speak with no one, sir.'

James began to wonder if all his womenfolk had gone mad. But Lanne was a grown woman. If, as appeared obvious, she had had a quarrel with her stepmother, it was not for him to interfere. Again, all would be revealed tomorrow, no doubt. He had always operated on the basis of letting people get on with their lives, so far as they did not interfere with him getting on with his own life. 'Very good, Wilton. Then I shall be lunching alone, it seems.'

'Yes, sir,' Wilton agreed, clearly very relieved that the master was taking this domestic upheaval so calmly.

James picked one of the newspapers from the stand by the door, folded it under his arm, and went through to the back terrace. Here all was peace, as he looked out at the lawns and flowerbeds, and beyond, the woods, that fringed the back of the estate. He drank some sherry, sat down, unfolded the paper, and gazed in surprise at the figure of Claudette, flitting by at the far end of the terrace, apparently attempting to regain the house without being seen. He put down both sherry glass and newspaper, stood up. 'Claudette!' he bellowed. She hesitated, then turned to face him and gave a little curtsey. 'Come here,' he called.

Slowly she advanced towards him, a trim figure in her black gown and white apron and cap; her hair, caught up in a tight bun, was reddish-brown—he had never seen it loose but he estimated it was fairly long—and her features small and pretty enough, although at the moment they were twisting themselves into all manner of grotesque expressions. 'What are you doing here?' James enquired.

''Ere, Sir James? I live 'ere.'

'I meant, what are you doing here, when Lady Martingell has gone to London?'

'Her ladyship say I am not to go, Sir James.'

Odder and odder. 'She must have given you a reason.'

'She just say I am not to go, Sir James.'

He knew she was lying. 'One of these days, Claudette, I am going to put you across my knee and spank you.'

'Ooh, la-la, Sir James.' She gave a little shudder, from neck to ankle, her gown rustling. But the shudder was not entirely of distaste.

'Would you like it to be today?' he asked. Because while he had never looked at Claudette twice before, as she was invariably in the company of his wife, he suddenly found the idea attractive himself.

'Ooh, Sir James.' Another little shudder.

'Because it will be if you do not tell me the truth. Where has Lady Martingell gone?'

Claudette looked at the floor, hands clasped in front of her stomach. 'I think it must be the Savoy 'Otel, Sir James.'

'Why has she gone there, without taking you?'

'She did not say, Sir James. She just say I am to stay 'ere.'

'Right,' James said 'Upstairs.'

Claudette's head came up. 'You are going to beat me, Sir James?'

'Unless you tell me the truth, yes.' Would he do it? The last woman he had ever clashed with, physically, had been Lanne's mother, and there had been ample reason for that; it was not in his nature to ill treat women. Yet the idea attracted him. Was he becoming a vicious old man? Or was he just suddenly angry at the mystery that was surrounding him, on a day which so far had gone so well?

Claudette went into the house and up the stairs. James followed, watching her hips moving beneath the heavy skirt. Had this been what Winston had felt when he had followed the Allardyce girl upstairs yesterday? He had dismissed Winston as a vicious young fool. Then what would he say of himself? He simply had to get out of this impasse, somehow. Because if he laid a finger on her, he was not going to stop at a whipping.

On the gallery Claudette hesitated, looking from his bedroom to that of her mistress. 'In there.' He pointed.

She went to his door, opened it, and checked. They had both heard the sound together.

'What was that?' James demanded.

'That, Sir James?' Now she was definitely trembling.

'It came from Miss Lanne's room. Who has she got in there with her?'

'I don't think there is anybody in there with 'er, Sir James.'

James glanced at her, then strode to Lanne's door, tried the handle. It was locked. He knocked. 'Lanne? What are you doing in there?' The noise came again, a kind of high-pitched but inarticulate moaning. 'Lanne!' Now James was shouting. He banged on the door. 'If you do not open this door I shall break it down.'

'Mmmmmm,' was the only reply he got.

James stood at the balustrade. 'Wilton!' he shouted. 'Fetch two of the gardeners and come up here.'

Claudette had been shifting from foot to foot. Now she gasped, 'I 'ave the key, Sir James.'

James turned towards her, slowly. 'You have the key? You mean she is locked in? My daughter is locked in her room. Why you ...'

He stepped forward, his expression suddenly so angry Claudette burst into tears. 'I 'ave only done what 'er ladyship wished, Sir James.'

'The key,' James snapped. Claudette took the key from the pocket of her apron. 'Thank you,' James said. 'Go into that bedroom and wait there.' He returned to the balustrade, looked down at the men assembling there, together with several downstairs maids and Mrs Beacham. 'There is no need, now,' he said. 'Go back to your work.'

He inserted the key into the lock, turned it, stepped into darkness. He strode to the window, drew the curtains, flooded the room with light, and gazed at his daughter. Lanne lay on her back on her bed in her nightdress, spreadeagled, her wrists bound to the upper bedpost, her ankles to the lower. She was gagged. Both her hair and her nightgown were disarranged where she had tried to free herself by tossing to and fro, and she made an evocative sight. It was something of a surprise to James that he had never seen his daughter's legs before, certainly not since she had reached puberty. 'In the name of God!' he remarked, and freed her wrists. She brought her arms together and gasped as he pulled the gag free. 'Who did this?'

'My stepmother,' Lanne said, in a low, angry voice.

James freed her ankles, pulled down her nightdress. 'Anne? Why on earth ...'

'To stop me going up to London,' Lanne said, sitting up and rubbing her feet as circulation returned.

'But she has gone to London.' James was trying desperately to keep his emotions under control.

'I suppose she has, the bitch,' Lanne said.

James scratched his head, unwilling at that moment even to reproach the girl for so speaking of her stepmother. 'There is some mystery here. Would you explain it to me?'

'I want something to drink,' Lanne said. 'God, my mouth tastes like a sewer. And I'm starving.'

James went to the door. Several of the servants, including Wilton, were still gathered in the downstairs hall. 'Wilton,' he said, 'a jug of orange juice. And two large brandies.' He returned to the bedroom. 'When you have had something to drink, you can get dressed and join me for lunch. But first, I wish to know what is going on. I've had enough evasion from Claudette.'

'Claudette?' Lanne snapped. 'She helped Mother tie me up. Then she was left here, as my gaoler. When I get my hands on her, I am—'

'I think you should leave Claudette to me,' James said. 'Now tell me what is happening.'

Lanne hunched her shoulders; she was not certain what his reaction was going to be. 'Richard invited me out to dinner, in London. But Stepmama said I couldn't go. When I told her I was going anyway, she forced me in here, she and that bitch Claudette, and tied me to the bed. My God, just as if I was some schoolgirl.'

'By Richard, I assume you mean Captain Elligan.'

'Yes,' Lanne said sulkily.

'You were meaning to go up to town, alone, and have dinner with this fellow.'

'I'm a grown woman,' Lanne said.

'There are still certain things one does and one doesn't do. What were you planning on doing after dinner?'

Lanne glared at her father, her cheeks

103

pink. 'I have absolutely no idea.'

'But you're fond of this fellow.'

'Well ... he's very nice. Very handsome.'

'True. You know he was sent here to talk me out of doing business with the Afghans?'

'Well ... yes. He told me that.'

'And when I refused to accept his warning, he threatened me? Did you know that?'

'He never told me that.'

'It's something you should know. So your stepmother has gone off to meet him herself.'

'She wouldn't dare!'

'Anne is a woman who has spent her life daring to do what others might think too risky. I wonder what she proposed to tell him?'

'What are you going to do?'

'Nothing.'

'Nothing?' she shouted.

'I certainly do not propose to go charging about the country like a demented lover, if that's what you mean.'

'She's taken my place,' Lanne said, now speaking quietly. 'Suppose she sleeps with him?'

'Is that what you were proposing to do?'

Lanne tossed her head. 'If he asked me to, yes.' Just like her mother, James thought, and wondered if he had indeed made a mistake in keeping the truth from her all of these years. But now was certainly not the time. 'She'd be committing adultery,' Lanne pointed out.

Not for the first time, James reflected. But that was before their marriage. She had been the most chaste of women since. 'If she does find that necessary, I'm sure she'll tell me of it when she comes home,' he said, and went to the door.

'But you'll punish Claudette,' Lanne insisted. 'Her creature.'

'I might well do that,' James said. 'Now, you get dressed, and come down to lunch.' He closed the door behind him.

James went to his own bedroom door, which was shut. He opened it, and Claudette, who had been sitting on the bed, rose like a startled pheasant. They gazed at each other for several seconds, then she slowly licked her lips. What am I going to do? he wondered. He knew what he wanted to do, a sudden surging desire compounded by the sight of his nearly naked daughter and the knowledge that Anne might be doing the same thing in London. With that scoundrel Elligan? He couldn't believe that. He couldn't see a reason for it.

She was still acting entirely on her own, pursuing her own plans ... and he did not know what those plans were. He was angry with her, and because he knew he could never vent that anger, it was turning against her servant, compounded by lust and the knowledge that he could never touch Lanne, either. Their combined whipping girl, he thought. But he had got entangled with servants before. Not merely Lanne's mother Martha. There had been Cecile von Beinhardt's maid, Lisette. Cecile had chosen him as a husband, but had died, tragically, before they could be married. He wondered how differently his life might have turned out had she not insisted on making that senseless journey to East Africa and a malarial grave? He would probably have been on the wrong side in the war! And Lisette had been waiting, knowing of his crimes, determined to use that knowledge for her own ends.

He wondered, as she had willingly wound up in the Mullah's harem, how she was faring now. For the Mullah still lived, and carried on his endless war against the British and the French and the Italians in the Horn of Africa. Idle thoughts. A man should always learn from the past, from his experiences. But they should never be allowed to determine his future.

'Do you wish me to undress, Sir James?' Claudette's voice was soft. She could see the desire in his eyes.

106

'You'll stay here,' he said. 'Until I return.'

'I 'ave not 'ad my lunch,' Claudette pointed out.

'You won't have any lunch today. You'll stay here, until I am ready to ... speak with you.'

'You think I am a schoolgirl?' Claudette demanded. 'To be sent to bed without any supper?'

'I think you are my servant, who will do as she is told,' James said, and closed the door.

'Where are Mbote and Winston?' Lanne enquired over the meal. She sat next to her father at one end of the long oak table.

'Looking for that Allardyce girl. I suppose they have had to go further than we thought.'

'I still don't understand what the fuss is about, regarding her,' Lanne said. 'She's just a maid.'

'Did you know that Winston assaulted her?'

Lanne's eyes grew large as saucers. 'Assaulted?'

'I think you know what I mean.'

'Oh, good Lord.' She crumbled bread between her fingers, but could say nothing as Wilton, who had been at the far end of the room, came up the table to remove their plates. When the butler had gone into the kitchen for the next course, she whispered, 'You mean Winston raped her?'

'He claims it was with her consent. But she ran off. So I have sent them to find her.'

'Finding her won't stop her bringing charges,' Lanne said.

'There are other reasons.'

'Tell me, Daddy?'

'I don't think I should, right now.'

She pouted. 'Everyone treats me like a child. Or a halfwit. Suppose Richard were to ask me to marry him?' She held her breath.

'I think that might be a very good idea,' James said.

Lanne dropped her bread in consternation, but had the time to recover while Wilton served the meat course. Then she said, 'That is what Stepmama is determined to prevent.'

'Yes,' he said thoughtfully.

'Why, Daddy?' She was using her most winning tone.

'We'll discuss it when Anne gets back,' James said, in a tone that allowed no further argument. But Richard Elligan had not appeared the sort of man who could be seen off by mere argument, or even warning. It would have to be something far stronger, quite decisive. Would she do

108

it? Meanwhile ... he finished his meal and got up. 'I suggest you just relax this afternoon.'

'I shall go for a ride.' Lanne also got up. 'You *are* going to punish Claudette? I mean, a servant, tying me up.'

'I am going to punish Claudette,' he promised.

But he went first of all to his study, to use the telephone. Curiosity, and anxiety, was getting the better of even his controlled personality. 'Savoy Hotel.'

'Good afternoon. Can you tell me if Lady Martingell is staying with you?'

'I'm afraid we do not divulge the names of our guests, sir.'

'This is Sir James Martingell speaking,' James said mildly. 'My wife telephoned this morning to make a reservation.' He was guessing, but there was no way Anne would have gone up to London without an hotel reservation.

'Ah. Lady Martingell is expected, Sir James. As you say, she telephoned to make a reservation this morning. But she has not yet arrived.'

'Can you tell me if there is a message for her?'

'Ah ...' Presumably the man was looking through various envelopes. 'Yes, sir, there is. To be delivered to her on her arrival.'

'Thank you.'

'Shall I ask Lady Martingell to telephone you, Sir James? When she arrives?'

'No, no,' James said. 'I shall be out this afternoon. I shall probably call her this evening. And by the way, there is no need to tell her I called. Do you understand me?'

'Of course, Sir James.' The clerk had had sufficient experience of dealing with husbands keeping a watchful eye on their wives—or vice versa.

'Thank you,' James said, and hung up.

Whatever was going to happen, was going to happen. Anne had either taken a shine to Richard Elligan herself, or she was prepared to go to any lengths to stop him and Lanne having an affair. Because that might lead to marriage?

His alternatives were unchanged. He could, despite what he had said to Lanne, go galloping up to town armed with a horsewhip, or he could behave like a civilised human being and wait for his wife to return and provide him with a full explanation of what had happened. He had never really been a civilised human being, however hard he tried. But this time ... he could occupy his time.

He went upstairs. Claudette was now lying on the bed, but she sat up and swung her legs to the floor as he came in. 'I am so 'ungry,' she said.

'You can eat as soon as I am finished with you.'

Another quick circle of her lips. 'You are going to beat me?'

'I haven't made up my mind yet. Undress.'

''Ow much?'

'Everything, Claudette.'

'Ooh, la-la. You 'ave no right to do this, Sir James.' But she was taking off her pinafore.

'So what will you do afterwards? You will not find a better job than this one.'

She bit her lip as she unbuttoned her gown and let it sink about her ankles. Daintily she picked it up as she stepped out of it, then took off her petticoat. She was certainly a practised coquette; she hesitated when the garment was about her waist, as if she had struck a snag, allowing him a long look at the black-stocking-clad legs, the suspender belt, the white drawers, before she placed that garment too on the chair. Then she turned to face him, hands at her side so that her breasts were exposed, waiting. To discover if he was a typically perverted English gentleman, he supposed. 'Everything,' he said.

She had small breasts, but very watchable, as was the rest of her, when she slid down her drawers and sat to remove her

111

stockings. 'Will you tell 'er ladyship?' she asked.

'Of course. We do not have secrets from each other.'

'Ooh, la-la. Then I will be sacked.'

'No, you will not be sacked, Claudette. I give you my word. Come here.' Slowly she stood up and moved towards him, still uncertain whether she was to be caned or raped. But then, so was he. Oddly, she still wore her cap. But this enhanced the piquancy of her naked body. When she stood immediately in front of him, he reached up and pulled the cap off, then pulled out the pins holding her hair, which fell in titian profusion about her shoulders. He slid his fingers down her arm to hold her hand, and her fingers closed on his, tightly, while a ripple of relief, and perhaps anticipated pleasure, travelled from her shoulders to her thighs. And there was a knock on the door. 'Confound it,' James said. 'Who is it?' he called.

'Wilton, sir. There is an urgent message.'

'Eh?' James gestured Claudette to withdraw across the room, out of sight of the doorway, then went to the door himself. 'What urgent message?'

'A telephone call, Sir James. From a police inspector.'

James closed the bedroom door and went down the stairs.

Richard Elligan's appointment at the India Office was immediately after lunch. 'I'm afraid I didn't have a great deal of success with Martingell,' he told the Under-Secretary.

'He's a difficult man,' Clerkwell agreed. 'Has he seen Azam?'

'I would say almost certainly. Although he would not give me a straight answer. But I believe he certainly is dealing with him.'

'Yes,' Clerkwell said thoughtfully.

'What I don't see is how he ships the goods without a licence,' Richard said.

'He uses forged licences, for the sight of his plant managers.'

'But surely that wouldn't work with a regular shipping line—at least, more than once.'

'He doesn't use a regular shipping line. He uses that yacht of his, the *Europa*.'

'But ... ' Richard scratched his chin. 'If you, we, know all this, why can't we just arrest him for illegally dealing in guns?'

'Simply because he has not yet illegally dealt in guns, Richard. He dealt illegally before the war, but was given an amnesty for that in return for turning his entire production over to the War Office. Since then he has done no deals, to our knowledge.'

'But if he is dealing with Azam, and means to ship guns, surely all we have to do is wait for him to do it, and then ... '

'You mean mount a round-the-clock surveillance.' It was Clerkwell's turn to stroke his chin. 'I am not sure we'd get permission to do that. The man is after all a knight of the realm, and a faithful servant of Great Britain. At least he has been a faithful servant over the past few years. No, no, Richard. I think we have done our bit. We have given him an unofficial warning that His Majesty's Government, certainly in India, will take a dim view of him selling arms to an Afghan Government which may not be willing to toe the line in Asia. If he determines to ignore our warning and goes ahead, well, we shall have to try to catch him in flagrante delicto, as it were.'

'That may be difficult without adequate surveillance.'

'We shall bring him down, never fear. You will bring him down, Richard. You'll be back in India before he can reach there with any guns. You'll be back in Afghanistan.'

'Do you suppose I will be welcomed?'

'Probably not. But they can't keep you out. You are a representative of HM Government. There's where we'll get the evidence to bring Sir James Martingell to trial.'

'And then?'

'Well, my dear fellow, he will go to gaol. Doesn't that thought please you?'

'Ah ... yes, of course. When do I return to India?'

'Tomorrow. We've arranged a passage for you.' Clerkwell frowned. 'That doesn't seem to please you greatly either.'

'It's a bit sudden.'

'It's where you are needed, Richard. India is where it's all happening, certainly compared with Europe. Big wars are history, Richard. We shall never see one again—they are simply too damned expensive. But little wars, now, they may well proliferate, simply because everyone knows they won't escalate. Afghanistan will be a little war, but still a place where one can pick up promotion and even a gong or two. Don't knock it. And incidentally, if there is a war out there, the rumour is that a Guards battalion or two may well be sent. Your own regiment, perhaps. With you in command? We will need men who know the ground.'

'And there is going to be a war with Afghanistan?'

'Oh, definitely. Unless this Amanullah Khan changes his tune. Which he won't.'

'And the Russians?'

115

'It is fashionable nowadays to refer to them as the Bolsheviks. Paints a more positive picture, don't you know. I don't think we need worry about the Bolsheviks, Richard; they have more than enough to do fighting each other. I'll wish you a good journey.'

Richard stood on the steps and surveyed the London traffic. What a tangled world it was, to be sure. But so many of the entanglements were of one's own making. He had known exactly what he was required to do when he had visited Martingell, and he had done it. He had known, or certainly suspected, that his warning would be ignored, in which case, as Clerkwell had just spelled out, the gun-runner would almost certainly wind up in gaol. So, knowing all that, what the devil did he mean by falling in love with Martingell's daughter?

Was he in love? He had been more instantly physically attracted to her than to any woman in his life before—but that life had not had too many opportunities for meeting beautiful women. There had been none in France, to his eyes, even had he had the time to look for them. There had been none in hospital, even had he had the strength to be interested. No doubt there were many beautiful women in India, but most of them were Indians, and he had been warned against inter-racial entanglements, other than when paid for. While white women in the subcontinent were either very firmly married, or equally firmly looking for husbands, few of the manhunters were beautiful. Thus he supposed that he had turned into something of a misogynist, which had made the impact of a woman like Lanne Martingell the more considerable.

But what had he intended? Or indeed, what *did* he intend? He was an officer and a gentleman. He had invited her to meet him in town, and she had accepted without hesitation. There was nothing wrong with that; it indicated that she might find him as attractive as he found her. And then? Get her into bed? Hardly the way he had been brought up to treat gentlewomen. But there was always the niggling knowledge that her father was virtually a gangster, a man who had fought his way to the top, literally, leaving quite a few dead bodies strewn about the place on his way, and who was now again beginning a criminal career. Did his daughter deserve to be treated as a lady?

Probably not. But overriding every logical consideration was the knowledge that he did want to treat her as a lady, because he wanted to marry her. There

117

was the end of a promising career. He wondered what Clerkwell would have done had he told him that. In any event, the die was cast, had been cast the moment he had written that note, telling her he would be at the Savoy at five. He looked at his fob watch; it was half-past four.

'Good afternoon,' Richard said. 'Has Miss Martingell arrived?'

'I'm afraid we do not divulge the names of our guests, sir,' the clerk at the Savoy reception desk said.

'I left a message for her this morning,' Richard explained.

'Ah. Would your name be Captain Richard Elligan?'

'That's correct.'

'Lady ... ah, Miss Martingell is expecting you. She said you were to go up.'

'To her room?'

'That is correct, sir.'

Richard was escorted to the elevator, and rode up to the seventh floor. Now his emotions were even more jumbled. Calling at five instead of seven had been intended to leave a lot of room to manoeuvre, to take steps or to withdraw. It had presupposed a quiet cup of tea in a corner of the lounge surrounded by people, a decorous chat, with the decision as to dinner and what might come afterwards a safe distance in the future, to be mutually considered. To be invited to her room ... The car stopped, and he stepped into the hallway, to be greeted by a floor waiter. 'Captain Elligan? Number Fifteen, sir.'

Richard drew a deep breath and walked along the wide corridor. He knocked, conscious that the waiter was still standing by the lift doors, watching him. The door opened, and he goggled at Lady Martingell. She wore an undressing-robe and slippers, and her golden hair was loose. If there was a more attractive sight in the world than Lanne, he was looking at it. But ... 'I'm sorry, Lady Martingell,' he said. 'I seem to have made a mistake.'

'Not in the least.' Anne held the door wide. 'As my daughter seldom comes to town by herself, the hotel staff thought that whoever had sent that note had merely made a mistake as regards titles. After all, the room was booked in my name. Won't you come in?' He hesitated, then stepped past her, acutely aware of her perfume, but at the same time relieved to discover that this was actually a suite; he was in a very comfortable sitting room, and there was not a bed in sight—although there was a door on his right, open. 'Tea?' Anne asked. 'Or would you prefer something stronger?'

'Ah ... tea, please.'

Anne rang the bell, then gestured him to a chair. 'Do please sit down.'

Slowly Richard lowered himself into a chair. Hardly had he done so than the door was opening to admit the waiter, clearly briefed, and a trolley, which he carefully wheeled into the centre of the room, bowed, and withdrew. 'Darjeeling?' Anne asked. 'Or, as you are currently stationed in India, would that be boring?'

'Darjeeling would be splendid,' Richard said, trying to get his thoughts under control; but the only way to handle this was to come straight up. 'I imagine I owe you an explanation, Lady Martingell.'

'I imagine you do, Captain Elligan.' She set his cup at his elbow, and sat opposite, crossing her knees with a flurry of silk.

'I presume you know that Sir James and I are ... shall I say, on opposite sides of the fence. Or perhaps you do not involve yourself in your husband's business?' He was hopeful.

'My husband's business is my business, Captain Elligan.'

'Ah. Yes, well, as I am sure you appreciate, this made my visit somewhat difficult. For me.'

'So you invited my daughter to meet you, clandestinely. With what in mind?'

'I ...' Richard cursed his flush. 'I have never met any woman to whom I was more instantly attracted, Lady Martingell. Please believe that. But as I have tried to explain, I was in an intensely difficult position, in your house, opposing Lanne's father ... I thought that if we could meet, away from that problem, we might ... well, get to know each other.'

'There are some suitable eating places in Worcester, just for instance, Captain. To which Lanne could have gone to meet you, and returned the same night.'

'I had to return to London, you see ...'

'To report to your superiors. Some more tea?' She got up, poured. 'And some cake?'

'Thank you, no.'

'But you're not going to rush off, I hope? As I understand it, you were taking Lanne out to dinner. Will you not take me instead?'

He stared at her, unable to decide whether or not she was joking at him. 'If ... if that is what you would like, Lady Martingell.'

Anne smiled, and sat down again, with another flurry of silk. 'I think it would be delightful to be taken out to dinner by a handsome young officer. But before I accept, you must tell me, what are your plans? For after dinner? The plans you no doubt had for Lanne?'

'You are attempting to make me out a scoundrel, Lady Martingell.'

'I am attempting to find out if you *are* a scoundrel, Captain Elligan.'

Richard took a deep breath. 'I know that Lanne and I have only just met, but as I have said, I have never been so instantly attracted to anyone in my life. My thoughts immediately turned to marriage ...'

'And then turned away again, perhaps.'

'Well Lady Martingell, it would be a profound step, for both of us.' He leaned forward. 'Your husband refused to listen to my advice. You do understand that if he were to ship guns to Afghanistan, clandestinely, he could go to gaol?'

'And I would go with him, Captain. We are partners in our business. Sadly, I doubt the authorities would allow us to share a cell,' she said brightly.

He leaned back again. 'You can joke about it?'

'My husband and I have found it necessary to joke at matters like laws and prisons, danger and even death, several times in our lives, Captain Elligan. Lanne is of course aware of the problems we have had, from time to time. She has even shared in some of them.'

Richard frowned. 'You'll not tell me she is also engaged in gun-running?'

'No. But she is aware of what we do. If

you were to bring my husband and me to trial, she might very well be called to give evidence.'

'That would be tragic.'

'Oh, I agree. So you will see that marriage, as you say, would be a *very* difficult business. And as you cannot reasonably propose marriage to me, well, what is left?'

He flushed. Now she was definitely poking fun at him. 'Nothing is impossible, Lady Martingell. Would you take deep offence if I were to say that I would hope to take Lanne away from the sordid and criminal background to which she has been exposed?'

Anne regarded him for several seconds, and he almost expected her to ring for the waiter to show him out. 'That would be a very laudable and gentlemanly thing to do, Captain Elligan,' she said at last. 'You are to be honoured for it. But sadly, while that would provide a magnificent ending for a novel, it would really only be the beginning of your mutual problems. You are physically attracted to my stepdaughter—you are aware that she is my stepdaughter?'

'Yes. I understood that her mother is dead.'

Anne made a moue. 'She may well be. However, no doubt you suppose that the ultimate happiness for you would be to hold Lanne naked in your arms.' Richard's head jerked; he had not expected her to be so direct. Anne smiled. 'And it is very possible that she may feel the same about you. But obviously you cannot spend the entire rest of your lives naked in each other's arms. Thus, you would live happily, and raise a family ... in India, would it be?'

'For a short while.'

'Where there are even more rigid layers of society than here.'

He frowned. 'Well, of course. You mean they would take against Lanne if it became known that her father had been sent to prison?'

'And mother,' Anne pointed out. 'They might well do so. They would certainly take against her when they realised, as they very rapidly would, I fear, that she has African blood.'

Now it was Richard's turn to stare, for several seconds. 'That is impossible. With her colouring?'

'You do not know where to look, Captain. People who have lived their lives in places like India do know where to look, what to seek, to determine whether or not a person has colour. I suspect, quite apart from the effect on your social life, a marriage to Lanne might well terminate your career. At least upwards.'

'I shall never believe that,' Richard declared.

Anne sighed. 'My husband was engaged in running guns into the Transvaal just before the outbreak of the Boer War. The guns were for the so-called Uitlanders, the English fortune hunters who had accumulated in that country seeking gold, and who were being denied what they considered their full rights by the Boers. He was captured, and was being held for trial, but he escaped, with the assistance of the young woman who served his food. Her name was Martha Alexander, and she was the daughter of an itinerant Scotsman and a half-caste woman. Lanne's great grandfather was probably pure-blooded. Sir James and Martha endured various vicissitudes before they could regain civilisation, and in the course of that adventure Martha became pregnant. Lanne is the result of that pregnancy.'

Richard could not help but believe her; she spoke with absolute certainty, and it was too outlandish a tale not to be true. 'Soon after that,' Anne went on, 'when my husband was engaged by the German House of Beinhardt to run guns for them, he and Martha parted company. I'm afraid she had been a prostitute when she assisted

James to escape the Boers, and she could not stop herself reverting to type. So he abandoned her, but he took the child with him, and has brought her up as an English lady. So there you have it. But the fact remains that she is what would be called in the Deep South of America an octoroon, that is to say, at least one-eighth of her blood is black. Now you may claim, and I may believe you, that this makes no difference to your love for her at this moment, but I can assure you that it will mean a great deal to many other people. And in time to yourself. Lanne has yellow hair and blue eyes. This is not the least uncommon. However, equally it is not uncommon for the child of such a woman to be very clearly at least half-caste. There is no telling. Have you considered how you would cope with that?'

Richard got up and took a turn around the room. He didn't want to believe it. Yet it was true. And if it was true, did he not still want to hold her in his arms? Of course he did. But ... Lady Martingell had painted the possible future with chilling certainty. He stopped in front of her. 'Does Lanne know what you have just told me?'

'She has never been told the truth, if that is what you mean. She was several years old when James finally took her out of Africa, therefore she remembers her mother, and she may remember something about her mother's lifestyle. She has never spoken of it, and we have never asked her. But I should say it is extremely unlikely that she knows she has coloured blood. And I would be very angry with anyone who told her that.'

'So what do you mean to do, keep her locked away in Worcestershire, a spinster, for the rest of her life?'

Anne sighed. 'Of course we hope that will not happen, that in the course of time someone will come along, who, well ... is older, and more settled in his career or business, more able to cope, shall we say, with her circumstances.'

Suddenly he knew that, for the first time in their conversation, she was *not* telling the truth. But why she should now choose to lie? 'And you do not feel I am mature enough for that.'

'I do not feel your circumstances, a young army officer intent upon making a career for himself, allow you to fill that role, Captain Elligan. Especially with the burden of the additional crisis your relationship with her, with her family, may impose. So, now, if you have changed your mind about dinner, I shall quite understand. If you have not, I must ask you to amuse yourself while I dress. I have not brought my maid with me.'

She smiled. 'I did not know what was involved.'

Richard licked his lips. He had never felt so put down in all his life. But he had booked a table, and Anne Martingell was a most beautiful woman, and he was ... suddenly angry enough to do something stupid.

'I would very much like to take you out to dinner, Lady Martingell,' he said.

'I hoped you'd say that,' Anne said. 'It would have such a bore to have come all this way simply to turn round and go back again. Well, as I said, make yourself comfortable. There are some magazines on the table, and if you feel like a drink, just ring the bell and the waiter will be along. I shan't be too long.'

She went into the bedroom and closed the door, and Richard stood at the window, looking down at the Thames. His emotions were still in a turmoil. No doubt her remarkable frankness had indeed saved him a good deal of grief, and perhaps even misfortune. That did not alter his feelings for Lanne, nor did he wish them to; merely to accept the fact that the girl was unsuitable and walk away would have been utterly caddish. But if he did not do that, what *was* he going to do? He was leaving for India tomorrow. He had supposed he might leave behind him undying memories, undying love, and undying promises, too, for as soon as it could be done. Now ... he was being cast in the role of a cad without having a chance to prove himself otherwise.

He wondered what Lady Martingell would tell her stepdaughter. But what had she told her to stop her from keeping their assignation in the first place? It occurred to him that the Martingell family was a total, inward-turned world, and that any man who endeavoured to feel his way into that world was on a hiding to nothing. He certainly had been. So, what was he going to do with this splendid woman who had replaced her stepdaughter as a dinner date and seemed willing to replace her in more ways than that? She was a self-confessed gun-runner, an enemy of everything he stood for. She was undoubtedly going to wind up in gaol. Should he not take everything she had to offer, and sail away with at least the undying memory of her? Or at least give her the fright of her life? He had been trampled upon once too often for one day. He knocked on the bedroom door.

'Sorry,' she said. 'I'm not ready.'

'I don't think I can wait,' he said, and opened the door.

Anne turned to face him. She had been sitting on a chair rolling on her stockings, and wore only knickers and a short chemise. She quite took his breath away, with the length, and strength, of her thighs and legs, the swell of her breasts. And her utter coolness. 'You couldn't wait for what, Captain?' He hesitated, uncertain what to do next. 'You do realise,' she said, 'that a touch on that bell would have you thrown out of the hotel? And thence, I would suppose, the army?'

'Are you going to touch it?'

They gazed at each other. 'No,' she said at last. 'I shan't touch the bell. I think you have had sufficient misfortune for one day.' Her shoulders rose and fell. 'Come here, you silly boy.' He moved towards her, and the telephone jangled. He turned sharply. 'Don't answer it,' Anne said, brushing past him to reach it. 'Lady Martingell?'

'Anne!' It was James. 'I hadn't meant to interfere with your little adventure, but I think you should get back down here right away.'

'You sound like an outraged husband.'

'Perhaps I am. But that's not why I'm calling. Winston is under arrest.'

'Winston?' Her voice rose an octave.

'Seems he and Mbote caught up with Allardyce.'

'Oh, my God! They didn't assault him?'

'I'm afraid they did, or Winston did. Anne, he's been charged with murder.'

Chapter 4

Flight

Slowly Anne sank to the bed beside the phone. Richard frowned at her. 'I don't understand,' Anne said.

'I had a chance to speak with Mbote alone,' James said. 'They're being held in the station in Worcester, as this promises to be what you might call a high-profile business. Allardyce told him that you had killed his father, and he went berserk. Before Mbote could stop him, the damage was done. Unfortunately the assault took place before Jane, and she accused Winston of murder.'

Anne licked her lips. 'Couldn't Mbote do something about it?'

'Like killing her, you mean?'

'No, I didn't mean that, James. My God! If only ...'

'If only what?'

Her shoulders slumped. 'Nothing. I'll catch the late train. Is ... is Winston all right?'

'He's as right as you can be when sitting in a police cell on such a charge.'

131

'Have you seen him?'

'No. But I understand from the police that he only has a couple of bruises.'

'We must get him out of there.'

'No hope of that, until he's been charged. Even then it's going to be doubtful. Winston will be in court before the magistrate tomorrow morning. At that time Harbottle says he will make a formal application for bail, but he's not too hopeful. There's Jane, you see. She's also charged him with rape.'

Slowly Anne replaced the phone. Then she looked at Richard. 'Did you hear any of that?'

'Not really. I gather there's a crisis.'

'Yes,' she said. 'My son is in gaol, charged with murder.'

'My God!' He sat beside her on the bed, uncertain what was the more important in this instance, that Winston was her son or an officer in the regiment. 'Whose murder?'

'It's a long story.' Anne picked up the phone again. 'What time is the next train for Worcester?' she asked the desk.

'The next compartment train for Worcester leaves at seven, milady. There is the milk train tomorrow morning.'

'Thank you. Call me a cab, for the station, for six thirty, please. Oh, and I shall not be staying the night after all.'

'Of course, milady.' The Martingells were too good customers for the Savoy to be concerned about a cancelled booking.

'I am most terribly sorry this has happened,' Richard said.

Anne's mouth twisted. 'Your second escape in an hour. If I had not come, and you had proposed to Lanne, and then found yourself with a brother-in-law charged with murder ... if he is found guilty, will they hang him?'

'That is the penalty for murder, certainly. But aren't you prejudging your own son?'

'Would to God I were. There are circumstances of which you know nothing.' Another twisted grin. 'My closet contains more family skeletons than the average graveyard.'

'Well ...' He stood up, reluctantly. 'If there is anything I can do to help ...'

She looked up, almost fiercely. 'You cannot help, Richard. My advice to you would be to go far away and forget that you ever heard the name Martingell. Does not the Bible say, somewhere, that those that live by the sword must also perish by the sword? But you can alleviate. My train does not leave for well over an hour, and I need a man to hold me in his arms.' She grasped his fingers. 'Quite desperately.'

Quite desperately, Richard thought, as

he walked back to his club; it was on Piccadilly and only half a mile away. Immediately behind him, as he emerged onto the Strand, Anne's taxi rattled out of the Savoy Yard and turned for the station. He wished he knew just how desperately was quite desperately. He had sought a memory to carry him back to India. Well, he had that. Perhaps he did not know enough about women who wanted, and who knew what they were about. Anne Martingell had certainly known what she was about, and what she had wanted him to be about, too. She had maintained his erection for half an hour before allowing him entry, while playing with every part of his body and requiring him to play with every part of hers.

It had never occurred to him that an English gentlewoman could know so much about the male anatomy ... or about her own, for that matter, and just what excited each part of it. He would remember the round firmness of both breast and buttock, the damp warmth that lay between her thighs, for the rest of his life. But had she *wanted?* Or had she been acting out some elaborate game? Certainly he could never now go after Lanne, as he had bedded the mother. Even the stepmother.

So that was a brick wall, composed entirely of memories. From which he must now turn away, while looking over his shoulder to watch them go down, down, down. As she had said, those who live by the sword ... But he almost felt like weeping.

It was just on dark, and Anne stared out of the first-class compartment window and watched the countryside racing by. She did not see any of it, even when a light suddenly glowed from a passing hamlet or station. Having sex with that handsome young captain had indeed been an act of desperation. Quite unforgivable, except in these quite horrible circumstances. But hadn't she gone up to London with the idea of having sex with him? She had never cheated on James before. Because she had never wanted to, needed to? Or because she was afraid of his reaction when he found out? Obviously the secret was never to let him find out. But she had wanted it. Her first, loveless, marriage had corrupted her morals. She had supposed she had turned her back on that. And been overwhelmed by her desire for a young, handsome, virile man—as James had once been. And now ... at least she had gained her objective. And what did it matter? She had gone up to London to save Lanne for Winston, because that was the only way the pair of them could ever find happiness. Now there was no way they could ever marry. She should have let Lanne be carried off by Richard, and watch a couple more lives being ruined.

But Winston! However much she had recognised all the weaknesses he had inherited from his father, he was still her son. Her only son since the death of that nameless child both she and James had wanted so badly. Had that driven them apart? Undoubtedly, in bed, while publicly they had presented a more united front than ever. But Winston! Hanged by the neck until he was dead. The world would say, what a sad end for the son of so heroic a father! But now Winston would know the truth. What would he say to her? What would he wish to do to her? Yet he had to be seen.

The train was stopping at Worcester Central. James was on the platform to meet her. She fell into his arms, felt his strength go round her and embrace her. Oh, what a fool she had been! He kissed her. 'Can we go to the prison now?' she asked.

'He's not in prison yet. He's in a police cell, waiting for the indictment tomorrow. And they say you cannot see him until then.'

'Bastards!'

'Come on home. You look exhausted.'

He escorted her to the Rolls, which he was apparently driving himself. At least, she reflected, at this moment he would not ask her about the London jaunt. And yet ... it was something that needed settling, and quickly. 'Are you very angry with me?' she asked, as they drove out of the station yard.

'I have never been very angry with you, my darling. Nor can I conceive that ever happening.'

'I had to do it, don't you see? They were going to get married. I couldn't let that happen.'

'And so you found it necessary to tie Lanne to her bed?'

'Well ... you weren't there. Besides, I thought ...'

'That I approved.' He was looking ahead, following the headlight beams into the darkness. 'Why did you *have* to prevent it?'

'Well ... it would have been so unfair. On them both. And if he was intending to have you arrested, or something—you must see it would have been quite impossible.'

'And he accepted that? Then he couldn't have been too serious.'

Anne also stared ahead at the twin beams of light. 'He accepted it when I told him certain things.' James' head turned for a moment, then looked back at the road. He was waiting. 'About Lanne's background.'

'You told that bastard that Lanne has black blood?'

'I had to.' She paused, but he didn't speak. 'So I must ask you again, are you very angry with me?'

Still he did not speak for several seconds. Then he said, 'As he will undoubtedly tell all his friends and relations, there goes any chance of Lanne ever making a successful marriage.'

He had not actually answered her question. 'He promised that it would remain confidential.'

'Do you really believe he will be able to keep it to himself? Especially when it is his business to bring me down, if he can?'

She sighed, and watched the lights of the house appear through the trees. 'I don't think Richard Elligan, or anyone else, for that matter, could possibly bring you down by scandal. I did what I thought was best, for everyone. I didn't know about Winston ... Oh, James, I am so desperately unhappy.'

He parked the car, and Wilton opened the front door for them. James waited for Anne to enter, followed her. 'Have there been any calls?'

'No, sir.'

James nodded, followed Anne into the

drawing room. 'I think brandy would he in order, Wilton.'

Wilton produced a tray with a decanter and two balloons, then left the room; he guessed his employers would have a lot to say to each other, in private, even if he didn't know all the subject matter. 'Where is Lanne?' Anne asked.

'She has gone to bed. She is quite upset.'

'I am sure she is. Shall I go up?'

'Not right now.'

She hesitated, then sat before the fire and sipped her brandy. 'What are you going to do? Beat me?' James gave a short laugh. 'I mean it,' she said. 'If it will make things better between us, you are welcome. I do not wish us to quarrel.'

'I was just thinking you are the second woman who has invited me to beat her today. I should go into business: female-beater extraordinary.'

Anne frowned. 'The second woman?'

'Yes. When I discovered what had happened, I fully intended to take a whip to Claudette.'

'You didn't! She was only doing what she was told.'

'I didn't. I found her too attractive to risk it.'

They gazed at each other, and Anne's tongue came out and circled her lips. To tell, or not to tell. But *that* was too risky. She could make it up to him, though. 'Well,' she said, 'If you're that worked up ...'

Harbottle the solicitor arrived while they were breakfasting. Lanne had refused to come down and was sulking in her room. Claudette was also keeping a low profile; she had assisted her mistress to dress, but being her maid she had immediately deduced that her ladyship had had a satisfactory homecoming. It was all very confusing. 'The arraignment is at eleven,' Harbottle said. He was a dapper little man, who, reasonably, was always nervous when in the presence of the Martingells. 'Will you be there?' He looked from face to face.

Anne poured him a cup of coffee. Richard Elligan, for all his charm and good looks, and considerable anatomy, need never have been. She had not felt so contented for a long time, even if there was so much catastrophe hovering. Which now had to be addressed. 'I would like to see my son.'

'Ah ... obviously you can see him if you wish, Lady Martingell. But I am bound to ask, is it wise?'

'To see my own son?'

'Well he is in a peculiar mood. He does

not know whether or not to believe what the man Allardyce seems to have told him. He may well ask some awkward questions.'

'I understand that. Yet he is still my son, and is in mortal danger.'

'Oh, quite.' Harbottle gave James, at the far end of the table, an anxious glance. 'Would I be entirely out of court if I asked, Lady Martingell, if there was any truth in what Allardyce said?'

'You mean I could wind up in the dock beside my son, charged with murder?'

'Well, of course that will not happen, Lady Martingell.' Harbottle wiped his brow with a silk handkerchief. 'The ... ah ... incident, if it happened, took place outside of British jurisdiction, as I understand it.'

'I thought a British ship was always British jurisdiction?' James asked.

'But, again as I understand it, the incident did not take place on the yacht, but in one of the yacht's boats.'

'And that would make a difference?'

'It would certainly be a controversial question, because you see, again as I understand it, the boat was actually inside Somali territorial waters when Sir Winston died. As to whether, at the time, the waters were Somali or Italian, well ... the ramifications are endless. In any event, resting as it does on the testimony of one man, who is now dead ...' He drank some coffee as he looked at Anne's expression. 'That is, of course, supposing the evidence of what caused the fracas is even admissible.'

'May we ask how you know so much about it?' Anne asked, softly, 'if, as *we* understand it, my son is supposed to have assaulted this man in the middle of whatever he was saying? He must have been speaking very quickly.'

'Ah ... I had a long talk with your servant, Mbote.'

'Mbote is not our servant,' Anne pointed out. 'He is our friend. And he told you what had happened, did he? Before witnesses?'

'Good heavens, no.'

'But he did tell you. And no one else?'

'No one else. And he told me with the greatest reluctance. In fact, he would not speak at all until I had persuaded him that I had to know the truth if I was going to defend either Mr Winston, or you, Lady Martingell.'

'I see.' Anne looked at James.

'What about Mbote, Mr Harbottle?'

'Well, he is being held as an accessory, although even the girl Jane Allardyce agrees that he attempted to stop Mr Winston from attacking her father. But you know, being a black man, and, well ...' Once again he was impaled upon their eyes.

'Will he be charged?'

'I sincerely hope not. I hope to have the case against him dismissed. But even if I do not, I will certainly obtain bail.'

'But in either case, he is a material witness.'

'Well, yes, Sir James, he is.'

'Damnation,' James said.

'There is no question of a conviction against him, really.'

'No doubt. But I am obliged to leave the country on business within the month, and I usually take Mbote with me on these trips.'

'Hm,' Harbottle said. 'Yes. I'm afraid that will not be possible until after the trial.'

'Which will be when?'

'Oh, the next assize. Three months' time.'

'Too long for me.'

'James,' Anne protested. 'You cannot possibly be going to go off—'

He silenced her with a look. 'I'm afraid I must, my dear. Business is business. Will you excuse us, Mr Harbottle? You say my wife can see her son. Would this be before or after the arraignment?'

'Well, sir, in my opinion, it would be best left until afterwards.'

'I think we should go along with Mr Harbottle,' James said. Anne bit her lip.

'Well, then,' James said. 'We shall of course be in court. We shall see you there, Mr Harbottle.'

'Ah ... yes.' Harbottle hastily stood up, bowed to them both, and hurried from the room.

'James,' Anne said.

'I must go, my dear. Azam has already drawn the first cheque, the yacht is ready and the goods will be by tomorrow, and besides, every day I delay gives that scoundrel Elligan more time to catch me out.'

'He is about to leave the country and return to India,' Anne said absently.

'He told you this?'

She flushed. 'Yes, he did.'

'Well that is probably even more dangerous. In any event, he will certainly have informed his superiors that I rejected his advice not to go ahead. I need to be out of the country, with the goods, just as rapidly as I can.'

'Leaving me here to pick up the pieces.'

'I'm sorry, my dear, but ...'

'Winston is my son. Don't rub it in. I will also have to cope with your daughter.'

'She'll get over it. I'll have a serious chat with her. Well, I suppose we should make a move.' He got up, stood beside her chair, rested his hand on her shoulder. 'What are you going to do, or say, if Winston asks you straight out if Allardyce was telling the truth?'

'I shall say he was lying.'

'And if you are called as a witness at the trial, and have to take the oath?'

'I shall still say he was lying.'

He gave her a gentle squeeze. 'I didn't really expect anything else. But Harbottle will know differently.'

'He's our solicitor. He's hardly likely to accuse me of perjury. If Mbote will back me up.'

'Mbote will certainly support any line you wish to take.'

'And the rest of the crew?'

James grinned. 'Another reason for me to hurry. The rest of the crew will be upon the high seas, with me.'

Lanne, standing at her bedroom window to watch the Rolls drive away, turned as the door opened. 'Get out,' she said. 'I do not wish to look at you.'

Claudette sidled into the room and closed the door behind her. 'I am 'ere to say 'ow sorry I am.'

'Oh, yes?' Lanne walked away from the window. 'Are you sore?'

'Sore, Miss Lanne?'

Lanne frowned. 'Didn't my father beat you?'

'No, Miss Lanne.'

145

'Didn't he do *anything* to you?'

Claudette gave a pretty little shiver. 'Not really, Miss Lanne.'

'Oh ... I should beat you myself.'

'If it will make you 'appy, Miss Lanne.'

'Yes,' Lanne said. 'It would make me very happy.'

Claudette came across the room with a little sigh. 'Then you must do it, Miss Lanne.'

'But there are things that would make me happier,' Lanne said. 'First of all, tell me about last night. Did my stepmother meet up with Captain Elligan?'

'I think she must 'ave done so, Miss Lanne.' Claudette gave a little shrug. 'I can only say what I 'eard 'er ladyship saying to Sir James. She say she warn the Captain off.'

'How?'

'I do not know.'

'If you do not tell me, I shall whip you till you bleed,' Lanne declared.

'It is true. I could not 'ear what she told Sir James. But I do 'ear that the Captain leaves England tomorrow. Perhaps today. I am not sure.'

'Oh ... shit!' Lanne declared. 'Then we must find him, today.'

'We, Miss Lanne?'

'You and I, Claudette. My parents have gone to court. They won't be back until

146

late. We shall go to London—'

'London?' Claudette squealed.

'And find Captain Elligan, and sail with him to India.'

'But I do not wish to go to India, mademoiselle.'

'You won't have to. Help me find Captain Elligan, and you can do what you like.'

'What I like? Mademoiselle, what I like is to continue 'ere as 'er ladyship's maid. Anyway, there is no money.'

'I have some money,' Lanne said. 'And we will get more. Go to Lady Martingell's room and fetch her chequebook. She has a very easy signature. We will forge it and obtain money.'

'Ooh, la-la,' Claudette cried. 'I will be sent to prison.'

'Oh, really, Claudette. I will take the blame.'

'You may take the blame, mademoiselle. But I will *get* the blame.' Claudette retreated to the door. 'I cannot do it.'

'You are a wretched woman,' Lanne said, advancing towards her. 'Then I *will* beat you.'

'I cannot do it,' Claudette repeated, and before Lanne could reach her, she had backed to the door, taken the key from the lock, run into the gallery, and closed and locked the door.

'The charge against Mr Mbote will be dismissed,' said the magistrate. 'I agree with Mr Harbottle that there is no case to be answered.' There was a rustle through the courtroom as the big black man stepped down from the dock, to have his hand shaken by James, and the rustle grew as he was embraced by Anne.

The magistrate rapped on his table with his gavel. 'In the matter of the second defendant,' he said, 'there is undoubtedly a case to be answered. Mr Harbottle has argued that Mr Pennyfeather was provoked by the scurrilous nature of the attack made upon his mother.' He allowed his gaze to drift towards Anne, who was now seated between James and Mbote. 'However, the nature of the attack was so vicious as to leave no doubt in my mind that Mr Pennyfeather meant to commit at the very least grievous bodily harm upon Mr Allardyce. In addition, there is the charge of rape brought against the defendant by Miss Jane Allardyce, a charge which has not been denied at this time. I therefore commit Mr Pennyfeather to be remanded in custody until the next assize. Mr Harbottle?'

Harbottle was on his feet. 'I submit an application for bail, your worship.'

'These are very serious offences, Mr Harbottle.'

'We understand that, your worship. However, I would point out that Mr Pennyfeather has, up to now, had a blameless character, that he is an officer in the army who served with distinction in the recent war, and that he is the stepson of a prominent resident in this country, recently knighted for his services to the crown, and that it would be an unwarrantable burden upon Mr Pennyfeather to be confined in prison for what may well be a matter of some months. I am certain that Sir James Martingell would be prepared to put up a substantial sum to save his stepson from such an unfortunate turn of events.'

'No doubt,' the magistrate agreed. 'I am well acquainted with both Sir James' wealth and the manner of his obtaining it.' This time he gazed at James. His expression spoke volumes. 'The application is refused, Mr Harbottle. Next.'

'He supposes,' Harbottle said, 'that with your well-known penchant for disappearing yourself for months on end, you may well be prepared to sacrifice even a considerable sum of money to have Winston disappear as well.'

'You did your best,' James said.

'Now I wish to see my son,' Anne said.

Winston had appeared quite calm in court, although he had not attempted to look at her. And to her great relief there had been no sign of Jane Allardyce. Of course Jane was entirely blameless, and was now an orphan, but as far as Anne was concerned, the wretched girl was an enemy—she could walk the streets or starve now; there was no longer a place for her at Martingell Hall. When the chips were down, Anne could be even more selfishly single-minded than her husband.

'Ah, yes,' Harbottle said, still uncertain. But he had made the necessary arrangements, and James and Anne were taken down to the cells.

They were met by an anxious police inspector. 'Sir James, Lady Martingell, I'm afraid, well, when we told Mr Pennyfeather that you were here to see him, he said, "Tell them to go away."'

'Obviously he is very upset,' Anne said.

'I'm afraid he is. I do think it would be better to give him a chance to, how shall I put it, come to terms with his present circumstances. There is also the matter of your own involvement, milady ...'

'Well?' Anne demanded aggressively.

The inspector looked more apologetic yet. 'You see, milady, the situation is that while at this moment what was actually said by the late Mr Allardyce to your son is known to very few people, when the case comes to trial, unless Mr Pennyfeather were to change his plea to guilty and pre-empt the hearing of any evidence, just what Mr Allardyce said will become very well known indeed.'

'Just what are you trying to say?' James inquired.

'Well, sir, we have felt it incumbent upon us to forward the papers in this case to the Director of Public Prosecutions. Purely for his information,' he added hastily, 'so that he may determine how we should treat the matter. When it becomes public knowledge.'

'You mean you're not going to arrest me at this moment,' Anne said.

'Well, milady, of course we are not going to arrest you ... at this moment. But should you insist upon seeing your son, it will have to be in the presence of police officers, and should anything be said, well, it could prove very awkward.' Anne snorted, and turned to leave the office. 'I assume you will be remaining in the country until the trial, milady?' the inspector asked.

Anne looked over her shoulder. 'I am not going to run away, sir.'

'Well, there it is.' Harbottle walked with

151

them to the car. 'Very unfortunate. But—there it is.'

'You are absolutely certain of what you told us at breakfast?' James asked.

'Oh, absolutely. I think the DPP will know he will be taking on something immense if he attempts to bring Lady Martingell to trial, which will include arraigning the entire company of the *Europa* on charges of perjury, and Heaven alone knows what else. No, no. He will never do it. But what Inspector Watkinson said was, I'm afraid, perfectly true. Once this case comes to trial, the facts will have to come out ...'

'And all the world will know I killed my first husband,' Anne said.

Harbottle gulped. He had not anticipated such an open admission.

'That was confidential,' James said.

'Of course, Sir James. But ... ah ... am I to go ahead and brief? It should be done right away.'

'Of course. The best man you can find.'

'I will do that, sir. But ... he will of course have to have all the facts.'

'Which will also be confidential, at least until the trial,' James reminded him.

'I am so frightened,' Anne said, as they drove back to Martingell Hall. 'I wish you could be here, James.'

'I will be here, just as soon as I can,' he promised. 'The delivery should take about four months. The trial will not have been finished by then. I will be here.'

'In time to see me accused of murdering my first husband.'

'As Harbottle said, I don't think it'll come to that. And if you are, why ... we'll emigrate.'

'Oh, James.' She reached across to squeeze his hand. 'Here I am, worrying about myself, while poor Winston is locked up with a whole lot of robbers and murderers ...'

'He's going to a remand centre, not a prison. Yet.'

'Will he have a cell to himself, James?'

'That I can't say. Some of these places get pretty crowded. But he's a grown man, a war veteran; he should be able to cope.'

'His career is over. If he was your son, would you be so casual about it?'

'I would hope so. If he were my son, I assume he would make a fresh career.' He grinned at her. 'We could take him into the business.'

They could tell by the look on Wilton's face that they were returning to another crisis. 'You had better listen to what Claudette has to say, Sir James, milady,' the old man suggested.

'Miss Lanne 'as been banging and crashing on the door,' Claudette told them. 'But what was I to do, Sir James? Milady?' She looked from face to face, seeking sympathy, or at least acceptance.

'I think you did entirely the right thing, Claudette,' Anne said. 'Thank you. Brandy, Wilton.' She led James into the drawing room. 'Now this is your crisis.'

'Yes,' James said. 'But I'll have a drink first. Who'd have children, eh?'

'What are you going to tell her? If she is going to run away behind that man, she is going to run away behind that man. I can't keep her locked in her room for the rest of her life. This is 1919, not 1819.'

'Yes,' James said thoughtfully. 'It will have to be the truth.'

Anne put down her glass. 'You'll destroy her.'

'Then what's the alternative?'

'Take her with you. That will at least stop you having to tell her she's a mulatto. And on such a long voyage you'll have the time to talk with her, make her see sense.'

James stroked his chin. 'You want me to kidnap my own daughter?'

'Isn't that better than kidnapping someone else's daughter?'

'I don't really think it's very funny.'

James finished his drink, got up, took a turn abut the room. But he was realising that was the only possible solution. He simply could not saddle Anne with defending her son, and perhaps herself, against charges of murder, and coping with Lanne at the same time. Nor could he really contemplate the girl running away. Girl! She was a grown woman in every sense save experience of the world.

He had never been sure of his feelings towards her. He was not even one hundred per cent sure she was his daughter. He had only discovered that Martha Alexander had been pregnant some three months after the mulatto had helped him escape from the Boer prison. Her pregnancy, and time of delivery, had seemed to fit all the facts and timings, but it had never been very carefully worked out. Martha had been a prostitute. She could easily have slept with someone else, and become pregnant, at any time during the week or so before the escape—it would have been unlike her not to do so. Nor was Anne's colouring any guide. There were many more blond Boers than Englishmen—he had not been particularly fair haired himself: Martha had suggested that the girl's colouring came largely from her vanished grandfather.

Yet because at that time he had been both intensely fond of Martha, and intensely grateful for her help, he had never questioned his parenthood. And having once accepted Lanne as his child, he had never had second thoughts about the matter. He was not a man who had ever had many second thoughts about anything; he couldn't afford to. One made up one's mind what had to be done, and one did it, looking neither to left nor right, and certainly never over one's shoulder. Anne of course had never questioned Lanne's parenthood either; she believed what he had told her.

Now he wished her well, and all the happiness in the world, providing her search for happiness did not interfere with his own life. He supposed he was an intensely selfish man. But that was the only road to success. 'Shall we have a word with her?' he asked.

'That girl!' Lanne shouted. Her hair was wild and she wore no shoes. At that moment she looked every inch Martha Alexander's daughter, save that she was much prettier than her mother. 'She locked me up. Again! If you don't whip her I am going to, Daddy.' She glared at Anne; it was the first time she had seen her stepmother since being tied to her bed the previous day.

'She was doing what she thought best,'

James said quietly. 'Now, we need to have a talk. About this infatuation you have developed over this fellow Elligan.'

Lanne tossed her head. 'Infatuation? Richard and I are in love. We intend to get married.'

'He told you this?' Anne asked.

Another toss of the head. 'I suppose he told you differently.'

'I think he intended to seduce you,' Anne said. 'And you stupidly agreed to it, virtually.'

'We were going to be married,' Lanne insisted.

'Do you suppose he is a gentleman?' James asked.

'Of course he is a gentleman, Daddy. Anyone can see that.'

'Then shouldn't he, as a gentleman, have done things properly, approached me and asked for your hand?'

'What would you have said?'

'Well, no.'

'Exactly,' she said. 'He knew that. I knew that. You're on opposite sides of the law. You're an outlaw, Daddy. You simply must realise that. It might have been great fun in the old days, but things have changed. This is 1919. You cannot give the middle finger to the law as you did for so long. Richard tried to tell you that, and you refused to listen.'

'And you honestly think that in those circumstances he would have married you?'

'Yes,' she said fiercely. 'He loves me. And we are going to marry. You can't stop me. I am twenty-two years old. You have no jurisdiction over me at all. You can't keep me locked up here. You are going to have to let me out some time, and then I am going to leave you, and go to Richard, and ... we'll be married.'

Father and daughter stared at each other, while Anne watched them both. She never doubted James' resolve, once it was made. She feared for the girl. 'Very well,' James said. 'But first you have to leave. That won't be tonight. Now I suggest you get yourself dressed and come down to dinner. And let me warn you: if you attempt to make a scene I shall both whip you and tie you to the bed.'

'I am not a child!' Lanne shouted.

'Then do not act like one.'

'Will she behave?' Anne asked.

'Tonight, yes. And then we must be away.' He led her downstairs. 'Mbote, you'll be ready to transport the guns tonight. Grayson will have loaded the wagons by now.'

Mbote nodded. 'But I can't come with you.'

'I'm afraid not this time, old man.

Otherwise the police will have a reason to come after me. You'll stay here and support Anne. But let's get those guns moving.'

Mbote nodded, and went to change into his riding gear.

'I am so scared,' Anne said.

'Darling ...' James gestured Wilton to pour champagne. 'You, who opposed the Mullah?'

'This is the British Government.'

'Who have nothing to go on, yet. I have been given a licence to dump those arms, or most of them, at sea. They are sending a man down to supervise the operation. But if I leave without him, they will have to prove that I have not done the dumping before they can interfere with me.'

'And Winston?'

'It was an unprovoked and unwarrantable verbal attack by Allardyce. As Harbottle says, we'll get it cut down to manslaughter, if we do not get an outright acquittal. And I'll be back, as I promised.'

She bit her lip, but accepted the glass of champagne.

James telephoned Azam's London hotel. 'No problems, I hope?' Azam asked. The news of Winston's arrest had not yet made the London newspapers.

'Some possibilities,' James said. 'So I am moving the shipment forward. We sail at dawn tomorrow.'

There was a moment's silence. 'This is not serious?' Azam asked at last.

'Not from your point of view. I should have thought the sooner you got the guns the better.'

'Oh, indeed.'

'So you will have to come up tonight to inspect the goods.'

Azam smiled. 'That will not be necessary, James. I trust you. I will see you in Chah Bahar, in ...'

'Two months' time,' James said.

'Agreed.'

'And the consignment cheque?'

'Will be paid into your bank tomorrow, with an advice to your good lady.'

There remained Lanne. As he had expected she would, she came down to dinner, looking her normal self, only giving a loud sniff when she happened to pass Claudette in the doorway. Mbote had by now returned, and signified to James that the transport of the goods was already in hand.

As was natural, Lanne wanted to hear all about Winston's appearance in court, and looking suitably shocked when she was told he had been committed for trial. 'But they can't actually convict him, can they?'

she asked, eyes wide at the suggestion.

'Of course they cannot. Harbottle is procuring the best possible barrister. But it is all very embarrassing. It means Mbote won't be able to come with me when I deliver the goods.'

'But you are going ahead with the delivery?'

'Of course.'

Her lips pursed. Something to tell Elligan, no doubt. Supposing she ever saw him again.

Lanne retired at about ten o'clock. 'I have been considering the situation,' James said. 'And while I agree with you, Anne, that there is only one solution, I feel it would be an intolerable situation for Lanne to be confined on board a ship for several months with only male company.'

'I wish I could come with you.'

'But as you can't, I am going to tell Philippe to bring Michelle.'

'But ... at such short notice?'

'Philippe works for me. He'll be available. And so will she.'

Philippe was in bed. 'Me?' he cried. 'Us?'

'I need you,' James pointed out.

'You will come to Marseilles?'

'No. I can't risk entering the Mediterranean; it would be too easy for us to be stopped at either Port Said or Aden.

161

Or Gibraltar, for that matter. I am going round the outside.'

'Ooh, la-la,' Philippe commented. 'This is a long voyage.'

'One which, having your wife along, you will thoroughly enjoy. Listen, leave tomorrow and take the train to Les Sables d'Olonne. Do you know it?'

'I know where it is,' Philippe said, dolefully. 'It is on the coast north of La Rochelle.'

'That's right. The harbour is small, but big enough for *Europa* if we do not hang about. You'll board there. And don't forget to bring Michelle with you.'

'Michelle gets seasick,' Philippe said, more dolefully yet.

'No one gets seasick for more than a couple of days,' James pointed out. 'Then she will have the time of her life. Lanne will be along.'

He packed, aware of a slowly rising excitement. Anne felt it too, although perhaps for a different reason. It was midnight before the house was quiet. 'The servants will think it strange, your disappearing in the middle of the night,' Anne said.

'The servants can think whatever they like,' James told her. 'Let's move.'

Softly they opened Lanne's door. She

was fast asleep, snuffling gently into her pillow. James stood above her, Anne beside him. Kidnapping my own daughter, he thought, and suddenly fervently hoped she *wasn't* his daughter. He glanced at Anne, who gave a quick nod, and placed the roll of cloth across Lanne's mouth. At the same moment Anne rolled her onto her face, grasping her wrists and bringing them behind her back. Lanne made a startled exclamation but could do no more than that as James secured the knot on the back of her head, then bound the wrists Anne was holding. Lanne kicked her feet helplessly and uttered a high-pitched moaning sound, but James tied her ankles together as well.

Then he and Anne, as the girl was wearing only a sheer nightdress, wrapped her in a dressing gown and tied the cord round her waist, rendering her even more helpless. She glared at them as Anne switched on the bedside light. 'I am sorry,' James told her, 'but desperate situations require desperate remedies. Now you are going for a long sea voyage, during which we will no doubt get to know each other better, so that at the end of it we can be friends.'

Anne was busily packing a couple of suitcases with whatever she could think of. Lanne rolled violently to and fro, but remained quite helpless. When Anne was finished, James lifted Lanne into his arms and carried her down to the car. The evening was warm, but Anne brought along a coat as well. The gear was loaded into the back, together with James' own, and Mbote got behind the wheel.

James placed Lanne in the back seat, then took Anne in his arms. 'Say this is the last time, James,' she begged.

'Half a million? Oh, yes, this is the last time, my darling,' he said. And kissed her. 'When this is finished, I go into honourable retirement. And so do you.'

Part Two

Business Affairs

'Misery acquaints a man with strange bedfellows.'

William Shakespeare

Chapter 5

The Decision

If Captain Petersen was concerned at the appearance of his employer with his daughter bound and gagged, he made no comment. The cargo was still being loaded, in any event, and James simply carried Lanne down to one of the aft cabins and laid her on the bunk. 'I will release you as soon as we put to sea,' he told her. 'But for the moment I'm afraid you'll have to remain as you are.'

She continued to glare at him. He knew she must be both thirsty and uncomfortable, but he couldn't risk upsetting either the crew or the men from the factory by having her cry out. He joined Mbote on deck. 'It is strange, not to be going with you,' Mbote said. 'This is the first time.'

'And the last,' James said. 'But you have more important things to do here, looking after Anne. And I'll be back before you know it.' They shook hands, and Mbote left, with the car.

It was dawn before the last of the

167

rifles, the revolvers, and the grenades were loaded, together with the machine-guns and the battery of crated mountain guns. These had been designed by James himself, and although light and easily dismantled to be carried on mules or camels over rough terrain, were equally easily put together by anyone trained to do so, and they fired a three-pounder shell which could be very effective. James shook hands with the foreman of the delivery crew. 'Many thanks, Tom. You have the note.'

'Goods to be dumped at sea, Sir James.'

'Correct,' James said, the two men grinned at each other; there would be a substantial bonus for everyone involved when he returned with the final payment. But he still reckoned on clearing four hundred thousand for himself and Anne. Properly invested, that would certainly mean they need never take risks like this again. 'Whenever you're ready, Captain,' he told Petersen.

Steam was already up, and the yacht stood out of the little cove into the choppy waters of the Irish Sea. James was exhausted, not having had any sleep, and it had been a pretty tiring day before. He went below, opened the door to Lanne's cabin, and removed the gag. It was some seconds before she could speak, and while she worked her mouth he poured her a glass of water. 'You are a fiend,' she said.

'This transaction represents all of our futures,' he told her. 'I simply could not risk it going wrong.'

'Don't you think I'll testify against you?'

'I hope you will not. But if you do, you'll have a problem proving whatever you say. Now, I have some good news for you.' He untied her wrists and ankles, massaged her feet while she rubbed her arms together to restore circulation. 'Philippe is joining us tomorrow morning. And he is bring his wife with him. So you will have female company for the voyage.'

'I don't like Philippe's wife.'

'Well, I am sure you will when you get to know her better. Would you like to come on deck?'

'Only to throw myself over the side,' she snapped.

'Then you had better stay here. I'll have some breakfast sent down to you.'

He joined Petersen on the bridge. 'I'm going to turn in, Captain. When do you reckon we'll make Les Sables?'

'It's not a coast I care to approach at night, Sir James. We'll stand in tomorrow morning. Is ... ah, the young lady all right?'

'The young lady is fine,' James said. 'You may as well know, Toby, that she was threatening to betray us. I did not see

169

any alternative to keeping her out of the way until the goods have been delivered. After that there'll be no proof.'

'Sad,' Peterson commented.

'Youth,' James pointed out.

When James woke up *Europa* was cruising towards the Bay of Biscay, standing well off from Ushant with its rocks and sharp tides, in a mist-shrouded afternoon and a calm sea. Petersen was sounding his foghorn every so often, but there did not seem any ships close to them. It was satisfactory to think that if they were being shadowed they must have lost their pursuer by now. Visibility was poor, but there was no fog, and they were maintaining a steady twelve knots. 'So there's nothing to worry about, Sir James,' Petersen said. 'Especially as we're not doing the obvious thing, and getting out of home waters just as rapidly as we might. Did you discover anything about Allardyce's whereabouts, sir?'

'I discovered Allardyce,' James said.

Petersen glanced at him. They were out of earshot of the helmsman. 'What did he have to say for himself?'

'Too much.'

'And?'

'He's dead.' Petersen's jaw dropped. 'Oh, I didn't kill him, Toby. Although I might have done. Young Winston did it.'

'Good heavens,' Petersen said. 'Then ...'

'Winston is standing trial for murder. Mbote is a witness, which is why he's not with us.'

Petersen scratched his head. 'Will the young gentleman be convicted, sir?'

'Obviously we are hoping not. Allardyce began to tell him the truth about Sir Winston's death, and young Winston lost his temper.'

'But it's all likely to come out.'

'Unfortunately, yes.'

Petersen gazed at the sea for several seconds. 'Is that why you were in such a hurry to leave England, Sir James?'

'It was one of the reasons.'

'I think that was a very sensible decision, if I may say so, sir. Does Miss Lanne know the truth of it?'

'Most of it.'

'But she'll not be talking to anyone?'

James frowned. 'What's on your mind?'

'Well, sir, this crew has sailed together for a long time. Most of that time just outside the law. They have always known that, and they have been well paid for it, so they have served you faithfully and well. But it makes a bond, sir, living that kind of life. Allardyce was a popular fellow. So he got their backs up when he got drunk and behaved stupidly, but he was still one

171

of them. If asked to choose between him and, well, anybody else, they'd close ranks around him.'

'Meaning, if they were to find out what happened, it'd be a jolly good thing Young Winston isn't on board. But Miss Lanne and I are. Is that it?'

'I'm sorry, sir,' Petersen said. 'But there it is. On the other hand, what they don't know can't hurt them. Or you.'

'Yes,' James said, thoughtfully.

He repeated the conversation to Lanne in the privacy of her cabin. 'I thought you should know just where we stand,' he told her. 'If it were to come to a crunch, you are one of us, right?' She clasped both hands to her neck. 'Exactly.'

'But when they find out—'

'There is no way they can find out until we return to England. The murder of one itinerant seaman is not likely to be front-page news in either Persia or Portuguese West Africa, where we are going to fuel. When we get back, hopefully the trial will be over, but in any event, this is our last gun-running voyage. The crisis will be over too. If necessary, I'll pay them all off.'

'And when they go to the police?'

'They won't have any proof, except at the cost of indicting themselves.'

She considered for some seconds. Then

she said, 'If you really are retiring after this voyage, then there is no reason why I should not marry Richard.' She glanced at him. 'Is there?'

James studied her. Just how much of her mother was contained behind those beautiful blue eyes? Was she attempting to blackmail him? For her to tell any member of the crew what had happened to Allardyce would be to endanger her life as much as his—she was his daughter. But perhaps she felt she could survive, by reason of her beauty—even if she had to sacrifice all else a woman should hold dear. He did not think she could do it ... but he really couldn't take the risk of her trying. 'I can't think of one at the moment,' he said. She kissed him.

They entered Les Sables d'Olonne just after dawn the next morning, having set the appropriate signals; they were an English yacht on passage to the Mediterranean, and if they chose to make this somewhat odd detour into the Bay of Biscay, that was their business. The entrance was long and narrow before opening into the fishing basin. Here they were able to lie alongside, briefly, while Philippe and Michelle came on board. 'Ooh, la-la,' Michelle commented. 'I do not like zee sea. I do not like ships.'

'You'll like this one,' James assured her. 'You remember Lanne?'

'Lanne!' Michelle screamed, and hugged and kissed the girl. 'I am so 'appy you are to come too. I had thought I would be alone wiz all zese men!' She rolled her eyes.

'We'll just have to share,' Lanne laughed. She was in the best of spirits since she had extracted what she considered a firm commitment from her father.

James and Philippe went up to the bridge. 'You may cast off, Captain,' James said. Petersen rang the engine telegraph and gave the orders, and *Europa* went astern up the channel; there was no room for her to turn.

Philippe and James stood on the bridge wing to watch the manoeuvre, while James told Philippe what had been happening. 'That you, we, are retiring is the best thing I have heard in a long while,' Philippe confessed; he was several years older than James. 'But this Winston business, it is bad, eh? Will I be called as a witness?'

'To the death of Pennyfeather? They may wish to call you, old fellow, but they'll have a job doing it.'

'Yes,' Philippe said thoughtfully. 'But if Anne becomes involved ...'

'Harbottle feels sure she won't be. And if the truth comes out, well, as I promised

174

her, we'll simply emigrate. It mightn't be a bad idea to do that anyway. We'll come and live with you in the south of France.'

'I think I would like that,' Philippe said.

'But first, let's deliver these guns and collect our money,' James told him.

'Mr Howorth,' Wilton said. Anne was in the study, going through her various accounts, but with only half her mind on what she was doing. Harbottle was bringing the barrister in today. Never had she felt so alone. And resentful. James had been gone more than a month; he and Lanne were heaven alone knew where, somewhere on the high seas; Richard Elligan was presumably almost back in India by now. Winston remained in the remand prison, still refusing to see her.

Were it not for the always cheerful presence of Mbote she thought she might have gone mad. She could only remind herself that it would all be over by the end of the summer. Surely. And one way or the other. Now this ... 'Who?' she asked.

'A gentleman from the ministry, milady.'

Anne frowned. 'Well, show him in.'

Mr Howorth was short and dapper, and wore a small moustache. But he was well dressed, and entirely confident. 'I am actually looking for Sir James,' he explained.

'I'm afraid Sir James is not here, Mr Howorth,' Anne said. 'Wilton, you may serve the Bollinger.'

Wilton bowed and withdrew. Howorth raised his eyebrows, but did not object. 'Will he be gone long, Lady Martingell?'

'I really have no idea,' Anne said. 'He is at sea.'

Howorth frowned. 'In his yacht? But ... when did he leave?'

'Oh, more than a week ago. Is it important?'

'I am supposed to be with him.'

Wilton reappeared with his tray, bottle and glasses, and poured. 'From the ministry,' Anne said, having had time to think. 'Of course.'

'I am to supervise the dumping of the surplus, ah, *matériel* from his warehouse,' Howorth explained, importantly. Perhaps this rather attractive woman did not know about such matters.

'Yes, indeed. So you were. But he decided to leave early.'

'But that is most improper,' Howorth declared. 'The dumping must be properly supervised.'

'Ah.' Anne drank some champagne, and almost as an afterthought Howorth did the same. 'You'll have to take it up with him when he comes back; I know very little about such matters. But I must warn you that my husband may not return for some time. After dumping the guns he was going to take a short cruise. Our daughter has gone with him.'

'Lady Martingell,' Howorth said severely. 'You do not seem to understand how serious a matter this is. The dumping of the guns must be supervised.' He flushed. 'We ... the Ministry ... must have proof that it was properly done.'

'You mean, when my husband returns with an empty ship, and tells you the guns have been dumped, you won't believe him?'

'I did not say that at all,' Howorth protested. 'It is simply that there is a correct procedure to be followed in these matters, and Sir James is not following it.'

'He never was very good at set procedures,' Anne said. 'Will you stay to lunch?'

'Ah ... thank you, Lady Martingell, but no. Do you have any objection if I go across to your factory and speak with your manager?'

'Of course I do not. I am sure you'll find everything in order.' Howorth finished his champagne and left.

'What do you reckon?' Mbote asked. He

had discreetly kept out of sight while the man from the ministry was about.

'As James said, no proof. Grayson will show that man the disposal order, and tell him the guns were loaded for dumping. He can do nothing more than that. Unless he is going to turn out the Royal Navy to look for one little yacht. I don't think that would go down very well with either the navy or the Ministry.' She looked out of the window. 'Ah, here are Harbottle and Mr Grimston.'

The solicitor and the barrister *were* staying for lunch. John Grimston was a surprisingly young man, with sharp features and an even sharper brain. He was fast gaining a reputation as a most brilliant man in criminal matters. He did not discuss business until after the meal, then settled himself comfortably with a glass of port. 'On the surface it appears a very open and shut case, Lady Martingell,' he said. 'As there are two witnesses, there can be no argument about the fact that your son did assault the man Allardyce, and that he continued to throttle him after Allardyce had ceased being able to resist. The crux of the matter is how severe was the provocation, and what was in Winston's mind at the time of the attack. That is as far as the charge of murder is concerned.

The other charge, that of rape, would be easily disposed of, were it not inextricably mixed up with the murder charge.

'Now, of the two witnesses, the young woman Jane Allardyce is clearly hostile. She is the one who has brought the charge of rape, and according to her deposition, which I have studied very carefully, this was a prime cause of Winston's attack on her father. That Allardyce may have made some derogatory remarks about you, and about the, ah, death of your first husband and Winston's father, is hardly mentioned by Jane at all. You'll understand that this could be quite serious.'

Anne nodded, and drank some coffee. 'On the other hand,' Grimston went on, 'I am assuming we may regard Mr Mbote as a friendly witness.' He gave Mbote, seated on the far side of the room, one of those uncertain glances with which most English people regarded the big black man. 'Unfortunately, Mr Mbote has testified'—he turned over the papers on his lap—'what I assume to be the exact truth, that Winston lost his temper when Allardyce accused you, Lady Martingell, of being responsible for his father's death. Now, obviously, such an extreme statement does constitute provocation, but in the hands of a capable counsel—and I believe they are going to lead with Kenyon, who

179

is a *very* capable man—the question may well be raised as to whether Winston's extreme reaction was not caused by a suspicion on his part that Allardyce may have been telling the truth.' He finished his port. 'What I mean is this, Lady Martingell. Our defence is going to be manslaughter, on the basis that Winston lost his temper and did not realise that he had already hurt Allardyce badly enough to seriously injure him, and thus went on throttling him until he was dead. I think we might get away with that. But if the prosecution can make the jury believe that Winston, as we say, went over the top on hearing what Allardyce said, because he already had a suspicion that it was the truth, then we are coming very close to premeditation.'

'So?' Anne asked. Her heart was pounding quite painfully, because she knew what was coming next.

'I very much fear that it may be necessary to put you in the witness box, Lady Martingell.'

'For what purpose?'

'To state categorically and under oath that everything the man Allardyce said was a lie, and that Winston had never accused you, in any shape or form, of having a hand in his father's death. Would you be prepared to make that statement, under oath?'

The room was absolutely quiet. 'We should also require such a statement, under oath, from Mr Mbote, as apparently he was present during the, ah, attack from the Socotran pirates. It is a pity Sir James and the crew of the yacht are out of the country, because supporting testimony from them would also be helpful. But I think the evidence of you and Mr Mbote should be sufficient.'

He knows I will have to perjure myself, Anne thought. And so will Mbote. To save my son. To save Winston's son. To risk my own liberty! For someone she basically despised, even if she had brought him into the world? 'Will you answer me a question, Mr Grimston?' she asked.

'Of course, my lady, if I can.'

'I assume that if Winston is convicted of murdering Allardyce, he will be hanged?'

'I'm afraid a sentence of death will be mandatory. However, I would hope that even in those desperate circumstances we would be able to accomplish something. Provocation is always a defence. It is not actually a defence to murder, but it is a possible reason for a commutation of the death sentence.'

'What would that mean?'

'It would be commuted to life imprisonment. I'm afraid we could hope for nothing better than that. Public opinion ... you must be aware, my lady, that this country is quite close to revolution. There have been mutinies in the army, riots and what have you in our major cities, people are singing the 'Red Flag' ... any suggestion that the judiciary was being especially lenient to a member of the upper classes would not go down very well. Any commutation would have to be strictly on a point of common law, i.e., provocation of a nature to which any man might be expected to overreact.'

'I see. And supposing I testified to the effect that Allardyce's accusation was utterly false, and that, as you have said, Winston merely lost his temper and strangled the man before he realised what he was doing?'

'Then I would hope the charge would be reduced to manslaughter.'

'And what kind of sentence would he receive for that?'

'Difficult to say. The attack was provoked, but it was a severe attack which resulted in death. The sentence could well be ten years.'

'Ten years,' Anne mused. 'Now tell me something else, Mr Grimston: supposing Winston were convicted of murder, and the death sentence was commuted to life, as you have suggested would be possible, would there be a chance of parole?'

'Oh, indeed,' Grimston said enthusiastically. 'The case would come up in about ten years, and if he had behaved himself during that period, he would have every chance of being let out on licence.'

'So, really, no matter what happens, we are looking at ten years in prison.'

'I'm afraid we are, yes.'

'Suppose the charge of rape is also brought against him? What sentence would that involve?'

'Jane Allardyce's word against his, but with the jury probably on Jane's side ... six years.'

'On top of the ten?'

'Oh, no. To run concurrently.'

'Well, then,' Anne said again, 'ten years at the very least, no matter how we handle it. In all the circumstances, Mr Grimston, I do not think it would be a sound idea for me to give evidence at my son's trial. I am not likely to be called by the prosecution, am I?'

'I shouldn't think so, as any evidence you might give would be in Winston's favour. But ... you mean you will not help your son?' He glanced at Harbottle.

'Mr Grimston,' Anne said. 'You have just explained to me that whether I help Winston or not, he is still going to prison

183

for ten years, but that he is very unlikely to be imprisoned for longer than that, as long as he does not do something utterly stupid.'

'Well, I suppose that is perfectly true. But still, for a mother not to appear in her son's defence ...'

'Perhaps it would be better if I were out of the country during the trial,' Anne suggested.

Once again Grimston glanced at Harbottle, who was waggling his eyebrows; both men were utterly taken aback by Anne's attitude. 'Well,' Grimston said, 'there is always Mr Mbote.' This time he managed a smile at Mbote.

'I do not think it would be a good idea for Mr Mbote to appear either,' Anne said.

'I'm afraid he will have to, my lady. He is already a witness, as he was present when the assault took place. His evidence is already in the possession of the police. In any event, he too would be an asset to the defence, in that he tried, and failed, to restrain Winston, which further indicates that your son had entirely lost control of himself.'

'Would either Mr Mbote or I be breaking the law were we unavailable?'

'Well ... no. Not until the subpoenas have actually been served.'

'And of course, if Mr Mbote were not in the country when subpoenaed, and was found to be unavailable for the trial, the statement he had already given to the police would be read in court, or could be called upon by the defence?'

'That is perfectly true. But it would cause a good deal of adverse publicity for him not to be there.'

'That cannot be helped. Thank you, gentlemen. I shall follow the case with interest.' She allowed them a smile. 'You will understand, of course, that I am still meeting the cost of the defence. Submit your accounts, and they will be paid, no matter where I happen to be.'

'Yes, well ... ' Grimston stood up, hesitated, then turned to the door without offering to shake hands. Harbottle did shake hands, with both Anne and Mbote, then hurried behind the barrister. 'That woman is a monster,' Grimston said as he got into the car.

'She is a realist, and a pragmatist, John. Nothing worse than that.'

Grimston glanced at him as the solicitor started the car and drove out of the yard. 'Just what do you mean by that?'

'That having established the best that can be hoped for Winston, she decided against risking being arrested herself, for perjury at the very least.'

'You mean she did murder Penny-feather?'

'I am certain she shot him dead. Whether it was murder, or self-defence, or in defence of James Martingell, only she and Mbote and Sir James know. And she didn't want to put them in the position of all having to commit perjury.'

'I still don't like to consider what Young Winston's reaction will be when he's told his mother refuses to give evidence on his behalf.'

'Yes,' Harbottle agreed. 'We have a tricky one there.'

'I think I need a drink,' Anne said. 'Wilton, some champagne.'

'Are you sure of what you do?' Mbote asked. 'You have made an enemy of your son for life.'

'Has that not happened anyway? At least he cannot be sure whether or not I killed his father.'

'Non-appearance will be taken as an admission of guilt.'

'But it is not proof.' She took a turn up and down the room, glass in hand. 'Don't you think I feel about what has happened? My God! If only James were here. But he acted as he thought best, and I must do the same.'

'May I ask—do you love your son?' Mbote asked.

Anne shot him a glance. 'I am his mother.'

'That is not quite an answer.'

'Oh ...' She waved her hand. 'He was the product of rape. Winston and I were married, but we already hated each other. When he came to me, usually when drunk, claiming his conjugal rights, I had to submit. That is rape, even if it is not recognised within marriage. And it so happened one of those frightful occasions produced young Winston.' She smiled at him. 'There, Mbote, you have the secrets of a so civilised British marriage.'

'So you hated the child,' Mbote suggested.

'Well ... one cannot hate one's own child. I loved the babe. I imagined him growing up as mine. But it was easy to see too much of his father in him. So ...' She sighed, and sat down. 'If only James and I could have had a child of our own. It was a son, you know. God, how I hate that crazy Somali chieftain. He was responsible.'

'You have too much hate in your heart,' Mbote remarked.

'Ha! My life has conditioned me to hate.'

'Do you love James?'

She glanced at him. 'Not as you love

him, Mbote. But ... we have good sex together, even now. I admire him.'

'You also fear him, I think.'

'Doesn't everyone? Don't you? No, I suppose you do not. You are not a man who fears people, am I right?'

'I was a slave when James chose me to be his servant. Since then we have become friends. Brothers, almost. I am proud of this. But I can never forget that had James not selected me, as a slave in central Africa I would undoubtedly have died long ago. Every day when I awake I say to myself, well, here is more profit. Can you understand that?'

'I can say I understand it, but I don't really. I have never been in that position. You mean that, as you should have died twenty years ago, you have nothing left to fear, least of all death. But there are other things to fear besides death. Yes, I fear James. He is the most ruthless man I have ever met. But ... we are yoked together. And I hope we remain that way, always. Without James I should go mad.'

'Then what are you going to do now?'

'You and I are going to take a trip on the Continent. Would you not like that?'

He grinned. 'People will talk.'

Anne gave the necessary instructions for the running of the household in her absence, put Claudette to packing. Claudette was wildly excited. For her the Continent meant France, and thus she was going home. But Anne was equally excited, as it was some time since she had left England. She had not set foot in France since the return from East Africa following Winston's death, a dozen years ago. Besides, she found the idea of travelling with Mbote exciting. Mbote was of course too much James' man ever even to flirt with her, but he was an excellent companion. She was quite looking forward to the air of scandal that would surround them. She craved adventure, and recently had been having too little of it, except for that odd evening with Richard Elligan.

Three days later they were ready to leave. She had not again heard from either Harbottle or Grimston and did not expect to. They thought her an unnatural mother. Having spent their lives in a society where conventions counted more than reality, they could not understand a woman capable of taking such a harsh but realistic decision. She felt quite sorry for them. But they were not the only men in the world who might be after her blood. 'Mr Howorth is here, milady,' Wilton said,

189

only an hour before they were leaving to catch the train to London and thence Dover.

'Oh, really,' Anne remarked. 'What can *he* want?' She received him in the drawing room. 'Well, Mr Howorth? Don't tell me, you have caught up with my husband.'

'No, I have not, Lady Martingell,' Howorth said. 'Would that I had. Have you not read a newspaper this morning?'

'I seldom read the newspaper, Mr Howorth. I find what goes on in the world of very little interest to me.'

'Well, I am sure what I have to say will interest you. Yesterday morning Afghan troops crossed their border and invaded British India.'

Anne had received him standing, but now she slowly sank into a chair. Mbote hurried forward to be at her side. 'Initial reports suggest they have met with some success,' Howorth went on. 'Which is not surprising seeing that our people were taken entirely unawares. The point is, however, that Great Britain and Afghanistan are now at war. It follows therefore that anyone who assists the Afghans in any way, and most especially by selling them arms and ammunition, is an enemy of Great Britain. If he happens to be a British citizen, then he is also a traitor.'

Chapter 6

Treachery

'The buggers,' said Captain Pope, 'are behind that ridge. What do you reckon?'

Richard Elligan crouched beside the company commander and surveyed the broken ground in front of them. He had been rushed up to the North-West Frontier Province immediately on his arrival in Bombay, the theory being that he knew the Afghans and would therefore be of great use to the commanders in the field. He felt that the commanders in the field could have done better with a few more battalions of infantry, and a few batteries of mountain artillery. While if they could get hold of some aircraft ...

Instead they had him. Or they would have him when this supply column to which he had been attached reached brigade headquarters. Supposing it ever did. The position was unpromising in the extreme. The company, detailed to escort the supplies to the battalion which was supposed to be entrenched a few miles away, was not very well acclimatised, and the men were pouring sweat and drinking far too readily from their canteens. The march to link up with battalion, and thence with brigade, had seemed straightforward enough on the map, but maps of this part of the world never actually corresponded with the terrain itself, nor were the guides as trustworthy on the frontier as they appeared in camp. Now he reckoned they were well and truly lost, and their march had been brought to a halt by a sudden flurry of firing from in front of them.

'I reckon we should move to the right, sir,' suggested the company sergeant major, kneeling beside them. 'Get round that hump, eh? Take the bastards in the flank.'

'What we need is a probe,' Pope decided, 'to make sure that way is clear. Lieutenant Avery.'

'Sir!' The boy, for he was little more than that, touched the brim of his pith helmet with great smartness.

'Take a corporal and ten men and move away to the right. Occupy that hillock over there. Once you are there, signal us, and the company will join you. We will cover you.'

'Sir!' Avery crawled away to select his men.

'Machine-gun,' Pope commanded, and the Lewis gun was brought forward and emplaced amidst the rocks. The firing from in front of them remained desultory, just the odd shot pinging off the rocks.

'How many do you estimate, Elligan?' Pope enquired.

'Difficult to say. But these people generally move in some force.'

'We'll smoke them out. All set, Avery?'

The lieutenant crouched several feet away, sweat staining his khaki tunic, revolver clutched in his right hand. Immediately behind him were his ten men and the corporal, bayonets fixed, but also sweating and looking distinctly uneasy. 'Go,' Pope commanded. 'Open fire, Sergeant.'

The machine-gun chattered as the belt of bullets was fed through its chambers. The rest of the company also began firing, and pieces of rock flew out of the hill in front of them. Under this cover Avery and his men rose and raced across the relatively flat ground towards the hummock some quarter of a mile away. There were few shots from the Afghans, pinned down as they were by the machine-gun. Then the patrol was lost to sight. 'Made it,' Pope said triumphantly. 'Now ...'

There was a whoosh and a bang, and earth and rock flew. Someone began screaming. 'What the fuck was that?' asked the sergeant major.

For reply another shell burst just in

front of the British position, showering them with rocks. 'Heads down,' Pope bellowed. 'Wounded!' He lowered his voice. 'Artillery. Where in the name of God did they get artillery?'

'We're fighting a reasonably modern army,' Richard pointed out. 'With old-fashioned methods.'

'We can't stay here and get blown to bits. Well, Sergeant?'

'Private Watkins, sir, hit. He's lost an arm. Private Emmett, sir, hit by splinters. He's got a nasty gash. Sergeant Creese, sir, hit by splinters. He's not too bad.'

'What about Watkins?'

'We're binding him up, sir, but it don't look too good.'

Pope chewed his lip. 'Make up a stretcher. Sergeant Major, prepare to withdraw.'

As if to confirm his decision, another shell struck the ground, this time further back, to set the mules and the bearers screaming and shouting.

'What about Avery and his people?' Richard asked.

'Shit,' Pope said. 'What bad luck.'

'What perfect timing,' Richard suggested.

Pope glared at him. 'They can hold till we can get back to them.' Richard forbore from asking just how he intended to do that, lacking artillery of his own. 'Rifle fire,' Pope commanded. 'Sergeant, dismantle that gun and move it back.'

Behind them the cacophony was growing, and the two captains turned to see several of the mules galloping away, followed by their drivers and the bearers. 'God damn it,' Pope snapped.

'You can't blame them,' Richard suggested. Nor were they going to get very far, he thought, as another shell burst in their midst, sending men and animals scattering to and fro in bloodied disorder. While now they were being shot at by rifle fire ... from behind.

'Good God,' Pope said. 'They're all round us.'

They were in a complete trap, Richard thought, and cursed his ill fortune to have been attached to such an inadequate command.

'What should I do?' Pope asked. 'What *can* I do?'

'Keep your head down,' Richard snapped. 'Form a perimeter, facing both ways. Set that machine-gun up again. Hold fast.'

'For how long? My God, for how long.' Tears were dribbling down Pope's cheeks.

'We are due at battalion for lunch. It's lunchtime now. They'll realise something is wrong in another hour or two.'

'And then an hour or two to decide

what's to be done, then an hour or two to get the relief together. My God ... we could be talking about tomorrow morning. We'll all be dead by then.'

'Sit tight,' Richard said. 'They won't rush the machine-gun.' And from the slow rate of fire he estimated there was only one field gun, and not too many shells. 'What we need to do is get Avery's patrol back.'

Pope stared at the distant hummock, again chewing his lip, while the sergeant major arranged the remaining seventy-odd men of the command in a square, making sure every man had a rock to hide behind. 'Just relax,' he told the raw soldiers. 'Make them come to you. Mark your target. And go easy on the water; there ain't all that much left.'

'Avery must know what's happened,' Pope muttered, levelling his binoculars. 'Bugler. Sound recall.' The notes of the trumpet disappeared into the various ravines and gullies around them. There was no response from beyond the hummock. 'They couldn't have heard it,' Pope decided. 'We'll signal him with flags. Signalman?' His agitation was disturbing.

A very young private crawled up to them. 'Signal the patrol to return,' Pope said. 'Sergeant, open fire with the Lewis gun.'

Once again the machine-gun chattered, while the signalman very bravely stood up and went through his flag drill, again without eliciting any response from the hummock. 'All right,' Pope said. 'The idiots can't be looking. Cease fire.'

But as the chatter of the machine-gun died away there was a flurry of shooting, accompanied by screams and yells, from beyond the hummock. 'Oh, Jesus Christ,' the sergeant major said. 'Begging your pardon, sir.'

The explosion of sound only lasted a few seconds, then the noise died. 'Now they'll come back, surely,' Pope said.

'If they can,' Richard said.

Pope glanced at him, then levelled the binoculars. 'Movement,' he said. 'They're coming. They—' The glasses dropped from his hand.

Richard levelled his own binoculars. A figure had appeared at the side of the hummock, thrust there because it was not capable of movement itself; it wore a British army uniform, but lacked a head. Richard swallowed, and listened to the most unearthly sound he had ever heard, a combination of a scream of agony and a howled prayer, it seemed, as of an animal in despair. He turned the glasses to one side, and caught the flutter of a garment. It might have been a tribesman's cloak, but it was brightly decorated. Then it was gone again. 'Oh, shit,' he muttered, recalling Kipling's lines:

'When you're wounded and left on Afghanistan's plains,
An' the women come out to cut up your remains,
Just roll to your rifle an' blow out your brains,
An' go to your Gawd like a soldier.'

Pope's fingers were trembling as he picked up the glasses to look in his turn. As he did so, there came another scream, and this spoke English. 'God!' the voice shrieked. 'God, no! Please ...' the voice rose into a screech of shame and agony.

'That was Avery,' Pope said. 'My God, Elligan, what are we to do?'

'Sit tight,' Richard told him, and looked around him at the enlisted men. They had all heard the screams, they all knew that their comrades were being castrated by the Afghan women. At least, Richard thought grimly, none of them will have any temptation to run away or surrender.

The screams lasted for the better part of an hour; the Afghans were enjoying what they were doing and not hurrying. The company lay, and shuddered, and occasionally drank water. Some of them fired at random, to relieve their spirits; there was no answering fire. The Afghans knew they weren't going anywhere. 'Do you think they're all dead?' Pope asked. He sounded almost hopeful.

'Yes,' Richard said. He didn't, actually. After cutting away a man's genitals, he knew there was a tendency to cut away his tongue, and leave him to bleed to death. But perhaps they were dead.

Was he afraid? Of being taken alive, certainly. But he was always an optimist. He tried to consider it as being a realist. The Afghans reckoned they had the company, if not today, certainly tomorrow. They didn't know there had been a scheduled rendezvous. Of course they would understand that when the battalion sent to find out what had happened to the supply column, but then they would probably withdraw—otherwise they would be faced with fighting a pitched battle against superior forces. His real worry was that the battalion would not move down here in strength. But he had to believe they would. He had not come here to die.

He lay on the hard earth, and took a sip of water, and stared up at the cloud-flecked sky. He wondered if the arms being used against them, and especially the mountain gun, had been manufactured and sold by the Martingell Arms Company. Of course it was far too soon for any current shipment to have been delivered, but Martingell had supplied the Afghans with guns before the war. The bastard! But would it not be poetic justice for him, having cuckolded the bastard, to be killed by one of the bastard's guns?

His feelings about that night had until now been mixed. He had been heartily ashamed of what he had done, but it remained about the most glorious memory of his life.

How much more glorious would it have been had it been Lanne instead of her stepmother? Her wicked, wicked stepmother. Who had actually saved him from an unimaginable fate. If she had been telling the truth. But he had to believe that, because he could not believe that any woman could so destroy her own stepchild if it were not true.

He wondered if either of them ever thought of him. Lanne would have, he supposed, for a while, and would then have dismissed him as an utter cad, who had attempted to seduce her and been talked out of it and then just disappeared. Lady Martingell ... as he was not the first man she had ever laid, and would certainly not be the last, he did not suppose he filled any great memory in *her* mind. If she learned that he had been killed in a skirmish with the Afghans, she would say to herself, better luck next time. That was how she lived her life.

But he was not going to be killed, he thought fiercely, rolled on his stomach, and in doing so awoke Pope, who had been dozing. 'What, what ... '

'Nothing yet.'

It was dark, but not quiet. The mules had all scattered now, and with them their drivers; various whinnyings could be heard in the distance as the Afghans rounded them up. There were night birds, and there were distant calls too, and the occasional shot, just to let them know that they were still surrounded. The British did not reply; they were well-disciplined troops, and however anxious or even afraid they were still going to obey orders. 'Sergeant Major,' Pope said.

'Sir!'

'Check the perimeter.'

'Yes, sir.' The sergeant major crawled off into the darkness.

'What time is it?' Pope asked.

Richard studied his watch. 'Coming up to ten.'

'My God, you'd have thought the battalion would have come looking for

201

us by now. They'll be here by dawn, won't they?'

'If they are here by dawn, then we have only about six hours to wait,' Richard agreed.

'And those bloody wogs will have missed the bus. Damnation. I'm out of water.'

Richard hesitated, but the fellow was really in a very bad way. 'I've a little left. Just one swig, mind.'

Pope took the offered canteen, drank, handed it back. 'I suppose situations like this are commonplace to you.'

'Happily, not.'

'But you were in France. I never got to France.'

'We didn't often lack water, in France,' Richard said.

The night drifted on; there was no moon. Richard nodded off again, then jerked into full wakefulness. Now what had done that? The catcalls had increased, and the firing had altogether ceased. He looked at his watch. A quarter to three, and utterly dark. But it would soon be light, and the Afghans were stirring. He touched Pope's shoulder, and as usual the inexperienced captain sat up with a start. 'They'll be coming any minute,' Richard said.

'Eh? How do you know?'

'Listen.' To go with the catcalls there was a dribble of dislodged rocks.

'Sergeant Major,' Pope snapped. 'Have the men stand to.'

'Sir.'

'Do you think it would be a good idea to blow the bugle?' Pope asked.

'Why, yes, that might be a very good idea,' Richard said. 'Show them we're not asleep.'

'Bugler. Sound reveille,' Pope said. The notes soared through the darkness, and were overtaken by a gigantic hum as the Afghans spoke amongst themselves. 'Volley fire,' Pope shouted, as the night became filled with white forms. 'Machine-gun.'

The Lewis gun chattered, and a wave of bullets swept into the darkness. The white-clad figures checked, but only for a moment, then they were coming on again. The British emptied their magazines, but much of the shooting was wild in the darkness and the growing fear of the coming minutes. 'Fix bayonets!' Pope yelled, and the rasp of steel rippled across the morning, which had suddenly lightened.

Richard rose to his feet, levelled his revolver, and shot one tribesman through the head. The man's turban seemed to dissolve in blood and bone. He shot another man who immediately filled the position, and emptied his revolver before he was bowled over by two men, both of whom thrust at him with curved tulwars. But he was still alive, he realised as he struck the earth. His revolver had flown away, so he rolled over and drew his sword, a weapon he had only used once on the Western Front.

Now he was surrounded by bearded, white-clad figures, as the lightness grew and he could see their faces. He swung at them, and they evaded the blow easily enough. They all carried swords or rifles, but he realised that they meant to take him alive; they had seen his officer's badges. He could never allow that. He swung the sword again, then reversed it, meaning to fall on the blade, and had it knocked from his hands by a swinging blow. He went with it, landed on his hands and knees, and before he could recover was seized by a dozen hands, forcing him to the ground and keeping him pinned there. He could only pray for succour, but there was none to be had. The brief battle was already over, with the Afghans cheering and yelling and laughing, and the British only screaming or moaning in pain.

My God, he thought, the entire command has been wiped out! He forced his head up, looking right and left, and saw Pope. The captain had been lucky; his eyes stared from a dead face. And now Richard was rolled on his back, and saw the flutter of skirts.

Richard had been picked as an attaché to the court of Amir Habibullah because he spoke Persian, which was the official language of Afghanistan. But these tribesmen, and their women, were speaking a dialect he didn't know, chattering happily. Why had they not killed him, when they had killed Pope? But perhaps the death of the company commander had been an accident; one of the Afghans, who seemed in some command, kicked the dead body with a scowl and made several derogatory comments to his men, who defended themselves with sly grins, and then dragged Richard to his feet and presented him. Now he could hear sound from behind him, bestial sounds as the victors moved amongst the wounded and their prisoners. God, he thought: this cannot be happening!

The Afghan captain was surrounded by women, giggling and whispering, pointing at Richard. They were asking for him. His legs felt weak, and had his arms not been so tightly gripped he would have fallen. I must not scream, he told himself. I must not beg. No matter what happens, I must not beg.

The Afghan chieftain came closer, peered

into his face, slapped his cheeks to move his head to and fro, and made a remark to his fellows. The women, most of them were hardly older than girls, chortled and came closer. One, bolder than the rest, pushed her way in front of her chief and tore open Richard's tunic. Her face was so close he could smell the garlic on her breath; he felt he could have bitten her nose, and had an enormous temptation to do so. But before he could make up his mind the face had slid lower, and she began to unbuckle his belt. Her companions now surged forward to join her, tearing at his pants, dragging them down, while the chieftain grinned at him ... and there suddenly came a crisp command, cutting across the morning like a whip.

The women stopped, and turned their heads, as did the chieftain, while Richard's own head jerked upwards, and he realised that his eyes had been filled with tears, for he could only see dimly. The newcomer was mounted, and he wore a green uniform and a peaked cap. 'Sandor?' Richard whispered. 'Sandor Galitsin?'

The Russian dismounted, and whipped his riding crop to and fro. The women shouted with pain and indignation as the leather landed on back and shoulder and backside and thigh, but they scattered to either side, while the men holding Richard let him go. He sank to his knees, trying to control himself, dragging his clothes into position. Galitsin! His saviour. But ... his military instincts were still working. 'You?' he demanded. 'Fighting with the Afghans?'

'You should be happy about that,' Galitsin remarked. 'In these circumstances.'

'My men ...'

Galitsin nodded. 'It is their way. I will see what can be done.' He walked away from Richard, giving orders. The women he had whipped glared at their would-be victim, eyes like live coals. Richard felt he was in a cage filled with lionesses. But they would not defy the Russian, and the cries of anguish from behind him were dwindling. Galitsin returned. 'They make war differently from us,' he remarked. 'But I have persuaded them it would be for the best to leave their prisoners here, unharmed. Your entire brigade is moving this way.'

'And they will obey you?'

Galitsin grinned. 'Oh, indeed. They rely on us for their weapons. Pending the arrival of others, to be sure.'

'Are you saying that Russia is fighting beside Afghanistan in this war? My God, Sandor, you do not realise what you have taken on.'

'We are military advisers, Richard. As

were you, for so long. Swings and roundabouts, eh? Now come, we must get out of here.'

'You said my men were to be left unharmed.'

'That is true. But not you, Richard. You know too much about me, and us. You will come with us.' Another grin. 'With me. I will look after you.'

'I do not think I have ever enjoyed myself so much,' Michelle Desmorins remarked, sitting on the quarterdeck and sipping iced tea as the *Europa* made her way towards the Persian Gulf, across a calm ocean and beneath a cloudless sky. 'When I think how seasick I was, those weeks ago ... you will have thought me a fool.'

'I entirely sympathised,' Lanne said. 'I was equally seasick the first time I made this voyage.' She frowned at the sea. 'My circumstances were different.'

'Philippe has told me.' Michelle reached across to squeeze her hand. 'You were kidnapped, by that madman in Somalia. My heart bleeds for you. Even if I ... well ... you survived very well.'

'Because I was a hostage for my father's delivery of weapons.' Lanne looked up the ladder to the yacht's bridge, where James was standing with Captain Petersen, who had just taken a noon sight; the end of the

voyage was near. 'If he had not come ...'
She gave a little shiver.

'It must be a terrible memory for you.'

'It isn't, because it never happened.'

'Ah, to have lived,' Michelle remarked.
She gave her friend a sideways glance.
'You are very close to your father.' It
was a question she had probed, constantly,
during the several weeks that had elapsed
throughout the voyage from England.
Weeks in which, as James Martingell
had forbidden any radio contact with
the outside world, the ship had become a
totally self-contained world of its own. The
only time they had broken the voyage had
been to fuel in Lusaka, and that had been
a very hasty affair. Since then, rounding
the Cape of Good Hope, standing out to
sea to avoid even the possible crowding of
the Madagascar Channel, they had scarce
seen another ship.

As she had told Michelle, Lanne
remembered her voyage in the Mad
Mullah's schooner very well. That had
been continually traumatic, not merely
because of her own circumstances, but
because she had sensed the terror that
had surrounded her, even if at the age
of nine she had not known what physical
form that terror might take. But she had
had the company, and the protection,
of Anne, always massively calm, always

certain that her husband would rescue them. As he had done. Now he was in total command, no less massively confident, massively competent.

Lanne knew so little of her father. Memory really began with the house in Dar es Salaam, so many years ago, when she had lived with her mother, and James Martingell had been an entirely remote figure, sometimes present for days at a time but more often absent, who she hardly remembered. She recalled that her mother had been a loving, almost too loving woman. She remembered the smell of stale liquor that had surrounded her, the number of times Mother had fallen over, the men who had come to call, had dandled the little girl on their knees, before she had been packed off to bed so that Mother could enjoy their company. She had questioned nothing of that, because it had been the norm.

Then suddenly, without warning, Father had reappeared. She had been told that she was leaving German East Africa for Germany itself, where she would be educated as a lady. She remembered Mother weeping because she was staying behind. Father had been very much a stranger, then. But had he become less of a stranger since?

She had travelled to Germany in the care

of a stern-faced woman who had whipped her when she had stuck out her tongue. Then she had been placed in the care of a childless couple, in Cologne. They had been kind, she recalled. But only briefly, before Father had reappeared, with his current mistress, the German Lisette Uhlmann, and taken her away again; she had understood that his relationship with the German arms firm the House of Beinhardt had soured following the death of the Countess Cecile von Beinhardt, to whom he had been betrothed. In the first instance they had gone to live with Uncle Philippe, as she had always regarded him, and still regarded him. That had been before Michelle; Uncle Philippe had been living with a Somali woman named Atossa. Then Philippe and Father had gone off to Africa to regain some of Father's money, and she had been left entirely in the care of Lisette. It had been a strange relationship. She now knew that Lisette had wanted to influence her against Father, with whom she had pretended to be in love. Lanne had been too young to understand all the implications of that, or of some of the things Lisette had done to her and with her—save that she had enjoyed much of it. But then Father had whisked her off to live with Anne, and an entirely new life had begun for her.

The surroundings had been so elegant, the servants and the required manners so impressive—she had been terrified, and most of all of the tall, strong woman who had created the rules and insisted they be obeyed. Yet she had grown to love Anne as much as she admired and respected her, the more so after their joint ordeal in East Africa. And now ... had she always known they would have to quarrel one day? She did not doubt that Anne had masterminded everything that had happened since Richard had appeared in their lives. She hated her for that, the more so because she had for so long loved her. But Anne had herself come a cropper, in the wilful violence of Winston. So ... bugger her, she thought.

But where did that leave her? She felt like Pandora. After such a chaste childhood and young adulthood, a box had suddenly been opened in front of her—and she had been forbidden to sample any of the fruits, good or bad, that had issued from it. In so many ways this voyage had been a purgatory. She had been made aware of her beauty, her sexuality, and she had been trapped in the strangest of prisons. The sailors all looked at her twice; there was not one of them would not like to find his way into her cabin. While Father ... but

Father was working to a plan, that was obvious. No one could have been kinder, more solicitous of her well-being, than he had during the voyage. She had always feared him, had always, deep in her heart, hated him for his treatment of her mother, although she now knew that Mother had actually been a prostitute. On this voyage she had learned to respect him, and even perhaps to love him. Yet she now knew that he was indeed the renegade criminal people had always described him, that he was engaged in breaking the law on a massive scale ... did that matter, to her? Only if she was setting up to oppose him. Richard would have her do that. But Richard was lost to her, no doubt for ever, frightened away by whatever Anne had told him. Anne was the one she should hate.

'Tomorrow morning, sir,' Captain Petersen said.

James, studying the chart, nodded. 'I'll be glad when this is done.'

'Is it really the last, sir?'

'Absolutely. Don't worry, Captain; I'm not selling the yacht. You'll still be employed.'

'Thank you, sir. And the crew?'

'We'll have to make do with less, to be sure. We'll have to work that out.'

'Yes, sir,' Petersen said, doubtfully.

James went aft to sit with the two woman and Philippe, and drink champagne. 'We'll be at Chah Bahar tomorrow,' he told them.

'How long will it take to unload the guns?' Lanne asked.

'About two days, I should think. Depends on how many people Azam has working for him.'

'And then home!'

'I'm afraid not quite that soon. I have to accompany the guns up to the Afghan border, and have them accepted there.' He grinned. 'And receive my final payment.'

'But ... how long will that take?'

'A month, there and back.'

'Oh, good Lord!' she exclaimed. 'What do we do for a month?'

'The drill we followed last time, and which I propose to repeat, is that once the guns are unloaded, *Europa* will put to sea and cruise for a month, then return here to pick me up. You will stay with the ship. And you, Michelle. Philippe, you'll accompany me.'

'Into the mountains?' Philippe did not look too happy.

'These are all friends,' James assured him.

'What do you think?' Lanne asked Michelle.

'I think it sounds delightful. A whole

214

month, just cruising.'

'And when there is a typhoon or whatever it is they call them around here?'

'This isn't the season,' James told her.

'There!' James pointed into the darkness, at the winking light on the horizon. 'Chah Bahar. We'll be at anchor in the morning.'

Lanne held his arm as they stood at the rail. Michelle and Philippe had gone to bed. 'Daddy, couldn't I come with you? I'd love to see the interior, the mountains, the people.'

'Not on this trip, sweetheart.'

'Why not?'

'It will be arduous and uncomfortable. And possibly dangerous.'

'But these people are your friends,' she pointed out. 'And I'm not afraid of a little discomfort. Why did you bring me on this voyage at all, if I was not to be with you?'

He supposed she had a point. And actually, guarded as they would be by Azam's men, there was very little danger involved. 'What will Michelle say?'

'Michelle can come too. She won't want to be left all alone on the yacht.'

Michelle did not wish to be left all alone on the yacht, although she grumbled at the prospect of a trek through the mountains.

'It will be an experience you will never forget,' Philippe assured her, happy to have her along.

Chah Bahar had grown somewhat from the sleepy little fishing village James remembered from more than ten years ago. There was in fact another ship flying the red ensign at anchor in the roadstead. But there was the usual swarm of lighters surrounding *Europa* the moment she dropped anchor, and the usual total lack of interest from the Persian customs officials—Azam had as always done his work well. Yet the sheikh was strangely agitated as he came on board. 'We must make haste,' he said.

'Something the matter?' James asked, shaking hands.

'There are always problems,' Azam pointed out. The unloading commenced right away, the cases being craned out of the hold and over the side into the lighters, while on the shore James could see the carts waiting to receive them, and which would form the caravan. Azam was somewhat taken aback to learn that they were to be accompanied by the two ladies. 'We will make them as comfortable as we can,' he said. 'But you understand we must travel fast.'

'I understand,' James said. He sensed a

crisis, but no doubt all would be revealed in good time. He told the women to get prepared, and he and Philippe did the same. When they returned on deck, the first lot of lighters were already on their way to the shore, and Azam was pacing up and down the deck impatiently as he waited for them to return.

'Ahoy, *Europa!*' came a hail.

'Good morning to you,' Petersen replied from the bridge to the steam launch that was approaching.

'My captain sends his compliments,' the ship's officer called, 'and asks if you would lunch with him?'

'I will check with my owner,' Petersen said, 'but come alongside.'

'Send those people away,' Azam muttered to James.

He raised his eyebrows; Azam was not in the habit of giving him orders. 'Do you know them?' he asked.

Azam shrugged, somewhat sulkily, and retired aft. James went to the gangway.

'Sir James Martingell?' the officer said, coming up.

'How do you know that?' James asked.

'I looked your ship up in our Lloyd's Register, sir. John Hopkins, first officer, *Marchioness of Granby.*'

'Welcome aboard,' James said.

'Strange to see an English yacht in

217

these waters,' Hopkins said. 'In these circumstances.'

James frowned. 'What circumstances? Don't tell me we are at war with Persia.'

'No, sir. But ...' Hopkins glanced at Azam, who was staring over the rail. 'We are at war with Afghanistan.'

'What did you say? When did this happen?'

'Quite recently, as I understand it. About a month ago the blighters suddenly invaded India. There has been some quite severe fighting.'

'The devil,' James said. 'Thank you for that information. Yes, we should be delighted to lunch with your captain.' He ushered a somewhat bewildered officer back to the gangway, saw him onto the ladder, and then hurried aft. 'I think you have some explaining to do,' he told Azam.

Another shrug. 'The fools would act. I warned them against it, I told them to wait, but you see they are encouraged by Russian agents.'

'Were you going to tell me of this?'

'I did not wish to distress you,' Azam said.

'Well now you have. Captain Petersen!' James shouted. 'Tell that unloading to cease.'

'Aye, aye,' Petersen called back. A

moment later the crane ceased its grinding.

'What are you doing?' Azam demanded.

'The deal was, no war with Britain,' James said.

'My dear James, this has nothing to do with you.'

'My guns have everything to do with me, Azam.'

'You have been paid for them.'

'Half.'

'Here is my cheque for the next quarter.'

James chewed his lip. This had been going to be his last expedition, his last running the gauntlet of the law and public opinion. For half a million pounds. To give that up would mean starting from scratch all over again ... but he could not sell his guns to a country in arms against his own. He was not that much of a scoundrel. 'I will return your money,' he said. 'Have those guns reloaded.'

'That will not do, James. We need those weapons. And those munitions.'

'And I have said, no sale,' James said. 'You know the terms of our agreement.'

'Then I will have to take them,' Azam said. 'I am sorry, James. But there are times when a nation is more important than an individual.' James heard movement, and turned to see a large number of men, all armed, appearing over the rail of the yacht; he realised that while he had been speaking with Hopkins, Azam had anticipated what would follow and had alerted his men. There were a good many sailors on deck, but none of them were armed; nor were he or Philippe. The two women, who had been sitting on the quarterdeck, now stood up in alarm. Azam drew a revolver from inside his jibbah. 'Please do nothing rash, James,' he said.

'Do you really suppose you can get away with this?' James asked. 'This is not Afghanistan.'

'It is Persia, and in this part of Persia, as you know, we have many friends. No one will interfere with us. Tell your captain to resume unloading the goods.'

'And if I refuse?'

Azam gave an order in some dialect unknown to James, and two of his men came forward. They seized Lanne's arms. 'Daddy!' she cried. 'Azam! You're our friend.'

'I wish to be your friend, certainly, Lanne,' Azam said. 'But duty comes before friendship. You'll obey me, James, or my men will cut your daughter's throat.'

Lanne and her father stared at each other in horror. For a moment, indeed, as she gazed at his face, Lanne thought he would resist, regardless of the circumstances, of what might happen to her. She could see the emotions racing through his mind.

220

To supply arms to an enemy in arms against his country would put him for ever beyond the pale. To resist would mean the death of his only daughter. A biblical dilemma. But she could thank God that James Martingell was not, after all, a biblical patriarch. 'You'll resume unloading, Captain Petersen,' James said.

'That was very wise of you,' Azam said. 'Now, will you and your companions prepare yourselves to go ashore. I am sorry, but it will be necessary for my people to be with you while you pack.'

'You are kidnapping us?'

'How can I be doing that? Did you not just tell me you intended to accompany the arms to the border? This is something I think you should do. After all, I cannot have you sailing from here direct to Bombay to acquaint the Government of India of the weapons shipment my government has just received.'

'If I did that I would go to prison,' James said.

Azam nodded. 'I think that is very likely. But I also think that you are just sufficiently a patriot to risk that. I have said that we should make haste.'

Philippe, Michelle and Lanne were standing together. Lanne and Philippe had been in this position before, and even if they had never expected to be

221

in such a position again they were still placing their trust in his ability to get them out of trouble. Michelle looked ready to faint. 'Well,' James said. 'You'll be pleased to learn that our trip into the interior is still on. Ladies, would you get your gear together. Don't mind the chap who'll be standing at your shoulder. He won't harm you.' He looked at Azam.

'You have my word,' Azam said. 'Providing they do nothing stupid.'

'And what of my ship, and my crew?' James enquired.

'It will remain here, under guard, until your return,' Azam said.

'This is an open roadstead. It may be necessary to put to sea.'

'We are some months away from the monsoon season,' Azam pointed out. 'I think it will be quite safe here. As will your men, unless *they* attempt something stupid. Regrettably, I am afraid it will be necessary for my people to destroy your radio equipment. I will pay for the damage.'

'I thought you were my friend,' James remarked.

Azam gave a little bow. 'As I have said, James, there are certain eventualities that transcend friendship. But I would hope to be your friend again, when this is over.'

Chapter 7

The Captives

The two women dressed themselves for what might loosely be called a safari, in voluminous skirts, loose blouses, and topis tied firmly beneath their chins with chiffon scarves; how they had accomplished this while overlooked by the Afghan warriors James did not care to ask, but where Lanne had apparently taken it in her stride Michelle was all pink cheeks and mutterings in French. These grew when they were ferried ashore, stared at by Persians and Afghans alike, surrounded by whooping and scantily clad children and snarling dogs, to discover that while their journey was to be made on horseback there were no side-saddles. 'It never occurred to me to pack jodhpurs,' Lanne remarked.

'I cannot ride astride,' Michelle complained. 'I simply cannot.'

'We will add extra blankets to the saddle,' Azam said, and gave the necessary orders.

'What is going to happen to us, Sir James?' Michelle whispered.

'Nothing, I hope,' James told her. 'We are merely hostages, for the time being.'

'Hostages,' she muttered, clearly recalling Lanne's earlier adventures. Philippe said nothing, merely looked as doleful as only Philippe could.

The guns were loaded into the waiting wagons, and the caravan moved off. As on the previous occasion James had unloaded guns here, there was no interference by the Persian authorities, such as they were. 'I have a cheque here for a hundred and twenty-five thousand pounds,' Azam told James. 'Or are you going to refuse it?'

'What's the point? As I am to be a traitor anyway, I may as well have the money.'

'Absolutely. But it is no good to you here, eh? I will have it sent to your London bank.'

'Which will make sure that you can prove you bought the guns from me.'

'It pays to be careful,' Azam agreed.

He gave the signal, and the caravan moved out of the little town. Almost immediately the land began to rise, and by that evening they had virtually left the coastal plain behind, and were in arid, stony country, with only the odd stunted tree in sight, while in front of them the mountains began to rise. 'Oo la-la,' Michelle commented. 'We are not going up there?'

'I'm afraid so,' James said. 'Lovely country.'

'We have tents,' Azam said, when they stopped for the night and sat around the campfire, already necessary because the air was chill once the sun went down. 'They each will sleep two people. It is better to be in a tent than in the open.'

'I will sleep with my 'usband,' Michelle said.

Azam looked at Lanne. 'I will sleep with my father,' she said.

'What are you going to do, Daddy?' Lanne asked, as they lay beneath their blankets, one on either side of the tent pole; the tent itself was not very large, and neither had had the least desire to undress.

'Sit it out,' he said.

'Are we in any danger?'

'Not until we reach Afghanistan.'

'And then?'

'That depends upon a lot of things. But we must always be patient, and do nothing rash.'

She said nothing more, but he knew she was remembering how he and Azam had charged to the rescue of Anne and herself, into the very heart of the Mullah's encampment. There had been nothing patient about that, and everything rash. But that had been more than ten years ago. Was he still the same man?

They climbed higher every day, every hour, and as they did so the going got rougher and their progress slower. Now there was hardly any vegetation at all, only the odd herds of sheep or goats, and the odd goatherd as well. The villages they passed through were sparsely inhabited, but the people all gathered to watch the caravan rolling by. 'Do they know what is in the wagons?' Lanne asked.

'Probably.'

They had not spoken much over the preceding few days, simply because by nightfall they had been too exhausted. But he was pleased that both women were bearing up very well, far more so than Philippe, who was looking his age, his face grey and his breath short. 'This is not good for him,' Michelle complained.

'It'll be easier going back,' James promised her. Supposing they were ever to go back.

'Why were you and Mother so against my marrying Richard, Daddy?' Lanne spoke out of the darkness of the tent. 'It wasn't simply because he is an officer in the army, was it?'

'No,' James said.

'I had the feeling you were quite keen on

the idea, at the beginning. Mother talked you out of it, didn't she?'

'She convinced me that it would be a mistake.'

'Will you tell me why? I would have thought that had we got married he would have found it more difficult to ... well ...'

'Bring me to justice?' James smiled into the darkness. 'I did have that in mind.'

'Then what changed your mind?'

James stared into the darkness. Although he had let no one know it, he realised they were in a life or death situation, effectively prisoners of the Afghans, and thus at the mercy of Azam's superiors. For a people at war with Britain, the disappearance of one English gun-runner and his accomplices was not going to cause any traumas—the traumas would all be on their side, and especially that of the two women ... who he had brought along with his usual careless confidence. He had been quite certain, correctly he was sure, that Britain would never go to war with the Afghans. It had simply never occurred to him that the Afghans might go to war with the British.

Thus Lanne might very well be living the last few days of her life. Had he the right to perhaps make those last few days even more miserable by telling her the truth of her ancestry? But then, did he have the right to play God and *not* tell her.

He listened to the sound of her blankets being thrown aside as she crawled out from beneath them. It was very close to freezing outside, but within the tent it was fairly warm. She knelt beside him. 'It's to do with Mother, isn't it. I mean, my real mother.'

'What do you remember of her?'

'I know she was a whore. And British army officers, certainly in the Guards, can't marry the daughters of whores, can they? Even if he doesn't know it and her father is a KCB.'

James sighed, but he had been let off the hook. 'I suppose that's about it,' he said.

'Is there anyone I *can* marry, Daddy?'

He reached out for her hand, squeezed it. 'We'll find someone. That's a promise.'

'Someone who won't care what I am?'

'That's right.'

It was her turn to sigh. 'Do you know I have never had sex?'

'I should hope not.'

'For God's sake. I'm twenty-three years old, all but, and I have never been in a man's arms.' Suddenly she was lying down beside him, her arms round his neck. 'I'm so ...'

'Frustrated?' He hugged her and kissed her. 'Now go back to bed. Incest is the last thing we want.'

They came to the town of Duzdab, and after travelling some miles further north, rounded the apex where Baluchistan, a province of British India, met up with the borders of Persia and Afghanistan, crossed the River Shelga, hardly more than a trickle at this time of year, and camped in the ruins of the ancient city of Ramrod. Next day they crossed the border into Afghanistan. The road to Duzdab had taken them to some five thousand feet above sea level, but the last day had all been downhill, and James did not suppose they were more than a thousand feet high at the border, but the air was thin and the sun scorched out of a cloudless sky. They had not been on their way more than an hour, into Afghan territory, traversing what appeared to be a vast stony desert which stretched for as far as the eye could see, with the only mountains those behind them, when without warning Philippe slumped from his saddle and struck the ground with a thump. Michelle gave a scream of alarm, and scrambled down beside him, while the caravan came to a halt.

James and Lanne hurried forward, to find Azam already there. 'He has had, what do you call this?' Azam asked. 'An apoplexy.'

'A stroke,' James agreed. Certainly his old friend seemed to be hardly breathing, while his face was suffused. 'He needs a doctor.'

'I knew this would 'appen,' Michelle declared. 'The journey is too much for 'im, eh, Sir James. I knew it.'

'There is no doctor until Kandahar,' Azam said.

'How far is that?'

'Three hundred miles.'

'But ... that is a fortnight away.'

Azam nodded. 'We will do what we can.' He signalled his men forward, and they pitched camp, and lifted Philippe into one of the tents.

'What are you going to do?' James asked.

'A stroke is caused by too much blood, eh? We will bleed him.'

'Bleed 'im?' Michelle screamed.

'We must keep him alive until we reach Kandahar,' Azam said. Michelle collapsed into tears, and James detailed Lanne to comfort her, if she could. He himself remained by Philippe while the tribesmen opened a vein. He reckoned they removed something like a pint of blood, without any visible difference to Philippe's appearance, although his breathing was slightly less stertorous. 'Now we can only hope,' Azam said.

'But you intend to proceed,' James said.

'Of course. These guns are needed by my people.'

'I do not think Philippe will survive the journey. Can you not leave us here, and send a doctor back to us?'

'Do you think *you* would survive here?' Azam asked. 'Besides, you are prisoners of war. You must understand this, James.'

They resumed their journey, Philippe being carried on a litter between two horses, which meant that he was constantly jolted to and fro. Michelle walked her own horse immediately behind him, shoulders hunched, huddled beneath her cloak, for the wind in the desert remained icy cold. James had never been sure whether or not she had actually been in love with Philippe, or had married him for his money, but she was certainly upset at the prospect of his death. 'Do you know that I had almost been enjoying this safari?' Lanne asked her father. 'Up till now. Will Uncle Philippe die?'

'Yes,' James said.

She too huddled herself beneath her cloak.

A few days later they reached the River Helmund, a very broad and powerful flow of water. Unfortunately, as it rose in the mountains behind Kandahar, it was flowing the wrong way, and could not therefore be used for transport. However they would, James gathered, follow the river into the foothills below the city. This was not country he knew, as on his previous visit he had handed over the weapons at the border before returning to Chah Bahar. But at least they would not lack fresh water, he supposed.

That night there was a gale of wind, strange to a seaman like himself as it came howling down from the mountains and across the plain. The tents were blown down as fast as they were put up, until they were abandoned altogether. James and the two women huddled together beneath their blankets, standing guard over Philippe, while dust swirled around them, often enough accompanied by small pebbles and even small rocks. The horses whinnied and reared against the picket lines, the Afghans cursed, and but for the cold they might have been in the pit of hell.

'Will the ship be all right?' Lanne shouted into James' ear.

'We're a long way from the sea,' he reminded her.

'This is a nightmare,' Michelle wailed. 'A nightmare!' It became more so next day.

The wind had dropped at dawn, but the

camp looked like a collection of scarecrows. They resumed their journey, the river always on their left, but had not gone very far when Azam's scouts returned to him in some agitation. 'Prince Amaruddin comes,' Azam told James. 'Look to yourself.' He did not say more than that before hurrying off to greet his employer.

The Afghans had taken James' binoculars as well as his revolver, but even without the glasses he could make out a large body of horsemen approaching, followed by a caravan of wagons. 'Are they friends, Daddy?' Lanne asked.

'They're friends of Azam's at any rate,' James said.

'I am so afraid,' Michelle moaned.

Soon the caravan was surrounded by stamping hooves and swirling dust. James and the women dismounted, and Philippe had also been placed on the ground. Now, as the dust cleared, they faced the prince, who strode towards them, accompanied by Azam and several other men, all heavily armed with both swords and revolvers, bearded and turbaned, and wearing a good deal of jewellery. 'The famous Martingell,' Amaruddin remarked.

James did not like the look of him. He was a big man, and his huge curved nose and strong chin were no more than common to his people. But his eyes, green and deepset, were cold, and kept drifting to the two women. 'And the famous Prince Amaruddin,' James acknowledged.

He knew that Amaruddin, no matter what he chose to call himself, was not actually a prince; he was an out-child of one of the late amir's brothers. But he had always held a prominent part in Afghan politics because he was so vehemently opposed to the British interference in Afghan affairs. And if he had actually had a part in Habibullah's death ... 'Sheikh Azam tells me that you do not wish to sell us these guns any longer,' Amaruddin said, 'because they may be used against the British.'

'Our agreement was that they would not be so used, your excellency.'

'And they have not. Is that not correct?'

'As long as a state of war exists between Afghanistan and Britain, your excellency, I must assume that they will be used.'

'Ha ha,' Amaruddin shouted. 'The war between Afghanistan and Britain is over.'

James frowned at Azam, who was smiling broadly. 'Is that true, your excellency?'

'Of course it is true. Those fools in Kabul, that idiot nephew of mine, lost his nerve when he was defeated in a few battles. He is suing for peace. So you see, your fears are groundless.'

'Indeed they are, your excellency, and I

am mighty grateful for it. Then you have no more use for these weapons.'

'I have use for them, Martingell. So now you will sell the guns to me.'

'Your excellency?' Again James looked at Azam, who continued to smile, but not quite so confidently as before.

'I have not made peace with the British,' Amaruddin pointed out. 'And now I am going to make war upon my nephew as well. So you see, I need the guns more than ever.'

'This is not in our contract,' James protested.

'Then I will tear up your contract. I will pay you for these guns. In fact, you have already been paid for these guns, is that not so?'

'You intend to use these weapons to rebel against your Government.'

'Bah, I am already in rebellion against my nephew's Government. I intend to become the Government.'

'There is no need to concern yourself, James,' Azam said. 'When last you sold me guns, was it not to aid a rebellion against the Government?'

'I think circumstances were different then,' James said. 'But if your master wishes to steal these guns, there is nothing I can do about it. I wish for a doctor to attend to my companion, and then I wish for an escort to take my people back to the coast.'

'This man's effrontery is amazing,' Amaruddin remarked. He stepped past James to stand closer to the women. 'I will have this one,' he said, pointing at Lanne.

There was a moment's total silence. Then Lanne said, 'Daddy!'

James turned, and found himself looking down the barrel of a rifle held by one of Amaruddin's guards. 'Azam,' James said, 'you are a treacherous scoundrel.'

Azam shrugged. 'Events have been taken out of my hands, James.'

'Take her to my wagon,' Amaruddin said, and two of his men went forward to grasp Lanne's arms. She opened her mouth, and then closed it again. She knew her father could not help her at that moment, and she would not embarrass him by asking for what he could not give. Michelle began to scream, in a high-pitched wail. 'Flog that woman,' Amaruddin said.

Michelle fell to her knees. 'My 'usband,' she wailed. 'My 'usband. Will you not help my 'usband?'

Amaruddin stepped past her to look at Philippe, who had not regained consciousness. 'Bury this carrion.'

'Bury 'im?' Michelle screamed. 'But 'e is not dead!'

236

'Fifty strokes,' Amaruddin said.

Again James made a move, and this time his arms were seized while the rifle muzzle was thrust into his throat. Lanne was being dragged off to one of the prince's wagons, while Michelle, still screaming, was thrown to the ground, and her boots and stockings torn off. 'I am going to kill you, Azam,' James said, keeping his voice low.

'If you live that long yourself, James,' Azam said.

Philippe's body was dragged away to where men were already digging a grave; James could only pray that he was indeed dead. Michelle fought her captors with a desperate urgency, but could do nothing as there were six of them. She was stretched on the ground and the remainder of her clothing torn from her body. James knew that there was nothing he could do, save wait, and watch ... and hopefully avenge. Michelle? Or Lanne? Or both. And hate himself, for having exposed the two women to this.

The Afghans clustered round to gaze at the exposed white skin as Michelle was held on her face, still gasping and squirming, but no longer screaming, as she had run out of breath. There could be no doubting her courage, but even that was put to the test as the cane was slashed across her buttocks, bringing this time a howl of pain and embarrassment as well as anguish. Fifty lashes, Amaruddin had said. Michelle fainted four times before the number was completed, each time being brought back to agonising life by a bucket of water emptied on her head. When at last they were done she lay in the dust, a crumpled white mass, blood seeping from several open cuts on her thighs and buttocks.

Now the men holding her arms and legs released her, and moved away, laughing and chattering amongst themselves, leaving her to writhe in the dust and the blood. James was also released. The temptation to attack the Afghans with his bare hands was enormous. But the necessity to look to the woman was more important. He knelt beside her, raised her up, held some water to her lips. Her eyes flopped open as she looked at him, then closed again, then opened again with a shriek of anguish as he sought to touch her wounds. 'She will scream, but you must apply antiseptic and then bind her up,' a voice said, in English.

James raised his head, frowned at the man in the green uniform and the green peaked cap, revolver on his belt, who was standing above him. 'Colonel Alexander Galitsin, at your service.' Galitsin held out various bandages, and also a tin.

'This ointment will soothe the pain, and it is also antiseptic,' he said.

James opened the tin and scooped some of the ointment into his fingers, then onto Michelle's flesh, gently rubbed it. Her body bucked and she screamed again, but gradually subsided. 'Who are you?' he asked while he worked.

'Military adviser to His Highness Amaruddin Khan,' Galitsin said.

'Russian.'

'I am, sir. We have a mutual acquaintance. Major Richard Elligan, Second Irish Guards, seconded to the Government of India,' Galitsin explained. 'We are old friends, whose life I recently had the pleasure of saving.'

'I'm sure he's grateful,' James muttered, now passing the rolls of bandage round Michelle's thighs, between her legs and back over her buttocks. She seemed to have fainted; certainly she made no effort to resist him.

'Oh, certainly,' Galitsin said. 'He may well be pleased to see you.'

'I thought Amaruddin said peace had been made?'

'Peace is being made,' Galitsin agreed. 'But as I am sure his highness has told you, he does not subscribe to it.'

'And you will continue to serve such a monster. One can only hope you will hang

239

beside him when the day comes.'

'I serve Amaruddin because that is the wish of my government,' Galitsin pointed out. 'When they tell me to cease doing so, then I shall cease doing so. In the meantime, I hope I may be of some service to you.'

'Service?' James snorted. 'What of this poor woman? You couldn't help her. What of my daughter, presently being raped by that thug?'

'I should not think it has happened yet.' Galitsin indicated the now enormous caravan, which was beginning to move again.

'But it will happen.'

'I'm afraid so. The fault is yours for bringing her with you.'

James had no adequate answer to that, because the accusation was perfectly true. 'And are we to be abandoned here?'

'No. I have asked that you be placed under my guard. I have your horse.'

'And the woman? She cannot possibly ride.'

Galitsin nodded. 'She can travel in that wagon.'

One of the supply wagons had also remained behind. James lifted Michelle's naked body in his arms and carried her to the wagon. An Afghan lowered the tailgate and he laid her inside, on her face. She was now moaning again, and moving to and fro. 'Is there nothing we can give her, to ease the pain?'

'Let her chew some bhang,' Galitsin said, and spoke to the Afghan. He produced some hemp and gave Michelle a small piece. She chewed it eagerly, while still writhing and moaning. James covered her with a blanket. 'Now let us follow the others,' Galitsin said. 'I should inform you that in asking that you be given to me as my prisoners, I have taken the responsibility for you. Should you try to escape, Sir James, I will have to shoot you.'

'Am I not going to be executed anyway?' James asked.

'We must hope not. Amaruddin has the idea that British captives, certainly of rank, may be of use to him in any future negotiations. That is why he has retained possession of Major Elligan. Now you, Sir James, are a far more important bargaining chip.'

Not to the British, James thought, but he had no intention of letting the Russian know that. He would just have to be patient. He could not escape even if presented with the opportunity: it was going to be weeks, perhaps months, before Michelle would be able to sit a horse, and he could not consider abandoning either her or Lanne. But what a mess he had got

241

himself into, in his desire to make one last killing!

Lanne made no attempt to fight the men who were dragging her towards the prince's wagons; she guessed that would only involve her in a beating. Besides, she was less afraid than curious. To have lived such a sheltered life, and been so frustrated by it, and now to have that shelter ripped aside like a veil ... she wondered how she would react to what was to be done to her. But then she had no real idea what was to be done to her.

They reached one of the wagons, and the curtains at the back were drawn to reveal several women. They wore richly embroidered kaftans which flowed from their shoulders to the ground, but were not veiled. One or two had gold rings in their noses, all had gold bangles on their arms. They all looked delighted to see her, and when the men holding her arms apparently explained what she was there for, they burst into shrieks of laughter. She estimated the oldest was only in her middle twenties, and the youngest was hardly a teenager; all were swarthily handsome, even their hooked noses fitting into the general contours of their faces.

The men seized Lanne by the shoulders and buttocks and heaved her up; the women held her arms to drag her into their midst, clucking solicitously when her thigh struck the tailboard; before she could protest she had been made to lie on her back while her skirts were pulled up and the leg of her drawers also pushed up to allow them to see if she had been hurt. But there was scarce a mark, and they seemed relieved. She expected the assault to be continued, but after they had fingered the material, and exclaimed at both the texture and the form of the garments, she was released, allowed to straighten her clothes, and given something to drink. She was not at all sure what it was, but it certainly contained alcohol, and as it was now about lunchtime and her stomach was empty it made her feel quite drowsy.

The women kept talking to her and at her, but she had no idea what they were saying, and the curtain had been dropped over the tailgate so that she could not see out of the back; as there was another curtain behind the driver, she could not see out of the front either, and she suddenly realised that she was so bound up in what was happening, or might be about to happen, to her that she had given not a thought to what might be happening to her father and Michelle. She had heard a woman screaming as she had been taken to the wagon; had that been Michelle?

Perhaps she too had been raped ... and then murdered? And what of Daddy?

She felt quite sick, and made herself look around her, as the women apparently at last realised she was not able to converse with them, and moved away from her. She lay on a rug, as the entire floor of the wagon was covered in rugs, rich stuffs which would have been worth a fortune in England. There were various boxes and chests against the sides of the wagon, while at the front there was the barrel from which they had drawn the liquid, and which they now proceeded to use again, both for themselves and for her. She tried to refuse another drink, but they insisted, and she certainly didn't want to antagonise them. So she drank, and felt even more drowsy, and slept.

When Lanne awoke, for a moment unsure where she was, the wagon had stopped moving, and all around her she could hear the sounds of camp being pitched. Now that the creaking movements and the shouts of the drivers had ceased, she could also hear the rushing of water to tell her that they remained close to the river. But the wagon was empty.

She sat up, looking left and right, and the tail curtain opened. Amaruddin clambered up, kneeling on the rugs to gaze at her.

She remembered that he spoke English, and licked her lips.

'You are thirsty,' he remarked.

Actually she was. But she was also very hungry. 'I am starving.'

He looked back through the curtain and spoke in Persian. Immediately one of the women climbed into the wagon, bearing a tin plate of food. 'Eat,' Amaruddin commanded.

There were no utensils, but she remembered from her days as a prisoner of the Mad Mullah how to use her fingers, and the food was very good, lamb, or more probably goat, not curried but highly spiced. Amaruddin grinned at her. 'Now you are thirsty,' he suggested. He himself drew liquor from the barrel.

'Can I not have water?' she asked.

He looked at her in surprise, then spoke to the woman, who hurried off. Amaruddin drank the liquor himself. 'You are Martingell's daughter?' he asked.

'Did you not know this?'

He shrugged. 'I thought you were his woman. Why should a man bring his daughter upon such an expedition?'

'There were reasons,' Lanne said.

The woman returned with a cup of water, no doubt taken from the river, because it was fresh and cold. Lanne drank greedily, while Amaruddin waved the woman away. 'It is better that you are his daughter,' Amaruddin remarked. 'But you are not afraid of me.'

'I have been taken captive by ... enemies of my father before,' she said.

He frowned. 'You are not a virgin?'

'I was very young.' She could not resist a smile.

'You are amused?' Amaruddin asked.

'I was thinking. They were Muslims. And they did not touch me. Are you not a Muslim?'

'I am a Muslim.'

'Yet you drink wine.'

'That is not wine. It is fermented goat's milk. So, it is your fate to belong to a Muslim.'

She understood that he would take her no matter what she did. That he might very well hurt her seriously, if she attempted to resist him. That above all else it was her duty, to herself and to her father, if he still survived, to preserve her health and her strength, and the mental ability to use that health and strength the moment the opportunity presented itself. She tossed her head. 'It is my fate to be raped by a Muslim.'

'That is the fate of all women, whether they be Christian or Muslim.'

'Not if it is done with love. With gentleness.'

He frowned at her. 'You will not fight me?'

'Not if you will allow me to undress myself, and then use me with kindness.'

He gazed at her for several seconds. Not only would that be a new experience for him, she guessed, but he was not sure he would enjoy it as much. Then he sat away from her, and waved his hand.

Slowly, controlling her breathing as much as she could, Lanne unbuttoned her blouse and pulled it from her waistband, then she shrugged the garment from her shoulders. Amaruddin gazed at the exposed flesh, the swell of the breasts beneath the single petticoat.

Lanne rose to her knees, unfastened her waistband and slid the skirt down past her thighs. She sat down to slip it off. Amaruddin gazed at her legs.

Lanne sat up to unfasten her boots and pulled them off, then raised her petticoat to her thighs to slide the garters down past her ankles, and roll the stockings right off. Now his breathing was quick. Lanne rose to her knees again, gathered the petticoat, and lifted it over her head, laid it on the rugs beside her. Amaruddin's tongue came out and stole round his lips. 'By Allah,' he said. 'Do all white women have breasts like those?'

'Of course,' she answered, and remaining

on her knees, slid her drawers down before sitting down to take them off. Then she remained, lying on her elbow, gazing at him, as he loosed his breeches.

'I will remember this day,' he told her.

So will I, she thought.

As James had estimated, it took the caravan a further three weeks to reached Kandahar. During that time it assumed the nature of a triumphal procession. He guessed that Amaruddin's stature as the leader of a native opposition to peace with Britain had depended very largely upon his ability to create an army of his own as opposed to a band of guerrillas. To do this he had needed guns; thus his anxiety to find Azam's caravan and establish its success. Now he had the guns. Messengers rode far and wide to acquaint the hill chieftains with his success, and they came to see for themselves, bringing their warriors with them. Each group was given some of the modern rifles and ammunition, presents celebrated by a good deal of firing into the air; James reckoned if they kept that up long enough they might run out of bullets before they ever faced a foe.

Far more than the rifles and ammunition, however, were they delighted with the hand grenades, which again were sampled with screams of delight while the horses and mules neighed and bucked, and the machine-guns. Fortunately the four mountain guns had not been assembled; the tribesmen could only stand and stare. During this time James never saw Azam, who he gathered had been sent on ahead to establish conditions in Kandahar, and he never spoke to Amaruddin, and indeed only saw the prince occasionally. He was of no more interest. But Amaruddin was of interest to him, because he did not see Lanne either. 'She is alive and well,' Galitsin assured him.

'And has no doubt been reduced to a wreck.'

'Not so far as I am aware. His highness seems delighted with her. I am sorry to say this of your daughter, Sir James ... but who can fathom the ways of a woman.'

Especially one whose mother practised sex as a profession, James thought; heredity would out. On the other hand, he reflected, but for that hereditary background, could she possibly have survived? Reassured about Lanne, if only in the short term, he could devote most of his time to Michelle, about whom he had serious doubts. Her background was entirely different from Lanne's, in that she had had a Roman Catholic upbringing as the daughter of a profoundly middle-class Provençal family. No doubt the greatest and most daring event of her life up to this time had been her marriage to such a raffish character as Philippe.

Now she had watched her husband buried alive, and had herself been stripped naked and humiliated before jeering men. The wounds on her back healed very well, thanks to Galitsin's ointment—but James wondered if the wounds in her mind would ever heal. She seemed grateful for his attention, submitted to his gentle massaging of her back and buttocks and thighs without protest, smiled at him when he gave her food and drink, allowed him, again without protest, to lift her down from the wagon and carry her to the river bank to perform her necessaries ... and never, he felt, actually saw him at all. While the future remained as bleak and uncertain as at any time in his life.

Amaruddin's army entered Kandahar with a huge beating of drums, blowing of bugles, and clashing of cymbals, always accompanied by a good deal more firing into the air. James knew that the city, at some three thousand feet above sea level, lying in the midst of a fertile plain watered by the River Tarnak, and situated where three of the most important roads in Asia crossed each other, from Kabul, from Herat and from Quetta in India, had been founded by Alexander the Great more than two thousand years before, and had been brought to its apogee by Ahmad Shah Durrani in the eighteenth century; indeed the remains of his mausoleum could still be seen. Its decline had begun with the sack by Nadir Shah in 1738, during that conqueror's rampage through central Asia. Yet even after that it had been, briefly, the capital of Afghanistan.

Now it remained a great city, teeming with people and animals, with sounds and smells, all at the moment seeming pleased to see Prince Amaruddin, and his well-armed soldiery. He made his headquarters in the old citadel, and it was here that the caravan was also taken. 'What happens now?' James asked Galitsin.

The Russian grinned. 'At least you can stop moving for a while. Bring the woman.'

James lifted Michelle and followed his captor down a series of corridors hewn from the living rock, and lit by guttering torches. On the third level they made their way along a corridor, accompanied now by several gaolers, one of whom carried a huge bunch of keys. With one of these he finally unlocked a door, into darkness. 'I am sorry I can offer you nothing more than this at the moment,' Galitsin said. 'But I have saved your life, and that of the woman. Remember this.

And if it is possible to help you again, I will do so. I promise you that I shall endeavour to persuade Amaruddin that if he truly wishes to be accepted as amir, supposing he can overthrow Amanullah Khan, his stature will depend upon his being accepted internationally, and that this can only be accomplished by humane treatment of his prisoners.'

'Will you succeed?'

'One must hope so, for all our sakes. But my friend, until you hear from me again, do nothing rash, I beg of you.'

He made to turn away, and James touched his arm. 'One more thing, comrade. Can you get a message to my daughter?'

'Perhaps.'

'Then tell her I am well, and that I hope we shall be reunited.'

'I shall give her that message,' Galitsin said. But his tone was pessimistic.

Then the door was slammed, and they were in darkness. And James immediately heard movement. For a moment his skin crawled, then he reminded himself that he had faced a number of potentially dangerous adversaries in his time, successfully, that if he was no longer a young man he was still a very tough one, and that there was little prospect of whoever was in here with him being armed. Carefully he laid Michelle on the straw-covered floor. 'James,' she whispered. 'James.'

'Ssssh,' he told her, because again he could hear movement.

'Who is there?' he demanded.

'English, by God,' a voice muttered.

It was a remarkably familiar voice. Besides, James had half suspected who it was in advance. 'Elligan?'

'My God! Sir James! But ... that bastard spoke of your daughter. Is she—'

'She is not with us,' James said.

'Thank God for that.'

'But she is in this citadel. A prisoner of Amaruddin, like us.'

'A prisoner? But that means ...' Elligan's voice was so stricken James could believe the young man had indeed been in love with Lanne. Perhaps he still was.

'That she has become another man's mistress,' James said.

'You can say that, so calmly ... you *are* just a thug, Martingell.'

'I am sure you're right,' James agreed. 'But I am also a man who has learned to survive, as I am sure Lanne has also learned that. But you, of course, being an officer and a gentleman, would never dream of accepting another man's leavings.'

'You can say that to me?'

'Especially, of course, as she is a lady of colour,' James added. The straw rustled as the movement came closer.

'If you attack me, sir, I shall break your fucking neck,' James told him, still speaking evenly. The movement ceased. 'I think we need to pull together,' James said.

'Yes,' Richard muttered. 'If only to get even with that bastard Galitsin.'

'He told me he saved your life.'

'Yes, he did. He saved me from the knives of the Afghan women. But did he really save my life, throwing me in here, to exist?'

'You *are* still alive,' James pointed out. 'And now you can have a purpose in life, helping me to care for this lady.'

Elligan moved closer. 'Who is it? Not your wife?'

'Not my wife, thank God,' James said. 'But nonetheless, a very dear friend, who has suffered badly. She shall be our charge, yours and mine.'

'Well, now, you see, these are for you,' Homaira said. She was an intelligent, handsome woman in her early thirties, and she was Prince Amaruddin's principal wife. Being a woman of considerable authority, she had chosen not to accompany her husband in his search for the arms caravan, but had remained in the relative security of Kandahar. A Persian, and of high birth, she was dark haired and dark eyed, and her face was strong; she presented a formidable aspect, and Lanne had been terrified when she had been virtually delivered into her power. But she had been kindness itself—Lanne wondered if she did not welcome any addition to Amaruddin's harem, which necessarily reduced the number of occasions he summoned *her* to his bed. She also spoke English!

Now she laid the richly decorated kaftans before Lanne, who could not stop herself kneeling and eagerly fingering the material. 'These are splendid.'

'Our lord is pleased with you. Are you not pleased with our lord, Lanne?'

Lanne looked up, caught unawares. It was not a question she had dared ask herself, in the past few weeks. Every instinct in her culture and upbringing had told her she should hate the prince, and everything he did to her, from the service he commanded of her lips—an unthinkable thought with regard to any man only a month ago; could she possibly kneel before Richard to take him into her mouth?—to the manner in which he mounted her, quite literally. Again, she could not imagine kneeling naked before Richard, while he spread her legs ... Did this stately, elegant, *powerful* woman undergo those torments, those pleasures? But of course she did; she was the prince's wife. Who had powers of life and death over the lesser women. 'Our lord pleases me, highness,' she said.

'Then dress yourself well, and enjoy yourself,' Homaira recommended. 'While your fortune, our fortune, lasts.'

Lanne's head jerked. 'Are we in danger, highness?'

'Indeed we are, child. Did you not know that the Amir Amanullah marches upon Kandahar, with a mighty army?'

Lanne clasped both hands to her neck. 'But ... what will happen, highness?'

'There will be a battle. A great battle,' Homaira said. 'Which we must hope and pray our lord wins.'

Lanne licked her lips. 'And if he does not?'

Homaira smiled. 'Why, then we will belong to the victor. As we are our lord's women, we shall no doubt be given to the Amir's soldiers, should he lose.'

'You can just say that, highness?'

'That is a woman's lot. Even in your country, perhaps. But because it is long time since England has fallen to a rampant foe such matters have been forgotten. In central Asia we are closer to the stuff of life.' She smiled. 'And death. But whatever your fate, Lanne, you will accept it as an

Afghan noblewoman, because that is what you are, now.'

'Will you be at my side, highness?'

Homaira's smile grew grim. 'Very probably.'

To Lanne's relief, Amaruddin's harem was not as she had imagined it would be. His women were segregated from the rest of the world, but they were not expected to wear the veil, nor were they entirely cut off from male company, provided they were adequately chaperoned. Thus often, when he conferred with his principal officers, various of his women were allowed to be present, and even to engage in idle conversation, always under the eye of himself, Homaira, and his eunuchs. Particularly was the beautiful blonde European woman allowed to be present; Amaruddin regarded her as a badge of office—follow me, his attitude indicated, and you too could possess one of these rare, entrancing, exciting creatures.

Lanne enjoyed the exposure, even if she knew it was just that, and she was invariably given a glass of vodka to drink before one of these soirées, to ensure that her eyes glittered and her conversation sparkled. She soon came to identify the leading warrior chieftains who had attached themselves to the rebels' cause. But most interesting she naturally found the Russian, to whom the others deferred when he spoke of military matters. He was the man who above all others would know about her father and Michelle.

And soon enough, one evening, he sat beside her, engaging in small-talk, while never actually looking at her. And suddenly speaking English. 'Do not become startled, I beg of you, dear lady,' he said. 'But I have a message from your father.'

It was all she could do to keep her head still. 'You know where he is?'

'He is in this very palace. With the Frenchwoman.'

'How do you know?'

'I put him there. He shares the cell with another Englishman. He wishes you to know that at present he is alive, as well as he may be.'

'Will he stay alive?'

'Hopefully.'

'May I see him?'

'That could be arranged. But not now. After the campaign.'

'When is the campaign?'

'We leave tomorrow.'

'Tomorrow! And when you come back ...'

Galitsin grinned. 'All things may be possible. All things are always possible. For a price.'

Now at last she did turn her head. 'I have no money.'

'You have all the wealth in the world, Lanne,' he said. 'Under that kaftan. Remember this.'

'Listen,' James said.

'I heard it earlier,' Richard said. 'That is an army, preparing to march.'

'I wonder if Galitsin is marching with them.'

'It is his duty to do so,' Richard pointed out.

Over the weeks of their incarceration the two men had become friends. It would have been difficult to remain indifferent to each other, as they had shared every aspect of life, or perhaps survival in their black and half-starved existence would have been more accurate. But they had been brought closer together by the necessity to care for the woman. James reckoned, as far as he could tell from feel, for in the perpetual gloom of the cell he could see very little, that Michelle was all but physically well again, although there remained little ridges of scar tissue on the pale flesh. Her mind remained a different matter. She certainly knew James, and she had come to accept Richard as a necessary companion, but she seldom spoke, seldom moved; her food, such as was passed underneath their door, had to be conveyed to her lips—she would never seek it herself.

No doubt she found it difficult to contemplate the future. But that applied to all of them. They had but a single hope, and ... 'Has it occurred to you,' James said, 'that should Galitsin go to war at Amaruddin's side, and be killed, we may well spend the rest of our lives in here? Not that I suppose that would be for very long.'

'I have been thinking about it,' Richard said. 'And Lanne?'

'Yes,' James said sombrely. And fell to listening.

When the army had left the city to wind its way through the mountain passes separating Kandahar from Kabul, there was a strange and foreboding quiet. The people knew their fate was being decided, and that there was nothing they could do about it. The women of the prince's harem prowled the high porches of the citadel, and stared to the east. Because of the mountains they could not see very far, but every so often there was a false alarm, as one of them thought they saw a horseman spurring down the pass towards them.

As day succeeded day, however, their excitement dwindled. This was a case where no news was definitely good news. And with Amaruddin and Azam and all his high officers gone, Lanne began to wonder if it might not be possible to find out something about her father, without waiting for Galitsin to return. What had he meant? Almost had it seemed that he wanted, and intended, to have her for his own. The thought made her shiver. Somehow, where submitting to Amaruddin had always been just that, submission, where she accepted what was done to her and from time to time even enjoyed it, she knew there would be more to sex between herself and Galitsin, if it ever came to that. But how could it ever come to that?

Meanwhile, he had told her that Daddy and Michelle were somewhere in this building. Could that be true? She felt it was. She was sure that if Daddy had been executed Amaruddin would have told her. She did not dare raise the matter directly with Homaira, who had the authority to have her bastinadoed, and was quite capable of doing so, for all her superficial kindness; Lanne was aghast when one of the other young concubines was discovered speaking with a guard, clandestinely, and was promptly caned till she bled. Therefore for her to talk to one of the guards was out of the question. Yet there had to be a way. 'This is such a fantastic castle,' she remarked one day as they lounged on their cushions while a musician strummed a sitar, under the watchful eye of two eunuchs. Harem discipline was somewhat lax, in that whole men were allowed within the walls, but it was none the less regulated. 'I should love to explore it.'

'One castle is very like another,' Homaira said. 'Do you not have great castles in England? I have heard this.'

'There are some,' Lanne agreed. 'But none like this, hewn out of the living rock. It must go down for miles.'

'That is absurd,' Homaira said.

'But it goes into the rock?'

'Well, of course. The dungeons are in the rock.'

'Dungeons? Are there really dungeons down there?'

'Yes,' Homaira said. 'But you would not enjoy them. They are stinking, noisome places, where felons are confined to await execution.'

She must know if my father is down there, Lanne thought. But she gave no sign of it. And leaving the harem without permission was impossible. There were the eunuchs, and then there were the outer guards, and then ... any young woman found wandering the stairs and corridors on her own would receive very short shrift.

She had not yet solved her dilemma when a horseman *was* discerned galloping down the pass through the hills. And more than one, shouting and waving. 'A victory,' Homaira announced. 'It must be a victory. Our lord will be amir.'

The gates swung open to admit the galloper, and a huge hubbub swelled out of the city, soon punctuated by screams and yells of terror. 'A victory?' Lanne asked.

Homaira scowled at her, and ran to the door of the harem. 'Go quickly,' she commanded one of the guards. 'Find out the news and bring it to me.' The rest of the women huddled round her, clamouring anxiously. 'Be quiet!' she bawled. 'Be quiet. Our lord ...'

One look at the face of the returning messenger was sufficient. 'A defeat, lady,' he gasped. 'A rout.'

'Prince Amaruddin?'

'They say he is dead, lady. The army of Amanullah Khan comes.'

Chapter 8

The Escape

The group of women dissolved, rushing to and fro, screaming and shouting, wailing their anticipated misery. Homaira stood still, biting her lip, uncertain what to do. Lanne ran with them. She chose the balustrade, looking down on the now seething city, and beyond, at the hills, out of which, even above the screaming noise beneath her, she could hear the clashing of cymbals, the thudding of drums, the blowing of bugles. The victors, come to seize the spoils of war.

The gates remained open, because there were still fleeing tribesmen entering the city, firing their rifles into the air, shouting their own despair, a motley mass of leaderless and terrified men. And with them ... Lanne's eyes narrowed. A man in a green uniform, with pale skin and a green peaked cap hiding his red hair. The Russian who had brought her the message from her father!

Without a moment's hesitation she turned and ran back to the doorway.

Homaira still stood there, biting her lip. But the eunuchs had fled. 'Stop!' Homaira shouted. 'You cannot go out there. Your place is here, with us.'

Lanne shoulder-charged her and knocked her from her feet, then she was through the arched doorway and running towards the outer doors. She braced herself for more opposition, but the guards here had also fled, while the entire place swelled with terrified noise, over which the sounds of the approaching army rose triumphantly. She came to the great staircase, and looked down at a scene of utter chaos. The soldiers and the domestic staff were abandoning the palace, but they were taking with them everything that was of any value that they could; men clutched statues of gold and ivory, women carried baskets of rich stuffs and jewels.

No one paid any attention to her, as she ran down the stairs, reached the bottom, was knocked over by one fleeing soldier, his arms full of valuables, regained her feet, gasping, and saw the Russian entering the great hall from the outer doors. 'Colonel!' she shouted. 'Colonel Galitsin!' His head jerked, and then he came towards her, pushing people out of his way. 'Please,' she gasped. 'Help me! Help my father! Help us!'

He held her shoulders, his fingers eating

through the silk of the kaftan into her flesh. 'And if I do?'

'Anything,' she said. 'Claim it. But help us to escape this place.'

'You,' he said. 'I would claim you.' He grinned at her. 'You are very beautiful.'

As you are young and handsome, she thought. Certainly compared with Amaruddin Khan. Her fate! To belong to men, rather than to share with them. Because of her mother? Or her father? Or both! 'Yes,' she said.

'Swear it. You will come to me of your own free will, and lovingly.'

'I swear it. When you have taken us to safety, I will come to you, of my own free will, and lovingly.'

Galitsin considered for a moment, unsure whether he needed to accept her terms when he could take her by force. Then he grinned. 'Then come.'

He held her wrist, led her across the still crowded hall and into a corridor. Here there were less people but even more noise, welling up from the dungeons below, as those incarcerated shouted for freedom. But presumably anyone who was a prisoner of Amaruddin Khan had little to fear from the amir—save for the man who had sold Amaruddin the weapons with which to wage war.

Now they were in the lower regions of

the palace, and most of the noise was coming from above them. A gaoler loomed in front of them, and without hesitation Galitsin drew his revolver and shot him dead. Then he knelt beside him to unstrap his bunch of keys. Lanne leaned against a wall and panted, afraid to believe what she was experiencing. Galitsin was on his feet again, again seizing her wrist to drag her onwards, and down another flight of stairs. Now the noise from above them had all but dwindled, and instead they were surrounded by unspeakable odours, their way lit by guttering sconces.

'Here!' Galitsin paused before a door, fumbled for the right key, and thrust it in, turning the lock with an immense effort. Lanne stood behind him, trying to hold her breath. 'Sir James,' Galitsin said. 'Hurry. We must leave this place. Bring your companions.'

There was movement in the gloom, and then Lanne saw her father emerge, blinking in the clear light of the corridor, an emaciated, white-haired and bearded figure, shoulders stooped. He was alone, but behind him there came two people, a man and a woman, the man leading the woman by the hand. 'Daddy!' she gasped, and held him in her arms, filthy as he was. Then she reached past him to hug Michelle. 'Oh, Michelle,' she said. 'I thought you were dead. Forgive me, sir ...' She peered at the black-bearded figure of the younger man who was supporting Michelle, frowning as she recognised him even beneath the hair. 'Richard? My God, Richard!'

'I did not know you knew each other,' Galitsin said. 'Now let us make haste and escape this place.'

He was very much in command as he led them back along the corridors. When they encountered another gaoler he shot this man too, and from him took a sword, which he gave to Richard, and a revolver, which he gave to James. Then they were in the upper regions of the palace, mostly deserted now, as all the staff had fled. Lanne's brain was tumbling. Richard! Alive and now safe, with her. After her promise to Galitsin? But Richard had rejected her.

Now they were in the open air behind the palace façade, hurrying towards the stables. The horses were wildly excited, and rearing and neighing, kicking against the doors to their stalls. 'You know horses?' Galitsin asked Lanne. She nodded. 'And I know you do, Richard. Come. Sir James, stay with the woman.'

They began picking out their mounts, calming them, and saddling them, while the noise from the city rose to a crescendo.

'Lanne!' screamed Homaira, standing on the rear balcony of the harem. 'Lanne! Help me!'

'Get down here,' Lanne shouted back, leading two horses to where her father and Michelle waited. Homaira disappeared. Galitsin and Richard now came out with three more mounts. 'We need another,' Lanne said, as Homaira emerged from the back of the palace, clothes disarranged, black hair floating behind her as she ran towards them.

'For her?' Galitsin asked, contemptuously.

'She was good to me,' Lanne told him.

Another horse was saddled, and they rode for the gate. Now the first of the amir's people were in the city, and the confusion, and the noise, was greater than ever. 'Stay close!' Galitsin shouted, and shot a man who tried to grasp his bridle. They forced their way through the teeming narrow streets, thrusting people left and right, defending themselves from angry blows. Lanne was afraid the strength of the three rescued prisoners, especially her father, might not be sufficient, but they were spurred on by the thought of freedom. They burst through one of the city gates to find themselves in the midst of another screaming crowd of refugees, while from behind them there now came the sounds of concerted gunfire, as the amir's troops dispersed the last of Amaruddin's men. 'The hills,' Galitsin shouted, and led the way over the uneven ground.

By nightfall their horses had taken them clear of the refugees, and they reached a stream bubbling down from the higher peaks above them. James, Richard and Michelle stripped off their vermin-infested rags and plunged into the water, while Galitsin levelled his binoculars at the city, now several miles away below them. 'It is burning,' he said. 'In many places. There will be a great massacre tonight.' He looked down at Homaira. 'You are fortunate, lady.'

Homaira lay by the stream to drink, her plump body a great glow from the cold water. 'Where will you take us?'

'I am returning to Russia,' Galitsin said. 'My business here is finished. You will come with me. But first ...' He gazed at James as he emerged from the water. 'We need clothes for these people.'

'And food, I hope,' James said.

'We will have to play the bandit,' Galitsin said. 'Listen.'

They could hear the sound of hooves, and voices. The refugees were starting to catch them up.

'Homaira,' Galitsin said. 'You and

Lanne take the horses behind that hummock. Wait for us.'

Lanne was reluctant to go. 'Daddy,' she said. 'Are you all right?' He nodded. 'And Richard?'

'Him too. Thanks to Galitsin.'

'Yes,' she said. 'Thanks to Galitsin.' She shuddered, and took the horses out of sight.

'Now remember,' Galitsin said. 'It is them or us. No pity, if you intend to live.' He reloaded his revolver, gave some shells to James. Richard had the sword. A few minutes later a group of people emerged round the bend in the track; three men, four women, and three children. They had two donkeys on which were loaded a variety of goods. Two of the men carried matchlock rifles, but they were in no mood to fight, perhaps as taken aback at the sight of two naked, bearded white men brandishing sword and revolver as by the weapons themselves.

Galitsin gave orders in the local dialect, which he spoke fluently. The Afghans threw down their weapons, while the women and children huddled together. James selected kaftans for Richard and himself, and for Michelle, as well as boots, while Galitsin rummaged through the packs and located food. One of the Afghans spoke to him, and he snapped a reply. 'They say without food they will starve. But then, so will we.'

Richard and James exchanged glances. But the Russian had spoken nothing less than the truth. 'Leave them half,' James said. 'We will find some more.'

'You British,' Galitsin said contemptuously. But he divided the food. 'Now let us make haste,' he said. 'It would not be good for these people, or any of their friends, to catch up with us again.'

They rode, or walked beside their horses, all night. Then they camped, and ate, before pressing on again. As the crow flew it was three hundred miles from Kandahar to the Russian border, and another two hundred to the ancient city of Merv, within Russian-claimed territory, where Galitsin was sure of finding friends and shelter. It was summer, but as their route took them through some very high mountains it remained cold at night, and soon it began to rain to add to their misery. But they did not dare turn off for places like Herat, where they gathered from those people they encountered that the amir was firmly in control.

They seldom made more than ten miles a day, as it was necessary both to continue acting the highwaymen to secure food, and equally to avoid encountering any of Amanullah's troops, who were now ranging all over the country, seeking rebels; they came across more than one gibbet from which hung a score of rotting bodies. To add to their problems, the loyalists had got hold of some aircraft, and these biplanes, flying quite slowly, ranged up and down the valleys; on one occasion the fugitives had to lie hidden in a ditch for several hours while the planes zoomed above.

Both James and Richard noticed quite early on that Galitsin had assumed a proprietary air towards Lanne. But in the early stages of their march they were always in a state of such exhaustion and mutual filth that they merely huddled together at night for warmth, so that his suggestion of ownership remained superficial—it even extended over Homaira, and presumably, James thought, over all of them. Richard was more concerned. He made several attempts to find himself alone with Lanne, but she always refused the implicit invitation, either to hang back on the march or to follow him away from their encampments.

He reckoned he knew the reason, of course. Anne must have told her of their brief but so memorable encounter. What puzzled him was that Anne should have told her stepdaughter, but not apparently her husband. Because if she had, then James Martingell was a most remarkable fellow, who in all the weeks had never once referred to the matter. Or was he just biding his time?

He found himself in an intensely difficult situation, the more so as Michelle had definitely taken to him. He did not suppose this was surprising, as James was old enough to be her father, and he had allowed Richard to take over most of the business of nursing her back to health; Richard reckoned he knew Michelle more intimately than any previous friend or acquaintance, male or female. And he had, in turn, grown very fond of her, but it was the fondness of a man for a favourite dog. Quite apart from the fact that he remained totally in love with Lanne, Michelle's mind had not recovered from its frightful experience—he did not think it ever would.

He supposed they really composed the oddest collection of refugees that could ever have prowled these mountains. Sir James Martingell, whose activities had, almost literally, blown up in his face, and who was now engaged in a desperate struggle for survival, far removed from his ship and his money, and his beautiful wife.

Michelle Desmorins, half crazed by her misfortunes, and by the loss of her husband, going through the motions of living. Homaira, so recently the greatest lady in Kandahar, grimly playing her role in their group, preparing food, washing clothes when they reached water—(she had no soap but would beat the cloth between two flat stones)—stripped of all her finery as well as her power, keeping her thoughts to herself, but clearly relying on James more than any of the other men for survival, both now and later. He wondered if James understood that.

Lanne Martingell, far removed from the spruce young woman with whom he had ridden that estate in Worcestershire, her kaftan torn and dirty, stripping off in front of the men to wash it when she could, or to bathe. She had been a prisoner of Amaruddin as long as they, and if she had lived in luxury she had also clearly been raped again and again, so that her sex was no longer a matter of importance to her. Had she truly been raped? But whether she had or not, her acceptance of her fate had driven a wedge between her and himself, and even her father, he fancied. No wonder she found the Russian more congenial company; she would have met him in Amaruddin's company.

Alexander Galitsin, urbane and good-humoured, anxious always to be friendly, a man who had saved his life from the Afghan women, and again in Kandahar. Thus a man to whom he should always be grateful. And who he was now finding himself growing to dislike.

And Major Richard Elligan, a man whose career had come to a thumping stop. He had undoubtedly been listed as missing presumed killed; he did not suppose Amaruddin had ever forwarded a list of his prisoners, even to the amir, much less the British who were the enemies of both of them. There would have been a memorial service, and his father and mother and sisters would have wept. Presumably the War Office would have been ethical enough not to spell out exactly how he had probably died.

But what did the future hold for him? Oddly, he was not as concerned with that distant prospect as with the immediate present. If one could forget past and future, this was the adventure of a lifetime, spent in the company of a man he had come wholly to admire, and of the woman he most wanted to marry. The future had to be there. He could not believe that Galitsin had gone to such trouble and taken such risks to save their lives in Kandahar if he did not intend to see them back to safety and even home. But there had to be a reason.

At last Richard could contain himself no longer, and he tackled Galitsin as they trekked through the valleys between the serrated peaks. They had now been on the road for more than a fortnight. Amazingly, they were all very fit, however sore their feet might be from time to time. The fresh air and constant exercise had restored both their health and the strength, and their food, if often high, was well prepared by Homaira and Lanne; even Michelle was able to help with the cooking. They even looked fit, now that he and James had managed to scrape away their beards.

They had camped beside one of the innumerable streams that watered the hill country, hardly more than trickles now as they approached the end of the summer, but still providing the sustenance they needed. Galitsin took off his boots and allowed his feet to drift in the water; Richard had no such problem as he was wearing open sandals taken from the refugees. 'Where are we?' he asked, kneeling beside the Russian, who was studying his map. Galitsin prodded the stiff paper. 'Isn't that a village marked?'

Galitsin nodded. 'We should be able to obtain some food. We are very short.' He jingled the bag of coins he had obtained from their last raid on a lonely farm.

'You will go into the village?'

Galitsin grinned. 'I will send Homaira.'

'You're sure she won't betray us?'

'Not her. She is probably wanted more than any of us.'

'They are courageous women,' Richard remarked. 'All of them.'

'They are terrified,' Galitsin countered. 'Their courage is the courage of terror.'

'And are we not terrified?'

'I would hope not.' Galitsin grinned.

'How much longer will our journey take?'

'To reach Merv? Not less than a month. Maybe longer. But we need to get there before winter.'

'Medieval,' Richard remarked.

'We are in a medieval part of the world.'

'I have been thinking,' Richard said. 'As we have so long still on the road, perhaps we should divide up the women.'

Now Galitsin laughed. 'You have recovered all your strength, eh? Why not? Martingell can have Homaira. She is the oldest. And I will bet she is good in bed. Or even on the ground.' He glanced at Richard. 'And you can have the Frenchwoman. Or have you already had her, in that cell? She is good, eh?'

'While you have Miss Martingell. Is that the idea?'

'That seems an equitable arrangement.'

'There is something you should know.

Miss Martingell and I have an understanding,' Richard said. 'We were to become engaged to be married, in England.'

'But you did not.'

'I was ordered back to India, and it was decided to postpone the engagement.'

'You expect me to believe that?'

Richard drew a deep breath. 'Ask her.'

Galitsin pulled his feet from the water, and looked past Richard to where the women were preparing the meal. James, back against a rock beside them, might have been asleep. 'I do not believe you.'

'I said, ask her.'

'I have already asked her, Richard. I have asked her to be my woman when we get to Merv, and she has said yes.'

Richard stared at him in consternation. 'You expect me to believe *that?*'

Galitsin shrugged. 'There is something *you* should understand, Richard. Perhaps you did know the girl in England, when no doubt she was a typical English rose, eh? All pink cheeks and vigorous virginity. This is no longer the same woman. Any woman who has shared Amaruddin's bed for any period of time is different from how she was before. Believe me. You would not enjoy her. Or perhaps more to the point, she would not enjoy you. But me, well, you see, I too am from central Asia. My mother was a Tartar. I

279

know how to please a woman, and I know how to make a woman please me. It does not matter to me how many men she has slept with, before me.'

'I ought to punch you on the nose,' Richard said.

'That would not be a good idea.'

'If you think you are going to get your hands on Lanne, you are mistaken.'

'I told you, she has already agreed to it.'

'And when did she do this?'

'On the day I took you out of Kandahar.'

The penny dropped. 'You bloody bastard!' Richard shouted. 'You made her agree, before rescuing us.'

'Before rescuing her father, certainly,' Galitsin agreed. 'It was a straightforward business transaction. One that I intend to honour.'

'Honour!' Richard shouted, and leapt at him. 'You wouldn't know the meaning of the word.' His body cannoned into Galitsin's, and the two men fell together, Richard on top, while he drove his fists into Galitsin's body.

The women started up with shouts of alarm, and ran forward. Even James woke, and got up. 'What the hell is going on?'

'They're fighting!' Lanne cried. 'Stop them!'

'Why they do this?' Homaira asked. Michelle giggled.

Galitsin was panting, as he had taken several severe blows to his chest and stomach, but he made an immense effort and threw Richard off. They were on the banks of the stream, and Richard overbalanced as he tried to sit up, and fell into the water. 'Richard!' Lanne screamed, and ran forward, herself entering the stream to seize his arm.

Galitsin made a remark in Russian, as he gained his feet and drew his revolver, levelling. 'Stop right there,' James said, levelling his own pistol. Galitsin half turned.

'Are you all right?' Lanne had Richard back to the bank—the stream was only a few inches deep—and was peering at him.

'I'm all right,' Richard panted. 'But that bastard ...'

'Holster the gun, Galitsin,' James suggested. Galitsin hesitated, but he had heard enough about James Martingell, from Azam ud-Ranatullah, to know that he was a dangerous man. Slowly he replaced the revolver in its holster. 'Now suppose you tell me what this is all about,' James requested, keeping his own weapon drawn.

'This ... this bastard has made Lanne agree to go with him,' Richard spluttered.

'Those were the terms on which he agreed to save us.'

'Is that true?' James asked his daughter.

She sighed, and then shrugged. 'I wanted to save your life, Daddy. I didn't know Richard was with you.'

James looked at Galitsin, who also shrugged. 'I have fulfilled my side of the bargain. I will continue to do so. I am to deliver you to Merv.'

'At which time you intend to claim my daughter.'

'That is our agreement, yes.'

'For how long?' James asked, quietly.

'My God, sir!' Richard scrambled to his feet. 'You cannot possibly agree to such a bargain, even for a single night.'

'I asked for how long,' James repeated.

'I will marry her,' Galitsin said.

'Over my dead body,' Richard snapped.

James looked at Lanne, who shrugged again. 'We made a bargain. And why not? There is nothing for me in England. There is nothing for me anywhere.'

'And you reckon there is something for you with Galitsin?'

'Out here, in the mountains and the steppes ... will you treat me well, Sandor?'

'I will treat you like the queen you are,' Galitsin promised.

'This cannot be happening,' Richard pleaded.

Lanne gazed at him. 'Will you offer me marriage, Richard?'

'Well ...' He licked his lips. James could sympathise with him. The young man knew the history of her ancestry, and he knew she had been Amaruddin's sexual plaything. He had to know there was no way she could ever enter a society ballroom in London on his arm, as his wife. But he was so obviously in love with her. Richard drew a long breath. 'Yes, I will offer you marriage. I ask you to marry me, now.'

Homaira clapped her hands.

'I do not believe you,' Lanne said. 'And I have given Sandor my word.'

'And suppose your Sandor doesn't survive this journey?' Richard asked.

'You wouldn't dare,' Lanne said.

Richard looked at James. 'There are two of us, sir, and one of him.'

'Killing me would mean the death of all of you,' Galitsin said. He did not look the least afraid. 'Who else can lead you to Merv?'

'We have your map,' Richard said.

'I think even with the map you would get lost,' Galitsin said. 'Whereas I have made this journey before. And when you get to Merv, what then? My compatriots would shoot you out of hand, and take the women anyway. Only I can return you to safety.'

'I think Colonel Galitsin has us over a barrel,' James said. 'So we had better forget this little fracas.'

'You would force your own daughter to submit to this monster?'

'I am forcing Lanne to do nothing,' James said. 'She seems content with the arrangement. Which is not to take effect until Merv, as I understand it.'

Galitsin grinned. 'By which time you hope something will have developed to your advantage. You are a wily one, Sir James. But I am content to wait until Merv to claim my bride. Providing you undertake to keep this young firebrand under control.'

'He'll be under control,' James said.

'You don't give a damn what happens to Lanne,' Richard said angrily. 'Simply because she's ...'

'Shut up,' James recommended. 'Or I'll deal with you myself.' Richard bit his lip.

'I do not mind, Daddy,' Lanne said. 'Yes, simply because I am the daughter of a whore. Is that what you were going to say? Well, then, knowing that, your conscience should be clear.'

'Now you listen to me, you young fool,' James said to Richard, as they resumed their march. 'I am putting you on your honour to attempt no further assaults upon

284

Galitsin. He is our salvation, and you want to remember that he has already been your salvation.'

'It is the thought of Lanne undergoing ...' Richard gave a little shudder.

'She will undergo nothing she has not already experienced. We have been dealt a hand and we must play it. Lanne will come back to us, eventually, if she wishes to do so.' He grinned. 'By which time you will be happily married and the father of twelve. Now go back to looking after Michelle. She trusts you, and she needs you. Regard it as a duty.'

He had to believe the young man would be sensible. As would everyone else. But that night, as he lay beneath his blanket, he became conscious of movement close at hand. Instantly he drew his revolver, and then realised it was Homaira, who promptly snuggled into his side. 'Listen,' she said. 'Sir James. You do not need the Russian. You have me.'

'Not quite the same thing.'

'You do not understand. I also have made this journey. I can guide you to Merv. You could kill the Russian now. I will take care of you.'

He was suddenly tempted. But ... 'And when we get to Merv?'

'We are refugees, fleeing Afghanistan. The Russians were supporting both the

285

amir and Amaruddin. Then they withdrew their support from Amaruddin. But they know Galitsin was with him. They will accept us as refugees.'

Again, temptation. But he was not sure just what would be solved by murder. It was not a game he had ever played; no matter how many men he had gunned down, it had always been in self-defence or a fair fight. Besides, Merv was only the beginning. They would still have a very long way to go to regain England, Home and Beauty.

There was only Lanne. But he knew he had lost his daughter. She had been set adrift in a world which, for women, was as far distant from the life of a daughter of an English country squire as if she had been translated to another planet. When she returned, *if* she returned, it would have to be of her own free will. Was that a fatherly attitude? But then, was Lanne truly a daughter, in any sense of the word? 'We'll go along with Galitsin,' he said.

Homaira sighed. 'And what will happen to me? I am your woman, now.' Her hands slid over his body.

'Ah,' he remarked.

Merv had been one of the famous cities of antiquity, and indeed, the Middle Ages. Astride the trade route in and out of central Asia and thence China, it had been a great city under the Achaemenid Persians before the Christian era, and had reached a zenith fifteen hundred years later under the Seljuk sultans, before being destroyed by the Mongols in 1221. Since then some attempt had been made to rebuild the aqueducts and other parts of the infrastructure, and the Tsarist Russians, who had taken possession in 1883, had done more, but it was no longer of a great deal of importance, having been replaced as a trading depot by the towns and cities situated along the Trans-Siberian Railway. Since the revolution, it had degenerated again, as had nearly all of Russia, but it was at least occupied by a garrison loyal to the Bolsheviks. This was safer for the refugees than had it been held by the Whites, who were still in force in central Asia, because they welcomed Galitsin. 'Well, now, Sir James,' he said. 'I have arranged for your transportation to Persia and thence home. Here are your passes, and some money. I do not know if we will meet again, but I will wish you good fortune.'

James shook hands. 'We owe you our lives, and we shall always be grateful,' he said. 'Look after Lanne.'

'I have said, I intend to make her my wife,' Galitsin said. And peered at him. 'Is she really your daughter?'

'Probably,' James said.

'I will be all right, truly, Daddy,' Lanne said. 'Sandor is really a very kind man.'

'I'm sure,' James said. 'You understand it was not my plan to abandon you in this situation.'

'It was my decision,' she said. 'Don't *worry*.'

'You know where to find me, if you ever wish to come home.'

'Medieval,' Richard grumbled, not for the first time, as they took the road west.

'It's a medieval country still,' James reminded him.

'And you have sold your daughter, like a slave.'

'She did the selling,' James pointed out. 'And I've a notion she'll be much happier with Galitsin than she could possibly be with anyone in England, or Europe for that matter. And that includes you.'

'Because of her black blood.'

'Partly. But also because of the life she has been forced to live these last months. I think we need to concentrate upon getting out of here ourselves.'

This, if tedious, was surprisingly easy to do. Russia was in a state of utter chaos, with many people supposing that the various White armies, composed of conservative elements who paid lip-service to tsardom but whose commanders were really thinking how they could carve out independent principalities for themselves, would soon prove victorious over the murderous rabble commanded by the Jewish revolutionary who called himself Leon Trotsky, and who had absolutely no experience of warfare. Galitsin had realised that to send his new father-in-law north to Moscow might be to have him and his companions shot out of hand by the first group, of either side, with whom they came into contact. Fortunately, Merv was only seventy-odd miles from the Persian border, and he had them escorted by his people. Crossing into Persia was not difficult, as the borders were in any event being flooded with refugees from Afghanistan, and although they had their hairy moments, since Galitsin had also well supplied them with money they managed to link up with a caravan and reach Tehran in another month.

Here there was a British consul to whom they explained their plight; that they were two Englishmen, accompanied by two Frenchwomen, who had been travelling, with others, in Afghanistan, been caught up in the war and then the revolution, and been robbed of all they possessed—including their passports and all forms of identification. The consul naturally needed to do some investigating, but he was clearly impressed by James' presence. 'Sir James Martingell,' he mused. 'I have heard the name, sir.' James could only hope it was not in connection with his recent departure from England. 'And Major Richard Elligan. Yes, indeed.'

He found them board and lodgings, sent off various telegrams, and two days later announced that he had been empowered to issue the four of them with temporary passports to enable them to reach England, when their affairs would have to be sorted out. He also informed James that he had been unable to contact Lady Martingell, because she had packed up and left England. 'There was some trouble with her son,' he explained, somewhat anxiously. 'Your son?'

'No,' James said. 'My stepson. Who has been charged with murder.'

'Convicted,' the consul said. 'It really looks rather bad.'

'All the more reason I should hurry home.' James had other things on his mind. The consul allowed him to send some telegrams, but whether these were to Bombay or Aden—there was no telegraph office in Chah Bahar—there was no word of the *Europa*, or her crew.

Getting back to England remained difficult, as Turkey was now engulfed in a war with Greece. So they took a very slow train south to Abandan, Mesopotamia still being under British control while the various mandates were being sorted out. But at least they felt they were safe at last.

'You loved that girl, eh?' Michelle asked Richard, as they sat together staring out of the window at the mountains through which they were descending towards the delta of the Tigris and Euphrates. It was the first time she had raised the subject, or indeed any subject, since their journey had begun.

'Yes,' he said. 'I did. I do.'

She sighed. 'What is to become of me?'

'Well ... we will see that you are returned to your family.'

'I 'ave no family.'

'Say again? There must be someone.'

'My family did not approve of Philippe,' she explained. 'When I married 'im, they said, out. So I left. I loved 'im. Just like you loved that girl,' she reminded him.

'Ah, yes. Well, I am sure Sir James will sort something out.'

'Sir James,' she pointed out, ''as a wife.'

Damnation, he thought: how am I going

to get out of this? The trouble was, he knew all of her most intimate secrets save the ultimate. And she was an attractive, cuddly little thing, who had just made him the most blatant offer. And he had been without a woman for too long; he was grateful the train was so crowded.

'You 'ave been so good to me,' Michelle confided, leaning against him. 'Without you, I would 'ave died. I 'ave come to consider you almost as my 'usband.'

'Yes. Well, a chap does what he can, don't you know. But we really can't consider the future until we're back in England. Or France.' But he put his arm round her shoulders and hugged her close.

Homaira also had the future much in mind. When James asked if she would not like to be returned to her family, here in Iran, she vehemently declined; as a discarded wife or widow she would be ranked lower than a sheep. 'In England,' she remarked, 'is it true that a man may only have one wife?'

'Quite true,' James assured her.

'And how many concubines?'

'Ah ... concubinage is not generally recognised, in England.'

'You mean a man has to be satisfied with one woman, all of his life?' She was aghast.

'Actually, no. Most men have at least one mistress in the course of their lives. But they usually have them one at a time, not in a group, if you follow me. And they are usually very discreet about it. If the wife finds out, it is grounds for divorce.'

Homaira considered this for several minutes. Then she said, 'I do not think that is a good place to live. If I am to be your mistress.'

'Are you?'

'Well, you say I cannot be your concubine.'

'And you really would like to be one or the other.'

'Am I not deserving of it?'

'I am sure you are, Homaira. But the fact is, I am not sure I need a mistress right now. It will have to wait until we return to England.'

'But that is a long way away. And we are to go by boat, you say. I have never been on a boat.'

'This will be a very comfortable boat,' he promised her.

'And we will share a bed on this boat?'

'Ah ... we'll sort that out when we get to the boat, all right?'

She did not seem totally mollified, but like Richard, he was protected by the crowded train.

'What the devil are we going to do with these women, Sir James?' Richard asked. The train had by now descended from the mountains and was crossing the desert.

'Pension them off,' James said.

'You think they'll accept that?'

'Certainly. Right now their horizons are limited, by us. Once they get into the wider world and have a little money to spend, they'll change their perspectives.' He glanced at the young man. 'Unless you would like a different arrangement?'

'Good Lord, no. Michelle is like a sister to me. And I will have a great deal to do.'

'Like rejoining the army?'

'I have never left the army.'

'Save to be posted dead,' James said with a grin.

'They'll have unposted me by now, since that consul told them I'm still alive.'

'Yes,' James said thoughtfully. He wondered where Anne and Mbote had got to. If they had fled England it could only be because people like Hazlitt had been pressing too hard. 'What is going to be your attitude to me?'

Richard flushed. 'Well sir, I will attempt to say as little as possible, save that we were both prisoners of the Afghan rebels, and are lucky to have escaped with our lives.'

'Your superiors will know that you were sent to warn me off.'

'As I did.' It was his turn to grin. 'Unwisely, in my opinion, you did not take my advice.'

'But I was in Afghanistan with a shipment of guns.'

'I cannot prove that, Sir James.'

James chuckled. 'Maybe you would have made a good son-in-law after all.'

Richard sighed. 'I don't think I can ever forgive you for that.'

'Damnation. I was going to offer you a job, if the army ever paled. How about a drink instead?'

Two days later they were in Basra. As they disembarked, they were met by a Consulate officer, backed up by four policemen. 'Sir James Martingell?'

'I am he,' James acknowledged.

'I have a warrant here for your arrest, Sir James.'

Part Three

The Last Gamble

'Ambition, in a private man a vice,
Is, in a prince, the virtue.'

Philip Massinger

Chapter 9

The Separation

Harbottle, as always, looked embarrassed. And hot. That was because Rome was extremely hot. There was hardly any breeze, and the effluvia rose from the streets, together with the noise. Italy was in a state of constant excitement, and Rome was more excited than anywhere else. Some said the country was on the verge of revolution. Harbottle wished Lady Martingell had not chosen it as her hiding place. As for what she was doing with that black chap ... But he was pleased. He only wished she would also look pleased. 'Life imprisonment, at hard labour?' she enquired.

'It was the best we could do, Lady Martingell. And it was a damn near run thing. In the absence of, well ... any evidence to support Mr Winston's claim ...'

'I assume my name came into it?'

'Well, it had to, Lady Martingell. Caused a considerable sensation.'

'And how did you treat it?'

'Well ... exactly as you instructed us, my lady. We dismissed it as the ravings of a madman. But you see, that loaded the case against Mr Winston.' He looked more embarrassed than ever. 'But there is the chance that he may be paroled, if he behaves himself. You may remember we discussed this, Lady Martingell.'

'Ten years,' Anne muttered. 'And what is the news of my husband and stepdaughter?'

'Ah ... I'm afraid, nothing.'

'For twelve months? Are you saying they're dead?'

'I'm afraid we have to consider that possibility, milady. As you know, Afghanistan has been in a state of turmoil for some time now, first when they launched that abortive attack upon India, and then when they descended into civil war themselves.'

'The Amir Amanullah has announced that the civil war is over,' Mbote pointed out.

'I believe it is, in effect. Which does not mean there are not bands of dangerous revolutionaries roaming the country. There always have been, in that part of the world. We know that Sir James was taken by one of these bands, as was Miss Lanne. And nothing has been heard of them since.'

'However,' Anne said, 'legally my husband is not dead.'

'No, milady. He cannot legally be

300

considered dead until he has disappeared for seven years. But your finances are all jointly held, are they not, so there should be no difficulty there.'

'Oh, your account will be paid, Mr Harbottle.'

'I never doubted it for a moment, Lady Martingell. Will you ... ah, be returning to England at any time in the near future?'

'You mean, am I coming back to see my son? Are visitors allowed at Dartmoor?'

'Oh, indeed, with permission from the governor. I have no doubt I could obtain such permission for you.'

'And no doubt there will be questions asked?'

'Not by the police, Lady Martingell. As far as they are concerned, the matter is dead and buried. I cannot answer for the press, of course. *Will* you be coming back?'

'Does Winston wish to see me?'

'At the moment, probably not. But I am sure he will wish to see you.'

'When I decide on it, I will let you know. And again, many thanks for your trouble.'

Harbottle gathered he had been dismissed. He shook hands, gave a nervous bow, and was escorted to the door by the waiting Claudette.

Anne went onto the balcony, looked

out over the Roman morning mist. Her apartment was just off the Via Veneto, and she could hear the rumble of the traffic, although the street beneath her was fairly empty. She heard movement, but only half turned her head. 'Do you condemn me as utterly as Harbottle, Mbote?'

'I understand your reasoning, Anne. We must hope that Winston does also, in the course of time.'

'But you still condemn me.'

'I would have handled it differently, yes.'

'And submitted to being pilloried the length and breadth of England, if I had not actually been arrested. If only James had been there to advise me. Do you think he is dead, Mbote?'

'We can only hope, Anne. He has always proved a very difficult man to kill, in the past.'

Now she did turn, her hips against the balustrade. 'And you do hope.'

'Don't you?'

She gave a little sigh. 'In some ways, yes. We have been partners a long time. From time to time I believe we even loved. But he always loved the trade more. And I ...' She shrugged. 'I am forty-five years old, Mbote. I have lost my son, and now I seem to have lost my husband and my stepdaughter. It seems to me that it is

302

necessary for me to begin my life all over again, and make what I can of it.'

'You mean, marry again?'

'No,' she said. 'I don't think I shall ever marry again. Two husbands, both of whom died violently, as we must suppose, are sufficient for any woman, surely. I shall find my happiness outside of marriage.' She gazed at him. 'With people who are utterly loyal to me, who I know I can trust.'

'Everything I have, including my life, I owe to James,' Mbote said.

'And I am offering you everything he left behind.'

'That is too big a concept for me to consider, at this time.'

Anne squeezed his hand. 'So consider it. I am not going anywhere.'

Was she being criminal, and crazy, as she had been so often in the past? She remembered the first time she had met James, before even her first marriage to Winston Pennyfeather, when he had just been refused employment by her uncle in Cape Town. She had thought then, there is a man I would like to take me to bed. She had been just twenty, and had instinctively rejected such a forward thought. And then asked herself, why should I not think such things, if I honestly feel them? It had been safe enough for her to risk: James Martingell had disappeared from her life and she had never expected to see him again. When he had reappeared, and she had sought him out, on Winston Pennyfeather's instructions, with an eye to a business deal, she had been surprised, and a little afraid, to discover that her desire for him had only grown. And could now be brought to fruition, in view of the disaster that was her marriage.

That it would also lead her into paths of adventure she had never anticipated, and even to murder, had never crossed her mind. If it had, would she still have carried it through? She rather felt she would, because, like James, she craved adventure, risk, and excitement. And she had carried hers to extremes. First with that young officer, so gallant and so confused. And now ...

Mbote was her oldest living friend, she supposed; she could no longer call Winston a friend. She had long admired him for his physical presence as well as his steadfast loyalty to James. Now she did not wish any wild, uncertain, and almost certainly disappointing, adventures with younger men. But she still craved sexual adventure. There would be none greater than with Mbote. Of course she had taken him by surprise. But she had no doubt he would agree. She knew her beauty, the compulsion of her frenetic personality. And then ... she thought that going to bed with Mbote would be the most exciting thing that had ever happened to her.

No doubt the world would consider her the most dissolute woman in the world. But did not the world, or that part of the world which knew of her, already so consider her? And perhaps in Mbote's arms she could forget all the demons from the past which haunted her sleep. ''Ere is the newspaper, madame.' Claudette placed *Il Tiempo* on the breakfast table. 'It is all this Signor Mussolini.' Claudette was in a high good humour nearly all the time, nowadays; she enjoyed living in Rome.

'Mr Mbote out?' Anne asked, as she opened the newspaper.

'Yes, madame. I think 'e is gone.'

Anne raised her head. 'Gone? What do you mean?'

'When I go in 'is room this morning, 'e is not there.'

'You mean he has gone for a walk.' Mbote often went for a constitutional before breakfast.

''E 'as gone, with all 'is clothes, madame.'

Anne got up and went to Mbote's bedroom; it was a large apartment, with

305

three bedrooms as well as the reception and dining rooms. But Mbote's room was as if it had never been occupied. 'You see?' Claudette asked at her shoulder. ''E 'as taken everything. I think this is good, eh? The people downstairs, they talk, you know, about us 'aving a black man living with us. Do you not think it is a good thing, madame?'

Anne slapped her face, and she gave a little shriek, which became a louder shriek as she was thrown across the bed and hit several more times. 'You 'ave no right to treat me so, madame,' Claudette sobbed.

'I have every right to treat you as I please, wretched girl,' Anne snapped, and hit her again.

Where could that stupid man have gone? Anne paced her balcony in a frenzy of anger and uncertainty. And shame? That she should have driven him to such an extremity? Their oldest friend, turning his back on her. Because she wanted what to him was unacceptable. She wondered if he would feel any different if James *were* dead?

But now he could be lost for ever. Where would he go? What would he do? How would he live? He had always been entirely dependent upon them. Or at least, James. Not for the first time she reflected what a fool she had been, in following her instincts rather than her brain.

Claudette stood in the doorway. 'I wish to give my notice, madame.'

For a moment what she was saying didn't register; then Anne realised the maid was wearing her street clothes. 'What on earth are you talking about?'

'You should not beat me so, madame.'

'Oh, really, Claudette. How may a lady not beat her servant?'

'It is not right.'

This is 1919, not 1819, Anne remembered she had told Winston. But she couldn't be left alone. 'All right. I won't beat you again, if it upsets you so. I'm sorry. I lost my temper. I was feeling depressed.'

Claudette considered. 'I think I should 'ave a rise in pay, madame. If I am to stay.'

'Very well. I will pay you an extra ten shillings a week.'

'Thank you, madame. Will we be staying in Rome?'

'For the time being, yes.'

'You think Mbote will come back?'

'I have to give him the time to do so.'

But a month later Mbote had still not returned. Anne was so lonely she was even giving some thought to returning to

England, as quietly and inconspicuously as possible, when Claudette appeared. 'That gentleman is 'ere, madame.'

'Mbote?' Anne leapt to her feet.

'The English gentleman,' Claudette said, stiffly; she regarded Richard Elligan as the seed from which a great deal of trouble had sprouted.

'Richard!' Anne would have hugged him, but he took a step back.

'Lady Martingell.'

'My God, to see you. How did you know where to find me?'

'I enquired of your solicitor, Mr Harbottle. He was reluctant to give me your address, until I convinced him that it really was most important that we meet.'

'You're home from India. Do you have news of James? And Lanne?'

'May we sit down?'

'Of course. Forgive my manners. If you knew how distraught I have been, these last few months, with no news other than James was missing, believed dead, and Lanne ... *do* you have news?'

'I have spent a good part of the last six months in your husband's company, Lady Martingell.'

Anne stared at him with her mouth open. 'You mean he is in England too?'

'I'm afraid he is. Sadly, he is under arrest.'

'You turned him in!'

'No, I did not. In fact, I intend to defend him. But we both felt it would be best for you to be kept fully informed.'

'He's well?'

'Oh, indeed. Sir James is indestructible.'

'And Lanne?'

'I think I had better tell you the whole story,' Richard said. And did so.

Anne listened in silence, did not speak for some seconds even when he had finished. Then she said, 'What a catastrophe. Poor Philippe. You say Michelle escaped with you? Where is she now?'

'Michelle and Homaira are in France. We deemed it best for them to stay there until this business has been sorted out.'

'Who is this woman Homaira?'

'Ah ... she was Amaruddin's principal wife.'

'You mean she is an Afghan.'

'No, she is a Persian.'

'And why did you waste your time bringing her out?'

'It seemed the right thing to do, Lady Martingell.'

Anne snorted. 'And Lanne, carried off into the wilds of Russia.'

'I mean to get her back,' Richard said.

Anne raised her eyebrows. 'After letting her go?'

'That was Sir James' decision, and it

309

was the only one he could have taken, in the circumstances, if we were to get away with our lives.'

'He sold his own daughter,' Anne remarked.

'As I have said, he had no choice. So there it is. Sir James would love to see you, of course, if you would go to England.'

Once again, Anne thought, they are attempting to involve me. After all, James was the one who had said, if the going gets too rough, we'll emigrate. She had done nothing more than obey his instructions. 'I think it would be best if I remained here,' she said. Richard raised his eyebrows. 'What is likely to happen to him?'

'He is being charged with selling guns to an enemy of Great Britain, at a time when Great Britain was at war with that enemy. If that is proved, he could receive a lengthy prison sentence. However, I believe he has a defence to that. Unfortunately, he has no defence to shipping arms out of the country without a licence. So he may have to suffer a fine. But it will be a heavy one.'

'Are you in his confidence?'

'I don't think anyone is fully in Sir James' confidence, Lady Martingell.'

'I wish you would stop calling me Lady Martingell. My name is Anne. Are you going back to England?'

'As soon as possible.'

'Well, you can tell him, and it may help in his defence, that we never received the last payment for those arms from Azam. Where is Azam, by the way?'

'Nobody knows. I suspect, knowing that gentleman, that he has made his peace with the amir. In which case we will probably hear from him again at some stage. I will give Sir James that information.' He stood up. 'I heard the news of your son's conviction. I am sorry.'

'He was guilty,' Anne muttered. 'But you're not rushing off already? At least stay to supper. I'm sure we still have a great deal to discuss.'

'I am booked on the night train.' Richard looked at his watch. 'Which leaves in an hour.'

'And you arrived only a few hours ago? You came all this way for an hour?'

'I came all this way in the hopes of persuading you to come to your husband's side, Lady Martingell. But as you consider this unwise, why, I must return to advise him of it. There are some other matters as well.'

'Richard!' She caught his hand. 'Have you no feelings at all for me?'

'I am sure I do. But after six months in Sir James' company, often in dire extremity, I have more for him. Good day to you.'

He left the room, and Anne remained staring at the door for several minutes, until it was opened by Claudette. 'Is the gentlemen not staying to supper, milady?'

'Oh, you ...' Anne ran at her.

Claudette gave a little squeal, and also ran. But she had the sense to run into her mistress's bedroom and throw herself across the bed. After all, it meant another rise in pay.

'I find your attitude very difficult to understand, Richard,' Clerkwell said. 'We have spent a lot of time and money, and you have risked your life, to bring this man to justice. Now you will not testify.'

'Correction, sir,' Richard said. 'My life was risked on behalf of the Indian Government, not to bring down Sir James Martingell. And I am perfectly willing to testify. But I can only give the truth as I know it. Sir James sold a shipment of guns to Prince Amaruddin, who was in rebellion against Amir Amanullah. As Amir Amanullah was at war with Great Britain, I would describe that as an act of patriotism, an effort to help us, rather than our enemies.'

'That, sir, is specious,' Clerkwell said. 'You know as well as I that when Sir James sold those guns, they were for the use of Amanullah in his war against Britain.'

'You can never prove it, Mr Clerkwell.'

Clerkwell gazed at the young man. 'You realise you are jeopardising your career by adopting this attitude.'

'I would be jeopardising my entire character did I agree to perjure myself, sir.'

Clerkwell's face reddened in anger. 'Very good. But we will still have him, you know. His licence was to dump those guns at sea. Not sell them.'

'One hundred thousand pounds,' James said. He stood at the window of the solicitor's office and looked out at the busy Piccadilly beneath him. 'It could have been a lot worse. My congratulations, Mr Grimston. And you, Harbottle.'

'It is still a sizeable sum of money,' Derrick Blount, James' chief accountant, said. 'Especially as that last cheque was not negotiated.'

'So what have I got left?' James returned to the table and sat down.

'Ah ... with what you have on deposit, after the fine is paid, and taking into consideration your other investments, you are worth just over three hundred thousand pounds. But a hundred thousand of that remains in cash, the residue of the Afghan

313

money, and that is being transferred, at five hundred pounds a month, to Rome for Lady Martingell's living expenses. So it is not going to last very long, unless that drain is stopped. It is presently earning two per cent interest, but that is a drop in the ocean. The sooner you get it properly invested, the better. Then there is the house in Worcestershire. That is worth a few thousand if you decide to sell. Then of course there is the factory.'

'Which is currently closed,' Harbottle pointed out. 'It will cost a considerable sum to get going again, and ... who are you going to sell the weapons to? There is absolutely no prospect of your ever getting a licence again.'

'What has happened to my people?' James asked.

'Well, they have all lost their jobs.'

'I want them found, and paid a gratuity. Two hundred pounds a man.'

'My dear Sir James, it was a government decision to close you down. You have no further responsibility to the workforce.'

'Those are my instructions, Derrick.'

'Two hundred pounds per man,' Blount muttered. 'There is eight thousand gone. And then there is the yacht,' he went on. 'I certainly recommend that you get rid of her, Sir James, because she has always been a considerable drain. And if you cannot use her for deliveries any more ...'

'I'm afraid the yacht is already gone, Derrick,' James said. They stared at him in consternation. 'Nothing has been heard of her since she was taken over by Azam's people,' James explained. 'When we reached Persia, I tried contacting her by radio, but there was no reply, and we were informed from Chah Bahar that she had put to sea just before a severe storm. It looks somewhat grim there. So there will be payments necessary to any widows that may be left. Two hundred pounds each. And two hundred pounds to that unfortunate Allardyce girl.'

'Her?' Harbottle cried. 'She is undoubtedly walking the streets by now. She'll only blow the money on gin.'

'Nevertheless, she will receive a gratuity the same as everyone else. I'm afraid this entire expedition has turned out to be a catastrophe.' In every possible way, he thought. It had not occurred to him that Anne might so resent his abandonment of her as to kick over the traces as she had in her youth. But the reports coming out of Rome were damning.

'It's not all that bad, Sir James,' Blount protested. 'Even with these, ah, unnecessary payments, you are still a relatively wealthy man. Your investments are improving ... well, so is everyone's. The stock market is the place to be today. Far safer than selling arms, what?'

'I can't argue with that. Thank you for all your assistance, gentlemen. I'll take my leave.'

Harbottle went with him to the door. 'What are you going to do?'

'In the first instance, sort out my wife,' James told him.

He lunched with Richard. 'I haven't properly thanked you for the evidence you gave on my behalf.'

'I simply told the truth.'

'Maybe. I'll wager it hasn't gone down very well with your superiors.'

Richard grinned. 'No, it hasn't.'

'So what are you going to do?'

'Oh, I haven't lost my commission. I've done nothing actually wrong. It's just that I shall probably end my days what I am now, a major.'

'You mean you'll stay in the army?'

'For the time being, certainly. I've volunteered to return to India. And, if possible, Afghanistan. Now we're all officially friends again, they will need an attaché, and I know the country and the people.'

'I wouldn't have thought you'd want to return there,' James remarked.

'I mean to find Lanne.'

James frowned at him. 'You think she is in Afghanistan?'

'I think she is in Russia.'

'That's a big area.'

'I'll find her. And I mean to marry her,' Richard said.

'Would you forgive me if I remarked that that is an utterly absurd, if romantic, notion. If you find her, and it's a very big if, she'll have been Galitsin's wife for some time, after having been Amaruddin's concubine for some time. Do you really suppose she'd make you a good wife?'

'Yes. I believe she loves me.'

'I see. And her husband?'

'If Galitsin gets in my way,' Richard said, 'I shall kill him.'

'Then I will wish you every success in the world.'

'Do you wish to become involved?'

'Yes,' James said. 'Find Lanne, or find where she is, and I'll join you to get her out.'

James returned to his hotel. It was not an expensive hotel—those were things of the past, he supposed, until he could sort himself out. But it was very respectable, and it had been necessary to take two rooms, one for himself and one for Homaira—Michelle had bitten the bullet and gone home to her family, some negotiation having convinced her that

317

they would take her in. But Homaira remained. Of all of them, he supposed she had benefited most from the disaster. She had not loved Amaruddin, so his demise did not affect her emotions. She had been freed from the harem and travelled the world, to her obvious fascination. And now she had him, without a care of what might lie ahead.

As he had taught her, she did not come to his room, which adjoined hers, until midnight, when the hotel had settled into sleep. Then she shrugged off the nightgown he had bought for her and slid beneath the sheets. She was a quite beautiful woman, and knew how to use her beauty. But tonight he was not to be aroused.

She rested her head on his shoulder, half hidden beneath the mass of glossy black hair. 'I am glad you did not have to go to prison, my lord.'

'So am I.' He stroked her breast, which swelled to fill his hand. 'What would you have done, had I been locked up?'

The breast swelled again. 'What could I have done, my lord? I would have killed myself.'

'Because of me? You didn't kill yourself when Amaruddin died.'

'You are far superior to Amaruddin, my lord.'

He held her close to bring her on top of

him, moved hair from her face. 'I'm afraid we have a difficult time ahead.'

'Because of your wife? I will be your number two wife, my lord.'

'I doubt that will really be practical. But ... tomorrow we will go and find out.'

A mad quest, the man had said, Richard thought, as he strolled along Shaftesbury Avenue. He had been talking about his own daughter! But presumably it was, a mad quest. And a futile one. Even if he found her, what was he going to do? She would be married, to a man who obviously satisfied her needs ... she was acting her true self. She would not wish to come back to him, or the life he would offer her.

And what sort of life could he possibly offer her? Yet to think ... 'Do pardon me, sir, but aren't you Major Richard Elligan?'

He had been in such deep thought he had all but bumped into the young woman. Now he stopped and stared, because she was a singularly attractive young woman, nearly as tall as himself, slender, with piquant features and a mass of red hair, standing out in a street full of bobbed and permed tresses; hers were straight and gathered with a blue ribbon on the nape of her neck. She wore a white dress, well below the knee, and white stockings, and a broad-brimmed hat. All of which helped to convince him that she was not English, although she spoke the language perfectly. But he had never seen her before in his life; he would certainly have remembered. 'You will think me very ill mannered,' she said. 'But I was in court at the trial of Sir James Martingell, and I saw you give evidence. The person sitting beside me said that what you had done was very brave, as it would virtually mean the end of your career.'

'I don't think it will be quite as drastic as that,' he made a stab at her nationality, 'Fräulein?'

She smiled, and doubled her beauty. 'You are very observant, sir. You are, therefore, a friend of Sir James?'

'I think I may claim that honour. And you?'

'I have only met him once. But he once did business with my family. Perhaps you have heard the name Beinhardt.'

'Beinhardt!' Richard said. James had spoken of them in prison, when they had reminisced together. 'My God! And you are the girl Sophie.'

'That is right, sir. Now, again, I must ask you to forgive my impertinence in accosting you on the street. I but wished to congratulate you on the assistance you rendered Sir James.'

'You are going to have to explain that,'

Richard said. 'May I offer you lunch?'

Somewhat to his surprise, she accepted. But he gathered that she was in London attending a business school, that she was nineteen, and that she was feeling extremely lonely and vulnerable. Equally that it had been that loneliness that had led her to attend the court at which James had been tried. 'But forgive me,' he said as they sipped their wine, 'I was under the impression that the House of Beinhardt rather regarded James Martingell as a scoundrel.'

She gave another of her charming smiles. 'But a most attractive one, don't you think? He is supposed to have embezzled a large sum of money owed to my parents, yes. But at the time he was engaged to be married to my aunt.' She gave a little sigh. 'I never knew my aunt Cecile; she died before I was born. But I understand that she was very beautiful.'

'Then you must take after her,' Richard ventured.

'Why, Major Elligan, what a nice thing to say. She died young.'

'I know. James told me. We spent quite a long while together, in an Afghan prison.'

'That must have been a terrible experience.'

'Being with James alleviated it.' The

meal was over. Never had he spent such an enjoyable two hours. Not that he had much idea what he had eaten; looking at Sophie von Beinhardt had that effect on a man. What am I thinking, he asked himself? I am bound to Lanne. Was he?

'Well,' Sophie said. 'Thank you so much for the meal, Major Elligan. I have enjoyed meeting you.'

'I would like to meet you again,' he said. Sophie raised her eyebrows. 'I feel we have not touched on half the subjects we might have,' he said, somewhat lamely.

'Why, I am sure you are right,' she agreed.

'Trouble is, I am due to leave the country in a week.' How the year rolled back. But never had he been so instantly attracted to anyone before. Had he not thought that about Lanne?

'Ah,' she said. 'Well, then ...'

'Dinner? Tonight?'

She considered him for several moments. Then she smiled. 'I should like that, Major Elligan.'

'I think, perhaps, you could try Richard,' he suggested.

What am I doing? he needed to ask himself, urgently. Easy to say that his commitment to locating Lanne, if possible, and then rescuing her, was merely an act of stubborn gallantry, which would depend entirely upon whether or not Lanne wished to be rescued, and this he doubted. Well, then, this girl, young, innocent, eager to be friends ... and German! One of her countrymen—it could even have been a relative—had fired the bullet on the Somme that had landed him in hospital for a year and left him with a permanent scar.

The temptation to avenge himself, to take anything she offered or might accept and then forget her was immense. He had felt the same way about Anne Martingell—and hated himself for it ever since. At least this girl didn't have a husband. 'How long will you stay in England?' he asked.

'I have another three months.'

'And then home to ...?'

'Hamburg is where my parents live now. Do you know it?'

'No, I have never been to Germany.'

'Not even as a member of the occupying army, when we were defeated?'

Was she mocking him? He couldn't be sure—her green eyes had all the depths of the ocean. 'When the war ended I was in India.'

'And that is where you are returning now?'

'Yes, it is.'

'It sounds very exciting.'

'It is not half as exciting as sitting here with you.'

Once again the eyebrows. 'I am exciting?'

'To me.'

'Well, then, as you are exciting to me, we are exciting to each other.' She bit her lip as if realising she might have said too much.

'I don't suppose you'd ever come to India,' he remarked.

'I should think that is very unlikely. It would be easier for you to come to Hamburg. Cheaper, too.'

They stared at each other. 'If I were to come to Hamburg ...'

'We would make you most welcome.'

'Then I shall come and visit you. Trouble is, when I return to India this time, I shall be there for at least three years, possibly as much as five. By then you will be married, and have children.'

'I doubt that.'

'A girl as beautiful as you? I am only surprised that you are not married already.'

'Are you married?'

'No.'

'I find that equally strange,' Sophie said. 'But perhaps you will marry, when you return to India.'

'I doubt *that.*'

'Well, then, it may not be so very long.'

'It will be for ever,' Richard said. 'Without ...' He hesitated. My God, he thought, and you considered James Martingell a scoundrel.

Sophie continued to consider him for some moments. Then she said, 'We have only just met.'

'I know. You are entirely entitled to slap my face and walk away.'

'Because you wish to have sex with me? I would say that is the greatest compliment that a man can pay a woman.'

He had to remind himself that this was not an English girl speaking. Such openness would have been impossible. But as she had said it ... 'I would like to do more than that, Sophie.'

'On the basis of a few meetings? You fall in love very readily.'

'Yes, I suppose I do.'

'So it is unlikely that these fallings-in-love can be the least permanent.'

'In my case ...' Before he knew it, he was telling her the story of Lanne.

She listened with hardly a change of expression, only occasionally sipping her drink. When he was finished, she said. 'And now you are seeking a replacement, no?' She smiled. 'Anyone will do, even someone you meet on the street.'

'That's not quite right,' he said. 'My life has at the moment a huge vacuum, and I suddenly realised you could be the one to fill it.'

'That is hardly mad, passionate love. What about Sir James' daughter? You say you are committed to finding her.'

'I suppose I am.'

'Well, then, I think you should at least make a stab at it.'

'And you will forget all about me.'

'I should prefer not to. I will give you, shall we say, a small remembrance of me. And then, when you have completed your quest, one way or the other, you may come to Hamburg and visit with me. And we shall see if it is possible for us to be together, always.'

'Oooh, la-la,' Claudette remarked, opening the door. James and Homaira had travelled overnight from London, via Paris, and it was very early in the morning. Claudette was in her nightgown, and her hair was loose. 'Sir James?' she asked, incredulously. And looked past him at Homaira, who was wearing a dress and laced boots, and a broad-brimmed hat. 'Oooh, la-la.' Now she was definitely terrified.

'We're not ghosts, Claudette,' James said. 'I suppose Lady Martingell is still asleep.'

'Ah ... yes,' Claudette said. 'You come in and 'ave a cup of tea, Sir James, and

326

I will wake 'er ladyship.'

'No, no,' James said. 'I will wake her ladyship.'

'Oooh, la-la,' Claudette said a third time. 'I will make zee tea.' Again she looked at Homaira, uncertainly.

'Have a seat, Homaira,' James invited. 'And a cup of tea.' He left the two women and walked down the corridor between the bedrooms. He reckoned the master bedroom would be the first, and he was right; when he opened the door he inhaled Anne's scent. And immediately knew an overwhelming sense of déjà vu.

'Claudette?' Anne asked, sleepily.

'James,' James said, standing above the bed.

The man was the first to realise the situation. He stared at James for a moment, then rolled across the bed and landed on his hands and knees. Anne also stared at him, then screamed.

'Sssh,' James suggested. 'You'll disturb the neighbours.'

The man—he was no one James had ever seen before—was dragging on his clothes. Anne sat up, the nightclothes held to her throat.

'I will wish you good day,' James said to the man, who sidled through the door and from the sound of his footsteps was running for the front door.

Anne licked her lips. 'I thought you were in London. Or in gaol.'

'Obviously.' He sat on the bed, and she moved away from him, sheet still held protectively, golden hair tumbling round her shoulders. 'Do you know,' he said, 'I have experienced this once before. With Martha Alexander. Of course, she was a whore, so I threw her out. I do not suppose one could possibly describe Anne, Lady Martingell as a whore.'

'Do you know how lonely I have been?' Anne demanded. 'How distraught? You went off, and left me with the whole world on my shoulders ...'

'Do you know another odd coincidence? When I walked in on Martha and her client, it was with every intention of ending our relationship, whether or not she had been unfaithful to me.'

Anne licked her lips. 'You came here to end our marriage?'

'Let's say I came here to alter our relationship, certainly.'

'We are partners.'

'In a partnership that is now dissolved, my dear. We have been put out of business. So, in all the circumstances, I think it best we go our separate ways. You have been spending money like water. I'm afraid that will have to stop. I propose to sell the house in Worcestershire, and with the proceeds buy two more modest establishments, one for you, and one for me. You may choose where you intend to live, but there is a purchasing limit of four thousand pounds.'

'You intend to divorce me?'

'I don't think that would be very good, for either of us, right this minute. We have both had a great deal of adverse publicity over the past year or so, and I think it would be best for us both to sink gently out of sight. If at any time you wish to marry again, then of course I shall give you a divorce. Now, as to income, I will settle three thousand a year on you. That will enable you to live very well, if perhaps not quite on the scale you are used to. If you are agreeable, I shall return to London immediately and have Harbottle draw up the terms.'

'And if I am not agreeable?'

He shrugged. 'Then I shall still return to England and have Harbottle draw up the terms. But you will receive not a penny until you *have* agreed.'

'I always knew you to be a ruthless man, James. I never expected to find that ruthlessness directed at me.'

'I prefer to think of myself as a realist, my dear. When a situation becomes untenable, it must be changed, sooner than later.'

'And all the adventures we have had in

partnership count for nothing?'

'They count for a great deal, as memories.'

'I saved your life.'

'I know. Thus I am giving you the best deal I can afford. Now tell me what you have done with Mbote.'

'He left.'

James frowned. 'You threw him out?'

'I did not throw him out, James. He left. I think he felt that he was an embarrassment to me.'

'I see. How long ago?'

'Several months.'

James nodded. 'I shall have to see if I can find him. Don't bother to get up. I am leaving now.'

He went to the door.

'What are you going to do?' Her tone was curious.

'Do? Why, I am going to retire, and hopefully enjoy my old age.'

Could he ever do that, after the life he had lived? The physical business of retiring was simple enough. The financial settlement was agreed on both sides, Anne received the necessary money for her to buy herself a London flat, her income was arranged, and she disappeared entirely from his orbit. Whether or not she was still entertaining young men was of no

330

further interest to him, in the abstract; he had Homaira, euphemistically described as his housekeeper, who cared for him in every possible way. But he also had too many memories, and nearly all of them involved guilt.

Lanne headed the list. It was easy to say now, as he had said then, that he had had no choice. And that she had not seemed concerned about her fate. Lanne had always wanted to adventure, and no doubt now she was doing that. If she lived. Yet the fact remained that he had allowed her to sacrifice herself to save the life of an ageing father, a life which had then simply fallen apart. Of course, if he had refused to accept Galitsin's terms, he would have died on the spot and Lanne would still have wound up with the Russian. But at least he would have tried. He sprang up whenever the postman came, hoping for news from Richard. But there was none. No doubt that young man had very quickly realised that finding someone in the vastness of Russia was not something to be done unless one possessed an army of agents.

Then there was Anne. She had indeed saved his life as she had earlier saved his career. They *had* adventured together, time and again, always with total mutual support. It had taken that murderous son of theirs to blow them apart. Although the signs had been there earlier. They were both too restless to live simply together. But it had been his decision to go for a last killing that had completed the dissolution of their relationship.

Then there was the *Europa*, and Captain Petersen, and the crew that had served him so faithfully and well for so long. All gone. And then there was Philippe, and by projection, Michelle. Philippe was another faithful supporter who had died in his service. And Michelle would never fully recover from her ordeal.

And lastly, Mbote, disappeared into a world innately hostile to anyone with a black skin. All for that last killing, that had not materialised.

At least his oldest enemy, the Mad Mullah, was finally dead. Not that it seemed either the Italians or the British were making any great headway in the Horn of Africa. And for him, the creeping advance of old age, as he entered his sixties. Without Homaira, he would have gone mad, a forgotten man, living on his memories.

It was almost a relief at last to receive a letter from Richard.

'I am sorry to say that my tour is completed. When I say that, I do not mean I shall be

sorry to leave this confounded country, but that my endeavours to find Lanne, or any trace of her, have quite failed. As you say, Russia is a vast country. I did hear some news of Galitsin, but it appears he is now peddling Communist propaganda in China, of all places. No doubt his wife is with him. So, I shall be returning to England, and leaving the army. My father has died, and I have a modest income. I shall devote myself to ... well, I have some ideas on that. On my way home, I have decided to take a short holiday in Germany. They seem to be becoming civilised. When I come home, I should like to call, if I may.'

He was as ebullient as ever, James thought, as he laid down the letter. But that was the final chapter in his life. It was all history now.

It was the following spring when he received the surprise of his life. 'Mbote?' he asked, as his friend was shown into his study by a somewhat nervous Homaira. 'Is it really you, old fellow?'

'Bits of me,' Mbote said with a grin. His clothes were shabby, and he had lost weight.

'Where in the name of God have you been? What have you been doing?'

'Working at this and that. Surviving.'

'Why didn't you come to me sooner?'

Mbote looked embarrassed. 'Is it true that you and Anne have separated?'

'Why, yes it is.' James frowned. 'You quarrelled? She did not mention it.'

'We discovered that we could not live in the same house without you,' Mbote said. 'I discovered that.'

'By God,' James said.

'If you would like me to leave again ...'

'I want you at my side, for the rest of my life. Believe me, old friend, the reason that Anne and I have separated is because I learned about her proclivities.'

The two men clasped hands. 'I heard you'd been fined for that shipment,' Mbote said. 'How it all went bad.'

'That's history. Now you're back, and that's all that matters. Just let's enjoy life a little.'

Chapter 10

The Offer

Hamburg, Richard decided, was a dump. As he was not looking for sexual adventure he had no interest in the red light district. Nor was he impressed by the house to which he was directed, a rather small building in not the best of neighbourhoods. But if it was where Sophie lived ... Of course she would be married and a mother by now, whatever her promise. Or the 'token' she had given him of her willingness to wait.

He had not known what to expect, had been willing to obey her every wish, and in the event, had been taken utterly by surprise. And back into history, he supposed, two or three centuries, when welcome had been given on lonely farms to equally lonely travellers, without any risk to the daughter of the house, either as regards virginity or pregnancy. They had bundled. Sophie had shared his bed, but with her lower half, from the waist down, encased in a pillowcase, its string drawn taut. Then he had been permitted full access to her body, without any risk to her.

It was a night he would never forget, the second such event. But how could Anne Martingell, probably the more beautiful woman but totally different in character, compare with Sophie von Beinhardt? He had climaxed in her hands, and she had kissed him and smiled into his mouth.

'Do you think you will remember me?' she asked.

'For ever and a day.'

'You say the sweetest things. And if you

happen to find your mistress?'

'Lanne was never my mistress. And if I find her ... I will return her to her family. And then come for you.'

'Five years,' she whispered.

Which had now elapsed. Sophie herself opened the door, cheeks pink and breasts heaving. 'I saw you from the window.' She was in his arms, and he was holding her close. 'I thought you would not come,' she said.

'I thought you would not be here.'

'Did you find the woman?'

He shook his head. 'I shall not think of her again.'

'Then you must never leave me again, either.' She pulled him into the living room. 'Mama! Papa! This is Richard Elligan.'

They obviously knew all about him. 'Why, sir,' Clementine von Beinhardt said, 'welcome to our home.'

'It is a humble home,' Claus von Beinhardt said, offering Richard a cigar. 'Times were when we owned vast estates. When the arms business was good, eh?'

'I've heard of them,' Richard said.

'From James Martingell, eh? Oh, yes, those were the days. And now you wish to marry our daughter. You will at least not be expecting some great dowry, Major Elligan.'

'I'm retired,' Richard reminded him. 'No, Count, I am not expecting anything. Sophie and I love each other. That should be sufficient.'

'Are you a wealthy man, Major ... I beg your pardon, Mr Elligan?'

'No, Count, I am not a wealthy man. But I think I have enough to keep Sophie in the style to which she is accustomed.'

Claus smiled, sadly. 'Because this is the style. Would you not like to be a wealthy man?'

'Who wouldn't?' Richard asked. 'If it could be done, legally.'

'For you, it would be legal.'

Richard frowned. 'You will have to explain that, sir.'

'I have an arsenal of weapons,' Claus said. 'Waiting to be sold. And now, do you know, I even have a buyer. Or at least, an agent acting for a buyer. You have an acquaintance with James Martingell, of course.'

'As we spent several months in an Afghan gaol together,' Richard said, 'and then had to walk five hundred-odd miles to safety, I think you could say we have an acquaintance.'

'Did he ever mention the name Azam ud-Ranatullah to you?' Richard's frown deepened. 'Or perhaps you know the fellow yourself,' Claus suggested.

'No,' Richard said. 'We have never met. But the name has been mentioned.'

'Sheikh Azam is what we might call an entrepreneur of war and violence. He is presently an outlaw in his own country for his attempt to aid the late Prince Amaruddin in taking over the Afghan throne, an attempt which failed. You know of this?'

'Yes,' Richard said, grimly.

'Thus the sheikh has had to cast his net further afield, one might say. Have you ever heard of a man named Ma Chung-ying?'

'Sounds Chinese.'

'Yes, he is Chinese, after a fashion. He is the leader of a, how shall I say, tribe? Of Muslim Chinese who have taken over Chinese Turkestan. You know of Chinese Turkestan?'

'It's one big desert, isn't it?'

'Well, not entirely. Kashgar was one of the great cities of antiquity, when it controlled the trade routes in and out of China. The point is that there is a big desert that separates what might one call the main part of China from Chinese Turkestan. Apart from the religious differences I have indicated. Now, as I am sure you know, since Sun Yat-sen's death, China has descended into anarchy. Sun Yat-sen, if not a Communist, was certainly leaning heavily on Soviet Russia for support. This young man who seems to have taken up his mantle, his son-in-law, Chiang Kai-shek, appears less interested in Communism than in uniting China under his banner. The ultimate warlord, eh? The trouble is, not everyone goes for this idea. There are other warlords seeking the ultimate power. Not to mention the Communists.'

'And this fellow Ma Chung-ying is one of these,' Richard ventured.

'Only in a degree. Ma seeks to create, out of the chaos that is China, an independent Muslim state in Turkestan.'

'For which, of course, he needs guns.'

'Absolutely. And being a Muslim, who should he turn to but that well-known Muslim entrepreneur, Azam ud-Ranatullah.'

'Who in turn has turned to that once well-known German arms producer, the House of Beinhardt.'

'Absolutely,' Claus said again. 'We have, in our warehouses, sufficient arms and ammunition to provide Ma Chung-ying with the weaponry to defeat any attempt by Chiang Kai-shek to recover Turkestan.'

'Then I wish you good fortune.'

'There is a problem,' Claus said.

'There always is.'

'Chinese Turkestan is an entirely land-locked country,' Claus said. 'It can only be reached overland. To attempt to land the guns in Shanghai and move them west, overland, would be as ridiculous as to attempt to move them east, through Germany and Poland and Soviet Russia. Even if we could get them to Soviet Russia, through say the Black Sea, it would be an enormous task. Sheikh Azam however believes he knows a way it can be done, and the man who can do it.'

'Through Persia and Afghanistan,' Richard said. 'Have you any idea of the difficulties, and the dangers, of that route?'

'I am persuaded that they are the lesser of all the other evils. Providing the shipment is in capable hands.'

Richard regarded him for some moments. 'I am sure Azam knows what he is about,' he said at last.

'He has a somewhat dubious reputation,' Claus suggested.

'He does indeed. But I can assure you that I know nothing of the business.'

'You have told me that you are well acquainted with someone who does.'

'There are a couple of points of which you may be unaware, Count,' Richard said. 'One is that Sir James has retired.'

'And is in somewhat straitened circumstances, I believe. Do you not think that you, an old comrade-in-arms, could persuade him to undertake one last, shall we say, adventure? Which would restore both him and the House of Beinhardt to prosperity? Especially as you wish to be my son-in-law.'

'I hope you are not suggesting that your consent to my marriage with Sophie depends on my persuading Sir James to engage in this venture?'

'By no means. Sophie is a determined young woman who will do as she pleases. If you knew the number of prospective suitors we have brought to this house over the past three years, and she has rejected them all. No, no, you are her choice, and neither her mother nor I would dare stand in her way. I am merely suggesting that you have, half opened, in front of you an opportunity to obtain immense riches. A partnership in the House of Beinhardt, with a full half-share in the profits from this, and all our future ventures. It would seem a shame to forgo such an opportunity.'

'And you would trust Sir James? After the last time?'

'I would trust you,' Claus said, and poured them each another goblet of brandy. 'As my son-in-law. But I also need Sir James, to deal with Azam, and to command the caravan. There is no man more capable, and he already knows the country through which you would have to pass. You mentioned another point.'

'Simply that I would say Azam ud-Ranatullah is Sir James Martingell's most bitter enemy, at this time.'

Claus von Beinhardt smiled. 'Enemies can be reconciled.'

'Will you do it?' Sophie asked, nestling in his arms. The wedding had been small, civil, and private. The Beinhardts were keeping a very low profile, and not only, Richard suspected, for financial reasons. As if he cared, when he could lie naked in his marriage bed, with Sophie in his arms.

'I have agreed to try. Would you not like me to be your father's partner?'

'I think that would be splendid.'

'But it all seems to depend on James Martingell wishing to return to the field, as it were.'

'But you think he will say yes.'

'I don't know. His circumstances are not as straitened as your father may suppose. But James is like an old warhorse. Give him the sniff of gunpowder ...'

'And you will go with him?'

'That is part of the deal. To keep him in order.'

'Then I will come with you.'

He pulled his head back. 'That is impossible. Do you know what happened to the last women who accompanied Sir James on such an expedition?'

'They adventured. As I wish to adventure. And besides, we agreed that we would never lose sight of each other again.' She snuggled closer yet. 'Are you going to England, to see Sir James?'

'It is necessary. And this I need to do alone.'

James sat in the study of his small house in the outskirts of Cheltenham, reading a letter from Richard. The young blighter, married to Sophie von Beinhardt! James distantly remembered her, a red-haired beauty, at Buckingham Palace in 1919. She was probably even more beautiful now. He wished them well, even if it finally meant the end of the quest for Lanne. Had there ever been any chance of success, there? James laid down the letter. Something else to lay at the foot of his conscience? But perhaps it was the other way around, in this instance. Had Richard Elligan never arrived on his doorstep to warn him off, a great deal of what had followed might never have happened.

Certain it was that Lanne would still be in England, perhaps happily married. And now asking if he could call ... he wondered if he would bring his bride with him?

Homaira stood in the doorway. 'There are two gentlemen to see you,' she said. 'One of them is Mr Elligan.'

343

James nodded. 'I was expecting him. And the other? You're sure it is not Mrs Elligan?'

Homaira rolled her eyes.

'Tell me.'

'Sheikh Azam ud-Ranatullah.'

James stared at her for a moment, then rose and went to his bureau to take out the service revolver and check that the chambers were loaded. Mbote was out walking.

'You are going to shoot him?' Homaira's eyes were wide even as her tone indicated full approval.

'My intention is to stop him shooting me,' James said, and thrust the revolver into the back of his waistband. 'Show them in.'

Although the rascal deserved to be shot on sight. As to what he was doing in England ... and brought here by Richard?

'James.' Richard held out his hand, and after a moment's hesitation, James took it. But he was looking past him.

Like himself, Azam had aged, but perhaps not so much. He was, as always, very well dressed, in European clothes, and did not look the least apprehensive. 'James!' he said, advancing in turn with outstretched hand, only checking when James did not take the offered fingers. 'You bear a grudge.'

'Should I not? I am astounded that you have the audacity to show your face.'

'In England? I have committed no crime here.'

'I meant in this house. As for you, Richard, bringing him here ...'

'The sheikh has an important proposition to put to you,' Richard said.

'He has put important propositions to me before,' James pointed out.

'Ah, James,' Azam said, 'but do we not know when times are extreme, it is every man for himself?'

'And are you now a representative of the Amir?'

'Sadly, no. I tried to make my peace with him, but he would not have it. The last few years have been difficult. But also for you, eh?'

'I have retired,' James said.

'Does a man like Sir James Martingell ever retire? I, we, have a proposition for you. Do you know anything of China?'

'Very little.'

'China, as I am sure you do know, James, is in chaos since the death of Sun Yat-sen. Chiang Kai-shek claims the country, but only controls a small part of it, in the east. In the south he is plagued by the Communists. In the north, the warlord Hsian Feng-yu holds sway, and he is reputed to be in Japanese pay; the Japanese would like to see China dismembered, of course. And in the outlying provinces there are local warlords who are busily carving out little kingdoms for themselves. China is entering a period of fragmentation, James, much has happened in Europe after the collapse of the Roman Empire. I assume you know of a place called Sinkiang and the warlord Ma Chung-ying?'

James looked at Richard. 'All very true,' Richard said.

'You'll forgive me if I say that I have very little idea of where Sinkiang is,' James said. 'And I have never heard of Mr Ma Chung-ying.'

'Sinkiang, James, is the westernmost province of China,' Azam said. 'It lies just north of Tibet, and comprises an area as large as France, Spain and Germany put together.'

'And Mr Ma is the ruler of this huge area? I don't really see where Chiang Kai-shek comes into the picture at all.'

Azam tapped his nose. 'Ma would like to be the warlord of Sinkiang, yes. To this end he already calls himself the supreme ruler. But the area he actually controls is only a few hundred thousand square miles in Chinese Turkestan. That lies at the western end of the province. What he needs are modern weapons with which to substantiate his claim.'

'How on earth do you propose that anyone should be able to get guns from Europe into a province of China?' James was interested despite himself.

Again Azam tapped his nose. 'It is not so difficult as you suppose, James. If the guns were shipped to, say, Chah Bahar as before, and taken up to Afghanistan, and then taken along the border with Russia, when you have reached the north-eastern corner of my country, there are only about a hundred and fifty miles of Russian territory between us and Chinese Turkestan.'

'Now I know you're crazy, Azam,' James said. 'You need to remember that I have been over some of that country. It is the toughest land in the world. And even suppose we got the guns to Pamir, don't you think the Russians would stop us going any further?'

'Supposing they knew of it. And supposing they had any armed forces in the vicinity. Russia is itself still fragmented. Lenin's death has done nothing to help this. Now, as I am sure you know, there is a power struggle going on both inside and outside of the Kremlin to see who succeeds Lenin, Stalin or Trotsky. They have little time for their borders. This gives us a great opportunity.'

What a temptation, James thought. But ...

'Dreams, Azam,' he said. 'Sweet dreams. I am retired. I have sold my factory, I have no staff, no organisation—and no guns to sell you.' He grinned. 'Even if I wanted to.'

Azam looked at Richard.

'Suppose we were to tell you that we can obtain the guns,' Richard said.

'By God,' James said. 'The House of Beinhardt. Into which you have now married! I think you are just as big a scoundrel as I ever was, Richard. But I do not see why you have come to me, Azam, after the way you betrayed me.'

'I saved your life. All of your lives. Who do you think gave that Russian his orders?'

James' eyes narrowed. 'You expect me to believe that?'

'I do, because it is the truth. I am very sorry for what happened, but I believed I was acting in the best interests of my country. Now I am simply acting as a businessman.'

James stroked his chin. 'And these guns? The House of Beinhardt was closed down when Germany surrendered.'

'Officially, yes,' Richard said. 'But Claus von Beinhardt is operating again, secretly, to be sure. He is accumulating a large stock of merchandise, just waiting to be sold.'

'And you suppose he will give this stock to me, for delivery?'

'As in the past,' Richard said.

'My dear Richard, that *was* the past. I would say that were you to mention my name to any Beinhardt they would immediately have a fit. They blame me for Cecile's death, and they still consider that I owe them a large sum of money.'

'Which, perhaps, they feel they can only recoup by dealing with you again. You are Claus von Beinhardt's own choice to command the expedition. He will have none other.'

'They have the problem, you see,' Azam went on, 'that while they are desperate to conclude the contract, they do not know the ground or, one might say, the form. As you will undoubtedly remember, in the old days the House of Beinhardt operated through agents on the ground, men who knew the terrain and the customers, of whom you were the very best. They have no organisation for delivering their merchandise. They have in fact been desperately trying to create one since the end of the Great War, without success. You can do that for them, and you will make a handsome profit for yourself. You will be paid an agent's fee, twenty-five thousand

349

pounds down, twenty-five on delivery.' He smiled. 'I'm afraid the House of Beinhardt, after their previous experiences, require that the actual payment for the guns be made direct to them.'

The temptation was enormous. But could he do it? Did he wish to risk so much, after the last time? He sighed. 'I'm sorry, Azam, but I'm not your man. I'm retired. I'm getting old. Trekking with a load of guns across the roof of the world is no longer appealing to me.'

'And that is your final word?'

'It is.'

Azam sighed. 'That is a shame. Now I have to look elsewhere. But I still hope you may change your mind. I keep an accommodation address in London. Here is my card.'

James took the piece of pasteboard. How the adrenalin was racing through his arteries. How he wanted to adventure, one last time. But he would be on a hiding to nothing, and he did not know if he any longer had the will, much less the physical strength, to carry it through, after the fiasco of the last time.

'It is a pity you will not work with us, Sir James,' Richard said. 'I was looking forward to one last adventure, with you.'

'You mean you were intending to accompany me?'

'That was the plan. As my father-in-law's representative.'

'Then I am again sorry. Take my advice and enjoy your beautiful bride.'

'I am glad you will not go back to Asia,' Homaira said. 'It has nothing but bad memories for me. For us.' Then she asked, ingenuously, 'If you had gone back, would you have taken me?'

'Not unless you wanted to come.'

Her mouth puckered, most attractively. 'I would wish to be where you are, James. Always.'

He ruffled her midnight hair.

Mbote said nothing when he was told of the interview. But he was clearly as tempted as his friend.

Mbote understood how deeply James had been affected by the events of 1919-20. Even as they walked and talked and fished he could see the evidence of the psychological damage James had suffered. It was, he felt, less the break-up of his marriage, less perhaps even the loss of his daughter, about whom he had always been ambivalent, than the failure of his expedition, the first complete failure he had ever had to endure. There had been disasters, even catastrophes, enough in the past, but always James Martingell had risen above them, like a phoenix, to move on to new triumphs. Now those days were done. James was sixty-five. There was nothing left save an old age which he could only share.

Now, by refusing Azam's latest proposal, he was accepting that old age sooner than was really necessary. And with every day he was becoming more aware of that.

'What *are* you going to do?' Mbote asked, a fortnight after Azam's visit.

James stared into the fireplace, then suddenly snapped his fingers. 'Adventure,' he said. 'One last time, old friend.' He opened his desk drawer, sifted through the papers and cards, and found the address Azam had given him in London. 'Just let's hope it's still on.'

'My dear friend,' Azam said. 'My dear old friend. I knew you would come round.'

'Cut the smarm, Azam,' James said. 'The job is still open?'

'Oh, yes. More than ever. Have you been keeping your eye on events in China?'

'When they happen to be reported.'

'Well, it would seem that Chiang Kai-shek has determined to eliminate Communism in his country. As you may know, the Communists are principally concentrated in the south. Now he has launched a series of attacks on their communes, building fortifications to hem them in, and then systematically destroying them. As a result they are starting to flee, and it is rumoured that a large body of them are moving west. Thus you will see that Shensi could be in some danger, if the fighting spreads that far. Ma Chung-ying must be in a position to defend himself.'

'I am ready to leave tomorrow,' James said. 'Are the goods ready for shipment?'

'There is a ship in Hamburg already loaded and ready to sail, for Chah Bahar, as before. Once she is there, you will take command of the goods. My people will be there to help you.'

'And yourself, no doubt?'

'If it is possible. But it will all be arranged. You will have guides and adequate protection.'

'How do I get to Chah Bahar?'

'That is up to you. You may go with the ship, if you choose. Or you may go across country. That will get you there more quickly. However, you will have to go to Hamburg in the first instance: von Beinhardt wishes to meet you.'

'That should be fun. When is the first instance?'

'You say you can leave tomorrow. I told you, it is a most urgent matter. I assume you will be taking Mbote?'

'Of course. And maybe one or two others.'

Azam shrugged. 'That is up to you. A personal bodyguard?'

'Don't you think, after the last time, I may need one?'

'Ah, but this time you have me on your side, irrevocably.

'You have no idea how much that reassures me. There remains payment.'

'As we have agreed, twenty-five thousand now, and twenty-five thousand when the delivery has been completed.'

'That was not an agreement, Azam. That was an offer you made to me, which I declined.'

Azam's eyes narrowed. 'What is it you wish?'

'A hundred thousand, fifty now and fifty on completion of the delivery.'

'You think you are worth that much? When I know you are destitute?'

'I am worth that much,' James said. 'Because you need the guns, and only I can get them to you.'

Azam stroked his beard. 'One day your arrogance will get you into serious trouble, James.'

'I think it may already have done so, on one or two occasions,' James said. 'But I am still here. And still in demand.'

Azam grinned. 'As you say. Fifty now,

and fifty on delivery. You will leave for Germany tomorrow?'

'No, the day after. That will give you time to make the deposit in my bank and for me to make certain arrangements.'

'You are a suspicious fellow, James. However ...' He stood up and held out his hand. 'I will see you in Chah Bahar.'

'Just like old times,' James commented.

Obviously the business had to be kept as secret as possible, but he had to have a back-up, apart from Mbote. He telephoned the number Richard had given him. 'James!' Richard appeared genuinely pleased to hear from him.

'Has Azam been in touch?'

'No. Should he have?'

'I've changed my mind about the job. Are you still interested?'

'Of course. As I told you, I am the House of Beinhardt's representative.'

'Yes,' James said drily. 'When can you be ready?'

'I'll need a day or two.'

'Right. I'm off tomorrow to check things out with your father-in-law. Will you be there?'

'Do you wish me to be?'

'No,' James said. 'I am not going with the shipment, but overland. You do the same. I'll meet you in al-Jagdub in one month's time. That's our real kick-off point.'

There remained Homaira. 'This is country I know well,' she argued. 'You think I cannot travel as well as a man, and shoot as well as one too, if we have to?'

'It is going to be dangerous,' he pointed out. 'And I thought you were against the idea.'

'What is danger? I am used to danger. And who is going to keep you warm on those cold mountain nights?'

She had a point there. But he was more interested in the thought that he would have, always at his side, or at his back, a built-in bodyguard, even closer than either Mbote or Richard. 'You'd better pack,' he told her.

They were at dinner when Anne rang. It was the first time in several years he had heard her voice, and it was agitated. 'Listen,' she said. 'I've just heard. Winston is out.'

'Already?'

'He's escaped.'

'Where did you learn this?'

'Inspector Lucas called. You remember him? He felt I should know. Just in case he's bearing a grudge.'

'I imagine he is. But he doesn't know where you live.'

'Don't you think he can find out?'

'Hm. You'd better ask for police protection till you see how his mind is working.'

'Really, James. What good is police protection going to do me? I want to move in with you.'

'Eh?'

'Just until, as you say, we find out how his mind is working. I won't be any trouble. Your girlfriend need not be upset.'

'It's not quite as simple as that,' James said. 'I am not going to be here.'

There was a brief silence. Anne was thinking things out. 'James! You're back in business.'

'As a matter of fact, I am,' he said. 'For a last time.'

'You said that the last time.'

'Yes, I did. But this is definitely it. So you'll see I cannot help you. Sit tight, ask for police protection, and we'll sort things out when I come back.'

'You said that the last time, too.'

'This time I mean it.' He hung up. No matter what might have happened, he could not believe Winston was so much of a thug as to wish to harm his own mother.

But just in case Anne had any idea of stopping him leaving, he and Mbote and

Homaira left that night, taking the train to Harwich, the night ferry to Rotterdam, and hiring a car the next morning to drive to Hamburg. Claus von Beinhardt was in his office when they got there. He was, as always, flawlessly dressed and groomed. As he shook hands, he said, 'I received the message from Richard. We are ready to sail as soon as you have inspected the goods.'

They went on board. James was a little taken aback by the steamer, which was most certainly of the tramp variety, but her engines looked sound enough, and he could not fault the merchandise in her holds. 'As good as when you worked with the House, eh?' Beinhardt suggested.

'Oh, absolutely. And there is no problem with a licence?'

Beinhardt tapped his nose. 'In today's Germany, everything is possible. I am a supporter of the local Nazi Party. You have heard of this?'

'Vaguely. But it is not a serious political force, surely?'

'It will be,' Beinhardt assured him. 'And it is already, in certain parts of the country. As here in Hamburg. So I say to you, there is no problem with licences. Now, you are sailing with us?'

'I shall be in Chah Bahar to greet you,' James said.

'That is a pity. I had hoped to make your acquaintance more, shall we say, intimately, on the voyage.'

It was James' turn to raise his eyebrows. 'You are sailing with the goods?'

'Of course. This is our first big sale, or first big delivery. This either makes the House of Beinhardt prosperous again, or it finishes us for ever. I, we, bear a heavy load of responsibility. Now come, my wife would like to meet you, again. But ...' He glanced at Mbote, who was standing some distance away. 'We would like you to come alone, if you don't mind. Clementine does not care for black people. Well, it is official Party policy, you understand.'

Clementine von Beinhardt was now in her mid-forties. She had been plump when last James had met her, and she had remained plump. She had none of the beauty of her sister Cecile, but she was the heiress to the Beinhardt fortune. Or what had been the Beinhardt fortune, before the catastrophe of the Great War. When he remembered the vast country mansion he had visited outside Cologne, the rolling parkland, the white-gloved servants, the crystal chandeliers, the lavish dinner parties at which twenty or more uniformed and bejewelled guests had sat beneath the benign gaze of old Adolf von Beinhardt ... now he was entertained to an intimate supper in a rather small house close to the Hamburg waterfront. A suitable comedown for a woman like Clementine von Beinhardt, James thought. Not that Mbote had taken offence at being excluded. 'They are not people I ever did like,' he pointed out.

'James Martingell,' Clementine said. 'Sir James Martingell. But for the grey hair, I swear you have not changed at all in the past seven years. How do you keep your figure?'

'I worry,' James told her, and she giggled as girlishly as ever he remembered.

'And now you and Claus are off on another great adventure, to restore the fortunes of the House,' Clementine said. 'With Richard. Dear Richard. He is such a lovely man. Do you not think so? Sophie has done well. You remember Sophie, James?' Her husband was not able to get a word in edgeways, but he seemed content enough.

'I remember Sophie very well,' James said. 'Although I have not met her since her marriage.'

'Oh, she is very happy. She even enjoys living in England.' She peered at him. 'You will bring Richard safely home to her?'

They have not forgotten, he thought. Or forgiven. But then, neither have I. They will seek to use me to obtain what they wish, and then discard me. But two can play at that game. It was a game he had played once before, with the House of Beinhardt—and he had won. The question he had to determine was: if it came to the crunch, which side would Richard support?

'What we have done,' said Inspector Lucas, 'is put an extra man on the beat along this street, milady.'

'And you really think one unarmed policeman is going to keep out my son, should he wish to come in?' Anne enquired.

'It will be a deterrent, milady. And should he turn up ...'

'You'll put him back in prison, where he belongs, for the rest of his life.'

'Well, yes, milady,' Lucas said, surprised. 'That is what we shall do, certainly.'

Anne saw him muttering to his driver as he got into his car. Am I an unnatural mother? she wondered. I never wanted to be a mother at all, save for that child of James'. If she could not have that, then she wanted nothing. Save to live as she chose, as she had done for the past four years, with the companion she would have chosen, too. They had been together so long; and now she was in her fifties, Claudette was in her thirties. They were intimates in the most total of senses, even if their roles had slightly changed, from mistress and maid to partners in erotica. It was Claudette who nowadays made the running, picking up young men and bringing them home for her mistress's amusement—and her own, to be sure; sometimes they were three in the bed.

Total hedonism. What she had always wanted, with not a care in the world ... until that terrifying telephone call last week. And once again James had swanned off into the sunset, or in this case the sunrise, she supposed, and left her holding the baby. A very big baby.

'You think 'e will come 'ere?' Claudette asked.

'I hope he has more sense. But just in case ...' She went up to her bedroom, opened the bottom drawer of her bureau, and took out the box in which she kept the revolver James had given her so many years ago. It was loaded, but as she had paid very little attention to it over the years it was beginning to rust.

She removed the bullets, and carefully oiled it, watched with wide eyes by Claudette. 'You will shoot at your own son?'

'If I have to. And if this goddamn thing will fire. We need adequate protection,

Claudie. We need a live-in man for the next month or so.'

'Oooh, la-la,' Claudette commented. 'But it 'as to be someone 'o will protect us, yes? Not 'o will escape out of zee window when Mr Winston is coming in through zee door.'

'Yes,' Anne said thoughtfully. Claudette had a point; most of their male friends were of the lounge-lizard variety. She snapped her fingers. 'Richard Elligan!'

''Im? 'E walked out on you.'

'He had a lot on his mind at the time.'

''E is probably married and a father ten times.'

'Somehow I doubt that. Anyway, it's worth a try.'

She got his telephone number from directory enquiries, waited with some excitement as she was put through. Richard would be in his late thirties now, the same age as James had been when they had finally got together. And he was just as exciting a man. Equally, he was a far more gallant man. He was a gentleman, where James had never been quite that. He would certainly come to the aid of a damsel in distress, especially when he had once shared a magic moment with that damsel. 'I am sorry, madam,' said the voice on the end of the phone, a woman's

363

voice. 'Mr Elligan is not at home.'

'It is most important that I speak with him,' Anne said. 'Would this be Mrs Elligan I am speaking to?'

'No, madam. This is the housekeeper.'

Anne gave a brief sigh of relief. 'Well, when he comes in, will you ask him to telephone Lady Martingell. I will give you my number.'

'I am sorry, Lady Martingell, but Mr Elligan is actually out of the country.'

'Out of the country. For how long?'

'I cannot say, madam.'

'Well, where has he gone?'

'I understand Mr Elligan was planning to visit Persia, madam.'

Persia! And James was back in business! Obviously selling to the Afghans, again, and no matter how badly the last time had turned out. Oh, the fool. But Richard was clearly going to join him; the old enemies had become partners!

'Thank you,' she said, and hung up.

'What is 'appening?' Claudette enquired.

Anne told her, while she paced up and down the room. But she had nowhere to turn, now. Unless she also left the country. And thanks to James' parsimony, she lacked the funds to do that.

'What are we to do?' Claudette asked.

'Go out and find a man,' Anne said. 'And make him a good one.'

Claudette always enjoyed dressing up and going down to the pub, where she would sit demurely in a corner of the lounge bar sipping a glass of white wine, certain that if there were any unattached men about one of them would try to pick her up. Even those in the public bar could see her through the hatch, and as she had surmised it wasn't long before one of these found himself on the right side of the partition. 'Hello,' he said. 'Haven't I seen you before?'

Which was not quite as hackneyed as it sounded; if he was a regular he could well have seen her before. 'Per'aps,' Claudette said.

He wasn't very big, and he didn't look very macho, but he was well dressed and reasonably sober. 'You're foreign,' he said.

'Do you not like foreigners?'

He stood in front of her. 'I like foreigners more than anything. Visiting, are you?'

'I live 'ere.'

'Is that a fact. Not married, are you?' He was studying her hands, but she was wearing gloves.

'I live with my mistress,' Claudette said. 'Will you buy me another drink?'

'Surely.'

'And then,' Claudette suggested, 'you

can walk me 'ome.'

Clearly he could not believe his luck, told her his name was Clive, and that he was a bank clerk, held her hand while they finished their drinks, and then escorted her out into the night with a most proprietory air. They rounded the corner from the pub ... 'Going some place?' asked Winston Pennyfeather.

Claudette goggled at him, while her stomach seemed to fill with lead. But even after seven years, and wearing shabby second-hand and ill-fitting clothing, she recognised him instantly. 'What's this?' Clive asked, somewhat anxiously. 'Who're you?'

'I'm Claudette's husband,' Winston said.

'You said you weren't married,' Clive protested.

'I am not married,' Claudette said. ''E is lying. 'E is also a murderer.'

'A what?' Clive's voice rose an octave, and he released her hand.

'As she said,' Winston agreed. 'You'd better be off before I add you to the list.'

Clive licked his lips, glanced at Claudette, then turned and almost ran down the street. 'Fetch a policeman,' Claudette shouted after him, and had her throat gripped.

'Now you listen to me, you pretty little

French tart,' Winston said. 'One more squeak out of you and they'll find you in the gutter.' Claudette panted, but she had more sense than to attempt to fight him; she remembered that he could be very violent. 'So now I'd like you to take me home. It's time I saw my darling mother again, don't you think?'

'And if I refuse?'

'As I said, they'll find you in the gutter, with your knickers round your throat, pulled tight.'

Claudette licked her lips. 'Will you let me go?'

'No. We'll hold hands, like honeymooners should.'

Claudette submitted and they walked up the street, while she tried to think. People. That was the first requirement. 'It is down 'ere,' she said, seeking to turn back into the street which led to the pub.

'You are a liar,' he told her. 'I know where it is. I just need you to get me inside.'

Claudette found she was panting again, as they turned through a succession of side streets and back alleys. But she was running out of options. 'Listen,' she said. 'She 'as a gun. 'Er ladyship. She will shoot you.'

'Her own son? Who she so shamefully betrayed, all those years ago?'

'She is a desperate woman,' Claudette said.

'I'll charm her,' Winston said.

They had reached the house before Claudette could think of anything else to try. She was very fond of Anne, but she was fonder of herself, and it seemed to her that survival was the key here. If she didn't antagonise him, Winston had no reason to harm *her*. 'Ring the bell,' Winston commanded.

'I 'ave a key,' Claudette said.

'Of course. That is much easier. Where will my mother be?'

'I should think upstairs, in 'er bedroom.'

'Well remember, if you attempt to take her side I am going to kill you.'

'Oooh, la-la,' Claudette said. She unlocked the door, entered before him, toying with the idea of attempting to slam it on him, and deciding against taking the risk.

'Is that you, Claudette?' Anne called down the stairs.

'It is me, madame,' Claudette said.

'And do we have company?'

Claudette took a deep breath as Winston nodded. 'I 'ave a gentleman with me, madame, who would very much like to meet you.'

'Then tell him to come up, and you bring a bottle of wine.'

'Yes, madame.'

Claudette glanced at Winston, who nodded again. She went towards the kitchen, he went to the foot of the stairs. Claudette went into the kitchen, opened the larder, and took out a bottle of red wine. This she uncorked, listening to the stairs creak as Winston climbed them. She arranged three glasses on a tray, added the bottle, and followed him. And heard Anne give a startled exclamation. 'You? How the hell did you get in here?'

'I persuaded Claudette to let me in, Mother.'

Claudette reached the landing, and looked into Anne's bedroom. Anne had backed against the bureau where she kept the revolver; but Winston was too close for her to risk opening the drawer. He had to be distracted. By her? She could wind up an accessory to murder. She placed the tray on the table just inside the door. 'You let him in?' Anne demanded. 'You little bitch!'

''E made me,' Claudette said.

'I can't imagine why you are all so agitated,' Winston said. 'Pour the wine, Claudette.' He smiled at her. 'She is a pretty little thing. And do you know how long it is since I have had a woman?'

'You came here for that?' Anne was regaining her composure. 'Well, then, have it, and get out.' Claudette gulped, and spilled some of the wine as she poured.

'What a welcome,' Winston said. But he drank some wine. 'The person I want is my illustrious stepfather. Because it was he who really killed my father, isn't it?'

Anne licked her lips and looked at Claudette. This was an easy way out. 'How did you find out?' she asked.

Winston grinned. 'I reasoned it. You wouldn't have shot Father, would you, Mother dear?'

'I ... of course I would not,' Anne said.

'Well, then, tell me where I can find Martingell. I found out where he lives, in Cheltenham, but the house is boarded up.'

'He is out of the country.'

'Oh, yes? Where?'

'By now I would say he is in Persia, or Afghanistan.'

Winston's eyes narrowed. 'He is running guns again?'

'Yes,' Anne said.

'At his age? I thought he had been put out of business after the last time. We get news in prison, you know.'

'It is some deal he has done with Sheikh Azam,' Anne said.

'I see,' Winston said.

'So you will have to wait for him to come back. If he ever does.'

'I think you are lying.'

Anne's head jerked. 'I am telling the truth.'

'I do not believe you have ever told the truth once in your life, Mother,' Winston said.

'You bastard,' Anne said.

Winston grinned. 'Now, you see, you are lying again. You know that I am not a bastard.' He moved forward, drawing a long-bladed knife from inside his coat, and in the same instant seizing Anne by the throat. 'I don't know the truth of what happened in that boat off the Somali coast,' he said. 'I believe Martingell actually shot Father. But you went along with him, didn't you?'

Anne gurgled and tried to hit him, but subsided as he held the knife to her face. 'You went along with that bastard,' he said. 'And you handed over to him Father's factory and Father's money, and you supported him in everything he wanted to do. So you are just as guilty as him.'

The fingers slightly relaxed, and Anne could breathe. Her knees gave way and she sat on the bed. 'Do you have any idea how your father treated me?' she muttered.

'Not badly enough, I reckon.'

Anne raised her head. 'What are you going to do to me?'

'Well,' Winston said. 'I think I will have to kill you, Mother dear. After all, if I do

371

not, the moment I leave this house you will be on the phone to the police, won't you? The only thing I have to consider is how to do it. I did think of strangling you, to feel your life ebbing away under my fingers. But then I thought, wouldn't it be better to stab you, and watch your blood gathering on the floor?'

'You're mad,' Anne gasped. 'Stark, raving mad! Claudette!'

Claudette had already realised she would have to do something; she could not just stand there and watch her mistress murdered before her eyes, especially as Winston would certainly kill her afterwards, if only to stop *her* calling the police. Thus she upended the bottle, spilling red wine everywhere, and advanced on Winston's back. But Anne's shout alerted him, and he turned towards the maid, knife thrust forward. Claudette uttered a shriek and jumped backwards, cannoning into a chair and sitting down heavily, eyes wide in horror as she saw the knife coming at her.

Anne thrust herself upwards, and hurled herself at the bureau. Now Winston again checked, and turned back to face his mother. But Anne had reached the bureau and wrenched the drawer open, so hard it came right out and her underclothes spilled on to the floor. But she had had time to close her hand on the revolver, and as Winston reached for her, lips drawn back in a snarl, she squeezed the trigger. And again and again and again.

'This is surely the most civilised way to travel,' Mbote remarked, gazing out of the window of the Orient Express as the Balkan countryside unfolded. It was early evening, and they both wore black tie, as did all the other men in the dining car, while the women were in long dresses, and at the far end of the car a piano tinkled; the movement was so smooth the champagne in their glasses hardly trembled. 'Can there ever be a better?'

'Yes,' James said. He too was feeling expansively content. The last great adventure, and then he could just sit back and watch the years slipping by. He would have wished one or two things could have been different. He would have wished he had not lost Lanne, and he could wish that perhaps he and Anne could be reconciled—after all, as they both grew older she would surely become a little less desperate for sexual variety. But that was something that could be attended to on his return, when he would again be well off, if not as well off as he had once been. For the time being, he could enjoy himself. 'Airship,' he said. 'I believe in another few years we will travel everywhere by dirigible. Think of the comfort, and the quiet ... and of course the greater speed.'

'Just so long as they serve meals like this,' Mbote said.

But the luxury ended in Istanbul the following morning, after which they had to cross the Bosphorus and take the ordinary train winding its way across the Turkish highland, through Eskisehir and down to Konya, the old Iconium, where they spent the night. Iconium had been the capital of the Seljuk sultanate eight hundred years earlier, and remained a place of veiled women and religious processions, no matter how hard Kemel Atatürk might be trying to drag his people into the twentieth century. From Konya they wound their way down to the coast at Adana before heading north again, into real mountains now, with peaks towering more than five thousand feet to either side. The railway wound its way through places like Malatya, the ancient Melitene, and thence through the Armenian mountains to Tatvan on Lake Van.

They crossed the lake by ferry to Van itself, a matter of sixty miles, over a surprisingly choppy sea as a wind had sprung up, but in Van they were able to rejoin the train, wrapped up in topcoats now, as they were some ten thousand feet above sea level. This was a long and painful journey, as the train had to stop every few miles to catch its breath, as it were, before it peaked and they began to descent to Tabriz. If the journey was slow, it was also intensely interesting. Quite apart from the scenery, which in places was spectacular, their travelling companions varied from businessmen and government officials, uncomfortable in the Western-style lounge suits they were required to wear, again by order of Kemel, as opposed to the far more comfortable kaftans of their ancestors, through groups of somewhat ragged soldiers, armed with weapons which both James and Mbote could see at a glance needed modernising, to other groups of armed men, not in uniform, but with very modern rifles indeed, to masses of farmers, with their wives and children, their dogs and cats and goats, their bicycles, and their weapons as well. For their part, the Turks and the Armenians and the Persians all regarded the two somewhat elderly Westerners, one black and the other white, with equal interest. But as they were as well armed as anyone on the train, no one interfered with them.

From Tabriz the railway wound south, to Maragegh and then again east, through Minaneh to Zanjan, and then at last Tehran. Here James discovered that things had improved as regards amenity since the overthrow of the boy sultan by the Cossack colonel Pahlevi, but equally there was more officialdom and much inspecting of papers before they were allowed to proceed; James could only hope that Azam would have his usual success in bribing the officials in Chah Bahar. Which they reached a week later. They did very well as far as the railway went, past Qom and Yazd, but the line ended at Kerman, four hundred and fifty miles short of their destination. There was a road, and they managed to travel by bus, uncomfortably, most of the way, making very slow progress, as they climbed up and down steep hills and crossed the bottom end of the Kerman Desert, and cheek by jowl with large numbers of Persians, even more askance at the presence of these two strangers than had been the people on the train. But at last, two months after leaving Folkestone, they arrived at Chah Bahar.

Azam was waiting for them, but then they all had to wait for the arrival of the Beinhardt ship. 'Now you are on the other side, eh?' Azam asked. 'It is the more difficult. But you will be comfortable.' He eyed Homaira, who merely gave him a dirty look.

The ship duly arrived, and the cargo was

unloaded. As usual, the Persian officials paid no attention to what was happening on the beach. James had used his spare time to try to discover what had happened to the *Europa* and her people, but could get nothing more than that they had put to sea, without warning, and had not been seen again. 'I am very sad about this,' Azam said. 'I cannot imagine what can have happened.'

Neither can I, James thought; unless their murder had been planned from the start.

'Sir James!' Claus von Beinhardt embraced him. 'It is good to be here. What a voyage. There were times I thought it would never end. Are you satisfied, Azam?'

Azam inspected the various cases. 'It all seems in order, Count. Here is the third payment.'

Beinhardt folded the cheque into his pocket. 'Then I will wish you godspeed.'

James raised his eyebrows. 'You are not coming with us to deliver the goods?'

'What, me go up into those mountains? I have no head for heights, Sir James. That is why you are along. To oversee the delivery.' He grinned. 'Do not worry, my friend. There is no money involved this time. Azam will forward the final payment to our bank in Hong Kong. Is that not correct, Sheikh?'

'There is one hell of a lot going on that I do not understand,' James said, as he stood beside Azam and watched the steamer fade into the heat of the Indian Ocean.

'Such as?'

'My involvement.'

'It is very simple, as Count von Beinhardt explained. You are in charge of the final delivery of the goods.'

'Cannot you do that, personally?'

'Sadly, it would be too great a risk. I have made my peace with the Amir, but on condition I never engage in gun-running or any political activity again in my life. If he were to find out about this shipment, it would go hard with me.'

'And you do not suppose he'll be unhappy to learn that I'm back in business?'

'He knows nothing about you. Oh, there are rumours, legends if you like, but then, you have always attracted legend, have you not, James? All that is *known* is that you delivered a shipment of guns to Amaruddin Khan, assuming that they were for the Afghan government, that when you discovered they were for use against your own soldiers, you attempted to back out of the deal, and that Amaruddin Khan, and I, sadly, then seized the weapons. That they were later used against the legitimate

378

government is not your fault. As for you, you disappeared. Many people suppose you dead. And of those sufficiently up to date with news from England to know that you survived, why, that was five years ago, and most of them are dead now too.'

'And just how do I get to Shensi?'

'I will supply you with a guide. An absolutely trustworthy man.'

'As trustworthy as yourself, no doubt,' James remarked.

'Of course.' Azam grinned.

'The whole project stinks. I have a mind to say, forget it.'

'You have accepted a large retainer.'

'And of course, at the moment, I am in your power.'

Azam bowed. 'I am sure you will go through with our deal, James, because I know you to be an honest man. Besides, I think you will like Shensi. Or parts of it, certainly.'

'I'm not going sightseeing.'

'Of course not. You are delivering certain goods to a great friend of mine. However, James, I have a piece of information which I hope may be of use in enabling you to stick to our agreement. Ma Chung-ying, as with so many Chinese warlords, not excluding Chiang Kai-shek himself, employs Russian military advisers. In Ma's case, he has obtained the services of one of the most experienced of all military attachés, a man with vast experience of what it is like to war in central Asia.' James' head jerked.

'Oh, indeed, James. Your old friend Galitsin is at the other end of your journey. There is a rumour that he has his wife with him.'

Chapter 11

The Rescue

'I should inform you,' Azam said, 'that Colonel Galitsin does not know that you are in charge of the guns. All he or Ma Chung-ying are aware of is that the guns will be delivered, and that they are coming from the House of Beinhardt. As far as they are aware there is no British involvement whatsoever. No doubt he will be surprised to see you. How you handle your future relationship with him is up to you. But I should tread carefully.'

'How long have you known this?' James asked.

'For some time.'

'But you did not see fit to tell me.'

'To have told you, in England, might have—how shall I put it?—clouded the issue. Now you are here, the guns are here, and your daughter is there. I do not think you will back out now.'

'I told you one day that I was going to strangle you, Azam,' James said. 'You constantly bring that day closer.'

Azam smiled, and glanced at the armed tribesmen with which they were surrounded. 'Then I must take care not to place my neck within the reach of your hands, eh?'

'What are you going to do?' Mbote asked. It was not the first time during their long acquaintance he had felt James was faced with a difficult situation.

'Deliver the goods,' James said. 'And collect our money.'

'And Lanne?'

'We'll play that by ear. But if she wants out, then we shall bring her out.'

'Regardless of what Galitsin might wish?'

James grinned. 'I owe him my life, twice, I think. But I reckon he's been paid in full over the past few years. If Lanne wants out, she comes out. However,' he added. 'I do not think it would be a good idea to tell Elligan the situation, right now. Just in case she doesn't want out.'

As agreed, Richard was waiting for them at Jagdub, but James was totally astonished at the sight of the young woman who stood at Richard's side. 'You have met Sophie,' Richard said.

'Are you out of your mind?' James enquired.

'Did not your wife accompany you on all of your expeditions, Sir James?' Sophie asked, demurely.

'Have you any idea where we are going?' James demanded. 'How long it will take? How difficult, and indeed dangerous, it is going to be?' And that Lanne could be at the end of it? he wondered to himself.

'I am sure we will manage, Sir James,' Sophie said.

'Of course we will manage,' Homaira declared. 'I will look after the child.' Richard waggled his eyebrows.

'You have some explaining to do,' James said, when he got his friend alone. 'Do her parents know she's here?'

'Her parents think she is at our home in England. We'll be back before they find out. Now where do we go, first?'

'Meshed,' Azam told them.

The city lay another five hundred miles to the north, and it took them five weeks to get there, as the road wound up into mountains five thousand feet and more above sea level, where even the camels were uncomfortable, the more so as their encampments were surrounded at night by the wailing of wolves, and more than once they sighted bears in some numbers. It was exhausting work, and this time it was James and Mbote who were the oldest in the party, and the most easily tired. But Homaira was a tower of strength, looking after their domestic affairs with great energy, and backed up with willing hands by Sophie, anxious to prove to the great Martingell that she was as good as her late aunt. 'Meshed,' she said. 'It is a place I have always wanted to visit.'

Meshed's fame rested on the fact that it was the site of the tomb of the most famous of the Abbasid caliphs, Harun al-Rashid, as well as that of his son-in-law, 'Ali al-Rida, who had been the imam, or leader of the Shiah Muslims. His shrine was an edifice of remarkable beauty, the pale golds and blues of the inscribed arch being striking. 'Amazing,' Richard commented. 'When you think that this city was virtually razed by the Mongols.'

'It has a history of being sacked and then restored,' Azam explained. 'The first restoration was actually by a Mongol, Shah Rukh, Timurlane's son. Then it was sacked again by the Uzbeks a hundred years later, and restored again by Shah Abbas the Great. It was Abbas who made it a place of pilgrimage. And now, my friends, here I must leave you. This man will be your guide to Shensi.' The Afghan was tall and powerfully built, in his early forties, James estimated. He had a hooked nose, and his beard was streaked with grey. He wore a turban and a belted kaftan, and from the belt was suspended both a tulwar and a knife half as long, while on his shoulder was slung a Lee Enfield .303 rifle, as currently used by the British army. 'His name is Zahir,' Azam said. 'He speaks English. I have taught him this myself.'

'And what else have you taught him?' James asked.

Azam grinned. 'To shoot. He is the best marksman I have ever known.' James glanced at Richard, who shrugged. 'He is utterly faithful to me,' Azam said. 'And because I have told him this, he is now utterly faithful to you. He will take you to Shensi, and he will bring you back out again.'

'All by himself?'

'He has done this before.'

'Now tell me about my final payment.'

'When the guns have been delivered, Zahir will bring you to me, and I will pay you myself. You have my most solemn word.'

'Which I am obliged to accept. Well ...' James held out his hand, and Zahir squeezed the offered fingers; he had a powerful grip. 'We place ourselves in your care, Zahir.'

Zahir bowed. 'It will be my pleasure to guide you safely, my lord.'

'I do not trust that man,' Homaira said, as she and James slept in a bed—for the last time for several months, he supposed.

'Actually, neither do I, sweetheart,' James said. 'But beggars cannot be choosers. Have you ever seen him before?'

'He came to the palace of my lord Amaruddin, from time to time,' Homaira said. 'I never spoke with him. But there was a rumour that he was the assassin who killed the Amir, Habibullah Khan.'

James rose on his elbow. 'You are serious?'

What a silly question. Homaira was always serious.

'It is what I have heard,' she said.

'What do you reckon?' James asked Richard the next morning. 'You were there.'

'I never saw the assassin. No one did, to my knowledge.'

'Except the man who employed him, perhaps. The man who taught him to shoot. "The best marksmen I ever saw," Azam said.'

'What do you mean to do?'

385

'Remember. And watch him like a hawk.'

'Snap,' Richard said.

They left at dawn the next day, the caravan filing out from the gate of the city, and taking the road to the east. Which soon became a track. But this was the easiest part of their journey. They made south-east first of all, to cross the Afghan border just south of where it abutted Russian territory. 'But it is very uncertain,' Zahir told James and Richard. 'Lines on a map, eh? There will be no difficulty.'

This journey was roughly a hundred miles, and took them five days. The route lay mostly across high ground, although at the end it descended sharply to the valley of the Tezdhen, south of the border town of Jennatabad. The caravan consisted of a hundred camels, but no wagons, as the country they would have to cross later on was too rugged for wheeled transport. Even so it stretched for a good quarter of a mile, but as each camel had a rider, and the whole was overseen by Richard and Zahir, also mounted, there was little risk of any interference, even from the groups of fierce-looking mountain men who occasionally gathered by the roadside to stare at them.

When they camped for the night the

camels were hobbled in a vast laager, and two men were on watch all the time—but that was more to keep off wolves than human marauders. 'One feels that we're on the roof of the world,' Richard commented, pulling his cloak tighter around his shoulders as the cold wind whistled through the camp. 'But by God the air is clean.'

'It'll get cleaner, for a while,' James promised him. 'Remember the last time we passed this way?'

'Yes,' Richard said. 'Do you suppose Lanne is anywhere about?'

'I think Lanne is best not thought about, until this is over,' James said. But he could not resist asking, 'Does Sophie know of her?'

'Actually, yes.'

James grinned. 'Back to secrets. Do you love her very much?'

'I think I love her more with every day,' Richard confessed.

James pulled his nose.

They crossed the river and through the Zulfiqar Pass. Now they were in Russian-claimed territory, but as Zahir had said, and as Richard and James remembered from the last time they had been in this part of the world, there was little evidence that anyone possessed any real ownership of this vast bleak land. They made their way across the vast Vozvyshennost Karabil, miles and miles of empty stony desert, keeping the Afghan border always fairly close on their right as a possible refuge, but heading always just north of east, aiming to cross the great Amudar'ya, famous in history as the River Oxus, a safe distance south of the town of Kerki.

Day after day they plodded on their way; the river was three hundred miles distant. But Zahir knew the country, and the best routes, and where water was to be found. Even so it was utterly exhausting, as the land was by no means as flat as it appeared on the map, and their route took them through a succession of gullies and over a succession of low hills, meaning that they were always going up or coming down. James began to feel his sixty-five years catching up with him. His last safari, he thought. Supposing he survived it. But he had survived so much. He was not going to let a bit of cold and altitude and hard work do him down.

It was on the twentieth day of their month-long trek across the desert that Zahir brought the caravan to a halt with a raised hand, and levelled his binoculars. James and Richard did likewise, to study the dust cloud on the horizon. 'Horsemen,' Zahir commented.

'Brigands?'

Zahir grinned. 'In this part of the world, Sir James, all men are brigands. But those are Russian soldiers.'

James studied the approaching cavalry. 'How many?'

Zahir also studied them. 'Perhaps fifty. They will wish to see our goods.'

'And that cannot be,' James said, remembering a similar encounter a long time ago, with Italian lancers in Somaliland. 'Pitch camp. Quickly.'

Zahir frowned. 'You will resist them?'

'I will destroy them,' James said. 'It is necessary. Pitch camp. Richard, unlimber three of the machine-guns and set them up.'

'Yes, *sir*,' Richard said.

'There,' James said, pointing to a sizeable hillock a hundred yards to their left.

The camels were hobbled, as well as the horses. Of their drivers, half were left to watch them, the others were armed with rifles and placed along the low ridge. James did not suppose they would be any great use in the coming skirmish, but they would add firepower. The two women were placed with the camels and the guards, although both equipped themselves with rifles and seemed prepared to defend themselves to the last.

The machine-guns were set up and

manned by Richard, Mbote and James himself; Zahir took up his position close by the guns, and they studied the horsemen, who were quite close, but who now slowed to a walk as they saw the preparations in front of them. But they could not see the machine-guns, nor could they tell how many men were opposed to them. They approached to within two hundred yards before they halted, and one of their officers walked his horse forward. He wore a khaki greatcoat, from the belt of which was suspended both sword and revolver. His hat was a curious conical shape, rather like pictures James had seen of Scythian warriors of antiquity. But then, these Russians were direct descendants of those Scythians.

The officer shouted at them. James looked at Zahir. 'He wishes to know our business,' Zahir said.

'Tell him we are a caravan for Kerki,' James said.

Zahir translated, also shouting. The officer replied. 'He says he wishes to inspect our merchandise. You intend to fight these people?'

'I have said, we need to destroy them.'

'Well, then ...' Zahir sighted his rifle, and squeezed the trigger. Azam had not exaggerated when he claimed his protégé was an excellent shot. The Russian officer threw up his hands and tumbled from the saddle.

'Open fire!' James shouted. The machine-guns crackled, the rifles exploded, the drivers getting into the act with great gusto. As James had anticipated, they did not do a great deal of damage, but they certainly gave the impression of a considerable force. The machine-guns tore into the surprised Russian squadron, which had not deployed in any way and was totally vulnerable. At least half of them fell in the first volley, and the others, having fired a few shots, broke up and fled.

'Bring them down,' James commanded. Again the machine-guns scoured the landscape. The Russians had over-confidently come too close before opening negotiations, and there was no escape. Only one man emerged from the hail of bullets, kicking his horse to gallop back to the east. 'We must have him,' James said. Zahir grinned, and sighted. A moment later the Russian tumbled from his saddle. 'There can be no survivors,' James said.

The Afghans grinned, and went forward with the knives. Homaira clapped her hands. Richard scratched his head. 'I always knew you were a ruthless man, Sir James,' he said, 'but this was a massacre. I've been on the receiving end of one of those.'

'And it's not pleasant,' James agreed. 'So have I. Let's move out.'

'You mean you're not even going to bury them?'

'Our business is to reach China,' James reminded him.

Zahir was more practical. 'It will be dangerous for us to come back this way,' he said.

'But you know another?'

'I will take you back into Afghanistan. Without the guns, you will just be travellers, eh?'

And I will be in your power, James thought. But that was a bridge he would have to cross when he came to it.

Now they travelled as fast as they could; James wanted to be across the Oxus before any serious pursuit was mounted. Now too there was no more chaff around the campfires; they all stared at their leader as if he were from another world. Sophie particularly was affected. 'Do they hate me?' James asked Homaira.

'They fear you, my lord,' she said. It was a long time since she had called him that. 'But they also respect you. They say, with such a man in command, how can we fail?'

They had a week's grace, but eight days after the battle they were spotted by an aircraft, circling overhead. 'They don't know it was us, as yet,' James said. 'Keep going.'

The plane was back the next day, and this time flew low over them, while they were inspected through binoculars. 'Do you suppose they mean to strafe us?' Richard asked.

'Whenever they're certain it was us killed their people,' James said. 'How far, Zahir?'

'We return into Afghan territory tomorrow,' Zahir said. 'And reach the river the day after. Then we can follow the river, in Afghan territory, all the way to the mountains.'

'Will the Russians follow us into your country?' Richard asked.

Zahir grinned. 'Not if they are wise.'

Two days later they stood on the banks of the Amudar'ya.

The flowing water was lined with poplars. It looked utterly peaceful. 'The longest river in Asia,' Zahir said reverently.

'Ah, no,' James said. 'The Yangtse-Kiang is the longest river in Asia. But this is a big river.'

'Do you think I could have a bath?' Sophie asked. 'I would so love a bath.'

'I think we could all have a bath,' James said.

He arranged privacy for the two women, but he and Richard joined them, upstream of the rest of the caravan, to splash about in the water. More and more James was reminded of Cecile, in the sea off the Horn of Africa. But this girl was even more beautiful. Richard was a lucky man, he thought, and fervently hoped that Lanne would not be in Kashgar.

That evening they all went fishing, and dined off carp.

They had another three-hundred-mile trek in front of them, along the northern Afghan border, which was formed by the river, as Zahir had said, until they reached the foothills of the Himalayas, which was where the great river actually rose. The going was less tiring than before, and less tense, as well, as Zahir could represent them to his people as a caravan out of Herat—not that they met many people other than goatherders. Occasionally they saw Russians on the far bank, but they were no threat. Their principal problem was the weather, for it was now late summer and there was a good deal of rain, while the wind sweeping down from the east bore a chilling indication of what they might face in another few months.

'We will be in Kashgar before the first snow,' Zahir said confidently.

Obviously he meant the first snowfalls, James thought, for as they began the climb there was already snow on the ground; they were now some nine thousand feet above sea level. 'I did not know people could live this high,' Homaira panted. 'The air is so thin.'

Richard was starting to worry. 'Are you all right, Sir James?' he asked.

'Of course I'm all right,' James said testily. 'Just a little short of breath.'

'Join the club,' Richard said.

'Tomorrow we cross the Pyemdah,' Zahir said, 'and are back in Russian territory. But I do not think they will know who we are.'

The water in the river was fairly close to freezing, and there was no temptation to have another swim. It took them an entire day to get all the camels across; Richard supposed it really was a miracle that they had not lost any so far; he put it down to the expertise of the Afghan drivers. Not for the first time he found himself wondering what he was doing here, especially with Sophie. Partly he supposed it was his desire for adventure, that had so abruptly ended when he had left the army. Partly it was a genuine love for this country, despite his harrowing experiences. And of course there was the money.

But the main reason he was here was James Martingell, he knew. Easy to say that having had an affair, however brief, with his wife, his code demanded that he serve the man wherever possible. Easy to say he still felt guilty at having been unable to find Lanne. But that was history. And the girl he was now holding in his arms had made up for all that lifetime of misery. Yet he could not stop himself considering might-have-beens. Supposing ... Lanne would be almost thirty now, and after more than five years, supposing she was still alive, she would be several times a mother and become an entirely Russian housewife, overweight and abusive. No, he realised, the main reason was a total admiration for the man, for his guts and his determination. Of course he was a thug, and the most ruthless man Richard had ever met. Equally was he a charmer and a leader any man would be proud to follow.

Another three hundred miles lay between the river and the Chinese border. Now they were in the Himalayas, although the great peaks such as Everest and K2 lay a long way to the southeast. But the land was high enough, and the winds were cold and blew incessantly. They were not required to do any mountaineering, which would have been impossible anyway with the laden camels. Zahir led them along river valleys and hidden gorges, but even these were several thousand feet above sea level. 'Do you think Sir James will survive?' Homaira asked Richard.

'Yes.

'If he were to die ...' She rolled her eyes.

Richard was more worried about Mbote, who was quite unused to both the heights and the cold. But the big black man, only a few years younger than James himself, pressed on with an equal determination. Oddly, he was not worried about Sophie. Almost invisible beneath her furs and her hat, wrapped in scarves, she resolutely followed him, with never a word of complaint. This was the adventure she had always sought. This was how she wanted to live.

This last leg of the journey took twice as long as any of the others, as they could only travel for a few hours at a time before having to camp and regain their strength. They passed isolated, huddled villages, and were scowled at by greatcoated men wearing the red stars of commissars in their schlems, but no one attempted to question them, much less stop them. Here they were beyond the reach of the Soviet system, and they were clearly both heavily armed and determined. Time ceased to have any meaning as they plodded on, until the morning Zahir pointed to the east. 'Muztagata,' he announced.

They blinked through the sunlight at the huge peak, which seemed to touch the sky. 'We don't have to go up there, do we?' Richard asked.

'No, no, that would be quite impossible. That mountain is more than twenty thousand feet high. But it is in China!'

Suddenly they were rejuvenated. The end of their trek was in sight. Four days later they crossed the border, and the next day came to a village. People turned out to greet them, with their dogs and their yaks, which necessitated hobbling the camels a good way off. But the people were definitely Chinese. 'I am Hsuan Wu-ling,' announced the big man, who wore a round flat hat and a kaftan, and carried a sword. And spoke excellent Persian. 'You are Zahir?'

'I am he.'

'We had given you up.'

'It is a long journey. This is Sir James Martingell, and Captain Richard Elligan, and Mbote.'

Hsuan Wu-ling embraced them each in turn. 'Don't tell me we're expected?' James asked.

'But of course. And those are the guns?' Hsuan asked.

'As promised. You will take delivery?'

'Not I. You must go to Kashgar. But I will send to tell them you are coming. They will be very happy. There is much fighting in the east, and we need the guns.'

'Fighting with who?' Richard asked.

'The Communists,' Hsuan said. 'But come, you must be hungry.'

They were fed, and then shown to an enormous communal bathtub, into which Homaira and Sophie plunged without hesitation, regardless of the men around them. But soon they were naked as well, less intent on getting clean than on feeling the heat from the water seeping into their systems. 'How far is it to Kashgar?' James asked.

'Fifty miles,' Hsuan said. 'My people will guide you. But I have already dispatched a messenger. They will come down to meet you.'

'And in Kashgar we make the delivery?'

'That is my understanding, yes.'

James would have preferred to leave the two women with their present hosts, as he had no idea what might lie ahead. But it was too risky, with war going on apparently all around them. Anyway, he doubted they would have stayed; they had become firm friends, and both were determined to be with their menfolk, always. So they moved out a few days later, greatly refreshed by their stopover.

They travelled now in the shadow of the Pamirs, whose peaks reached skywards. They went east for a few miles, descending all the while. Now they could see the vast desert stretching in front of them, and that night they camped on sandy soil, with hardly a tree in sight, and only the vultures for company. Next morning they turned up to the north, following a well-marked track, but always on the edge of the desert, with the mountains on their left. It was that evening that they saw a body of horsemen approaching. 'How do we handle this?' James asked Zahir.

He gave one of his invariable grins as he studied the approaching group through his binoculars. 'These are Ma Chung-ying's people.'

The two of them rode out in front to greet the rebels, as James presumed they had to be considered. He deliberately left Richard in command of the main body, as he had an idea who they might be going to meet, and sure enough, there was a familiar green uniform. 'Sir James!' Galitsin cried, leaning from his horse to grasp James' hand. 'Or should I call you Father? When I was told you would be commanding this caravan, I was overwhelmed with delight.'

'And Lanne?' James asked.

'She too,' Galitsin said.

'She is here with you?'

'She is in Kashgar, certainly. Should a wife not be with her husband?'

'Quite so. You understand that we come as friends.'

'But of course.' He gave a shout of laughter. 'You come as merchants, bearing gifts of great importance.'

'Yes. I have Richard Elligan with me.' Galitsin's eyes narrowed. 'He is working with me, now,' James explained.

'That is natural, after your adventures together,' Galitsin conceded. 'I will not trouble him, if he will not trouble me. Does he still wish to possess Lanne?'

'I do not think so,' James said. 'He is married. Indeed, his wife is with him now. But I suspect there may still be some resentment,' James said.

'I have said, I will not trouble him, if he will not trouble me. This is in your hands, James.'

'Yes,' James said. They walked their horses back to the caravan, followed by Galitsin's bodyguard. 'Will I be able to see Lanne, in Kashgar?' he asked.

Galitsin's eyes were hooded. 'If she wishes to see you, certainly,' he said.

'Sandor?' Richard was astounded.

'Richard, my old friend. And is this your beautiful wife?' For they all felt so much warmer after their descent from the mountains that Sophie was for the moment hatless, her auburn hair floating in the breeze. 'My dear lady, you *are* beautiful.' He kissed her gloved hand.

Sophie looked at Richard for an explanation. 'I saved your husband's life,' Galitsin explained. 'Once. No, twice. Is that not true, Richard?'

'Yes,' Richard said.

'And then we both fell in love with the same woman,' Galitsin went on. 'Sir James' daughter. But I won out, did I not, Richard?'

'You are a swine, Sandor,' Richard said evenly.

'Gentlemen,' James said. 'I think we should have a drink to celebrate our meeting, and a successful conclusion to our safari.'

'You knew he was going to be here,' Richard said, when he and James had a moment alone.

'I was informed, yes.'

'But you did not think it necessary to inform me?'

'I was toying with the idea when we met up in Meshed. But when I saw that you had Sophie in tow, I decided to let it lie. Why start trouble where it may never be necessary? Galitsin could have died before we got here.'

'What are you going to do about it? About Lanne?'

'Is she still your concern?'

Richard flushed. 'I suppose not. But she is your concern.'

'What I do about Lanne will depend on Lanne,' James said. 'But if it becomes necessary to do something about her, will you back me?'

'To the hilt.'

'And Sophie?'

'If you wish to rescue Lanne, I will help you, James. It will have nothing to do with Sophie and me.'

'I think you should explain that to Sophie,' James suggested. 'Before we get to Kashgar.'

'There is so much in your life of which I have no share,' Sophie said, as they lay together beneath their blankets, surrounded by the sounds of the camp.

'I had not expected ever to have to see him again,' he said. 'Or Lanne. But as I have ...'

'You must support Sir James.'

'Can you understand that?'

'Yes. As I must support you. You are

403

all I have left in the world. Can you understand that?'

'Yes. And I am grateful for it.'

'As for afterwards ...' She sighed.

'Afterwards, I shall love you for ever,' he promised.

If we survive, she thought.

They reached Kashgar two days later. It was a large town, famous in history, for as far back as a thousand years and more it had controlled the silk route west, to Europe. Now it bustled with eager people, flying green flags and determined in their allegiance to Ma Chung-ying, but revealing its medieval links in the six men impaled outside the walls, their bodies rotting in the wind.

Sophie turned her head away in disgust, and Richard squeezed her hand.

'These people live on the edge of time,' Zahir commented.

Ma Chung-ying himself came to greet the caravan as it proceeded through the city gates. He was a thickset man with heavy moustaches who wore a Chinese kaftan and a Muslim turban and bristled with revolver and dagger and sword, as well as a rifle slung over his shoulder. He was accompanied by a dozen men, each as clearly bandits as himself. 'Zahir!' he shouted, leaning from the saddle to embrace the Afghan. 'By Allah, I had given you up for lost.'

He seized James' hands. 'Martingell! The famous Martingell. You have my guns?'

'The best,' James assured him.

Ma ignored the rest of the party in his eagerness to dismount and be shown the weapons. He took the first rifle from the opened case and shook it above his head, and his people cheered. 'Now we will march east and resume the offensive,' he declared. 'But you, Martingell, and your people, we will feast tonight!'

'I do not trust that man,' Homaira remarked, as they bathed. Around them people danced and fired their guns, and the fires blazed, over which sheep were being roasted.

'Well,' James said, 'We have delivered the guns, and our business is done. All we need to do now is return south and collect our money. What I would like to do now is see my daughter. You will have to see if you can arrange it.'

'I will see to it,' Homaira promised. 'I too would like to see Lanne again. Once we were close friends. But the money for the guns ... when will it be paid?'

'My understanding was that it would be paid directly to Beinhardt. But I'll check that out before we leave. Lanne is what matters now.'

James left her to it while he dressed himself in a new kaftan, supplied by the Chinese, and soft kid boots, belted on a sword, a weapon he had never worn before but was apparently regarded as an important accessory, and went in search of Zahir, who he found similarly dressed, having been similarly attended with a good deal more enthusiasm by his maidservants. Not that he was the least impressed. 'Still,' he said, 'the food will be good.'

'When will Ma make the payment?' James asked.

'Tomorrow. He will give Mr Elligan a bank draft.' Zahir grinned. 'He has a lot of money in foreign banks. It will be honoured.'

'Well, if Richard is happy with that, so am I. My concern is my own payment.'

'It awaits you, Sir James, in Afghanistan. Now you must cease worrying, and enjoy yourself. Tonight Ma has commanded a great feast to be made ready for us, in celebration of our arrival, and of the guns.'

'Does he reckon this shipment alone will win the war for him?'

'I should think he understands that it will not. But it is a sign to his people that he is a power in the world, and will consolidate his hold upon the tribes.' One of his grins, accompanied by a slap on the shoulder. 'Come, my friend. We have triumphed over all the odds. Do you not think we should celebrate?'

The Kashgari certainly thought so. The entire city was *en fête*. Richard and Sophie, both also dressed in clean new clothes, joined James and Zahir for the feast, held in the central square in the open air despite the chill wind that came down from the mountains. 'This place could grow on a chap,' Richard said. 'When do we start home?'

'Just as soon as our host forks out,' James assured him. 'Or would you rather stay?'

Ma had that in mind as well. Richard was seated on his left, James on his right, with Sophie on James's left and Zahir on Richard's right. One of Ma's women was on Zahir's left, and beyond her, Galitsin. Of Homaira there was no sign, but she did not seem to be missed, at least by Ma. 'I am told that you were a soldier in the British Guards,' Ma said to Richard.

'I was, your excellency.'

'You are young to have stopped fighting.'

'Well, your excellency, we British have run out of people to fight.'

Ma gave a shout of laughter. 'There are

407

always people to fight. Here in China we have more than most. Suppose I offered you a commission in my army. Would you not stay and fight with me?'

'You tempt me, your excellency. But it is my duty to escort Martingell back to safety.'

'Martingell,' Ma commented. 'Ha. He is an old man. He will soon be dead in any event. Well then, escort him to safety, if it is your duty. And then return to me.' His sleepy eyes flickered over Sophie. 'With your so beautiful bride.'

'Perhaps that may be possible,' Richard said, diplomatically.

The evening became riotous, as Ma and most of his people got drunk on koumiss, fermented mare's milk, and sang and laughed and cheered, and clapped the various entertainments, which varied from performing bears to jugglers and dancers and contortionists, but which also descended into the bestial, as prisoners were brought out, wearing the cangue, or huge wooden collar, to which their wrists were fastened so that they were helpless to protect their bodies from the stones thrown at them, the sticks that poked and lashed at them, the hands that pulled away their clothing to expose their genitals, the contemptuous laughter with which they were surrounded.

Once again Sophie hid her eyes, and Richard asked Ma, 'Do any human beings deserve such degradation?'

'What does it matter?' Ma asked. 'Tomorrow their heads will be cut off. You will watch. It is much sport.'

James kept as sober as he could, as his eyes searched the crowd. And at last he saw Homaira, on the far side of the square. 'I must relieve myself,' he told his hosts, and got up, pushing his way into the people, knowing she would find him.

She held his arm. 'Are you sober?'

'Enough. Have you found her?'

'I have found where she lives. Do you not find it strange that she is not attending the feast?'

'Yes,' he agreed.

'I think she is a prisoner. We will have to break in. That may cause trouble.'

'Then we'll cause trouble. If she's a prisoner, it is our business to release her.'

'If she wants to come,' Homaira pointed out. She held his hand and led him through the throng, until they reached a comparatively open space. Then she took him down several side alleys, so that he loosened both his sword in its scabbard and his revolver in its holster.

But they were not accosted, and eventually came to a house, set, like all the other houses, close by its neighbours. 'This is the dwelling of Galitsin,' she said.

The place was closed and dark. 'How many servants?' he asked.

'I have only seen four. But that was much earlier. There has been no movement for the past hour, at least.'

'You had best go back to the square.'

'Why? You will need me here.'

'This could be dangerous.'

She smiled. 'It is always dangerous. My place is here, with you.' He didn't argue. He knew she could provide formidable assistance.

He knocked on the door, and then again. It took some five minutes of hammering to bring a response. Then they heard shuffling feet, and a moment later a small window was opened. Before the half-asleep maidservant could work out who was there, James had thrust his arm through the aperture and seized her by the hair. 'Unlock the door,' he said, speaking Persian, which he guessed would be used by Galitsin for his domestics, 'or I will break your neck.'

She gasped, and attempted to jerk free, but he had twined his fingers in the coarse black strands, and now he jerked her head against the door. 'Quickly,' he said. 'Or die.'

Her fingers scrabbled at the bolt, and the moment it was drawn Homaira had pushed the door in; James went with it, still grasping the woman's hair and holding her against the door. Then Homaira was inside, her dagger pressed against the woman's back. 'No killing unless we have to,' James commanded. He released the woman and entered himself, found himself in a large antechamber, lit by a single candle, already more than half consumed.

'Give me your pistol,' Homaira said. He handed her the revolver, and she reversed it and struck the servant a sharp blow on the head. Her knees gave way and she hit the floor with a thump, arms and legs scattered. 'Five minutes, maybe,' Homaira said.

There was a staircase in the corner. Homaira picked up the candle, and they ran across the floor, paused to listen, and heard a vague noise from the back of the downstairs part of the house. Presumably more servants. James jerked his head, and they ran up the stairs. At the top there was a landing and four doors. James nodded to the first one, and Homaira opened it; she had returned him the revolver, but kept her dagger thrust forward, while raising the candle above her head. But the room was empty.

Now there was noise from the foot of the stairs, and some more light. James went back to the stairhead, and looked

411

down, at two men coming up, the first carrying a candle; both were armed with swords. There was nothing for it, now. James levelled his revolver and fired. The first man took the bullet in the chest and went tumbling back down into the arms of the second, who also fell beneath the impact. The candle went clattering down the stairs and extinguished itself.

'Who's there?' someone called, in Persian. It was a voice he would have recognised anywhere.

'Lanne!' he shouted, and ran back along the corridor. Homaira was already at the door from behind which the voice had come.

'What's happening?' Lanne shouted. 'Sandor, is that you?'

'The door is locked,' Homaira said.

'Stand clear!' James shouted, and blew the lock apart with a single shot from his revolver.

The door swung in, and he stared at his daughter. 'Father?' she gasped. 'Daddy?'

Homaira was again holding the candle above her head, but for a few seconds James could not recognise who he was looking at. Lanne had grown into a massive woman; always tall, she was now stout as well—even her features seem to have enlarged. She wore a nightgown, and was barefoot. Her golden hair was a tangled mess, and even in the candlelight could be seen to contain streaks of grey. 'Father?' she asked again, incredulously. From the bed there came a wail. 'Ssssh,' she said, and came forward to be embraced.

He held her close, looked past her at the babe in the bed, and frowned. 'Your child?'

'One of them. I have had others. Galitsin sends them away.'

'But ...' He released her. 'That child is half-Chinese.'

Lanne shrugged. 'Galitsin likes me to entertain his friends.' She held on to him again. 'You have come to take me away. Please say that you have come to take me away!'

Chapter 12

Coming Home

James wasn't sure he was hearing right. 'You wish to leave?'

'Yes,' she said. 'Yes. My God, you have no idea what I have been through.'

'Then get dressed,' Homaira said. 'We need to hurry.'

Lanne tore off her nightgown and pulled

413

on her kaftan.

The baby wailed. 'He'll need clothes as well,' James suggested.

'Him? I'm not taking *him!* Sandor can give him back to his father.' James and Homaira gazed at each other. But Lanne was his daughter, and now she was fully dressed. And remembering. 'Galitsin!' she said.

'Presently occupied,' Homaira said. 'But we will have to get out of Kashgar tonight.'

'Without our money?' James asked.

'It is not *our* money, James. It is Beinhardt's,' Homaira said. 'We have done what you contracted to do, delivered the guns. Azam owes you fifty thousand pounds. All we have to do is get to him.' She was talking sense, but omitting all of the imponderables in between.

'Listen,' James told Lanne. 'If you want to get out, you must do exactly what we tell you.'

'Of course. Anything.'

'Right. Do you know somewhere you can hide for the next couple of hours?' She looked left and right. 'Not in this house. That maidservant will have gone for help. You must be out of the house.'

'Yes. I know a place.'

'Then go there, with Homaira. Homaira, you will remain hidden with Lanne, for two hours, and then come and find me and take me to her, and we will leave Kashgar.'

'How do I know when two hours have gone?'

He gave her his gold hunter. 'Don't drop it.'

'And you are going to do what?'

'I have to get hold of Mbote and Richard and Sophie. And Zahir, I suppose.'

'Richard!' Lanne cried. 'Is he here?'

'Yes, he is. With his wife, who he loves very dearly. Remember that. Now let's get out of here.'

He led them down the stairs. They stepped over the dead bodies of the two menservants, and Lanne gasped. The front door remained open, swinging on its hinges. 'Haste!' Homaira said.

There were people on the street, no doubt alerted by the gunshots. But they made no attempt to interfere, and Lanne led them down a succession of alleys. 'Over there,' she said, pointing at a pagoda-roofed building. 'There is a temple. We will wait in the temple.'

'Right,' James said. 'Then there'll be a change of plan, as I know where you'll be. You two go in there and sit tight, and I'll come to you.'

'Say you will come,' Homaira said.

He grinned at her. 'I will come.'

He left them and hurried back to the

square. This took him about fifteen minutes. The celebrations were continuing, and the noise was tremendous, but he saw that Galitsin had left his place; the maidservant had reached him. Both Richard and Sophie were looking somewhat agitated, as was Zahir, but Ma Chung-ying was even drunker than before, rocking to and fro as he sat, and continuing to drink and sing. James sat beside Mbote. 'Where is Galitsin?'

'Some woman came and spoke in his ear, and he rushed off. We figured you were responsible.'

'Yes. Well, we have to get out of here now. Can you fetch our horses? We need an extra one.'

'For Lanne?'

'Yes.'

He repeated the instructions to Richard. 'Is she ...' Richard hesitated.

'She's alive, and fairly well. But she's had a hard time. You'll find she's changed. Considerably.'

It was difficult to tell whether or not he was relieved about that. 'What about the money? Ma hasn't paid it yet.'

'We are going to have to forget the money,' James told him. 'It is that or our necks. If Ma is an honest man he will pay it anyway, to your father-in-law.'

Richard was obviously unhappy at having

416

to abandon his responsibility as the Beinhardt representative. But he squeezed Sophie's hand and the two of them stole away into the darkness, entirely unnoticed by their Chinese hosts—but not by Zahir, who had taken no alcohol. 'What is happening?' Zahir asked.

'We are leaving Kashgar,' James said. 'You coming?'

'We have not been paid.'

'Is that your concern? What we need to do is get out of here, now.'

Zahir stroked his beard. 'There is something happening that I do not understand.'

'I'll explain it later. Are you coming?'

Zahir grinned. 'It is my business to guide you, Sir James.'

Mbote and Richard had saddled seven horses. 'What about food?' Sophie asked, ever practical.

'We shall have to obtain that on the way,' James told her. 'The important thing is to get south before we are pursued.'

He led them to the temple, where Lanne and Homaira were waiting on the steps. 'Richard!' Lanne screamed, running down the steps to throw herself into his arms.

He fielded her as well he could, trying to avoid her eager kisses. 'We have to get out of here,' he said.

417

Lanne was looking at Sophie. 'I am told this is your wife.'

'I have heard of you too, Mrs Galitsin,' Sophie said, with her invariable composure.

Zahir had been looking at both of them. 'Your daughter, by Allah!' he said. 'Martingell, you endanger all our lives.'

'I have done what I came here to do,' James told him. 'As your master was well aware. Perhaps you were not. But it was Azam's plan that I should find my daughter, and perish in an attempt to save her. It is up to you whether you come with us, and surprise him, or stay here, and perish. You are certainly associated with us.'

'By Allah,' Zahir said again. 'I have been tricked.' Then he grinned. 'I will take you out of here, Martingell.'

They mounted, and, guided for the moment by Lanne, took side alleys to reach the gates. Here they were challenged by the guards, but these too had been indulging, and James did not hesitate to open fire, followed by Mbote, Richard, and Zahir. The men leapt for safety, leaving two of their number stretched on the ground, and then they were through, and galloping down the road towards Alto. After a few minutes James made them slow to a walk, as they could not risk exhausting the horses. Now they could look back at the city, where lights blazed and there was still an enormous hubbub. Whether or not they were being pursued was impossible to tell.

They dismounted and walked their horses for a while, then mounted again and rode into the night. By morning they had covered some twenty miles, James estimated, and he called a halt for a scanty breakfast. 'We'll obtain food in the village,' he said.

But before they had drunk the last of their tea, Zahir jerked his head. 'Horsemen,' he said tersely.

They mounted and rode on for another few hours, by which time the horses were very tired. Now again the desert loomed, this time on their left, while the land rose steeply on their right. 'We are going to have to check those men,' James said. 'Homaira, take the women further down the road and wait for us.'

'And if you do not come?' Homaira asked.

James looked at Mbote. 'I will stay with you, James,' Mbote said. 'Let Zahir take the women.'

'But I am the best shot you have,' Zahir said, and looked at Richard.

'We will all stay,' Homaira decided. 'Let us shelter the horses.'

They hobbled the horses in a gulley, and

took their places to either side of the road; everyone had a rifle.

'You understand that I have to kill Galitsin,' James told Lanne.

'I understand,' she agreed, without apparent emotion.

It was now daylight, and they watched the track. Richard was well aware that if there were a large body of pursuers, they would not survive. He reached out to squeeze Sophie's hand. 'Well?' she asked. 'Was she worth coming this far to rescue?'

'I came this far to support James, not to rescue Lanne.'

'And I believe you.' She seemed surprised at the admission. 'What will they do to me if they capture me? Will they impale me, like those people we saw?'

'You have a revolver. You must promise me, and yourself, that they will not capture you. Alive.'

'They will not capture me, alive,' she promised. And smiled. 'I have often wondered what it would be like to be impaled.' She pointed. 'There!'

They watched the road, and the dozen horsemen who came down it. Galitsin was at their head, studying the tracks. 'No one shoot until I do,' James said. 'We need to take them all.'

Sophie swallowed, and Richard squeezed

her hand again. He knew exactly how she felt, and he had been in this situation several times to her once. Galitsin raised his hand, and the horsemen came on, still walking their horses, still studying the tracks. James levelled his binoculars, but he could see no sign of movement behind them. Twelve men. And one of them had once saved his life. Twice, he supposed. There was gratitude. But that same man had then made off with his daughter! 'Now,' he said, aiming at the centre of Galitsin's chest, and squeezing the trigger.

Galitsin's tunic dissolved into flying crimson as he tumbled from the saddle. The rest of the fugitives were also firing now, several more of the bullets striking home, so that more than half of the pursuers were hit.

Horses galloped to and fro, men shrieked their agony, and four turned to ride back to Kashgar. 'Bring them down!' James shouted.

Zahir levelled his rifle, and one of the Chinese fell from the saddle. Richard followed his example, and brought down another. Both James and Mbote also fired again, but their eyesight was not so good, and the last two Chinese galloped out of range. 'Depend upon it, they'll have support in a couple of hours,' James said.

'Then we must make haste,' Zahir said.

They went down to the road, where the horses roamed to and fro, and the dead bodies lay scattered on the ground. James stood above Galitsin. The Russian had died instantly from the bullet in his chest. Lanne squeezed her father's hand. 'Are you not at all regretful?' he asked.

'Not now,' she said. 'At first, it was tremendous. He was a splendid lover. But then, he drank too much vodka, and he went with other women, and he beat me. He said all Russian men beat their wives, and that I should enjoy it. I hated him.'

'And now he's dead.'

'You killed him, Daddy. You avenged me. I always knew you would.'

He looked down at her. 'But for him, I would have died, long ago.'

'He served his purpose,' she said urgently.

James mounted, and led his people to the south.

They were at the village long before any word reached it of what had happened, either on the road or at Kashgar; there was no radio link down here. The elders were pleased to see them again, gave them food, and saw them on their way. They would have offered them lodgings, for winter was fast approaching, but James was too conscious that there would be a pursuit, and pressed on. They reached the Khunjerab Pass three weeks after leaving Kashgar, and were in India.

By now it was snowing fairly regularly at these high altitudes—the great mountains of the Himalayas, dominated by K2, soared away to their left, and wrapped up as they were in furs and fur hats and fur boots there was no means of telling that they were not Chinese. Zahir insisted to everyone they met that they were all Afghans, on their way home from a trading mission to Chinese Turkestan, and there were no border formalities—that they were well armed was not the least unusual in these remote regions. 'India,' Lanne breathed. 'Are we safe now?'

'Nearly,' James assured her, surveying the mountains of Jammu and Kashmir, through which led their road. 'We just have to pick up our money.' He didn't tell her that involved returning to Afghanistan.

They had spoken little during their weeks on the road. With an icy wind whistling about them there had been little temptation to speak in any event, and their encampments had been a matter of huddling against each other as best they might. James slept with Homaira on one side of him and Lanne on the other, all three fully dressed. 'To go home,' Lanne murmured. 'After all of these years. Will I be married, Daddy?'

'I really can't say. If you wish, I suppose.'

'It is a pity about Richard. Marrying that German girl, I mean. But ... is Winston still in prison?'

'He's out. But he'll be going back as soon as they catch him.'

'You mean he escaped? How romantic.'

'No doubt it is. But I must tell you that Anne and I have separated. I don't know where Winston stands in that.'

'Well, we'll just have to find out, won't we.'

He marvelled at her insouciance, the way she could just turn her back on the life she had lived for the past half-dozen years, the determination to resume her English life as if they never had been. 'Don't you want to find out what happened to your children?' he asked.

'Other men's children,' she said.

'You mothered them.'

'They were all bastards. Save two. Those were by Galitsin. One died young. The other, the girl ... I do not know what happened to her.'

'Don't you care?'

'She was Sandor's daughter. He sent her off to Moscow to be educated. I want to forget all that, start anew. Do you think that's wrong?'

James preferred not to answer that. He could hardly claim to have looked after her with extravagant love or care when she had been a child. But he had never deserted her. 'She will grow out of it,' Homaira whispered. Grow out of what? he wondered.

'Did you really love her?' Sophie asked, snug in Richard's arms.

'I think I did, once.'

'But not now?'

He kissed her frozen nose. 'Now I love you.'

'Are we going to survive this, Richard?'

He kissed her again. 'Put your trust in James. He has survived so much in his life. This is just another incident to him.' She hugged herself against him.

Lanne had been deep in thought for a few days. Then she managed to get herself alone with her father, on a morning Homaira was doing some very necessary washing in a mountain stream. 'I didn't properly understand what you said, the other day, Daddy. You mean that you and Anne have split up? Irrevocably?'

'I would say so.'

'Well, then, there is no need to find me

a husband. I will keep house for you.'

He glanced at her. 'I have Homaira.'

'Oh, really, Daddy. She is a common woman, and so *old*. I could do much more for you.' Her tongue came out and circled her lips.

'You have a lot of your mother in you,' James said.

She flushed. 'Is that so very surprising? Or wrong?'

'No, it is neither surprising nor wrong. But if you make a suggestion like that again I am going to remember that I am your father and put you across my knee.'

She giggled. 'Just like Sandor.'

Now they followed the course of the Indus, in valleys well below the freezing peaks, although it remained cold enough. They went through Chalt and Gilgit, Bunji and Chilas, before leaving the river and making for the Khyber Pass. Here the great peaks again looked down on them, and presumably there were Afghan warriors looking down on them too. But they were not molested until they were through the pass, and climbing to the high ground beyond. Then they suddenly found themselves surrounded by the turbaned, bearded tribesmen, well armed with modern weapons. 'Probably from your warehouse, James,' Richard could not resist commenting. But he stayed close to Sophie, well aware that they were in as great danger here as they had ever been in China.

But Zahir addressed the warriors, who soon began to laugh and joke, and the travellers found themselves invited to a feast. 'These people know me,' Zahir told James. 'As they know my master.'

'Where is your master?'

'He awaits us in Jalalabad. It is not far.'

Next day they were on their way, and two days later the battlements of the famous frontier town came into sight. Now they were accompanied by a guard of honour of Pathans, escorted through the gates, and through thronging crowds in the market place. There were several distinguished-looking buildings as well as mosques, and it was to one of these that they were escorted, gates in the wall opening to admit them to a large courtyard, entirely cut off from the rest of the city by the high-walled building which surrounded it. Here grooms were waiting to take their exhausted horses, and other men, and women, waiting to escort them into the house, where the appointments, from the mosaic floors to the great silk drapes that hung everywhere, depicted great wealth. 'The Sheikh has some rich friends,' Richard remarked.

Zahir smiled. 'This is the Sheikh's own house, Major.'

'The blighter,' Richard said.

James realised it had never occurred to him to enquire into Azam's domestic affairs. He had always known him as a highly educated and sophisticated man, who had the disposition of large funds to aid his various causes in Afghanistan; that he had also been a very wealthy man in his own right had not occurred to him.

A major-domo had appeared, resplendent in cloth-of-gold tunic and turban, bowing before them. 'Gentlemen, and ladies, will wish for hot baths,' he suggested in good English.

'Wouldn't I just,' Sophie said.

'Ladies will go with ladies,' the major-domo said, summoning two women, hardly less resplendently clad, with a snap of his fingers.

'Oh, but ...' Sophie looked at Richard.

'I think we had better go with local custom,' Richard said. 'Homaira will look after you.'

The three women were escorted into one of the inner rooms of the palace, which presumably was part of the harem, for they were immediately surrounded by more women and girls, who stripped off their clothing, with expressions of distaste, and then indicated the huge tub of steaming water that occupied a lower level. 'This is going to feel so good,' Lanne said, slowly lowering herself into the tub. Homaira followed, and Sophie, feeling totally isolated as she had never been so publicly naked before, hastily got in behind them.

The tub was large enough for the three of them to wallow without actually touching each other, but now, to Sophie's consternation, several of the Afghan women also stripped off and got in with them, making it very crowded indeed, especially as it seemed that the Afghans' function was to bathe them. 'Oh!' Sophie gasped, as soapy hands roamed over her breasts and down her back, and others slid up and down her legs.

'Sit back and enjoy it,' Lanne told her.

'It is true,' Homaira said. 'Does this not remind you of our days in the harem, Lanne?'

Lanne giggled.

Sophie closed her eyes and tried to relax as more soft hands were now washing her hair. Well, she thought, it desperately needed washing. Then suddenly the hands were withdrawn, leaving her slipping beneath the water. She sat up, spluttering,

429

scooping hair from her eyes, and discovered that the Afghan women were all standing up, rigidly to attention ... and that standing above the bath and looking into it was Azam ud-Ranatullah.

Sophie gave a little shriek, and sank back into the water, sufficiently soapy to be opaque, arms crossed over her breasts. Neither Lanne nor Homaira seemed so concerned. 'Welcome to my house,' Azam said. 'You have had quite an adventure. But Martingell has brought you out, as always, safe and sound. Leaving your husband behind, Madame Galitsin?'

'Yes,' Lanne said, and tilted her chin at him. 'He was a brute.'

'You mean you did not know that when you went off with him? You, Mrs Elligan, stand up that I may look at you.' Sophie sank deeper into the water until only her head was showing. Azam smiled at her. 'I was greatly taken with you when first we met. Now I am even more taken with you. I really had not supposed you would survive so arduous a journey. But as you have ...' He gave an order in Afghan, and four of the women promptly seized Sophie, two to each arm, and dragged her to her feet. Water slid down her arms and thighs and legs, and from her hair. She gasped, and tried to sink again, but the grip on her arms was too strong. 'Yes,' Azam said, 'a

430

true Western pearl. I will have you.'

'My husband ...' Sophie gasped, and checked herself.

Azam grinned. 'Of course, he must be attended to first.' He gave another order to his women, then left the room.

'He means treachery,' Homaira said, speaking English, which she knew none of the Afghans would understand. 'He has always meant treachery.'

The women were now dragging Sophie from the bath, to wrap her in towels and dry her. They were not paying very much attention to Homaira and Lanne. 'What are we to do?' Lanne whispered.

Homaira shrugged. 'I think, if he succeeds, we will die anyway, or be forced into common prostitution to his men. He has eyes only for Sophie. So ...'

There were three other women, waiting for them with towels, while the first four attended to a gasping Sophie with much giggles and shrieks of laughter. Homaira stood up, stepped out of the bath, and as one of the women stepped up to her with a towel, turned with tremendous violence, wrenched the towel from her grasp, and hurled her into the bath. There she was seized by Lanne, and held under the water by her hair, leaving her arms and legs flailing helplessly. Before the other women could grasp what was happening, Homaira was in their midst, kicking one behind the knee which brought a shriek of pain as she fell down, standing on her as she did so, and then throwing the towel over the head of the third, twisting it tight; the woman fell to her hands and knees, choking and gasping.

The other four women had at last realised this was no horseplay, and released Sophie to face up to Homaira, now supported by Lanne, crawling out of the bath. But Sophie had also sized up the situation, grabbed two of her attendants by the hair, and banged their heads together. They collapsed with shrieks, and Homaira and Lanne took care of the other two; they were both bigger than any of the Afghans. Sophie stared at the woman floating face down in the bath. 'Is she ...?'

'It's them or us,' Lanne explained.

Homaira was shepherding the half-conscious, terrified women together. 'In there,' she said, pointing to the cupboard from which she had seen them take the towels.

Lanne opened the door and more towels came tumbling out. These were torn into strips and used to bind and gag the unhappy women, then they were all thrust into the cupboard, being forced to lean against each other as there was no room to lie down. 'Now,' Homaira said. 'Let us find some clothes, and then go and rescue our men, eh?'

Azam ud-Ranatullah sat on the edge of the bath and grinned at the four men; Zahir was in there with the others. 'So,' he said, 'what are your plans now, James?'

'Once you have paid us the balance of the delivery fee, we shall return into British India, and thence make our way back to England.'

'I wonder if we shall ever meet again,' Azam mused.

'I would hope not. I am retiring, once we get home. I'm getting a little old for these long treks.'

'Of course. I too am so much older than when we first adventured together. Ah, those were the days. But you do understand, James, that if you are never going to work for me again, then I have no further interest in you.' He grinned at Richard and Mbote. 'Or your companions.'

James looked left and right, and an inner door opened to admit four men, armed with revolvers. 'Shit!' Mbote said.

'I also have in mind that once you swore to kill me,' Azam said. 'Well now, when it comes to killing, I have always held the view that it is better to kill your enemy before he can kill you. Is that not sensible?

Get out of the bath, Zahir.'

Zahir placed his hands on the surround, heaved himself up, and was seized from behind by Mbote, still by far the biggest man in the room, and lacking little in strength for all his age. Zahir gave a strangled exclamation as he was picked up and thrown straight into the group of armed men. They fired instinctively, and the assassin took three bullets in the chest.

James and Richard were by now also out of the bath. James seized an astonished Azam while Richard plucked the revolver from his belt. The Afghans, themselves astounded at having shot one of their own, now realised that if they fired again they would hit their master. 'Drop your weapons,' Richard said. They understood him well enough to obey, and as they did so Mbote gathered them up. 'Just don't move,' Richard advised.

The four men stood as if turned to stone, while Zahir gasped away his life at their feet. 'Our clothes,' James said.

Mbote gathered them up, and they got dressed, one of them always keeping a revolver pointed at Azam. 'What can you hope to achieve?' Azam asked. 'This is my house. This is my city. Where can you go?'

'We are going to go back to India,'

James told him. 'With our money, and our women.'

'You'll never get there,' Azam said.

'I think we will,' James said. 'Because you are going to take us.'

'There are people at the door,' Mbote said. Azam smiled in triumph.

'Open it,' James said. 'Remember, Azam, that you will be the first to go.'

Mbote opened the door, and the three women tumbled into the bathchamber. 'Richard!' Sophie cried with relief.

'You have taken care of yourselves,' Homaira remarked. 'Now we must leave this place.'

Azam was remarkably cooperative. Far too cooperative, in Richard's opinion. He hoped James was equally aware of this. As James sensibly declined to take a cheque, the money was counted out in gold and silver coin.

'We are going to charge you double,' James said, having seen the contents of Azam's treasure chest. 'For your treachery.'

Azam shrugged. 'A man does what he can.'

A caravan was prepared on Azam's instructions, seven good horses and two pack mules, and was provisioned. That Azam was under restraint was obvious to everyone in his house, as either Richard or Mbote or Homaira was always at his side, revolver pressed against him; he seemed far more afraid of Homaira than of either of the men, but then he did not really seem afraid of her either. 'He has something up his sleeve,' Richard muttered to James.

'Probably up both of them,' James agreed. 'But he is our only way out.'

The horses assembled, the gates were opened, watched by Azam's entire household, it seemed. 'Now stay close,' James told the women as they filed through.

They all wore heavy cloaks and the women were veiled, their hair entirely concealed so that no one could tell they were European. Slowly they walked their horses down the street, surrounded by the usual crowds, none of whom seemed the least hostile. 'You see,' Azam said, 'I am cooperating with you as much as possible. When will you let me go?'

'When we are through the Khyber Pass,' James said.

'Ah,' Azam commented.

They left the city just before dusk, and did not stop. The route was well marked, and there were few people about in the night; from time to time they caught sight of campfires in the hills to left and right. It was fifty miles from Jalalabad to the

Pass, and by dawn Richard reckoned they had covered half the distance. Now James called a brief halt for a meal and to water the horses. 'We'll be there by nightfall,' he said.

'At the Pass,' Azam said thoughtfully.

'What's he going to do?' Sophie whispered.

'Hopefully, nothing,' Richard whispered back.

But he knew that was being optimistic; it was late that afternoon when they saw that the road ahead was blocked by a group of horsemen. 'Well, now,' Azam said with a smile. 'You have a problem.'

'Yours?' James asked.

'We are not so primitive as you supposed, you see. My people have a radio, as do those people. Who are also my people. Now, Sir James, you and I have been friends for a very long time. I wish us to continue being friends. So I make you the same offer as I did before. Leave the money, ride out of here, and we may remain friends. Until the next time.'

'That is not quite the offer you made earlier,' Mbote said.

'I am amending it, to suit the circumstances.'

'You are forgetting that you are our prisoner, not we theirs,' James reminded him.

'Pouf,' Azam remarked. 'You kill me, my people will capture you. They will give you, Sir James, and you, Mbote, and you, Elligan, to their women. While they will take *your* women. I assure you that will not be a happy experience. When they have had them, they will cut off their breasts and noses and lips and eyelids, and expose them to the ants and the buzzards. Now really, there is only one sensible decision you can make, James.'

James stared at the men, who had advanced their horses somewhat closer. Then he looked at his own people. They waited on his decision, and would accept it, he knew, even if it meant their own deaths, however terrible those deaths. He was suddenly aware of having adventured too long, of having risked death too often. Why, that was all he had devoted his life to doing. Now he was tired. He was ready for the end of it all. But if he was going to accept that, he wanted at least some of those who had followed him, regardless of the odds, to the very end of the earth, to survive. 'Richard,' he said. 'Take the saddlebags.'

Richard obeyed, frowning. 'I am not leaving you, James.'

'Yes, you are,' James told him. 'You have important things to do with your life.' He smiled at Sophie. 'With your wife.

438

Maybe I was responsible for your aunt's death, Sophie. I know I did rob your family of a fortune, in order to create my own. I give it all back to you. Just remember, don't look back.' He looked at Homaira. 'See them out of here. And Lanne.'

'Daddy!'

'Will you do as you are told, at least once in your life?' Lanne bit her lip. 'Mbote ...'

Mbote grinned. 'Where you go, I go, James. Surely you know that.'

'Homaira?'

'You know that without you there can be no life for me.'

He had expected nothing different. 'Well, then ...' James drew his revolver. 'Remember, Richard, be ruthless. You must get the women out.'

Richard swallowed, but his face was grim; he was less afraid of the coming battle than of having to abandon his old friend. 'You are mad,' Azam said. 'I have told you what they will do to you.'

'Take him and ride,' James snapped.

Richard grasped Azam's reins. 'Go,' he shouted.

Both Sophie and Lanne kicked their horses and rode to the right.

'Charge!' James shouted. There were ten men in front of them, and he recollected that he had faced far greater odds in the past. Mbote was on his right, waving his tulwar. Homaira was on his left, firing her rifle as she galloped. The Afghans were taken aback by the sudden action. Three of them swung their horses to ride after Richard and the women, and Azam. The other five spurred their own horses forward to meet the coming attack. 'Aieee!' James shouted, the old urge to battle rising within him as he shot the first man through the head. He swung his revolver to aim at the second, but then they were too close. He fired again, and again, and then holstered his revolver to draw his sword. But as he did so he was struck a paralysing blow in the side.

With a gasp he tumbled from the saddle, striking the ground heavily, for the moment winded, while from the sharp pain he suspected he had broken something. But that was irrelevant as he touched his side, and his hand became sticky with blood; he had not yet felt the wound. A horse reared above him, and the bearded face glared down at him as the man leapt from the saddle, tulwar raised, to spin round and hit the ground as Homaira shot him at close range. But even as she did so, another man speared her between the shoulder blades. She gave a little shriek and fell on her face. At least, James reflected, she had died instantly.

'James!' Mbote had also dismounted, to try to reach him. But he was surrounded by flailing figures, and a moment later he went down as well, his head split open by a tulwar blow.

Richard had led the escape, but now the three pursuers were very close, and a bullet whistled past his head. He drew rein, and turned his horse, levelled his revolver, and shot the first man through the chest. He threw up his arms and tumbled from the saddle, and the second man fell almost at the same time, shot by Lanne. The third wheeled his horse and galloped back to his companions. But now Lanne looked past their pursuers at the mêlée behind them, and saw her father fall. 'Daddy!' she cried, and spurred her horse back to the action.

Richard glanced at Sophie, but she had also turned her horse and drawn her revolver. 'We can't abandon them,' she said.

Azam realised they were distracted, and kicked his own horse, hoping to escape, even if his hands remained bound. Without hesitation Sophie shot him. He tumbled from the saddle, but, still secured to the reins, was dragged by his horse. They left him to ride after Lanne.

The fight was over, with James, Mbote and Homaira all dead, but they had taken five of the Afghans with them. Now the sight of Lanne charging at them, firing her revolver, alerted the remaining three, who had been stripping their victims. Hastily they reached for their weapons, but before they could use them Lanne was in their midst, firing again and again, and bringing down two more before she herself fell to a tulwar cut. By now Richard and Sophie were close, also firing. The remaining Afghan leapt into his saddle and galloped off.

Richard drew rein and jumped down. Lanne lay on her face, her entire side split open. 'My God!' Sophie also dismounted, looking around her at the carnage. 'Is she ...'

'She's breathing,' Richard said, his hands wet with blood as he gently turned her over. But her lung had been exposed by the force of the blow, and even as she attempted to speak, she died. Richard laid her on the ground.

Sophie stood beside him. 'I think she died as she would have wished, at the end.'

'You're probably right.' He got up, and stood above James; Mbote and Homaira lay close. The closest and best of friends, united in death.

'Him too,' Sophie suggested.

'Oh, absolutely.'

'Did you love her?'

'I think, once upon a time, I did. But I think I loved him more.'

'I can understand that. Are we going to bury them?'

'No.' Sophie raised her head with a frown. 'Firstly, it would take us several hours to dig a dozen graves in this earth, and we want to be across the border before any other Afghans happen along. And secondly, I think James would rather lie here, in the open air, and be picked clean by the birds, than be eaten by worms.'

Sophie shuddered. I have married a reincarnation of that grim old man, she thought. But would she have had it any other way?

It took them six weeks to get home, travelling first of all down to Bombay, and then finding passages on a ship for England. And slowly, as the traumatic memories of what they had undergone over the previous six months, of what they had done, and seen done, began to fade, they fell in love, all over again. And Sophie could even understand. 'You loved that old man,' she said. 'Far more than you ever did his daughter.'

They sat in the stern of the liner, as it steamed slowly up the Red Sea, and watched the wake bubbling away. 'I think you're right,' Richard agreed. 'Although the daughter came first. But you ... you were magnificent.'

Sophie shuddered. 'Don't speak of it. Promise me you'll never speak of it.' He wondered which of her personal crises had most affected her.

She had felt obliged to wire Hamburg once they got to Bombay, to let her parents know that she was safe and well. The Beinhardts had not even been aware that she had accompanied Richard for some weeks after they had left, when Clementine had become agitated because none of her letters were answered. She had herself gone to England, to be informed by the housekeeper that Mrs Elligan had left the country—with her husband. Clementine had nearly had a stroke, had sent wires in every direction, had upbraided Claus for ever allowing the marriage to take place, but had been unable to do anything about the situation; Sophie and Richard had already disappeared into the empty wastes of central Asia.

Now her joy was as hysterical as her grief had been. Wires came bouncing back, and when they docked at Marseilles both Claus and Clementine were there to greet them. 'What an adventure,' Claus said, as they told their tale. 'But what a triumph, too. You know the final payment has been made. Ma Chung-ying is an honest man. Besides, I think he was happy to be rid of Galitsin. Now we must look to the future, eh?'

'Not for us,' Richard said.

'But ... I promised you a partnership. And you shall have it.'

'As you have said, Claus,' Richard said, 'it was some adventure. And it was a tragedy, for James, and Lanne, and Mbote, and Homaira. I want no more tragedies in our lives. Sophie and I are going to raise a family.' Sophie squeezed his hand.

But the Martingell tragedy was not over. Richard read the newspaper in consternation; his housekeeper had kept it for him, but it was only four days old. The other papers, in which the trial had been reported, were stacked on the table.

'Appeal refused?' he muttered. 'My God! Lady Martingell has been sentenced to death for the murder of her son. She pleaded self-defence, but her maid testified that she shot him down in cold blood.'

Claudette, he thought. He remembered her from their meeting in Rome. He had formed the impression then that she and Anne had been more than just friends. But also that Claudette had always been out for the main chance—herself. Now she had sent her mistress to the gallows!

'Oh, that poor family,' Sophie said. 'But does not the Book say, those that live by the sword shall die by the sword?'

'Yes,' he said, half to himself.

Sophie put her arms round him. 'I know you loved Sir James,' she said. 'Did you love Lady Martingell as well? I never even knew you had met her.'

'I met her,' he said. 'Once.'

And I loved her too, he thought, as he walked the downs beyond his garden fence. But she was the past. A different life, when he had had ideals, and standards, and beliefs. Before he had come to realise that life was a matter of survival.

And now ... thanks to James he was a very wealthy man. He had a beautiful wife, a future of sublime peace and contentment ... And nothing to look forward to.

He returned to the house, where Mrs Bright was waiting with a cup of tea.

'Mrs Elligan not in?'

'She went into the village, sir. But there is a gentleman to see you.'

Richard raised his eyebrows.

'A very foreign-looking gentleman,' Mrs Bright confided in a whisper. 'Dark. And, well ... I put him in the study.'

Richard drank his tea and entered the study, gazed at the man who stood at his entry.

'Mr Richard Elligan? Do forgive me. I have a letter of introduction, from Marshal Ma Chung-ying. There is some business he would like me to discuss with you.'

How his heart pounded. 'Then you must sit down and tell me what it is,' Richard invited.

This Large Print Book for the Partially sighted, who cannot read normal print, is published under the auspices of

THE ULVERSCROFT FOUNDATION